SHATTER THE BONES

Stuart MacBride is the bestselling author of the DS Logan McRae series, the most recent of which, *Shatter the Bones*, was a *Sunday Times* No. 1 bestseller.

His novels have won him the CWA Dagger in the Library, the Barry Award for Best Debut Novel, and Best Breakthrough Author at the ITV3 crime thriller awards.

Stuart's other works include *Halfhead*, a near-future thriller, *Sawbones*, a novella aimed at adult emergent readers, and several short stories.

He lives in the north-east of Scotland with his wife, Fiona, and cat, Grendel.

For more information visit StuartMacBride.com

Also by Stuart MacBride

The Logan McRae Novels
Cold Granite
Dying Light
Broken Skin
Flesh House
Blind Eye
Dark Blood

Other Works
Sawbones
12 Days of Winter
Birthdays for the Dead

Writing as Stuart B. MacBride
Halfhead

STUART MACBRIDE

SHATTER THE BONES

HARPER

Harper
An imprint of HarperCollins*Publishers*
77–85 Fulham Palace Road,
Hammersmith, London W6 8JB

www.harpercollins.co.uk

This paperback edition 2012
3

First published in Great Britain by
HarperCollins*Publishers* 2011

Copyright © Stuart MacBride 2011

Stuart MacBride asserts the moral right to
be identified as the author of this work

A catalogue record for this book is
available from the British Library

ISBN: 978 0 00 734424 6

Set in Meridien by Palimpsest Book Production Ltd,
Falkirk, Stirlingshire

Printed and bound in Great Britain by
Clays Ltd, St Ives plc

MIX
Paper from
responsible sources

FSC
www.fsc.org   **FSC™ C007454**

For Phil

Without Whom

As always, a lot of people very generously helped with the research for this book – anything I've got right is their fault, everything I've got wrong is mine.

I want to say a big thank you to Professor Dave Barclay at the Robert Gordon University, Dr Lorna Dawson and David Miller at the Macaulay, and Dr James Grieve at the University of Aberdeen whose help has been invaluable. The ever-wonderful Ishbel Gall went above and beyond (as usual).

Hats off to Lee Carr, Xavier Jones-Barlow, Christopher MacBride, Julie Bultitude, Allan 'Ubby' Davidson, John Dennis, Dave Goulding, and Alex Clark for all their trailer-tastic help. Mark McHardy, Chris Croly, and Andrew Morrisson for advice and snippets.

Allan and Donna Buchan for support and curry.

My groovy editors Jane Johnson and Sarah Hodgson, and everyone at HarperCollins, especially Alice Moss, Amy Neilson, Julia Wisdom, Wendy Neale and Damon Greeney; and everyone in the Glasgow DC crew. My agent Philip Graystoke Patterson, Isabella, Luke, and the rest of Marjacq scripts. Andrea Best, Susanne Grünbeck, Gregor Weber, and Andreas Jäger.

Several police officers were incredibly helpful; I can't name them, but I *can* thank them.

And saving the best for last – as always – Fiona and Grendel.

six days later

1

'Three minutes.'

'Fuck.' DS Logan McRae leant on the horn, its harsh *breeeeeeep* barely audible over the wailing siren and the burbling radio. 'Get out of the bloody way!'

'*...to show we're all thinking about them. So, this is Alison and Jenny McGregor with Wind Beneath My Wings...*' There was a swell of violins, and then the singing started: '*Did—*'

'Christ, not again.' DC Rennie switched the car radio off and ran a hand through his spiky-gelled mop of blond hair. Checked his watch again. 'We're not going to make it, are we?'

Another blast on the horn.

'Finally!' The moron in the Toyota Prius edged closer to the kerb and Logan floored the accelerator, sending the CID pool car roaring around the outside, hands wrapped so tightly around the steering wheel his left palm ached. 'Time?'

'Two minutes forty.' Rennie grabbed the handle above the passenger door as Logan threw the manky Vauxhall around the Hazlehead roundabout. A screech of tyres, the pinging clunk of a plastic hub-cap parting company with one of the wheels. 'Aaagh...'

'Come on, come on.' Logan overtook the 215 bus to Westhill – a Range Rover coming the other way slammed on its brakes, the driver wide-eyed and swearing.

Through the lights, ignoring oncoming traffic.

Logan wrenched the wheel to the left, the pool car's back end kicking out as he chucked it around the corner onto Hazledean Drive.

Rennie squealed. Closed his eyes. 'Oh God. . .'

'Time?'

'We're going to die. . .'

'TIME, YOU IDIOT!'

'One minute fifty-six.'

A group of schoolchildren milled about outside the swimming pool, turning to watch as the car flashed past.

Logan changed down, aiming the Vauxhall at a rust-red speed bump. Catch it dead centre and the wheels would go either side of the four-foot-wide lump. No problem. . . The car lurched into the air, and battered back down against the potholed tarmac.

'Are you *trying* to kill us?' Rennie checked his watch again. 'One minute thirty.'

The constable was right: they weren't going to make it. Logan took the next speed hump without slowing down.

'Aaaagh! One minute ten.'

Couldn't even *see* the phone box yet.

'Come on!'

The car slithered around the next corner, wheels kicking up a spray of grit as they fishtailed towards Hazlehead Park. No way in hell they were going to make it.

'Thirty-nine, thirty-eight, thirty-seven, thirty-six. . .' Rennie braced himself against the dashboard. 'Maybe they'll wait?'

Logan stuck his foot hard to the floor, rocking back and forth in his seat. 'Come on you piece of shit.' Left hand throbbing where it was wrapped around the wheel. Bushes flickered past the window, a drystane dyke little more than a grey knobbly blur. Sixty-five miles an hour. Sixty-six. Sixty-seven. . .

'Five, four, three, two, one.' Rennie cleared his throat. 'Twenty past.'

The police radio crackled. *'Control to Charlie Delta Fourteen, is she—'*

Rennie snatched up the handset. 'Still en route.'

'Still en. . . ? It's twenty past—'

'We bloody know!' Logan took another speed bump at seventy, the car jerking as it leapt into the air. This time when it hit the tarmac there was a loud metallic banging noise followed by a deafening growl. Then the whole car juddered, a scraping sound, and the rear wheels bounced over something.

Logan glanced in the rearview mirror. The exhaust was lying dented and battered in the middle of the road. 'Tell them to get roadblocks up all round the park – every exit!'

One more corner, the engine roaring like an angry bear, and there it was. A British Telecom phone box – its Perspex skin covered with spray-paint tattoos – sitting outside the grubby concrete rectangle of a public toilet. No sign of anyone. No parked cars. No passersby.

The Vauxhall skidded to a halt in a cloud of pale dust. Logan hauled on the handbrake, tore off his seatbelt, jumped out, and sprinted for the phone box.

Silence, just the crunch of his feet on the gravel.

He yanked the box's door open and was engulfed in the eye-watering reek of stale urine. The phone was sitting in the cradle, the shiny metal cord still in place. It was about the only thing in there that hadn't been vandalized.

But it wasn't ringing.

'Time?'

Rennie staggered to a halt beside him, sunburnt face an even deeper shade of pink than usual. Panting. 'Two minutes late.' He twirled around on the spot. 'Maybe they haven't called yet? Maybe they've been held up? Or something. . .' He stared at the padded brown envelope sitting on the shelf where a telephone directory should have been.

Logan dug a pair of blue nitrile gloves out of his pocket and hauled them on. He picked up the envelope. It was addressed to 'THE COPS'.

Rennie wiped a hand across his mouth. 'You think it's for—'

'Of course it is.' The flap wasn't sealed. Logan levered it open and peered inside. 'Jesus.'

'What? What did they. . .'

He reached inside and pulled out a crumpled ball of white paper, stained red in the centre. He eased the bundle open.

A little pale tube of flesh lay in the middle – a pink-varnished nail at one end, a bloody stump at the other. A little girl's toe.

The wrapping paper was covered in congealed blood, but Logan could still make out the laser-printed message: 'MAYBE NEXT TIME YOU WON'T BE LATE'.

2

'Did your mother find you under the *idiot* bush?' DCI Finnie jabbed his finger toward the graffitied phone box, where a lone Investigation Bureau technician in full SOC get-up was dusting for prints. 'Is *that* why you thought it'd be a good idea to compromise every tenet of *evidentiary procedure* by opening the envelope, when any halfwit—'

'What if it was instructions? Where to go next?' Logan jerked his chin forward. 'Would you have left it?'

Finnie closed his eyes, sighed, then ran a hand through his floppy brown hair. With his wide rubbery lips and sagging face, the head of CID was looking more like a disappointed frog with every passing year. 'If you'd been here on time instead of—'

'There was no way in hell we were ever going to make it all the way here from Altens in six minutes!'

'You were supposed to be—'

'We were *two minutes* late. Two minutes. And in that time they manage to print off a note, hack off a little girl's toe, stick it all in an envelope, address it to "The Cops", and bugger off without a trace?'

'But—'

7

'If they did the amputation here there'd be blood everywhere.'

Finnie puffed out his cheeks, then blew out a long, wet breath. 'Bloody hell.'

'We weren't *meant* to get here in time; it was a set-up.'

A shout echoed out from somewhere behind them. 'Detective Superintendent? Hello? Is it true you've found Jenny's body?'

Finnie sagged for a second, then narrowed his beady little eyes. 'Are these bastards *psychic*?'

It was a baggy woman, wearing jeans and a pale blue shirt that was stained navy under the arms and between the breast pockets. She lumbered up the dusty road, her greying hair tied in a puffball behind her sweaty face. A spotty man trotted along beside her, fiddling with a huge camera.

The head of CID squared his shoulders, voice a hard whisper. 'Get that envelope back to the lab: I want it run through every bloody test they've got. Not *tomorrow*, or *next week*, or when Peterhead stop clogging up the system with their bloody gangland execution: *today*. ASAP. Understand?'

Logan nodded. 'Yes, Guv.' He turned away, making for the phone box just as Spotty the Cameraman took his first picture.

'Is it her? Is it Jenny?'

Finnie's voice boomed out into the warm afternoon, 'DS TAYLOR, GET THIS BLOODY CRIME SCENE CORDONED OFF!'

The IB tech was busy lifting a print from the cracked Perspex wall of the phone box, just beneath a set of pornographic stick men done in black marker pen.

Logan knocked on the metal frame. 'Any joy?'

She peered up at him, a thin band of skin the only thing visible between her steamed-up safety goggles and white facemask. 'Depends on your definition of "joy". This thing's clarted with prints and I'll bet you a tenner none of them belong to our guy. But on the *plus* side: I've found three used condoms, a pile of fossilized dog turds, two empty Coke cans, it's like a microwave oven in here, and I'm kneeling in dried-up pish. Who could ask for more?'

'Condoms?' Logan wrinkled his nose. In a phone box that smelled like a urinal? And they said romance was dead. 'You got the envelope?'

She pointed at the case beside her. 'If you sign for it, you can have the lot.'

'You left it out in the *sun*? Why isn't it packed in ice?'

The tech wiped the arm of her SOC suit across her glistening forehead. 'Where the hell am I going to get ice from? Anyway, not like they're going to sew the bloody thing back on, is it?'

'No wonder Finnie does his nut. . .' Logan opened the battered metal case. A black Grampian Police fleece was folded up inside it, the padded envelope in its clear plastic evidence pouch resting in the middle. At least she'd had the common sense to keep it insulated. He filled in the chain of evidence form and stood. 'Right, if you see any—'

'MCRAE!' Finnie's voice was loud enough to make them both flinch. 'I SAID ASAP, NOT WHEN YOU BLOODY FEEL LIKE IT!'

Logan turned the rattling Vauxhall into Queen Street. They'd stuck the battered exhaust in the boot and now the pool car roared and bellowed like a teenager's first hatchback, the choking smell of exhaust fumes filling the interior.

Sitting in the passenger seat, DC Rennie tutted. 'Thought they'd all be out at Hazlehead by now. . .'

Grampian Police Force Headquarters loomed at the end of the road – an ugly seventies-style black-and-white building, blocky and threatening, the roof festooned with communications antennae and early warning sirens. The Sheriff and JP Court building next door wasn't much better, but even that was welcoming compared with the crowd gathered on FHQ's Front Podium car park.

TV crews, reporters, photographers, and the obligatory crowd of outraged citizens clutching banners and placards: 'DON'T HURT OUR JENNY!', 'THE WIND BENEATH OUR WINGS!!!', 'WERE PREYING 4 U ALISON AND JENNY!', 'LET THEM GO!!!!!' Tears for the cameras. Grim faces. What's the world coming to, and hanging's too good for them.

A few protesters turned to watch the Vauxhall grumble past.

Rennie sniffed. 'How come it's the ugly ones that always want to get on the telly? I mean, don't get me wrong: it's tragic and all that, but none of this lot ever even met the McGregors. So how come they're out here bawling their eyes out like their mum just died? Not natural, is it?'

Logan parked around the back, abandoning the battered car next to the police vans. 'Get everything up to the third floor.'

Rennie rummaged the evidence bags out from the back seat. 'I mean public displays of grief for someone you've never met are just creepy, they. . . Is this dog shite?' He held one of the bags up, peering at the grey-brown lumps inside. 'It is! It's dog—'

'Just get it up to the bloody lab.' Logan turned and made for the back doors.

'So how long's it going to take?'

'Urgh. . .' The man in the white Tyvek suit shuddered, then lifted the toe from the bloodstained note and slipped it into an evidence bag. His voice came out muffled from behind the facemask. 'A wee girl, for God's sake.'

The lab at FHQ was a fraction of the size of the main facility on Nelson Street and it looked more like a messy kitchen than a state-of-the-art forensic facility. It even had a fridge-freezer, gurgling away to itself by the door, covered in novelty shaped magnets. A little digital radio played Northsound One just loud enough to be heard over the whine of the vacuum table as someone dusted a length of metal pipe for prints.

Logan hauled at the crotch of his oversuit. Some funny bugger must've changed the label, because there was no way in hell this was a Large. 'So, how long?'

'Give us a break, we've only had the stuff fifteen minutes.'

'Finnie wants everything tested ASAP.'

'There's a shock.' The technician bent over the crumpled note again, taking a swab of sticky dark-red blood and slipping it into a little plastic vial. 'If I put a rush on the DNA you'll get it back in an hour—'

'There's a media briefing at six!'

'—hour and a half tops. Best I can do.'

'Can't you—'

'This isn't the telly, I can't just *magic up* a DNA profile in time for the adverts. Can probably do you a blood-type, though.' He took another swab, then wandered over to the work surface beside the fridge. 'As for the rest of it. . .' He sighed, adjusted his safety goggles, then looked across the room. 'Sam? How long for fingerprints?'

Nothing.

Logan peered at the shape huddled over the vacuum table. The baggy white SOC suit made her completely anonymous, even to him. 'Samantha?'

The tech tried again. 'Sam?'

Still nothing.

'SAM: HOW LONG FOR FINGERPRINTS?'

She looked up from her length of iron pipe. One end was

wrapped in a clear plastic evidence bag, the metal inside dark and stained. She hauled at the elastic on her suit's hood – exposing a shock of bright scarlet hair – and pulled a tiny black headphone out of her ear. 'What?'

'Fingerprints.'

'Oh.' She looked at Logan and smiled. . . Probably. It was difficult to tell under the full SOC get-up. 'That you in there?'

Logan smiled back behind his own mask. 'Last time I checked.'

'Got your envelope in the superglue box. Not holding my breath though, been in there ten minutes already and nothing's come up.'

'O rhesus negative.' The tech held up a card. 'Does that help?'

Same as Jenny McGregor.

'Post mortem?'

'No idea.' The man picked up the evidence bag with the toe in it – using two fingers as if it was a dirty nappy – handed it to Logan, then wiped his gloves down the front of his oversuit. 'The Ice Queen's off at a conference in Baltimore, and the silly sod they got in to cover for her's off with the squits. So. . .'

Logan tried not to groan. 'When's her highness back?'

'Tuesday week.'

Brilliant.

He signed for the toe, then headed down to the mortuary: quiet and cold in a subterranean annex off the Rear Podium car park. The duty Anatomical Pathology Technician was sitting in a small beige office by the cutting room, feet up on the desk, reading a celebrity gossip magazine.

Logan knocked on the door frame. 'Got some remains for you.'

'Ah, indeed.'

'WAG Love Cheat Exclusive!' went into a desk drawer, and

the APT unfolded herself from the chair. Tall, thin, and insect-like, with trendy glasses and wide flat face, fingers constantly moving. 'Is the hearse in the loading bay?'

Logan held up the bag containing the tiny chunk of flesh and bone.

'Oh. . .' She raised a broad, dark eyebrow. 'I see. Well, we've had a busy day; I dare say this will represent a change of pace when Mr Hudson returns from his illness.' She prowled through to the cold storage room, selected a metal door, opened it, and slid a large metal drawer out of the wall.

A waxy yellow face stared up at them. Swollen golf-ball nose; scraggy grey beard; the skin around the forehead and cheeks slightly baggy, as if it hadn't been put back properly.

The APT frowned. 'Now that's not right. *You* should be in number four.' Sigh. 'Never mind.' She opened up the next one along. 'Here we go.'

'I need the PM done soon as possible. We have—'

'Sadly, with Dr McAllister away, and Mr Hudson . . . *indisposed*, it may be a few days before we can do anything.' She reached towards him, fingers searching like the antennae on a centipede. 'May I have the remains?'

Logan got her to sign for the toe, then watched her solemnly place the little pale digit in the drawer. It looked vaguely ridiculous: a tiny nub of flesh in an evidence bag, lying in the middle of that expanse of stainless steel. Then she slid the drawer back into the wall and clunked the heavy door shut.

Out of sight, but definitely not out of mind.

3

'Rose Ferris, *Daily Mail*. You still haven't answered the question: did you find Jenny McGregor's body or not?' The gangly reporter shifted forward in her seat, nostrils flaring.

Up on the podium DCI Finnie opened his mouth, but the man sitting next to him got in first.

'No, Ms Ferris, we did not.' Chief Superintendent Bain straightened the front of his dress uniform, the TV lights glinting off the silver buttons and his shiny bald head. 'And I'd thank the more excitable members of the press to stop spreading these *unsubstantiated* rumours. People are distressed enough as it is. Is that clear, Ms Ferris?'

Standing at the side of the room, Logan scanned the sea of faces gathered in the Beach Ballroom's biggest function suite – the only place near Force Headquarters large enough to fit everyone in. TV cameras, press photographers, and journalists from every major news outlet in the country. All here to watch Grampian Police screwing everything up.

They were arranged in neat rows of plastic chairs, facing the little dais where DCI Finnie, his boss – Baldy Brian – and a chewed-looking Media Liaison Officer perched behind a table draped in black cloth. A display stand with the Scottish

Constabulary crest on it made up the backdrop: '*Semper Vigilo*', 'Always Vigilant'. Somehow Logan doubted anyone was buying it.

A rumpled man stuck his hand up: a sagging vulture in a supermarket suit. 'Michael Larson, *Edinburgh Evening Post*. "Unsubstantiated", right? So you're saying this is all just a big hoax? That the production company—'

Everything else was drowned out: 'Here we bloody go. . .', 'Hoy, Larson, your dick's unsubstantiated!', 'Tosser. . .'

Larson's back stiffened. 'Oh come on, it's obviously fake. They're just doing it to boost record sales, aren't they? There never *was* a body, it's all—'

'If there are no other *sensible* questions, I'm. . .' Chief Superintendent Bain frowned out into the crowd as a reporter in the middle of the pack stood up. The whole room turned to stare at the short, stocky bloke, dressed in an expensive-looking grey suit, silk shirt and tie, hair immaculately coiffed. As if he'd come shrink-wrapped in a box.

He waited until every microphone and camera was pointed in his direction. 'Colin Miller, *Aberdeen Examiner*.' His broad Glaswegian accent didn't really go with the fancy clothes. The wee man pulled out a sheet of paper in a clear plastic sleeve. 'This turned up on my desk half an hour ago. And I quote: "The police isn't taking this seriously. We gave them simple, clear, instructions, but they still was late. So we got no other choice: we had to cut off the wee girl's toe. She got nine more. No more fucking about."'

The room erupted.

'Is it true? *Did* you find Jenny's toe?', 'Why *aren't* Grampian Police taking it seriously?', 'How can you justify putting a little girl's life at risk?', 'Will you hand this case over to SOCA now?', 'When can we see the toe?', '. . . public inquiry. . .', '. . . people have a right to know. . .', '. . . think she's still alive?'

Camera flashes went off like a firework display, Finnie, Bain, and the Media Liaison Officer not getting a word in.

And standing there, basking in the media glow: Colin Miller.

Wee shite.

'Enough!' Up at the front of the room, Chief Superintendent Bain banged his hand on the desk, making the jug of water and three empty glasses chink and rattle. 'Quiet down or I'll have you all thrown out, are we clear?'

Gradually the hubbub subsided, bums returned to seats. Until the only one left standing was Colin Miller, still holding the note. 'Well?'

Bain cleared his throat. 'I think. . .'

The Media Liaison Officer leaned over and whispered something in Bain's ear and the Chief Superintendent scowled, whispered something back, then nodded.

'I can confirm that we recovered a toe this afternoon that appears to have come from a small girl, but until DNA results—'

And the room erupted again.

4

Shouts; telephones ringing; constables and support staff bustling about the main CID room with bits of paper; the bitter-sweet smells of stewed coffee and stale sweat overlaid with something cloying, artificial and floral. A little walled-off section lurked on one side, home to Grampian Police's six detective sergeants. The sheet of A4 Blu-Tacked to the door was starting to look tatty, 'THE WEE HOOSE' barely readable through all the rude Post-it notes and biroed-on willies. Logan pushed through and closed the door behind him, shutting out the worst of the noise.

'Jesus. . .'

He nodded at the room's only occupant, a slouching figure with an expanding bald spot, taxi-door ears, and a single eyebrow that crossed his forehead like a strip of hairy carpet. Biohazard Bob Marshall: living proof that even natural selection had off days.

Bob spun around in his seat. 'I had a whole packet of fags in here yesterday and they've gone missing.'

'Don't look at me: gave up four weeks ago.' Logan checked his watch. 'How come you managed to skip the briefing?'

'Our beloved leader, *Acting* DI MacDonald, thinks someone

needs to keep this bloody department's head above the sewage-line while you bunch of poofs are off being media hoors.'

'You're just jealous.'

'Bloody right I am.' He turned back to his desk. 'See when it's my turn to be DI? You bastards are going to know the wrath of Bob.'

Logan settled behind his desk and powered up his computer. 'You got that new pathologist, Hudson's number?'

'Ask Ms Dalrymple.'

Logan shuddered. 'No chance.'

'Hmm.' Bob narrowed his eyes. 'She still playing the creepy morgue attendant?'

'Three weeks straight. Started doing this weird thing with her fingers too, like she's got spiders for hands.'

Bob nodded. 'Like it. Dedication.' He scooted his chair forward. 'Did I ever tell you about the time—'

The door clunked open, letting in the sounds of barely-controlled chaos. Samantha stood in the doorway, the SOC oversuit gone, revealing a Green Day T-shirt, black jeans, and a mop of scarlet hair, fringe plastered to her forehead. Face all pink and shiny. The metal bar she'd been dusting for prints was slung over one shoulder, wrapped in a swathe of evidence bags and silver duct tape. 'Anyone in for a DNA result?'

Bob grinned. 'If you're looking for a sample, I've got some body fluids in a handy pump dispenser?'

'Logan, tell Biohazard I wouldn't touch his knob with a cheese grater.'

'Aw, come on – you're not still sulking are you?'

She turned and dumped a small sheaf of papers on Logan's desk. 'The blood's Jenny's. Ninety-nine point nine eight certainty.'

Logan flipped through to the conclusions page. 'Sod. . .'

'Sorry.' Samantha draped a warm arm around his

shoulders. 'You going to be late tonight? Big day tomorrow, remember?'

'Aye, well,' Bob rubbed a finger across his single hairy eyebrow, 'look on the bright side: imagine if it'd been someone else's? Then you'd have two kiddies missing.'

'Yeah, probably. . .' Logan put the report down on his desk. Jenny's DNA. Sod *and* bugger. 'Did you tell Finnie?'

Samantha backed off, hands up. 'Oh no you don't.'

'Please?'

'*Your* name's on the chain of evidence, tell him yourself.' She gave the length of pipe a little shake. 'Anyway, I've got to get down the store before that idiot Downie comes on. Wouldn't trust the rotten sod to file his toenails, never mind physical evidence. . .' Samantha blushed. Cleared her throat. 'Sorry.'

Bob pursed his lips and tutted. 'See that's the trouble with support staff these days: always putting their foot in it. Making jokes about toenails when there's a wee girl's severed—'

'Screw you, Bob.'

He grinned. 'See: you're talking to me again!'

She planted a kiss on Logan's forehead then marched out, giving Bob the finger.

Bob pointed at his crotch. 'So . . . you want a rain-check on that DNA sample?'

Samantha slammed the door.

The main CID room was broken up into a cattle-pen of chest-high partition walls, all covered in memos, phone lists, and cartoons cut out of the *Aberdeen Examiner*. Someone had vandalized the 'TERRORISM: IT'S EVERYONE'S PROBLEM!' poster on the wall – by the little recess where the tea and coffee making facilities lurked – the word 'TERRORISM' scored out and 'BOB'S ARSE' written in its place.

Logan paused in front of the huge whiteboards at the

front of the room, scanning the scrawled boxes of case updates. Apparently Jenny and her mum had been spotted in a Peterhead post office, a pub in Methlick, Elgin Library, the Inverurie swimming pool, Cults church. . . All utter bollocks.

Someone had updated the countdown, now it read, '8 DAYS TO DEADLINE!!!'

'Sarge?'

Logan glanced to his left. PC Guthrie was standing beside him, clutching a steaming mug of coffee that curled the smell of bitter burnt-toast into the room. Logan turned back to the board. 'If you've got bad news, you can sod off and share it with someone else.'

Guthrie handed him the mug, a wee pout pulling his pale face out of shape. With his semi-skimmed skin, faint ginger hair, and blond eyebrows he looked like a ghost that had been at the pies. 'Milk, two sugars.'

'Oh. . . sorry.' Logan took the offered mug.

The constable nodded. 'But while I've got you, Sarge, any chance you can take a look at tomorrow's drug bust? McPherson's SIO and you know what that means. . .'

Logan did. 'When you going in?'

'Half-three.'

'Well, at least it's an early morning shout. The buggers will still be. . .' He could see Guthrie's face pulling itself into an ugly grimace. 'What?'

'Not AM, Sarge, PM.'

'You're going in at half-three in the *afternoon*? Are you mad?'

'Any chance you could, you know, have a word with him?'

'They'll all be wide awake and ready for a fight, resisting arrest, doing a runner, destroying evidence—'

'Setting their sodding huge dogs on us, yeah, I know:

20

Shuggie Webster's just got himself a Rottweiler the size of a minibus.' Guthrie sidled closer. 'Maybe you could talk to Finnie? Tell him McPherson's being a dick?'

Logan took a sip of coffee. 'Gah. . .' He handed it back. 'Not that you deserve it, making coffee like that.'

Guthrie grinned. 'Thanks, Sarge.'

Logan pushed through the doors and out into the corridor. He paused outside Detective Chief Inspector Finnie's office, took a deep breath and knocked just as the door swung open.

Acting DI MacDonald froze on the threshold, flinching as Logan's knuckles jerked to a halt just short of his nose. 'Jesus. . .'

Logan smiled. 'Sorry, Mark, I mean Guv.'

MacDonald nodded, a blush turning the skin pink around his little goatee beard. 'Yes, well, if you'll excuse me, Sergeant.' Then he pushed past, limped back up the corridor to his new office and disappeared inside, slamming the door behind him.

Sergeant? Two weeks in the job and *Acting* DI MacDonald was already *acting* like a tosser.

Logan peered into Finnie's office. The head of CID was behind his desk, face creased into a scowl. Colin Miller, the *Aberdeen Examiner*'s star reporter sat in one of the leather visitors' chairs, smoothing the crease on his immaculate trousers. A pile of dirty laundry slumped in the other chair, mouth thrown open in a jaw-cracking yawn.

Detective Inspector Steel finished with a little burp and a shudder, then sagged even further. Her greying hair stuck up in random directions like a malformed Einstein wig. She ran a hand across her face, pulling the deep-blue-grey bags under her eyes all out of shape. Then let go and the wrinkles took over again. She sniffed. 'We going to be much longer? Only I've got a wean with a temperature to go home to.'

Finnie drummed his fingers on the desk. The note lay beside his keyboard in a clear plastic envelope, the paper pristine white and shining. He stared at Logan. 'Yes?'

Logan held up the report Samantha had delivered. 'DNA result.'

Colin Miller sat up straight. 'Oh aye?'

Logan looked at Finnie, the reporter, then back to Finnie again. 'Sir?'

'Some time today would be good, Sergeant, *before* we all lose the will to live.'

'Ah, right.' He cleared his throat. 'It's positive. DNA matches Jenny McGregor.'

Finnie nodded, his thick rubbery lips pressed into a down-turned line. 'There's no need to sound so *dramatic*, Sergeant. Where do you think the kidnappers got the thing from, *Toes R Us*? Of course it's Jenny's.' He sat back in his seat. 'What about the envelope and note?'

Steel held up a hand. 'Let me guess, sod all.'

Logan ignored her. 'Same as all the others: no fingerprints, no DNA, no fibre, no hairs, no dust – no trace of any kind. Nothing.'

'She shoots, she scores!'

'Inspector, that's *enough*.' Finnie peered down at the note on his desk. '"We gave them simple, clear, instructions, but they still was late. So we got no other choice: we had to cut off the wee girl's toe."' He pinched his lips together. 'Mr Miller, I take it we're going to be seeing this in tomorrow's paper.'

'Aye, got it all set up for the front page: Jenny Tortured – Kidnappers Hack Off Toe.'

'I see. . .' Finnie steepled his fingers. 'And you sure it's *wise* to print something like that? The public are already very upset, and—'

'Naw, you know the deal here: I *have* to print it. Just like I had to read it out at that bloody press conference. You

22

think I wanted to do that? Jesus, man, I'd've kept it secret till the paper came out tomorrow mornin'. Now I've got no exclusive and every bastard tabloid and broadsheet in the country's goin' to run it. No' to mention it's probably already on the bloody telly.' The reporter shrugged. 'Got no choice, but. I publish, or Jenny and her mum die.'

Finnie ran a hand through his floppy brown hair. 'Then the *least* you can do is put our side of things. We weren't given enough time to respond to the call, given the conditions. And the toe was severed long before we got there.' He looked up. 'Wasn't it, Sergeant?'

Logan nodded. 'We were set up.'

The reporter had his notepad out. 'That a quote?'

Finnie coughed. 'Call it, "sources close to the investigation".'

'Gonnae give us details?'

'DS McRae can fill you in on the way out – the usual restrictions apply. Now unless there's anything else. . . ?' The DCI turned back to his computer.

'Actually, sir,' Logan nodded towards the CID room, 'I need to have a quick word with you. About another operation?'

Steel hauled herself out of her chair, then stood there, bent almost double for a moment, before straightening up with a sigh. 'Come on, Weegie Boy, you can walk us to the front door while the lovers here have their wee tryst.' She lowered her voice to a theatrical whisper. 'That means they're going to have a shag.'

'Thank you, *Inspector*, that will be *all*.'

Logan waited until the door clunked shut. 'No offence, sir, but I'd rather keep our relationship platonic.'

Finnie glowered at him. 'I *allow* Steel a little latitude because, despite *everything*, she's an effective detective inspector. You however. . .'

'Sorry, sir.' He sank into the chair Colin Miller had just

vacated. 'It's about DI McPherson – you know he's got a drug bust on tomorrow? He's planned it for the middle of the afternoon.' There was a silent pause. 'When the targets are going to be—'

'Yes, Sergeant, I'm well aware of what *drug dealers* do in the afternoon.' Finnie sat back, tapped the flat tips of his fingers against his rubbery lips. 'And what do you propose to do about it?'

'Well, you could speak to McPherson, let him know. . .' Logan blinked. Licked his lips. Shifted in his seat. 'Sorry, what do *I* propose to do. . . ?'

'Well, clearly you know *better* than a DI with nine years' experience. What are *you* going to do with *your* drug bust?'

Oh bloody hell.

'I really . . . with the . . . and it's . . . erm. . .' Logan checked his watch. Just after seven. 'OK, well, I'm back in on Friday and—'

'I believe in striking while the iron's hot, don't you, Logan? How *else* are you going to get the creases in your jeans nice and straight?'

'But I've got a . . . thing on tomorrow. And it—'

'Where are we with the post mortem on the toe?'

'You see, I booked the time off so—'

'Do *try* to pay attention, Sergeant: post mortem.'

Logan could feel the heat rising in his cheeks. 'I phoned the pathologist, Hudson – spoke to his wife. Apparently he's not left the toilet all day. "Tube of toothpaste" was the term she used. She thinks he'll either be dead by the morning, or back to work.'

'Good.' Finnie clicked a button, bringing his monitor back to life. 'Now you trot along. I'm sure you've got a *great* deal of organizing to do.'

5

'. . . confirm, we are in position. Over?'

Logan scrubbed a hand across his gritty eyes and squinted out at the semi-detached house at the end of the quiet cul-de-sac. The neighbourhood had that slightly rundown feel to it: the grass left too long so it was going to seed, a battered washing machine sitting next to a pair of dented wheelie bins. The whole scene turned monochrome in the sodium glow of a dozen streetlights.

He keyed the button on his Airwave handset. 'OK, listen up people: we have three, possibly four, IC-One males inside. This has to be quick and clean – no sodding up, no getting hurt, no hurting anyone else. And Shuggie Webster's meant to have a new Rottweiler, so keep an eye out. We clear?'

'Team Two, Roger.'

'Team One, Rover.'

'Just don't come crying to me when there's a huge dog chewing your knackers off, OK?' Logan tugged his jacket sleeve back, exposing his watch. 'And we're live in: eight, seven, six—'

'Aww . . . who farted?'

'—three, two, one. GO!'

PC Guthrie shifted in the passenger seat. 'Don't see why I have to be—'

'You wanted me to do something about it, I did something about it.'

'But—'

'Don't push it, Allan. Wasn't for you I'd be snuggled up at home with my intended.'

Down at the far end of the cul-de-sac torches sprang into life, sweeping the front garden of a nondescript two-storey. White BMW 3 Series in the drive.

The dull crack of a mini battering ram slamming into a UPVC door.

'Fucking thing. . .'

A dog barking.

Another crack.

Then another.

'Why can't we use bloody explosives?'

A light clicked on in an upstairs bedroom.

Another crack.

'Open, you fucker!'

A muffled scream from somewhere inside.

Guthrie turned in his seat. 'You know, I saw this video on the internet once. Welsh police took twelve minutes to get through one of these modern UPVC front doors. Bloody stuff's tougher than steel, if you—'

Logan stabbed his thumb down on the Airwave's 'TALK' button. 'Go in through the window!'

A pause.

'Who's got the hoolie bar?'

'Thought you had it.'

'How? I've got the Big Red Door Key, you Muppet.'

Another pause.

'Sarge?'

26

Logan clicked the button again. 'I swear to God, Greg, if you make me come down there. . .'

'It's . . . er . . . in the back of the van.'

'You're *supposed* to be an MOE specialist!' Logan hauled open the pool car's door and scrambled out into the warm night.

The unmarked response van was parked off to the side, beneath a broken streetlight. Logan sprinted for it. Someone had finger-painted the words 'MICHELLE SUX COX!!!' in the grime that frosted the back windows.

Bloody thing wasn't even locked.

He hauled the back door open and snapped on his torch. Empty pizza boxes, a litre bottle of Coke – half-empty, with fag-ends floating in it – and then, mounted to the van's wall with a spider's web of bungee cords, the hooligan bar.

Logan unhooked it and dragged the thing out: a three-and-a-half-foot-long metal pole with a claw at one end and a spike-and-lever arrangement on the other, its coating of spark-resistant black chipped and flaking. He hefted it over his shoulder and ran towards the target house.

Lights flickered on in the other buildings as the curtain-twitchers woke up for a good ogle.

PC Greg Ferguson was at the head of the small, ineffectual clot of police officers – all of them dressed in ninja black. He thumped the Big Red Door Key into the shuddering plastic door again. Sweat rippled across his bright pink face, teeth gritted, eyes screwed shut as the mini battering ram slammed into the cracking UPVC. 'Come on, you *fucker*!'

Logan waded through the knee-high grass, making for the front window. 'Glass!'

He held the hoolie bar at the far end: just above the claw, drew the thing back, and swung as hard as he could. The big metal spike tore straight through the double glazing, turning it into an explosion of little shining cubes. Logan closed his eyes, covering his face with one hand as glass shattered down all around him.

The hoolie bar thunked into the window frame.

Keeping his face covered, he raked it around the edges – just like they'd taught him on the Method of Entry course – clearing away everything but the smallest chunks of safety glass.

'Don't just bloody stand there!'

PC Greg Ferguson dropped the Big Red Door Key and made an ungainly leap for the window ledge, only *just* getting his stomach over it, then clambered inside, legs waving about as if he was having a fit. Then there was a thump and some swearing as he hit the floor inside.

'Ow. . .'

One of the less useless team members stuck their back to the wall, hunkered down and cupped their hands together, giving everyone else a leg up as they barrelled inside. Then she looked at Logan. Nodded towards her gloved hands.

'Sarge?'

'Thanks, but I'll wait for the all-clear.'

'Suit yourself.' She turned and scrambled in through the broken window.

There was no point heading back to the car, so Logan perched himself on the bonnet of the BMW and fidgeted through his pockets for the packet of cigarettes that wasn't there any more. Four weeks, two days and . . . what time was it now? Just after half three in the morning. . . Eight hours. Not bad going.

He stifled a yawn.

The sound of a toilet flushing came from upstairs, just audible between the shouts, screams, barking, and the high-pitched wail of a young child. Brilliant – more paperwork. At this rate he'd be lucky to get home before lunchtime. Which was going to be cutting it a bit fine. . .

Bloody PC Bloody Guthrie. *Can't you have a quick word, Sarge?*

Speak of the devil.

Guthrie kicked his way through the grass until he was standing beside Logan, looking up at the house. 'We going to be much longer, Sarge? Only I've got—'

'Unless the next words out of your mouth are "I've got to go buy everyone a bacon buttie" I wouldn't risk it. Understand?'

Guthrie's chubby cheeks went a fetching shade of pink. 'Er . . . yeah, that was what I was going to say. Bacon butties. You back on the meat then?'

'Get onto Social Services – we'll need someone to take care of the kid.'

The words, 'PUT THAT BLOODY THING DOWN!' boomed out from inside. Then a portable television burst through an upstairs window in a halo of glass. The TV crashed into the garden three foot from where they stood, cathode ray tube giving an angry *pop* as it burst.

Logan smacked a hand against Guthrie's arm. 'Might want to stand back a bit.'

A full-grown man barrelled out of the upstairs window. He seemed to hang in the air for a moment, caught in the light from the bedroom. And then he slammed into the garden at their feet with a sickening thud and crack.

Pause.

No movement. Just some groaning and muffled swearing.

'Jesus. . .' Guthrie hunkered down beside the crumpled figure. 'Are you all right? Don't move!'

One of the forced entry team peered out over the window-sill. 'Everyone OK down there?'

'More or less.' Logan stood and dusted his hands together. 'Billy Dawson, you silly sod. When are you going to learn that drug-dealing toerags can't fly?'

'Urgh. . .' Billy's face was a mass of beard and gritted

teeth, his eyes wide, the pupils huge and dark. 'Think my leg's broke. . .'

'Lucky it wasn't your neck. So, come on then: how much gear have you got in the house?'

'How . . . I . . . don't know what you're on about.'

'We're going to find it anyway. Might as well save everyone the bother.'

'Aaaaargh, my leg. . . Ahem. You know?'

Logan hit Guthrie again. 'When you've finished speaking to Social Services, call for an ambulance.'

The constable upstairs waved again. 'Better make it two.'

Logan walked towards the house, stepping over the groaning body. 'And keep an eye on Billy here, don't want him doing a runner and injuring himself.'

'They tried flushing most of it, but the whole bathroom's clarted with the stuff.' PC Ferguson waved a hand at the once-blue suite, now layered with a dusting of dirty-brown powder. A small pile of torn plastic and parcel-tape lay between the cistern and the bath; more, unopened, packages on the grubby lino floor.

The room smelled of peppery ammonia, dirty toilet, and floral air freshener . . . with a dark, fizzy undertone that was making Logan's teeth itch. Probably better not to stand about breathing it in. He backed out of the room, hauling Ferguson after him, and closed the door. 'Leave it for Forensics.'

Ferguson peeled the black scarf from around his face, showing off an amateur moustache kit. 'Look, about earlier—'

'What, when you forgot the hoolie bar?'

'Er. . . yeah. Look, we don't have to mention that, do we? I mean—'

'So what am I supposed to say when Finnie asks why it took us so long to force entry the suspects had time to flush three bricks of heroin?'

The constable stared at his boots. 'Operational difficulties?'

'Greg, you're a disaster, you know that, don't you?'

He grinned. 'Thanks, Sarge.'

'Must be bloody mad.' Logan turned and looked down over the balustrade.

The flocked wallpaper was torn and baggy, a patchy coat of magnolia doing little to make it look any classier. Scuffed carpet dotted with brown stains and clumps of animal hair. Bare light bulbs. A bedroom door with a deep gouge out of the wood, showing off the hollow interior.

The familiar bitter-sweet-sweaty taint of cannabis hung in the warm, stale air. Which explained the size of Billy's pupils.

'Where's the rest of them?'

Ferguson pointed at the bedroom with the dented door. 'Got two in there; one in the kitchen – fell over and split his head open on the worktop, stoned out his tits; one in the other bedroom. . . Well, two if you count the kid; and—'

'One flat on his face in the middle of the front garden?'

'I *was* going to say, one handcuffed out back.'

Logan made for the nearest bedroom. 'Well bring him in then.'

'Ah. . .'

He stopped, one hand on the doorknob. 'Greg: what did you do?'

'It wasn't me! It was just . . . well we caught him trying to do a runner over the back fence, and Ellen was handcuffing him, when the biggest dog you've ever seen in your *life* comes tearing out of the bushes. And we kinda had to leg it. Barely got back inside with the arse still in our trousers. Left him cuffed to the whirly washing line thing.'

'In the name of. . .' Logan closed his eyes. Counted to ten.

'Sarge?'

'Whirlies aren't fixed to the ground, Greg: the metal pole

31

goes into a little hole. All he has to do is lift the thing up and he'll be off!' Logan wrenched the bedroom door open.

A woman crouched in the corner wearing nothing but a bra and a pair of ripped jeans. Stick thin, all elbows and ribs, sunken eyes glittering like polished coal. Hands cuffed behind her back. Chapped and faded lips, pulled back over yellowing teeth. 'We didn't do nothing!'

A small child – couldn't have been more than three-years-old – was perched in her lap, wearing a filthy pair of Ben 10 pyjamas. Snot silvered the wee boy's top lip, something brown smeared around his mouth.

One of the forced entry team was standing over them, fiddling with a mobile phone.

Logan brushed past, making for the window. 'You better not be updating your bloody Twitter account, Archie.'

The pudding-faced constable blushed and stuck the phone in his pocket.

Logan stared into the back garden. There was a man in the middle of the wilderness, fighting with a rotary washing line while a black dog patrolled the knee-high grass around him. Shuggie Webster.

At least Ellen had been bright enough to cuff him to the complicated lever joint that attached the four arms to the pole.

He was getting a bit *enthusiastic*. . . Hauling, tugging, swearing, trying to break either the handcuffs or the whirly, getting tangled up in dirty yellow washing line. A big ugly fly caught in a plastic spider's web. He turned himself upside down, both feet planted against the whirly's arms, straining.

Logan opened the bedroom window. 'He's going to dislocate his wrist if he isn't careful.'

PC Ferguson sidled up. 'Don't get any brighter, do they?'

'Hoy! Shuggie!'

The man froze, still dangling upside down.

'Cut it out. You've been caught.'

The dog stopped its patrolling and turned to bark and snarl up at them.

The constable with the mobile phone appeared at Logan's shoulder. 'Bugger me. . . That's a big dog.'

The stick-thin woman shoulder-charged Archie, hands still cuffed behind her back, sending him stumbling into Ferguson. Both officers went crashing to the bedroom floor in a tangle of limbs and swearing.

She shoved past Logan to the open window. 'Shuggie! Pull the thing out the ground, you daft fuck!'

Logan grabbed her, tried to haul her back, but she lashed out with a knee.

Boiling oil flared out from his groin, curdling in the pit of his stomach, making his knees buckle. He steadied himself against the tatty wallpaper. Oh *Christ* that hurt.

'Shuggie! PULL THE FUCKING WHIRLY OUT THE GROUND!'

Outside, Shuggie finally seemed to understand. He squatted down as far as he could with one wrist cuffed to the articulated joint, wrapped his other hand around the pole, and hauled the whole thing out of the ground. He teetered for a moment, turned through a hundred and eighty degrees, then fell on his bum, tangled in the yellow plastic washing line again.

'GET UP YOU DAFT CUNT!'

Logan cleared his throat, gritted his teeth, grabbed the skeletal woman again and threw her onto the bed – she bounced off the mattress and went spinning over the other side, disappearing from view with a thud.

The little boy wailed, tears and snot running down his puffy pink face.

PC Ferguson was back on his feet, leaning out of the window. 'COME BACK HERE YOU WEE SHITE: YOU'RE STILL UNDER ARREST!'

'Fucking police bastards!' The woman crawled upright, eyes thin slits, graveyard teeth bared, a smear of blood from her cracked lips. Then she charged, head down, like a greasy battering ram.

Logan lurched out of the way . . . or tried to.

She slammed into his stomach. Pain ripped across his scars, digging deep into his guts, tearing all the breath from his throat as they thudded into the bedroom wall, then down to the carpet. All he could do was curl up around the fire and try not to throw up. Barely feeling the harsh nip of her teeth sinking into his arm through his suit jacket. The dull thunk of her forehead battering into his right ear.

And then she was gone. Screaming. 'Let me go you bastard! Let me fucking go! RAPE! Fucking . . . RAPE!'

Logan peeled open one watering eye to see her a foot-and-a-half off the ground, legs flailing about. Archie was standing behind her, arms wrapped around her waist, holding her up.

'Calm down!'

'RAPE! RAPE!'

And all the way through it, the kid kept on screaming.

6

'How's the balls?' PC Ferguson handed Logan another packet of frozen chips from the gurgling freezer. The kitchen reeked of cannabis and stale fat, the extractor hood above the cooker covered in a dark-brown greasy film.

Leaning back against the working surface, Logan pressed the bag of frozen chips against his aching stomach. 'You found him yet?'

'We should maybe take you to the hospital?'

'Greg: have – you – found – him?'

The constable pinched his face into a painful chicken's bum. 'Well, there's a funny story, and—'

'You let him get away, didn't you?'

'It wasn't—'

'Why the hell didn't you have anyone watching the back? I *told* you to get someone watching the back!'

'But it—'

'For God's sake, Greg, did you sleep through the bloody risk assessment and planning meeting? Two out front, two out back to catch any runaways!'

PC Greg Ferguson stared at his shoes. 'Sorry, Guv. It all kinda got away from me. A bit. . .'

'A *bit*? He was handcuffed to a bloody whirly!'

'It's just. . . I've been having a tough time at home, with wee Georgie ill and Liz on the tablets, and her mum moving in . . . and I can't. . .' He ran a finger around the collar of his black fleecy top. 'I can't go up in front of the rubber-heelers again. Bain's thinking about making us up to sergeant, and we could really do with the extra dosh. . .'

Logan slumped back, stared up at a strange brown stain on the ceiling. 'Way I see it we've got three options. One: I dob you in.'

'Please, Sarge, you—'

'Two: *I* take the heat and let Professional Standards tear me a new one.'

Ferguson broke out a thin smile. 'Would you really do that for—'

'No I bloody wouldn't. Three: we come up with some sort of cover story. . .' Logan straightened.

Ellen, the officer who'd given everyone a leg-up through the lounge window, lurched into the kitchen, face all pink and glistening. She puffed and panted her way across to the sink, set the cold tap running, and stuck her head under the stream of water. 'Bloody hell. . .'

Ferguson licked his teeth. 'Did you. . .?'

She turned, dripping all over the kitchen floor. 'They should rope . . . rope him in . . . for the 2012 Olympics. If the bugger can . . . can run that fast handcuffed . . . to a rotary drier . . . he'll *walk* the five hundred metres. . .' She stuck her head back under the tap again. 'Swear I watched him hurdle a . . . six foot fence like it . . . like it wasn't even there.'

'Oh God. . .' Ferguson covered his face with a hand. 'I'm screwed.'

'Ellen?' Logan fidgeted with the bag of frozen chips. 'I think Greg here wants to ask you a favour.' He cleared his throat. 'Just make sure the pair of you've got your stories straight for Professional Standards, OK?'

A knock at the kitchen door.

It was Guthrie, clutching an assortment of white paper bags, most of them turned peek-a-boo with grease. 'Wouldn't believe how hard it is to find an all-night baker's in Kincorth.' He handed a bag to Logan.

'Bacon?'

'Fried egg. Us veggies got to stick together, right?'

Logan took a bite out of the soft, floury roll, getting a little dribble of yolk on his chin. 'What about the ambulance?'

'Out front. Got Billy Dawson in the back already, they say the other bloke just needs a couple of stitches.' Guthrie helped himself to a flaky-pastry-log thing. Speaking with his mouth full, getting little chips of pale brown all down the front of his black uniform. 'Social worker's here too, Guv. Wants a word.'

The social worker was in the lounge, poking through a twirly CD tower unit, her black hair streaked with grey: tweedy trousers, yellow shirt, red waistcoat straining over her belly . . . like something out of *Wind in the Willows*. She turned and sniffed at Logan. Then held out a clipboard. 'I need you to sign.'

He scanned the form, then scrawled his signature in the box with a cross marked beside it. 'It's a—'

'Ooh, I've got this one.' She pulled a copy of Annie Lennox's *Diva* from the stand. 'You ever meet her?'

'Er, no. We—'

'I was born in Torry, just like her. Even went to the same school: Harlaw Academy.' The social worker turned the album over, frowning at the back. 'Is Trisha still here, or have you carted her off?'

37

'Trisha?'

'Trisha Brown? The mother? Addict? Has a little boy about so high?' She held a hand level with her own swollen belly.

'Upstairs.'

A nod. 'I remember thinking, "When I grow up, I'm going to be that famous. Going to be on *Top of the Pops* and MTV and in all the papers." Sang in a couple of bands, nearly got a record deal.' She stuck the album back in the tower. 'Then my dad died, my mum fell apart, and I had to get a job in Asda. Here endeth the pop star's dream.'

'We're doing her for possession, resisting arrest, and assaulting a police officer.'

The social worker took the clipboard back from Logan, squinted at his signature. 'Loren McRoy? That not a girl's name?'

'Logan, and it's McRae, not McRoy.'

'God, your handwriting's worse than mine. Lucy Woods, nice to meet you.' She headed towards the stairs. 'Might as well get it over with.'

'Trisha? Can you hear me, Trisha?' She squatted in front of the stick-thin figure. 'Trisha? It's Lucy. I've got to take wee Ricky into care while you're with the police tonight, OK?'

Trisha swung her head around, like a lump of pasty concrete attached to a chain. Pupils like tiny bugs, heavy lids, mouth open, lips connected by little strings of drool. 'Whmmm?'

'I said I've got to take wee Ricky into care. While you're in custody?'

A frown crawled slowly across Trisha's pale face. 'Who're. . .?'

'Lucy. Lucy Woods? From the social?'

The frown turned into a glacial smile. 'But I'm comfy here.'

The social worker sighed, looked up at Logan. 'Heroin?'

'Probably. They tried to redecorate the toilet with it when we forced entry.'

'Oh Trisha, you *know* it's not good to you. Makes you do bad things.'

Trisha blinked. It seemed to take a lot of effort. 'Don't let them take Ricky! Don't. . .' She pointed a bony finger at the PC standing in the corner. 'He tried to rape me!'

Sigh. 'How much did you take, Trisha?'

'He did! He tried to rape me!'

'That's a woman, Trisha.'

Frown. 'Oh. . .' A string of drool spiralled its way to her sunken chest. 'Someone tried to rape me. . .'

Logan folded his arms. 'She's been like this for about an hour. Was fine before that.'

'Yes, well, it takes a while for drugs to be absorbed by the system, especially if you practise as much as Trisha.' Lucy Woods sat back on her heels. 'Might be an idea to get her up to A&E for the night, just in case.'

Which was a pain in the arse, but much better than her dying from an overdose in custody. 'I'll get someone to run her up.'

'Good.' The social worker stood. 'We're going to take care of wee Ricky for you, OK Trisha?'

Blink. Blink. She smacked her lips. 'No. . .' Frown. 'Mum. Mum'll take him.' Blink.

'Your mum? Thought she was still in Craiginches?'

'Someone raped me. . .' And this time, when her eyes closed they didn't open again.

'Craiginches?' Logan watched the social worker shake her head, check Trisha's pulse, then haul herself to her feet.

'Where's the wee lad?'

'Other bedroom. She going to be OK?'

'I took over her case when she was thirteen. She's

averaged about two ODs a year since. Better have the hospital pump her stomach too: never know what she's swallowed.'

Wee Ricky was huddled in the corner of the room, eyes darting back and forth as Logan followed the social worker inside. Clothes lay strewn across the scabby beige carpet, a line of syringes and flame-blackened spoons on the bedside cabinet.

One of the Forced Entry team was leaning back against an ancient-looking sideboard, black crash helmet sitting beside her while she flipped through a copy of *Hello!* She slapped it down on a pile of celebrity gossip mags.

Even drug dealers and addicts had aspirations.

'Sarge.' She nodded at the boy. 'Watch: he bites.'

The child bared his teeth, a small growling noise coming from his throat, filthy fingers clutching a plastic Buzz Lightyear like a claw-hammer.

'Ricky?' Lucy Woods lowered herself down in front of him, waistcoat groaning. 'You remember me, Ricky?'

The kid stared at her for a moment, then nodded.

'Good. We're going to take you to stay with your granny tonight, OK? While your mum's not feeling well.'

Logan hauled the pool car around onto Abbotswell Crescent and into a labyrinth of blank grey granite houses, silent in the dawn's pale glow.

Wee Ricky sat in the back with PC Guthrie, the constable looking every bit as wary and worried as the three-year-old.

Lucy Woods tapped on the passenger-side window. 'How much do you think that lot's worth then?'

Bunches of flowers wrapped in cellophane made a slick that nearly covered the pavement outside a nondescript semi-detached. Teddy bears were tied to the knee-high fence, along with angels, unicorns, and other assorted cuddly toys. Candles in glass jars flickered among the tributes, their light fading before the rising sun. A banner with, 'JENNY, WE'LL NEVER STOP BELIEVING!' was tied to stakes in the front garden. A smattering of the posters they'd given away with the *Scottish Sun* at the weekend: 'ALISON AND JENNY ~ NEVER GIVE UP!' stuck to walls, stapled to sticks.

A handful of people sat at one end of the display, wrapped up in sleeping bags and heavy parka coats, two of them were still awake, smoking cigarettes and sharing a Thermos. They stopped to stare at the pool car as it drifted by.

One raised a hand, gave a short wave of solidarity, then went back to their vigil.

The social worker nodded back. 'Course they never had anything like the *X-Factor*, or *Britain's Got Talent*, or *Big Brother*, when I was young. Could've made it if they had. Been properly famous.' She turned her head as the public display of grief faded from the rearview mirror. 'That could be me. . .'

Bloody hell.

Logan glanced at her, then back at the road.

Some people should watch what they wish for.

'You sure this is a good idea?' Logan looked around the living room, trying to find somewhere even vaguely clean to sit.

The sound of a dog scrabbling at the kitchen door, claws raking the other side of the wood. Deep growls and the occasional outraged bark.

'I'm not supposed to take a kid into care unless there's no other option.' Lucy Woods picked a CD from the littered coffee table, the shiny surface glittering in the overhead light. 'If we can place them with a member of the family we will. Means the kid doesn't get dragged through the system.'

'Yeah, but. . .' Logan lifted his foot, but the carpet didn't want to let go.

'Trisha's mum might not be perfect, but at least she's blood.' The social worker wrinkled her nose and dropped the CD back into the mess. 'Fleetwood Mac.'

A voice at the door behind them: 'What the fuck's wrong with Fleetwood Mac?'

Lucy Woods snapped on a smile. 'Hi Helen. He go off to sleep OK?'

'What she do this time?' Helen Brown lurched into the room, swigging from a tin of Tennent's Super, one leg stiff at the knee. Her face was every bit as thin as her daughter's, the same dark hollows under her bloodshot eyes, the same yellowy teeth spaced wide in pale gums. Pupils the size of pinpricks.

She was wearing a pale-grey long-sleeved T-shirt, tugging the cuffs down every time she looked in Logan's direction. Probably hiding the trackmarks.

He shifted away from the sticky patch. 'She's just helping us with an investigation.'

Trisha's mum howched, picked up a scummy mug and spat into it. 'Hooring, or drugs?'

'I can't—'

'You fucks is all the same.' Another swig of extra-strong lager. 'Hassling folk doing no harm to no one.' A dribble of liquid ran down her chin, dripped and made a clay-coloured stain on the long-sleeved T-shirt. 'Fuck is it to you if she's making a few quid down the docks? Not like she's robbing auld wifies' pensions, is it?'

The social worker cleared her throat. 'So, Helen, how are you coping? Doing OK?'

'You fuckers should be out there!' She jabbed a finger at the closed curtains. 'Looking for that wee girl and her mum. Not arresting my Trisha for giving someone a blowjob!'

'There was a drugs raid and—'

'What, she wouldn't give you a freebie, so you banged

her up? You make me sick! Fucking country's going to shit and it's bastards like you dragging it there!' She tipped the tin of lager to her mouth, glugging it down.

'—in accident and emergency for observation.'

Helen Brown scrunched the can up and threw it across the room. It bounced off Logan's chest. 'What, you going to arrest me too? That's about your fucking speed, isn't it? Arrest the *victims*, when there's illegal Paki bastards living two doors up, shitting in the street and stealing my fucking washing!'

Logan brushed the droplets of pale yellow liquid from his jacket. 'We'll see ourselves out.'

7

'Mmph. . .?' Logan peered out from beneath the duvet. The alarm clock radio stared back at him. He fumbled with the buttons on the top, but it didn't stop the noise.

Sat up.

Phone.

It was his mobile, in his jacket pocket, hanging on the back of the chair in the corner, warbling the *Danse macabre* at him.

God's sake. . . He hauled it out and squinted at the glowing screen: 'DI STEEL'

Logan stabbed his thumb onto the button. 'What the hell do you want?'

There was a pause. *'You know what costs sod-all in this life, Laz? A smile; a thank you; and my boot up your arse, you rude little—'*

'What – do – you – want?'

'Well seeing as the little hand is on the nine, and the big hand is on the twelve, what I want is you at bloody work!'

He slumped back on the bed, spreadeagled like a pasty starfish, the scars on his chest and stomach puckered and angry. 'I only just got *home* from bloody work.' A yawn drowned out whatever the inspector said next. Logan shuddered.

'—*round like a sodding mentalist. When*—'

'Had to pull an all-nighter. Finnie lumbered me with McPherson's drug busts; was stuck interviewing a smackhead called Shaky Jake till nearly eight this morning. So I'm going back to bed.'

'*You've no' seen the papers this morning, have you.*' Not a question.

'I don't care.' He dragged the duvet back into place, covering himself. 'It's my day off.'

'*Your mate Hudson's a no show.*'

'Who the hell is. . . Oh.' Dr Hudson – the pathologist. 'How's that my fault?'

'*Finnie's going mental – he's had three PCs in tears already, and it's no' even lunchtime.*'

'So get a pathologist up from Edinburgh.' Logan nestled down into his pillow, soft and cool. Yawned again.

'*Already tried it – going to be six hours before he gets here. Meanwhile some tosser from SOCA's turned up to "review the situation,", and you know what that means. . .*'

He draped an arm across his eyes. 'It's my day off!'

'*Now's no' the time to be missing in action, Laz. No' if you don't fancy working fraud cases for the rest of your natural. I'm serious: spreadsheets and accountants from here till retirement.*'

'But I've got a thing on this—'

'*Pick up something tasty on the way in, eh? And some decent coffee for a change.*'

The line went dead.

The sun glared down from a pale blue sky, a few thin wisps of white making sod all difference to the harsh light. Logan trudged up Marischal Street, hands in his pockets.

Bunch of bastards. An hour: was that too much to ask for?

An hour in his own bloody bed. Never mind actually getting to take some bloody time off.

High above, fat seagulls screamed and swore, spattering a rusty hatchback with stinking polka dots.

Logan came to a halt at the top of the hill, where the road joined onto the tail end of Union Street, and stared across the road. Lodge Walk – the little alley that ran between the Town House and the Sheriff Court – was choked with journalists, photographers, and TV crews. DI Bell was caught in the middle of them, a little hairy island in a sea of bastards, all shouting questions and waving cameras. Poor sod had probably been caught trying to sneak out of Force Headquarters' secret side door.

Well, he was on his own, because there was no way Logan was wading in to help.

A newsagents lurked on one side of the Mercat Cross, the windows dulled by a thin film of dust. One of those red-and-white sandwich boards was parked out on the cobbled pedestrian area in front of the shop: 'TORTURED JENNY LOSES TOE – POLICE POWERLESS' printed in thick black lettering above the *Aberdeen Examiner* logo.

Logan hesitated for a moment, then went in. Every tabloid newspaper in the place had something similar screaming from the front page. The *Sport* had gone for 'TOE HORRIBLE FOR WORDS', the *Press and Journal* – 'KIDNAP HORROR FIND', *Evening Express* – '"I CAN FIND JENNY" SAYS NE PSYCHIC'. . . He bought an *Examiner* and a P&J, then nipped next door to the baker's for a couple of bacon butties and something for himself.

Steel could get the damn coffees for once.

He dragged his phone out as he trudged along the pavement and made a quick call.

'What the bloody hell are you *eating*?' DI Steel had her feet up on the desk, one hand wrapped around a white floury roll with slivers of deep-fried pig sticking out the edges.

'Fish finger buttie. And I'm only here till twelve, understand?'

'You're no' right in the head, Laz: butties are all about the bacon.' She took a huge bite, getting a smear of tomato sauce on her cheek. 'So, come on then – what did you get out of Shaky Jake? He still on the crutches?'

'I mean it: twelve o'clock on the dot. I've got a thing on and I can't be late, or—'

'Focus for five minutes, will you? Shaky Jake.'

Logan frowned at her. 'It's McPherson's case.'

'Humour me.'

'Yeah, he's still on the crutches. They had to fuse his anklebones into one big lump after Wee Hamish's lads took a pickaxe to them. Walks like a penguin now. Lucky the hospital didn't just amputate his feet.'

'Silly sod shouldn't have helped himself to the merchandise then, should he? How much gear did you get?'

'Three bricks of heroin, two of cannabis resin, some E, a big suitcase full of mephedrone, two replica handguns, and some dodgy porno DVDs.'

'Oh aye?' Steel sat upright. 'Anything I should be reviewing?'

'Already sent them over to Trading Standards.'

She slumped back again. 'Sod.' Another bite of buttie. 'And which one of your daft buggers let Shuggie Webster escape?'

Logan squirted another sachet of tartar sauce onto his fish fingers, not looking the inspector in the eye. 'It's all in the report.'

'"Operational difficulties" my sharny arse – it was that useless bum-crack Ferguson, wasn't it?'

'We had to get the social out to—'

'Aye, Trisha Brown's wee lad. I do read these things, you know. How was her mum?'

'How do you think?'

'Pished, rancid, and racist?' Steel nodded. 'Her granny was the same. Trisha's your genuine third-generation drug user. Really makes you hold out hope for her wee boy, doesn't it? Other kids'll be showing each other their knickers behind the bike sheds: he'll be doing crack.' She sooked a greasy fingertip clean. 'What else you got on for McPherson?'

'Not till you tell me why you—'

'Laz, it always pays to keep an eye on what DI Disaster's up to: you never know when he's going to get himself bashed over the head, break a limb, fall down the stairs, be hit by a car, punched in the nose. . .' She wrinkled her forehead. 'Am I missing anything?'

'He got rabies once.'

'Exactly. And while he's off on the sick, who do you think gets lumbered with his caseload? Muggins. Like I don't have enough on my plate.' Steel puffed out her cheeks and slumped even further. 'I'm knackered the whole time; Jasmine won't stop screaming; Susan's nerves are in tatters so she's getting on mine; nobody's sleeping. . .' Sigh. 'Don't get me wrong: Jasmine's a wee darling, but *Jesus*. Now I know why some animals eat their young.'

Logan yawned again. 'At least you didn't get dragged out of your bed after an hour, by a grumpy—'

'Oh boo bloody hoo. For your own good, remember?' The inspector polished off the last of her buttie, swilling it down with another mouthful of coffee. 'Dying for a shag too. Bloody Susan's still no' up for it – they had to stitch her bits back together, and you know it—'

Logan held up a hand. 'I'm *eating*.'

'—like a doner kebab. If I don't get my end away soon I'm going to. . . Morning, Guv.'

Logan scrunched around in his seat. DCI Finnie was standing in the doorway, his face crumpled down at the edges. As if it needed a good iron.

'Inspector,' the head of CID held up a manila folder, 'why are there *still* no suspects in the Douglas Ewan case?'

Steel sniffed. 'You told me the McGregors took precedence. Remember?'

'I see. . .' Finnie's rubbery mouth became a thin-lipped line. 'Well, I'm *sorry* if I gave you the *impression* that you could drop everything and sit in here having a wee tea party instead. But perhaps, if it's not *too* much trouble, you wouldn't mind solving something?'

She put her mug down. 'It's no' that I haven't got any suspects for the Ewan case: I've got too bloody many. Dougy Ewan is a nasty raping wee bastard: half that bloody estate's got reason to kick the shite out of him. Interviewed fifty-two people so far, and they *all* think whoever did it deserves a knighthood. So coming in here "motivating" me's no' as helpful as you think.'

Finnie stiffened. 'I don't appreciate your—'

'Fuck's sake, Andy, I know you've got SOCA dancing on your bollocks with clogs on, but it's no' my fault, OK? We're doing our best here.'

Silence.

'And you. . .' The DCI turned on Logan. 'Tell me, Sergeant, did I imagine it, or did you swear to me that you could do a *much* better job on that drug bust than DI McPherson? Yet what do I find when I get in this morning? A matching set of signed *confessions*? A stack of seized drugs in the evidence stores?'

Logan shifted in his seat. 'Actually, sir—'

'No: I find half the evidence has been *flushed* down some junkie's toilet, and you let the ringleader get away!'

'It was . . . erm . . . we were—'

'Operational difficulties, Guv.' Steel tapped a fingernail against her mug. 'McRae was just debriefing me on the incident. Nothing he could've done without a firearms team: dirty big dog like that. It's remarkable he got the result he did, really. McPherson would've come back with half the team dead.'

Finnie's scowl slipped a bit. 'I see.' He looked at Logan in silence for a moment, raised an eyebrow, then back to Steel. 'We need to have a briefing for Superintendent Green.'

'Oh aye, and how is our friendly neighbourhood clog dancer?'

'Make sure the core team is in the boardroom at half eleven. And for God's sake send the no-hopers off somewhere. It *might* be nice if the Serious Organized Crime Agency didn't get the impression Grampian Police was *entirely* populated with morons, don't you think?' He turned back to Logan. 'And *you* can go chase up Lothian and Borders. I want that pathologist on the first flight to Aberdeen, *not* when they think it's convenient. Understand?'

'Actually, sir—'

'No: I don't want excuses, I want a bloody pathologist, and I want him here now!'

'But I—'

'Now!'

Someone out in the corridor cleared their throat.

Logan peered over Finnie's shoulder to see a bald man in a threadbare cardigan. The newcomer blinked watery grey eyes, then grinned: making the tufts of hair growing out of his bulbous nose bristle. 'Morning all. Sergeant McRae tells me you've got a wee girl's remains that need examining?'

8

Doc Fraser pulled a tartan hanky from his cardigan pocket, polished a pair of half-moon spectacles and slipped them on. The mortuary was cool and dark, the overhead lights blinking and buzzing as they warmed up. Something classical oozed out from the speakers of a new stereo unit, a black iPhone plugged into it. Violins and cellos casting dark and sombre sounds to echo back from the pristine white tiles.

The Anatomical Pathology Technician handed Logan a set of white Tyvec coveralls, then waved her creepy-spider fingers in the direction of a box of purple nitrile gloves. 'Please avail yourself of our . . . facilities.'

Doc Fraser slipped his feet out of his shoes, dropped his trousers, took off his cardigan and shirt, then clambered into his own SOC suit, getting the APT to help him with the zip. Hiding his baggy grey Y-fronts and string vest. 'Thanks, Sheila.'

A small bow. 'Shall I fetch . . . the *remains*?'

'Might as well, it's not. . .' He glanced down at the grey socks poking out from the legs of his SOC suit. There was a hole in one. 'You haven't still got my PM slippers, have you?'

She nodded, let her fingers creep through the air for a moment, picked up his discarded clothes, then turned and stalked from the room.

Doc Fraser waited until the door clunked shut. 'Is it just me, or has Ms Dalrymple gone a bit strange since I retired?'

Steel hauled up the hood of her oversuit. 'She's got a bet on with Biohazard.'

The pathologist shook his head, then looked around the low room. 'Can we get started, or are we expecting an audience?'

Logan snapped on a pair of gloves. 'Just Finnie.'

'Well, he'll have to get a shift on: I've got a three o'clock tee-time at Meldrum House and if I'm late there'll be trouble.' He picked a facemask from a box in the corner, stretched the elastic over his head, and let the mask dangle just under his chin. 'Can someone get the lights, please? And do something about the music, it's like a bloody funeral parlour in here.'

The spotlights above the cutting table blazed into life, glaring back from the stainless steel cutting table. The whole place reeked of disinfectant, bleach, and formaldehyde. The bowl of potpourri sitting next to the stereo didn't even make a dent in it. Logan flicked through the iPod, replacing Barber's *Adagio for Strings* with Del Amitri's *Move Away Jimmy Blue*.

'That's better.' The pathologist pulled at a roll of green plastic mounted on the wall, tearing off a length like a bin-bag and unfurling it into an apron. Putting it on as the door banged open. 'Ah, about time.'

Finnie bustled into the room and snatched up an SOC suit for himself, and another for the younger man who followed him in. 'Everyone, this is Superintendent Green from SOCA. He'll be observing.'

Superintendent Green – wavy blond hair, chiselled jaw, serious blue eyes, broad shoulders, narrow waist. Like something off the television. He gave a tight-lipped smile, a little tilt of the head. 'I'll try not to get in the way.' He even sounded as if he belonged on a cop show – a rich baritone voice with a faint London accent.

Steel leaned over and whispered in Logan's ear, 'Sodding hell: I would, wouldn't you?'

'No. And you're married.'

'Laz, I'm gay, no' dead. . .'

The head of CID zipped up his hood, then did the introductions – Steel holding onto Superintendent Green's hand for way longer than was either necessary or professional. When she finally let go, Finnie pointed across the cutting table. 'And last, but not least, this is Dr Duncan Fraser. Our forensic pathologist.'

Doc Fraser gave the superintendent a wave. 'Retired.' Sniff. 'Who's corroborating?'

Finnie pulled on a facemask.

Steel rocked back and forth on her heels.

Logan cleared his throat. 'You're it, Doc. Isobel's off at some conference and the new guy, Hudson's—'

'Indisposed.' Sheila, the APT, glided back into the cutting room, carrying a stainless steel tray with a pair of white plastic clogs on it. The kind with little holes in the top to let your feet breathe. She froze, then turned to stare at the stereo. 'Tsk. . .'

Steel nodded. 'Dose of the killer squits, apparently. Turning himself inside out as we speak.'

The APT rolled her eyes, then placed the clogs on the floor at Doc Fraser's feet. 'Most . . . *unfortunate*.' She stalked over to the iPod, and five seconds later Barber's *Adagio* was back.

Doc Fraser rolled his shoulders, an indistinct rustling

inside his white paper suit. 'Ah well, I'm not happy about it, but McRae said it was urgent, so I suppose needs must.' He drummed his fingers on the cutting table. 'Sheila, can you fetch the little girl's remains please? And can we *please* listen to something a bit cheerier? Bad enough as it is.'

The APT nodded at the tray, spotlights sparking off the shiny surface. A small evidence bag sat on one side.

The pathologist looked at her. 'What?'

She plucked the bag from the tray and lowered it reverently onto the slab. 'The remains.'

Silence. Just the mournful dirge of violins coming from the stereo.

'Seriously?' He opened the bag and tipped Jenny McGregor's toe out onto his palm. 'Is this *it*?'

Which probably made him the only person in the country who didn't know.

Doc Fraser held the digit up to the light, turning it back and forth, round and round. 'Unbelievable. . .'

It had been cleaned up since Logan last saw it, all the congealed blood removed for testing, the whole thing gone over with sticky tape to lift any fibres so they could be analysed. Nothing left but flesh, nail, and bone.

Steel tried to put her hands into pockets that weren't there. 'Do you no' read the papers?'

'Inspector, one of the best things about retiring – apart from the golf, the gardening, and the Viagra – is not having to wallow in society's filth every morning.' He raised his safety goggles, until they were sitting on top of his head, and peered at the pale yellow chunk of little girl.

Finnie stepped closer to the table. 'What can you tell us?'

There was a long pause. Then the pathologist placed the digit back on the slab.

'You see, this is why I retired.' Doc Fraser crumpled for

a moment. Sighed. Then peeled back the hood of his SOC suit. 'Sheila, I want the usual tests.'

'Yes, Doctor.'

Finnie leant over the cutting table. 'What?'

Doc Fraser shuffled over to the pedal bin in the corner, peeled off his gloves and dropped them in. 'We're finished here.'

That had to go on record as the shortest post mortem ever.

'Doctor?' Finnie straightened up. 'Where are you—'

'She's dead.' He removed his mask and apron, and sent them after the gloves. 'A wee girl. . .'

Steel groaned. Superintendent Green straightened his shoulders, chin up. Finnie swore.

Logan stared at the severed toe. Pale, bloodless, almost translucent. 'Are you sure she isn't just—'

'Look at the cut end.' Doc Fraser unzipped his SOC suit. 'No bruising, no discolouration, no lividity. Cut a toe off a living person and you make a hell of a mess: the tissue gets inflamed, blood flows to the damaged area, capillaries burst, subcutaneous bleeding makes a dark stain around the wound.' He struggled out of the suit, stood there in his vest and pants, one sock crumpled around an ankle. 'That toe was cut from a dead body. Your wee girl's dead.'

Logan followed DI Steel back up the mortuary steps and out onto the sun-bathed tarmac of the Rear Podium car park. It was bounded on one side by the seven-storey bulk of FHQ; the squat admin and mortuary blocks on two others; and – across a narrow lane – the dark granite wall of tenement buildings that made up the back of King Street. Normally it was wrapped in chilly shadows, but today it was positively Mediterranean.

Logan didn't bother stifling a jaw-cracking yawn. Shuddered. Blinked. Dug his hands deeper into his pockets.

Steel paused beside a CID pool car with 'Dirty Piggy Bastards!!!' spray-painted in dripping letters along the side, and produced a little plastic stick coloured to look like a cigarette. She stuck it in her mouth and tried for a puff. Then pulled the thing out and squinted at it. Had another go, sooking her cheeks hollow.

'Sodding bugger-monkeys. . .' She thrust the fake cigarette at Logan. 'You – man – fix.'

Logan watched DCI Finnie storm through the back doors into FHQ, Superintendent Green flowing along behind him. Like a cat in a reasonably-priced suit.

'When the press find out Jenny's dead, we're screwed. They'll—'

'Fix it, fix it, fix it!'

Logan twisted the fake plastic filter, and the e-cigarette went '*click*', then the end glowed an artificial ruby colour. He handed it back. 'SOCA's going to take over the investigation; we'll all be up in front of Professional Standards; and every newspaper, TV crew, and tosser on the street, is going to play Bash Grampian Police.'

Steel sucked on her fake cigarette. A thin wisp of vapour curled from the end. 'Aye, that's the real tragedy here, isn't it? No' a wee girl being dead or anything.'

Logan could feel the blush rushing up his cheeks, ears tingling.

Six years old, and they barely had enough to bury.

He looked away. 'Yeah, sorry.'

Fuck.

So much for the compassionate face of modern policing.

Steel patted him on the arm. 'Don't sweat it. I'll bet Finnie's arse isn't eating his frilly man-panties because Jenny's dead either. But do you no' think it might be nice if someone kept an eye on what actually matters?' Another sook. 'But you're right – we *are* fucked.'

'So what do we do now?'

'Well, I don't know about you,' Steel marched off towards the back door, sticking the fake fag back in her pocket, 'but I'm no' lying back and thinking of England.'

9

They pushed through the double doors into the custody area
– a bare concrete floor, breezeblock walls, 'HAVE YOU SEEN
THIS MAN?' posters, the smell of old sweat and stale biscuits.

A shrill, jagged, cry echoed down the corridor: 'I want a
fucking doctor!'

The reply sounded as if it was being spat between gritted
teeth: 'If you don't quiet down—'

'I'M FUCKING DYING!'

Logan turned the corner to the cell block. A Police Custody
and Security Officer was peering through the hatch of number
five, hands on her hips, white shirt rucked up at the back.
One epaulette nearly torn off. Hairdo all skewed to one side.
'You don't need a doctor, you need a good kick up the—'

'Morning, Kathy.' DI Steel paused on the way past to slap
the PCSO on the bum.

'Hoy!' Kathy glowered, both cheeks deep pink, eyes
scrunched into narrow slits. Then she saw Logan. '*You!*'

He backed off a step. 'What?'

'This,' she slapped a palm against the cell door, 'is *your*
fault. Trisha Brown – hospital turfed her out half an hour
ago and she's—'

'RAPE! I'VE BEEN RAPED! HELP!'

'Do you *see* what I've got to put up with?'

'I'M DYING!'

'Shut up!' Kathy hit the door again. 'I want her interviewed and out of here *now*!'

Logan held up his hands. 'It's McPherson's case – he's supposed to be interviewing the lot of them this afternoon.'

'This *afternoon*? I'm not—'

'I'M DYING IN HERE, YOU FUCKS!'

'Christ's sake!' The PCSO hauled the hatch open. 'Will you bloody shut it for five minutes!'

Steel glanced at the floor. 'You've sprung a leak.'

Logan followed her gaze, down to where a clear yellow puddle was seeping out from beneath the cell door and pooling around the PCSO's sensible shoes.

'Agh, you filthy cow!' She danced back a couple of steps, leaving damp footprints on the concrete.

They left her to it.

The Wee Hoose smelled of egg sandwiches left in the sun for too long, but Sergeant Biohazard Bob Marshall was nowhere to be seen.

'I can't – I've got a team briefing in half an hour.' Logan shifted his mobile from one ear to the other and settled into his seat, then froze, staring at his desk lamp. Someone had attached three socks and a pair of pale-grey lady's knickers to the metal shade with clothes-pegs.

Ha-bloody-ha.

DI McPherson's voice had that petulant sound kids used when their mums were dragging them past the sweetie aisle in the supermarket: *'But I don't know what you arrested them for! How can I interview them if—'*

'It was *your* operation: read the report.' Logan hauled the socks off his lamp, dumped them on the floor.

'But I can't—'

'And I'm not here this afternoon, anyway. You'll have to do it yourself.'

He reached for the pants, then stopped. Grabbed a blue nitrile glove from the big box by the door and used it to pull the pants from their peg. A thick brown skidmark ran the length of the gusset. He curled his top lip.

'Filthy bastards. . .'

'What?'

'No, not you, Guv; someone else.' He almost dropped the grubby knickers in the bin, then turned and stuffed them in Bob's top drawer instead. See how *he* liked it.

McPherson moaned for a bit, but eventually got the point and hung up. Logan slumped back in his seat, blinking up at the ceiling tiles. Be nice to just snooze for a couple of minutes. Not that there was any way in hell he'd risk it, not with Finnie storming around the place like an angry bull-frog.

Nothing for it, but to try and get some work done. He poked the power button on his creaky beige computer, listening to it bleep and groan and whir. Then the speakers made that psychic durrrrrrrrum-durrrrrrrrum-durrrrrrrrum buzz that meant his mobile was about to ring.

Sodding hell. What *now*?

But when the call came through the phone played the metal-chicken rendition of *Lydia the Tattooed Lady* Samantha had programmed into it for whenever she called.

'Hey, you.'

'*Logan? How come you're not home yet? Big day: you better not be getting cold feet on me!*'

'Two guesses.'

'*Oh for. . . You're in work, aren't you? You do know the Church's booked for half one?*'

'Yes, but—'

'Half one. On the dot.'

'Had to sort out a PM for Jenny McGregor's toe, and—'

'Don't make me drag you out of there, 'cause I will.'

'Doc Fraser says she's dead.'

Silence. *'Shit. . . I'm sorry.'*

'Yeah, me too.' Logan glanced up at the poster on the wall: 'HAVE YOU ANY INFORMATION?' The photo was a smiling mother and daughter, standing on Aberdeen beach, caught in a shaft of golden light, the cold grey swell of the North Sea foam-flecked and angry behind them. Now it was only a matter of time before the bodies turned up.

'Anyway, yes: half one. I'll be there, OK?'

'Good. Love you.' And the line went dead.

He checked his watch – just gone eleven – then his email. Memo; directive; memo; Sheriff Court times for everyone arrested last night at Shuggie Webster's house; general update on the hunt for Jenny and Alison McGregor's kidnappers; details of the emergency media briefing at half three; an invitation to PC Henderson's leaving bash—

A knock on the door.

Logan looked up from his screen to see *Acting* DI Mark MacDonald, clutching a little parcel – about the size of a hardback book.

Logan nodded. *'Guv.'*

MacDonald cleared his throat. 'Look, it's been a bastard of a week. . .' He clunked the door shut behind him and settled on the edge of his old desk, one finger tracing a figure-of-eight on the laminate wood surface. He held out the parcel. 'Peace offering?'

Logan unwrapped the brown paper. There was a brass plaque inside, mounted on a dark wooden plinth: 'THE WEE HOOSE'. A couple of screws and rawlplugs were Sellotaped to the back.

'I thought it could, you know: go on the wall outside.'

'Thanks.'

MacDonald nodded. Then sagged. 'Fuck me, being a DI is a pain in the arse. You don't want to swap do you?'

'Do I hell.'

'When it was Doreen's turn, what did she get? Two attempted murders and a run of unlawful removals. Three sodding months, Bill got nothing but break-ins. Me? I get the fucking *McGregors*.' He tugged at the edges of his goatee beard. 'It's not bloody fair.'

Logan powered his computer down again. 'Never is.'

'Sure you don't want to take your turn early?'

'Sorry, Mark – got a briefing to go to.'

'Three month job-share trial period my arse.' He picked the plaque up from Logan's desk. Held it against his chest. 'You remember how Insch used to take his pulse the whole time? Stick two fingers to his throat whenever he was going purple? I don't need to do that. I can hear the bloody thing pounding in my ears.'

'All right, that's *enough*.' Finnie stood at the front of the room with his hands up, until silence settled across the crowd again. Everyone involved in the investigation was jammed into FHQ's major incident room, the biggest in the building: CID, uniform, and support staff perched on chairs and desks, staring. The top brass sat at the front with Finnie, looking as if they were on their way to a funeral – Chief Superintendent Baldy Bain, the Assistant Chief Constable, the Deputy Chief Constable, and God himself – Chief Constable Anderson – all done up in full dress regalia, their silver buttons polished to a mirror shine.

One of the admin officers stuck up her hand.

Finnie stared at her for a moment. 'Yes?'

'Are you *sure* she's dead?'

The head of CID pursed his lips. 'No, I just *made that bit up*, because I thought it would be a *fun* excuse to get everyone together so we could plait each other's hair! Anyone have any *other* stupid questions?'

The admin officer went pink and lowered her hand.

Finnie scowled around the room. 'We are now investigating the abduction and *murder* of a six-year-old girl, and the abduction of her mother. Media briefing's at half three; Chief Superintendent Bain will be making the announcement about Jenny's death. I'm sure the media will do its usual *sterling* job of appealing for calm and reasoned reflection at this *difficult* time, but just in case: Acting DI MacDonald, you are now in charge of crowd control. I don't want some journalistic toss-pot using this to whip up a riot, understand?'

Logan watched Mark squirm in his seat.

'Yes, sir.'

'And I want every chiz handler we've got, out there pulling in their sources – someone, somewhere has to know something. DI McPherson, you can handle that.'

Which was bloody doubtful, McPherson could barely handle tying his own shoelaces. But at least this would keep him out of trouble: Covert Human Intelligence Sources were OK for burglaries and low-level drug trafficking, but whoever snatched Alison and Jenny McGregor weren't going to brag about it over a pint in Dodgy Pete's, were they?

Finnie pointed at the crumpled mess sitting next to Logan. 'DI Steel will be coordinating with all the other forces in the UK. Just because they were snatched in Aberdeen, doesn't mean they're being held here.' Finnie turned to his boss, Chief Superintendent Baldy Bain. 'Sir?'

Bain stood, gave the standard motivational – we're all in this together/everyone's depending on us/justice for Jenny – speech. Then he turned and nodded at the newcomer, sitting with the bigwigs. 'Right: we have Superintendent

Green from the Serious Organized Crime Agency with us. Superintendent, I think you want to say a few words?'

'Thanks.' He got to his feet and flashed them a smile, straight white teeth and furrowed brow. 'Before we go any further I just want you all to know that SOCA isn't here to tell you how to do your jobs, or take the investigation away from Grampian Police. I'm just here to provide a fresh pair of eyes, a sense-check, and all the support I can.'

And now Acting DI Mark MacDonald wasn't the only one squirming in his seat. But no one stood up and called Green a lying tosser.

'OK, so, while I'm up here: other options. How about background checks?'

Finnie's smile looked painful. 'Ongoing. I've got six teams working their way through Alison McGregor's colleagues and neighbours. We've already interviewed everyone on her course.'

'Family?'

'Adopted when she was three. Foster parents are both dead – one cancer, one heart attack. Husband's parents went in a house fire seven years ago.'

Green nodded, chewed the inside of his cheek for a moment. 'What about the production company?'

Finnie looked at Acting DI MacDonald.

Mark fumbled his way into a blue folder and pulled out a trembling sheet of paper. 'I spoke to the Met this morning and they say they've been through Blue-Fish-Two-Fish Productions with a nit comb. Company has a reputation for some pretty extreme publicity stunts, but DI. . .' Mark checked the sheet again, 'DI Broddur thinks they'd draw the line at kidnapping their own artistes. And they certainly wouldn't kill a wee—'

'OK.' Green nodded. 'Good work.'

Finnie cleared his throat. 'So, if there's nothing else—'

'Apart from the obvious? Don't just profile the offender, we need to profile the victim too.' Green turned, sweeping his arms out, indicating the scribbled whiteboards, scrawled flipcharts, and crowded corkboards that lined the incident room. 'We need to go back to the start, sift through everything we've got. There's a connection here – something that links Jenny and Alison McGregor to the bastards who kidnapped them. We just have to find it.'

Acting DI Mark MacDonald got as far as the window of DI Steel's office, turned round and paced back towards the door, about-faced and did it all over again. '"There's a connection here, we just have to find it."' Round again. 'Could that bastard be any more of a cliché if he tried?'

'Oh, park your arse and stop whining.' Steel pulled the e-cigarette from her gob, tilted her head back, opened her mouth in a wide 'O' and puffed. But instead of a perfectly-formed smoke ring, a mangled amoeba tumbled its way towards the ceiling. 'You're just jealous, because he's sex and chips.'

'He's a cock.' Mark slumped into the visitor chair next to Logan's and glowered. 'Coming up here, telling us how to—'

'Least *you're* on crowd control. *I've* got to play nice with Officer Tosser from every sodding force in the country.' She tried for another smoke ring. Failed. 'Laz, get a statement together: inter-force cooperation, agreed response times, service levels, utmost importance to catching Jenny's killer, blah, blah, blah.'

'Can't.' Logan stuck his mug on Steel's desk and stood. Groaned. Stretched. Slumped. 'Was supposed to be out of here at twelve, remember? I've got—'

'"A thing", aye, you've been banging on about your mysterious "thing" for weeks. It really more important than finding out who killed a wee girl and hacked off her toe?'

'Oh no you don't – I've been on duty for. . .' He checked his watch. 'Christ, thirty hours straight.' Well, with one hour off to clamber into his empty bed, but that hardly counted. He threw in a yawn for good measure. 'Shattered. . .'

She pursed her lips, narrowed her eyes. '*Fine*, I'll get Rennie to do it. Happy?'

'I've got to go.'

Steel pointed a finger at him, the skin stained yellow, the cherry-red nail varnish chipped. 'Tomorrow morning, seven o'clock, on the sodding dot. And bring—'

The phone on her desk rang.

'Sod. . .' She peered at the display, then snatched up the receiver. 'Susan? What's. . . No. . . Susan, calm down, it's. . .' Steel crumpled forward, until her head was resting on the desktop. 'No. No I'm not saying that, Susan, it's. . . Yes. . .'

Logan slipped out through the door.

10

'You sure you want to go through with this?' Samantha squeezed his hand.

Logan swallowed, blinked, cranked his smile up a notch. 'Yes. It's fine. Really. I want to do this.' He ran a finger around the inside of his shirt collar. 'Just a bit . . . you know.'

'You're . . . not just doing this for *me*, are you?'

Of course he was. Well, maybe. A bit anyway.

The Church was bathed in sunlight, the walls glowing with bright colours, a bunch of flowers in a vase perfuming the air.

'No. I really want to do this.'

'Only, if you want to back out, I'll understand.' She looked away. 'Because, you've got to commit to this for the rest of your life. . .'

A shadow fell across them, and Logan looked up to see a large bald man beaming at him through a Grizzly Adams beard, a dog collar just visible through all that hair. 'Are we ready?'

Sam squeezed Logan's hand again. 'Last minute nerves.'

The big man nodded. 'I understand. It's a big step, but I'm here to make it as easy as possible.' He patted Logan on the shoulder. 'Shall we?'

Deep breath. Glance at Samantha – smiling with her brows all furrowed, the silver ring in her nose sparking in the sunlight. Back to the Reverend. Nod.

'Excellent.' The big man steepled his fingers. 'So if you'll just take off your shirt and climb in the chair, we'll get started. Won't hurt a bit.'

11

Darkness. Black, like the cat that sleeps on the wall at the bottom of the garden. The one that hisses and scratches.

She blinks.

Teddy Gordon's eyes sparkle like a crow's. He's sitting on the end of the bed grinning at her. She *hates* Teddy Gordon. Hates his nasty blue fur. Hates his horrid stitched-on smile. Hates the way he smells of smoking.

Teddy Gordon knows she hates him. That's why he's friends with the monster.

If she had her way, Teddy Gordon would live at the bottom of the wheelie-bin, all dirty and stinky with the green-brown water that leaks out of the bin-bags. But Mummy says she has to be nice to Teddy Gordon, because Teddy Gordon was a present from a man Mummy likes. A man who gives her nice things. Much nicer things than Daddy ever did.

Daddy wouldn't let Teddy Gordon sleep on the end of her bed.

Her room smells of bananas and ice cream, but the little plastic thing plugged into the wall by the nightlight still can't

69

cover the old-man smell of the blue teddy bear. The window glows a pale orange, making thick shadows between the chair and the wall, behind the toy cupboard, down the side of the wardrobe. Creeping out from under the bed. . .

She tries to lie really still and quiet, like a dead person.

She's not awake. She's asleep, like a Good Little Girl.

Only Bad Little Girls wake up in the middle of the night.

That's when the monster comes out.

She shivers, even though she knows she mustn't move at all. Not even a tiny bit.

The monster doesn't like Bad Little Girls.

The monster with its sharp white teeth and bright-red claws.

Lie still. Don't move an inch.

She can hear it, out in the hallway, creeping on its soft hairy paws, making the floorboards creak. Creak. Creak.

She holds her breath.

Go away. No one's awake in here. Only Good Little Girls, fast asleep and dreaming of ponies.

Please go away. . .

But the monster knows.

A rattle. A clunk. And then the door groans like an old man.

A pause.

She holds her breath.

Go away. Go away. GO AWAY!

Good Little Girl. Sleeping.

The monster rustles, right beside her bed. Breathing.

Whooomph. . . *Hissssssss*. Whooomph. . . *Hissssssss*.

Standing right over her. In the dark.

Don't move. . .

But her chest aches, like a big purple bruise. And then her body tells on her, gasping in a great whoosh of air. And now it's too late: it knows she's awake. Her eyes snap open. . .

70

Light spills in through the open door. Teddy Gordon grins from the bottom of the bed.

But the monster's different. Its face is waxy-shiny, and it's naked – its skin all crinkly white, rustling as it breathes. Whooomph. . . *Hissssssss*. Whooomph. . . *Hissssssss*. One eye glows red in the darkness.

Daddy. . .

No. . .

Don't leave us. . .

The monster reaches for her with sticky purple fingers.

She screams.

12

Logan took another sip of coffee and clicked his mouse on the little red 'Replay' icon. A moment of darkness. Then the video started playing again. Fourth time in a row. The counter beneath it showed 6,376,451 views since the ransom demand was uploaded eight days ago.

The quality wasn't great. Better than a lot of things posted on YouTube, but still jerky and grainy. A low-light image, all the colour leached away by whatever setting they'd used on the camcorder to make it record in the middle of the night – and there it was: the most famous house in the country. Or the back of it, anyway.

A plain, two-storey, brick box, just like all the other plain, two-storey, brick boxes in the street, with a six-foot tall wooden fence running all the way along the back gardens.

He shifted the headphones again and turned the volume up full, but there was nothing there. Not even a hiss. Complete silence. At least for this bit. . .

'03:05:26' blinked in the bottom left hand corner of the screen.

The camera swung left then right – checking the little alleyway was empty – and then a pair of heavy-duty bolt cutters appeared on the screen. They crunched through the shackle of a massive padlock, then a pale-grey hand reached into shot and pushed the gate open.

The image shook as the cameraman hurried up the path to the back door.

Someone stepped in front of the camera – filling the screen with an expanse of grey-white – and then they were inside.

According to the time-stamp at the bottom of the screen less than two minutes had passed.

Kitchen: old fashioned units and a fridge freezer covered with newspaper clippings and childish drawings.

Hallway: floral wallpaper, a couple of generic pictures in cheap-looking frames.

Stairs: a photo halfway up. Logan couldn't see what of.

Landing: three doors leading off.

He clicked the mouse again, maximizing the window so the video filled the whole screen.

The camera went straight for the door on the right. It had a little wooden sign on it: 'JENNY'S ROOM'. Through into a child's bedroom: stuffed toys piled on a little chest; books on a shelf; a nightlight glowing by the wardrobe. A single bed against the wall.

A little girl lay beneath the covers. She was flat on her back, eyes closed, face all scrunched up, trembling in the grainy gloom, a teddy bear sitting at her feet.

The camera moved closer.

Her eyes snapped open, then bulged. Mouth open, gasping. Staring.

A grey hand reached into shot. Right hand: the skin completely featureless, just a couple of wrinkles between the thumb and forefinger where the latex glove didn't quite fit.

Jenny McGregor screamed, the sound booming in Logan's earphones. He winced. And then the footage went silent again.

The gloved hand darted forward, grabbing the duvet and ripping it away.

She scrambled backwards, her Winnie the Pooh pyjamas all tangled around her torso, little bare feet rucking the sheets as she shoved herself into the corner. Screaming, over and over again. Nothing came through Logan's headphones, just the faint buzz of silence turned up too loud.

The hand snatched a handful of pyjama top and—

Fingers wrapped around Logan's shoulder.

He flinched so hard he nearly fell out of his chair. Yanked off his headphones. Turned round and glared at DS Biohazard Bob Marshall. 'Very bloody funny!'

Bob danced back a couple of steps, both hands up, a grin on his face. 'Just asking if you wanted a coffee.'

'How long were you standing there?'

'From about the time they were going up the stairs. Good job you had the old headphones on, or you'd've heard me giggling.' Bob threw himself into his swivel chair, hard enough to make the wheels come off the ground on the rebound. 'Your face was classic.'

Logan stared at him. 'A wee girl's *dead*, Bob.'

Silence. Bob sighed. 'She was grabbed a week ago: you and I both know she's been dead for days. Lucky if she lived through the first night. . . Aye, well, maybe lucky's not the right word.' He twirled around, then pulled a newspaper from the pile on his desk and chucked it over. 'Front page.'

On Logan's screen another figure in a white SOC-style oversuit – the kind sold in DIY stores everywhere – was hauling a struggling Alison McGregor down the stairs: duct tape over her mouth, hands bound behind her back, legs bound at the ankle, curly blonde hair whipping from side to side as she tried to head-butt her abductor.

He hit pause, then picked up the newspaper. It was a copy

of the *Edinburgh Evening Post*, the headline, 'Hook Line And Stinker – Police Fall For "Jenny's Dead" Hoax'.

'God's sake. . .'

'Gets better. Check out the third paragraph.'

Logan skimmed the first two, swore, then read it out loud. '"It's obvious to anyone with half a brain – brackets – which clearly excludes most of Grampian Police – close brackets – that Blue-Fish-Two-Fish Productions are up to their old tricks again. This is the company that handed out used tampons at T in the Park last year, the company that projected a naked photograph of Benjamin Kerhill on Big Ben, the company that proudly tattooed a live pig in Trafalgar Square". . .'

'Keep going.'

'"The police need to understand that all they're doing here is helping an unscrupulous company whip up interest in the McGregors' upcoming album. What's next: the HMS Ark Royal, sponsored by Lamb's Navy Rum? The fire brigade, brought to you by Gaviscon?". . .' Logan crumpled the paper up and rammed it into the bin beside his desk. Then hauled it out again. 'Who wrote this?'

'You stopped before you got to the rant about "throwing away tax payers' money" and "institutional gullibility".'

'Michael Bloody Larson.' Logan stuck the thing back in the bin again.

'Ask me, the bastard needs a stiff kicking.' Bob stretched out his legs, crossed his ankles, then stuck his hands behind his head. 'Still, at least you're getting some media interest. I've been trying for days to get them to print something about my case. *"Sex-god sergeant leads hunt for missing alky."* or, *"Handsome Bob Marshall, twenty-four, in race to find Stinky Tam the Holburn Street tramp."*'

'Twenty-four?'

'Shut up. Poor old Tam's been gone two weeks now and no bugger's got any idea if he's sodded off for a fortnight in

75

glamorous Stonehaven, or lying dead behind the bins somewhere. Guess where my money's at?' Bob curled his top lip. 'And Stinky Tam wasn't exactly a bowl of lilies at the best of times.' He creaked his chair from side to side a couple of times, then pointed at Logan's screen: the figure in the SOC suit and Alison McGregor. 'Don't know how you can watch that over and over. Creeps me out.'

'What else can I do? We've got sod-all forensics. According to the lab there's not a single fingerprint in the whole house that doesn't belong to Alison, Jenny, the babysitter, or Alison's dead husband. No hair, no fibres, no DNA, footprints. . . Nothing.'

'Pfff. . . What do you expect? Look at them.' He pointed at the screen again. 'Course there's sod-all forensics: they're not thick, are they? No, they're wearing the same stuff we do: oversuits, gloves, booties, facemasks. That's what you get for having all this crime drama on the telly, every bugger out there's getting a weekly masterclass in how to get away with murder.'

The only forensic evidence the kidnappers had left behind was a faint dusting of tiny brass filings, caused by whatever they'd used to pick the lock on the back door.

Bob sniffed. 'You chase up YouTube?'

'Nothing. They can trace the upload back through to a couple of servers in Bangladesh, but after that. . .? Could've come from anywhere.' Logan picked the forensic report out of his in-tray. 'Everything: every note, every envelope, every video – it's like they've been put together in a vacuum by bloody ghosts.'

A gravelly voice came from the CID room outside, ruining a Fifties song, 'Oh yes, I'm the great pudenda; pudendin' I'm doing well. . .'

DI Steel pushed through the door to the Wee Hoose, huge mug of coffee in one hand, chocolate biscuit in the other.

'Morning, ladies.' She stuffed the biscuit in her gob and bumped the door closed with her hip.

Logan scowled at her. 'Seven AM *sharp*, you said. Where have you been?'

'It's your lucky day, Laz. Susan says she's probably up for a wild ride on the orgasm express this weekend, so I shall forgive your rudeness if you tell me you've sent that letter off.'

'You said you'd get Rennie to do it.'

'No I didn't.'

'You bloody well did! Bob, tell her.'

'Now, now, Laz.' Bob grinned and turned back to his computer. 'It's not nice to contradict a lady.'

'You rotten—'

A knock on the door, then PC Guthrie stuck his pasty head into the Wee Hoose. 'Guv?' He nodded at DI Steel. 'This just came in. . .'

Guthrie held up a clear plastic evidence pouch. There was a sheet of A4 in it, creased as if it had been folded into thirds, covered in jagged blue biro.

Steel grabbed it off him, squinted at the note for a bit, then held it out to Logan. 'Read.'

It was all in block capitals, the letters lopsided and sloppy, traced over and over again. Probably disguising their handwriting. 'Sodding hell. . .'

The inspector wrinkled her nose. 'Well? What does it say?'

'It's a tip-off. Says Alison and Jenny were snatched by a paedophile ring.'

Bob squeaked around in his chair and peered over Logan's shoulder. 'They've spelled "paedophile" wrong. And "snatched". . .'

'Says they're going to auction Jenny off – after they've all. . . Shite. After they've all "sampled the merchandise". They're going to kill her mum soon as they get the ransom.'

Guthrie nodded. 'Arrived in the post today. Finnie said I had to show you, then get it up to the lab.'

Steel crunched her way through her biscuit, frowning. 'Bit risky, isn't it?'

Logan read the note again. 'Could be a hoax?'

'Don't know.' Bob poked the evidence bag. 'If you're going to lust after wee girls, what could be better than screwing the pretty six-year-old off the telly? Bet there's paedos up and down the country recording *Britain's Next Big Star* and wanking themselves ragged every time she comes on.'

Celebrity paedophilia – why not, they'd had celebrity everything else. . . Logan handed the note back to Guthrie. 'Anything on the envelope?'

'Just the address. Didn't even have a stamp; lucky it got delivered at all.'

'Right,' Steel dumped her mug on Doreen's desk. 'Laz, get onto Bucksburn: I want the Diddymen hauling in every pervert they've ever dealt with. And no' just the ones on the register, the lapsed ones too. We'll start with the paedos, then try our luck with the rapists. And don't let them fob you off with—'

'Why would rapists—'

'Just because they've no' been done for kiddy-fiddling, doesn't mean they're no' into it. Sometimes you've got to convict the filthy fucks for what you can get.'

Logan thumped the wodge of stapled-together paper down on DI Steel's desk. 'Three hundred and thirty-nine sex offenders living in the north-east. That's them arranged by offence, in order of closeness to Alison McGregor's house.'

Steel prodded the paperwork with a stained finger. 'This all of them?'

'All the ones on the register. Ingram says he'll get the rest written up by close of play.'

'Sodding hell, that's a lot of perverts. . .'

'Can't drag them all into Bucksburn, or FHQ – someone's bound to notice and call the media, so I've booked a bunch of rooms at the Munro House Hotel. Told them we're interviewing for Special Constables; they're even doing us a discount on the corporate rate. If we haul three-hundred-odd people in there over a couple of days, no one's going to notice.'

She scrunched one eye closed, flipping through the wodge of printouts. 'Right, get onto Big Gary, I want—'

'Twelve-man team, all accredited interviewers, six video cameras, and an unmarked minibus. Ready to go whenever you are.'

There was a pause.

'Nobody likes a smart arse.'

The hotel was a huge Victorian mock-Scottish-Baronial mansion – a forbidding lump of granite with turrets, bay windows, and gable ends shaped like a staircase for crows – only a five-minute walk from the Bucksburn police station, where the Offender Management Unit were based.

Steel marched up the sweeping grey steps, past two carved lions. 'How many we doing?'

Logan checked the list. 'As many as we can get through. DI Ingram's lot are bringing them in from half nine.'

'All paedos?'

'A mixture. I've told him to bring them in based on how close they live to Alison McGregor's house.'

The unmarked minibus kangarooed into the car park, a grim-faced Rennie wrestling with the steering wheel. It jerked to a halt and a ragged cheer went up from the passengers.

'Fair enough.' She shoved open the heavy oak door and

79

barged through into the reception, with Logan right behind her.

The Munro's carpet was a muted blue tartan, with a pale groove worn into it leading away into the gloomy interior. Wooden panelling lined the walls, peppered with watercolours of mountains in heavy golden frames. A stag's head was stuffed and mounted above the reception desk, glaring out in mild surprise at Logan and the inspector.

'Can I help you?' A man in a charcoal-coloured suit appeared at the inspector's elbow. He stood slightly hunched and knock-kneed, as if his underwear was doing horrible things to his undercarriage.

Logan flashed his warrant card. 'I called earlier about running some interviews?'

'Ah, yes, of course: the Special Constables.' The man clasped his hands together in front of his chest. 'Your six rooms should be ready shortly, but I've taken the liberty of setting up a base of operations in the Crianlarich meeting room as well. There should be complimentary teas, coffees, and some pastries waiting for you.'

Steel wrapped an arm around the concierge, smiling up at him. 'Throw in a couple of steak pies and a bottle of Macallan, and I might never leave.'

Frank Baker (24) – Indecent Exposure, Lewd and Libidinous Practices and Behaviour

'I really don't see how this concerns me, Mr. . . ?'

'*Sergeant* McRae.'

'Ah. . .' Frank Baker crossed his legs, made sure the crease in his tan chinos was *perfectly* straight, then did the same with the parting in his floppy brown hair. 'Well, Sergeant, you see, I've never actually met—'

'You live on the same street.' Detective Constable Rennie crossed his legs, ran a hand through his own hair. Little flakes of skin were peeling off of his nose and forehead, glowing in the sun's rays. 'You have to see why we'd want to talk to you, Frank.'

'Yes, well. . .' He cleared his throat, then glanced at the little video camera mounted on a cheap tripod in the corner. 'It's really all just a silly mistake, you see, it was a mis-understanding, I really shouldn't be on the register in the first place, I just—'

'You just *happened* to expose yourself through the railings of a primary school?' Logan checked the notes pinned to his clipboard. 'Then did it again at the duck pond in Duthie Park.'

'Well. . .'

'And then you tried to get a little boy to come into the toilets with you in Hazlehead Park, didn't you, Mr Baker?'

Frank Baker's cheeks turned a fiery shade of pink. Then his chin came up. 'I don't see how that makes me a kidnapper!'

Rennie leaned forward and patted Baker on the knee. 'It's OK, Frank, no one's saying you kidnapped anyone, we—'

'They dragged me out of work to come here, you know! Two hairy constables, where I work!'

Logan checked his notes. 'Says here you're a welder?'

'They came to my *work*.' He uncrossed his legs, then crossed them the other way around. Went through the same routine with all his creases. 'No one there knows about . . . my misunderstanding. And I'd like to keep it that way.'

'A *welder*?' Somehow it was difficult to imagine the prissy floppy-haired neat-freak sitting in front of them doing anything as messy as that.

'They had no business bundling me into a patrol car like some sort of criminal.' Baker brushed imaginary lint from his sleeve. 'I know what you're thinking, and you're

wrong. I would never *ever* touch a little girl. They're not. . .'
He shuddered slightly. 'I never even spoke to her. Or her
mother. I wouldn't know them if I passed them on the
street.'

Rennie uncrossed his legs, then crossed them again.
Brushed something from his trouser leg. 'Not even when
they got on the TV?' He'd been doing this since the start of
the interview: every time Baker did anything, Rennie copied
it. Like a sunburnt reflection.

'Dear God, it was a nightmare. Soon as they made it
through the first two stages there were reporters *everywhere*.
I couldn't go out my front door without a half dozen of the
grubby little swines pointing cameras in my face. "Do you
know Alison and Jenny?", "What do they like to eat for
breakfast?", "Does Alison have a man in her life?" On and
on, every single day.' He took a deep breath, and Logan
watched Rennie do exactly the same thing.

Baker looked out of the window. 'It's very . . . inconven-
ient for someone in my position to be harassed by the media.
It makes me uncomfortable.'

Logan tapped his pen against the clipboard. 'So you're
saying you never spoke to, interacted with, or had anything
to do with Alison and Jenny McGregor?'

Baker closed his eyes, pursed his lips. 'I don't know them.
I've never known them. I don't *want* to know them.'

'Do you watch a lot of television, Mr Baker?'

'Sometimes.'

'Documentaries, the news, or are you an *X-Factor* and
Britain's Next Big Star kinda guy?'

Baker gave an exaggerated sigh. 'OK, OK. . . I watched
them. Every week, up there singing and dancing and getting
famous. For what? What the hell was so special about Alison
Bloody McGregor and her little girl? Oh, Jenny's daddy died
in Afghanistan, boo bloody hoo.'

'Iraq, Mr Baker. James McGregor died in Iraq.'

'Same difference.' He scowled at the floor. 'I never touched them. I didn't kidnap them. I didn't kill her, or her horrible little child. I wouldn't dirty my hands. . .'

Darren McInnes (52) – Exposing Children to Harm/Danger or Neglect, Possessing Indecent Images of Children, Theft by Housebreaking, Serious Assault

'No, that's not what I'm saying.' McInnes brushed his long, greasy yellow-grey hair from his face and tied it in a loose ponytail. He pursed his lips, the folds around his grey eyes deepening behind thick glasses. 'I'm saying I had nothing to do with them.'

At least he *looked* like a paedophile. Baker could have passed for a swimming pool attendant, but there was no mistaking Darren McInnes.

McInnes shifted in his seat, Rennie copying his every move. 'Can I smoke?' He pulled out a tin of tobacco.

Logan shook his head. 'There's a hundred and fifty pound fine for smoking in the hotel, Mr McInnes. Where were you last week: Wednesday night, Thursday morning?'

'Bloody government. I should be able to smoke if I want to, they're *my* bloody lungs.'

Logan banged on the arm of his chair, making the lanky man flinch.

'Where – were – you?'

'I don't know. I was at home. Probably. Watching TV. Maybe I had a couple of beers, it's not illegal is it?'

'How well do you know Alison and Jenny McGregor?'

'We've been over this. I don't, OK? Yes, I was aware of them, but I don't follow all that reality television shite. Whatever happened to the good old days, eh? When they used to make decent drama and comedy and documentaries? Now it's all about sticking a bunch of nobodies on the box and raking the cash in with dodgy telephone scams. Makes you sick.' He produced the tobacco tin again, popped it open and pulled out a packet of Rizla papers.

'I said no smoking.'

McInnes looked up at Logan. 'I'm not smoking, I'm rolling, OK? That still allowed in Nazi Britain?'

Rennie pulled a pen from his pocket and fiddled with it. 'And you never watched Alison and Jenny on the TV, at all?'

'Oh, I heard them on the radio. Everywhere you go, they're on the radio, singing that bloody awful song. They didn't even write it. Cover versions, that's all people can do these days.'

Logan stood and walked around until he was standing directly behind McInnes. Looming. Up close he smelled of unwashed hair and stale cigarettes. 'Do you know anyone who's selling a little girl?'

'Ah.' The lanky man pulled a sheet of translucent paper from the little packet, then dug into a pouch of tobacco. 'Well, sometimes one hears certain . . . *rumours*. Internet chat rooms, news groups, that kind of thing.'

'Anyone talking about Jenny McGregor?'

He fiddled a line of thin brown curls down the middle of the paper, then ran a pale yellow tongue along one edge. 'Celebrity child like that. . . Hmm. . . It *would* give things an extra kick, wouldn't it? Knowing everyone's out there, looking for her, but she's all yours. And you can do anything you want. . .' McInnes rolled the cigarette into a tight cylinder and pinched the excess tobacco from the ends. 'Can you imagine what she'd be worth on the open market?' He cleared his throat. 'If she wasn't dead.'

Logan stared at him. 'You tell me.'

McInnes popped the newly formed cigarette in the tin and produced another rolling paper. 'I really wouldn't know.

And before you ask: Jenny isn't my type.' He smiled, showing off a set of uneven brown teeth. 'Far too old.'

Sarah Cooper (35) – Lewd and Libidinous Practices and Behaviour, Abduction, Attempted Murder

'Such an awful thing to happen.' Sarah Cooper leaned forward in her seat, exposing a cavernous expanse of freckled cleavage, blue silk blouse stretched tight across her swollen belly and massive breasts. Her pork-sausage fingers traced a circle on her short black skirt, the nails as scarlet as her lips. 'I can only imagine what poor Alison must be going through. . .'

Rennie did his mirror thing again. 'Can you tell us where you were last Wednesday night, Thursday morning?'

She blushed, looked away. Pink cheeks clashing with her Irn-Bru-orange hair. 'To lose a child like that. . .'

Logan checked his watch. Half-eleven already and they'd only seen four people on the list. If the other teams were going at this rate it was going to take at least another three days to get through everyone on the Sex Offenders' Register. Assuming DI Ingram and the Diddymen could track them all down. And it was getting hot in here, making his arm itch beneath the wadding. 'You didn't answer Constable Rennie's question, Ms Cooper. Where were you the night Alison and Jenny were snatched?'

Not that she could have had anything to do with it. Her backside was far too large to fit in an SOC suit. Hell, it barely fitted in her seat: if she got up too quickly, she'd be wearing the thing as a bum warmer.

'I was . . . with a friend.' She shifted her buttocks, making the chair creak.

Logan smiled at her. 'Whom?'

'I don't see how that's any business of—'

'It's OK, Sarah,' Rennie shifted in his seat, arranging himself in a perfect reflection, 'we just need to eliminate you from our enquiries. You want to help us catch whoever hurt Jenny, don't you?'

The blush deepened. 'I. . . I read all about them, you know. When *OK!* did that big spread on them: Alison and Jenny at home. Such a cramped little house for such a huge talent.'

'We need a name, Ms Cooper. And an address.'

'I don't. . .' She ran a hand across her neck, sweat glistened in the crevasse between her breasts.

'Where were you?'

'Come on, Sarah, you can tell us.'

Another wipe of cleavage. 'Can I have a glass of water or something, it's very hot in here.'

'Might as well get it off your chest.'

Her eyes flickered across the room. The door, the window, the bathroom. 'I. . . I was babysitting.' Both hands clenched in her lap. 'A friend of a friend asked if I could watch her little boys. I didn't touch them, if that's what you're thinking. I didn't do anything. I just watched them. Nothing happened.'

Lee Hamilton (32) – Rape, Possession of an Offensive Weapon
'What the fuck would I want with a wee girl? The mother, *maybe*, but fuck's sake, the kid was only six!'

Duncan McLean (46) – Indecent Assault, Attempted Rape, Possession with Intent to Supply
'. . . would *never* touch someone like that. I mean, they're . . . *female*. How disgusting would that be?'

Logan hung his jacket on the hook in the bathroom, took off his tie, then unbuttoned his shirt. The wadding taped to the top of his left arm almost glowed, it was so white. He peeled back a corner and grimaced. Skin was still all red and inflamed – so much for 'it won't hurt a bit'.

He dug a little tube of antibacterial gel from his jacket

pocket, squeezed some into his palm and smoothed it on. Trying not to wince. At least it didn't look—

A knock at the door.

'Sarge?' It was Rennie. 'Next one's here.'

Alastair McMillan (42) – Indecent Assault, Possession of Indecent Images, Theft

'"I want to dedicate this to my husband John; you'll always be our hero. . ." I mean, who was she trying to kid? Like rainbows and puppies come out of her arse instead of shite like the rest of us.' Sniff.

Alastair McMillan leant forward, and tapped a dirty, chewed fingernail against Logan's knee. 'She fucking deserves everything she's got coming to her, know what I mean?'

Ross Kelley (19) – Indecent Assault

'You have very pretty eyes, Constable. . .'

Shona Wallace (26) – Taking and Distributing Illegal Images of Children, Lewd and Libidinous Practices and Behaviour, Attempt to Pervert the Course of Justice

'. . . shouldn't really be surprised, should we? There are some very sick people out there.' Shona Wallace flicked a strand of bleached blonde hair out of her eyes. She shrugged, bony shoulders rising and falling beneath her LITTLE MISS NAUGHTY T-shirt. 'I mean, it's like, you know, you stand up and do anything in this country and the weirdos just latch onto you, don't they?'

She smiled, her weak chin disappearing into the pale skin of her neck. The kind of girl-next-door you didn't want living anywhere near you. 'Oh: do you remember that woman? What was her name, you know, like, she was this big ugly heifer and she was saying all these horrible things about Alison? In the papers and that?'

Rennie nodded. 'Vicious Vikki?'

'Yeah, that's right. God, what a cow. Jealousy, that's all it is. Me I thought Alison and Jenny were the best thing on *Britain's Next Big Star*. I mean, like, they really *were*, you know: stars. The series is going to be *totally* crap without them.'

She scooted forward in her seat, until her knees were nearly touching Rennie's, blue eyes wide, a heavy layer of mascara making them look even bigger. 'What's her house really like inside? Is it cool? I bet it's cool. Bet they hid away all the really cool stuff when they got the cameramen round, you know, for the *OK!* magazine shoot, yeah? She's like on the radio all the time, she's got to have, I don't know, a jacuzzi and diamonds and champagne and that?'

'Bloody awful, that's how it's going.' Logan slumped into one of the chairs arranged around the long meeting table. 'What's happening about lunch?'

Right on cue, PC Guthrie backed into the room, carrying a cardboard box. The smell of fresh baking oozed out to fill the room. 'Get them while they're hot.'

Steel sniffed. 'You took your time.'

The box went on the table. 'Fourteen steak, six mince, four macaroni, four cheese and onion pasties, and a dozen sausage rolls.'

'Where's my change?'

'And about a million packets of tomato sauce.' Guthrie dug a hand into his pocket and produced a mound of coins. They rattled on the tabletop.

The interview team swarmed around the box, pulling out grease-spotted paper bags, checking the contents, and passing on anything they didn't fancy.

Logan rubbed his fingertips against his eyelids, trying to massage the grit away. 'Lots of rumours about Jenny being available for a price, but no one knows who's selling. Or they're not saying.'

Rennie appeared with a pair of paper bags, the green-and-gold Chalmers of Bucksburn logo going slightly transparent. 'Macaroni pie, or cheese and onion pasty?'

'Cheese and onion.' He took the proffered bag and scrunched it down around the golden flaky pastry like a makeshift napkin. 'I mean, what are we supposed to do? No one's going to stick their hand up and admit to kidnapping and murder, are they?'

Steel shrugged, then took a dainty bite out of her pie and chewed. 'Early days, Laz. Got a lot more perverts to get through.'

'Yeah, and at the rate we're going it'll take us three and a half days, minimum.'

'Oh.' She stared at the hole in her pie for a moment, then tore the top off a sachet of tomato sauce and squirted it inside.

Logan frowned. 'Unless we get the back shift to do some?'

A nod. 'Sort it out with Ding-Dong. Sooner we get a result the better.'

'Have you been to the scene?' The pasty was filled with savoury napalm, almost too hot to eat. He brushed pastry flakes from his fingertips as he chewed. 'I was thinking of paying a visit later. Get a feel for the ground.'

A lump-faced constable stuck her head around the meeting room door. 'Guv?' She waved at DI Steel. 'That's the next bunch arrived downstairs, you want me to get them up to the rooms, or let them stew for a bit?'

'Fuck 'em, we're eating pies.' Steel took another bite and the tomato sauce she'd so carefully squirted in squirted out in a blood-spatter, all over her hand. 'Bastard. . .' She licked at her wrist. 'Where's the napkins?'

'I mean, they must've checked out the house before the abduction, they went straight to Jenny's room and—' Logan

89

swore, his phone was ringing. He hauled it out with greasy fingers and checked the display: 'Unknown'.

'Hello?'

'Hello?'

'Who's—'

'Hello? Can you hear me?' Doc Fraser must have been fiddling with the buttons at his end, because a series of bleeps sounded in Logan's ear. Followed by, *'Logan? You there? I've just got the tox screen back from the lab. Thought you'd want an update before I went and spilled the beans to Finnie and his fellow wankers.'*

Logan opened his mouth, then shut it again. 'Er, Doc, are you sure you should be—'

'Now pay attention: we scraped every little vein in that toe for blood cells and found trace amounts of morphine. The fatty tissue contained a minuscule quantity of thiopental sodium. And I mean a tiny, tiny quantity. Damn lucky we detected anything at all.'

He dug his notebook out of his pocket, pinned the phone between his ear and his shoulder, and scribbled it all down. . . Taking a rough stab at the spelling, 'Thigh-o-penthal (sp?)'. 'Care to hazard a guess?'

'You buggers never change, do you? At a guess – and this is just a guess – she was given the morphine to keep her quiet. Compliant. It would work pretty well as a sedative. Thiopental sodium, on the other hand, is a general anaesthetic. They probably planned to put her under before removing the toe, but something went wrong. An allergic reaction maybe, or she'd eaten too recently, threw up, and choked. . . Either way, it was quick – if that's any consolation – otherwise there'd be more of the drug laid down in the fatty tissue.'

Logan closed his eyes. 'When?'

'Nearly impossible to tell. But from the look of it, I'd say it was severed at least six hours after death, then kept in a fridge. Maybe up to a week?'

So Bob was right – Jenny was dead before they'd even received the first ransom demand.

'The amputation's pretty good, certainly done by someone with medical training using a thin, fine blade. And thiopental sodium is used to knock people out before they go in for surgery – before they put you on the air and gas. So you're looking at hospitals: operating theatres, in-house pharmacy, neurology, the ITU. . . Or maybe a vet? I think they use it on animals too.'

'What about doctors' surgeries, GPs, people like that?'

'They don't get anything stronger than lidocaine. Same with dentists.'

'Thanks, Doc.' Deep breath. 'Can you do me a favour?'

'Depends.'

'When you tell "the wankers", don't call them that, OK? Just because you're retired doesn't mean they won't take it out on us.' Logan pressed disconnect, then looked up to see Steel staring at him.

'Well?'

He told her about the drugs and a smile broke across her face.

'Right.' She banged her hand against the table. 'Listen up you shiftless bunch of jessies – when you're interviewing your mongs and stots this afternoon, I want to know if anyone's got connections up the hospital or at a vet's, OK? Job, volunteer work, friend, family – the lot.' She stuck two fingers up. 'Hospitals, vets.'

Rennie frowned. 'How come?'

''Cos I say so. Laz, call Ingram – tell him we need everyone we've seen today back tomorrow morning.' She beamed, then punched Logan in the arm. 'We've finally—'

'Ow!' Bloody hell, that *stung*! He wrapped a hand around his deltoid, trying to squeeze the pain away. 'What was that for?' The skin underneath throbbed and burned.

'Oh stop moaning, you big girl's blouse. Barely touched you. We're actually going to catch the bastards.'

'That hurt!'

'Jesus, and I thought Rennie was a wimp.'

The constable paused, halfway through a huge sausage roll. 'Hey!'

Logan rubbed at his arm. 'I don't go around hitting you, do I?'

'Inspector?' The lumpy constable hooked a thumb over her shoulder at the corridor outside.

'Aye, I know.' Steel wiped her fingers down the front of her red satin shirt, leaving little greasy smears. 'Come on, Laz, *carpe pervertum.*'

13

Bruce Preston (46) – Possession of Indecent Images; Animal Cruelty; Obstructing, Assaulting, Molesting or Hindering an Officer in the Course of their Duty; Bestiality

'Well, I *suppose. . .*' Bruce Preston shifted in his seat, squiggling his bum left and right, as if he had worms, or an unreachable itch. He was slightly chubby, slightly balding; completely unremarkable in every way, except for the huge collection of photos of people having sex with dogs the IB had found on his computer. Apparently Bruce's home-made snaps all featured next door's Cairn terrier.

He gave a huge, overacting shrug, arms coming out to forty-five degrees. The bitter-oniony stench of stale armpits got even worse. 'But it's not really the same thing, is it? Besides, I don't really watch the TV any more. Not since that cow on Channel Five did that "Britain's Secret Sex Shame" show.'

'And you're sure you don't know anyone at the hospital, or a vet's?'

Preston rubbed his fingers along his thighs, cheeks flushing pink. 'Told you – I'm not allowed within a hundred metres of a veterinary surgery or dog-walking park.'

Logan logged the end of the interview, thanked Bruce Preston for his time, then told him he could see himself out.

As soon as the door clunked shut, Logan sprawled in his chair, hanging over the edges; arms dangling, fingertips brushing the carpet. 'That was fun.'

Rennie gagged. 'Bloody hell. . . Mind if I open the window?'

'Oh, God, *please*!'

Clunk. And the sound of traffic filtered in from the nearby dual carriageway, the rumble of a plane fading into the distance, the tweet and whitter of birds.

'Do you think Steel's right?'

Logan checked his watch – nearly twenty to four. He stretched, then flopped back again. 'Been rumours doing the rounds about the "livestock" market for years. Kids, women, snatched to order, sold in secret auctions. . . All we need to do is catch *one* of these bastards and the whole thing falls apart.' There was a creaking noise. He looked over to see Rennie slumped in the other seat, arms hanging over the edges, fingertips brushing the tartan carpet.

'Will you stop doing that?'

Rennie raised an eyebrow. 'What?'

'The bloody monkey-see-monkey-do routine. It's getting on my nerves.'

'NLP, my dear Sergeant McRae. Did it when I was on the Interviewer Accreditation Course last month. Got top marks, by the way.' He slumped back, just like Logan. 'It puts the subject at ease subconsciously, makes them think they have a connection, an ally in the room.'

'There's going to be a bloodstain in the room if you don't cut it out.'

Rennie sat up straight. 'What mark did you get?'

'None of your business.' Sixty-five percent. 'How many more on the list for today?'

'Three. Then it's DI Bell's turn.' He smiled. 'Hey, maybe we'll get lucky and crack the case before the end of the day? Interview Superstar Rennie and his sidekick: Sergeant McRae.'

'You're a dick, you know that, don't you?'

Henry MacDonald (24) – Assault, Possession of a Controlled Drug, Drunk and Incapable, Breach of the Peace, Public Indecency

'Yes, but only on the TV.' Henry sat completely still in the hotel chair, knees firmly clamped together, hands clasped in his lap. Someone had dressed him up in his Sunday best – a shiny grey suit that looked like a charity shop special. Didn't really fit him. Hair that he *must* have cut himself, probably with garden shears.

Rennie crossed his arms, then uncrossed them again. Rearranged himself into Henry's mirror image. It didn't take a perfect score in Neuro-Linguistic Programming to see the technique wasn't going to work this time.

Not that it made any difference. No one was admitting to knowing anyone at Aberdeen Royal Infirmary, Albyn, Wood End, Cornhill, or any of the other hospitals in the north-east. And it was the same story with the area's fifty-eight veterinarian practices.

Mind you, they were only a third of the way through Grampian's Sex Offenders' Register, not to mention the six or seven dozen more on DI Ingram's unofficial list.

But at least they were doing something. . .

Silence.

It took Logan a moment to realize both Rennie and MacDonald were staring at him. 'Hmm. . .' He cleared his throat. 'In what way?'

'Well,' Rennie shifted in his chair, 'I mean, it's not likely, is it?'

Nope, still no clue.

Logan shrugged. 'You never know.' Checked his clipboard. 'Erm . . . your social worker says you've applied for chemical castration?'

MacDonald shrugged, the barest twitch of his shoulders. 'I don't like feeling. . . I. . .' A long, hard frown. 'I don't want to *be* like this any more. Inside. . .' He clapped a bony hand to his chest. 'You understand?'

Not really.

Logan nodded. 'Well, if you're sure. And you're sure you've not heard anything about the McGregors?'

'It's like being broken all the time.'

'OK. . .'

Brian Canter (41) – Attempted Abduction of a Child, Possession of Indecent Images of Children, Attempt to Pervert the Course of Justice

'I'm sorry if that makes me an unsympathetic character,' Canter licked his lips – it was like watching a slab of liver slither across a rubber band, 'but my therapist says I have to be honest about who I am if I'm ever going to get better.'

Rennie cleared his throat. 'So you're saying, given the opportunity—'

'I'd tie Jenny McGregor to a sideboard and fuck her till she split: yes. Might even make her eat her mother out. You know? Do a threesome?' All said in the same tone of voice normal people reserved for talking about ordering a pizza. 'I'd probably video it too. You know, so it'd last? I mean, I wouldn't *kill* her or anything – they're no fun if they don't wriggle.'

Silence.

'. . . OK. . .' Rennie looked at Logan, Adam's apple bobbing up and down in his throat. 'Erm, Guv?'

'How often are you seeing your social worker, Mr Canter?'

That dark-purple tongue made another pass across the thin red lips. 'Every other week?'

'Right. I see. . .' Logan nodded, and wrote, 'IMMEDIATE 24HR SUPERVISION REQUIRED!!!' on the form attached to his clipboard and underlined it three times.

14

Logan climbed out into the sunny evening, then slammed the car door shut. Locked up. Followed Steel across the road to the McGregors' house.

There had to be thirty or forty people standing vigil by the garden fence. Men, women, children: all dressed as if they were just out for an evening stroll, enjoying the sun. An outside broadcast unit was setting up on the opposite side of the road, probably getting ready for the next live news bulletin.

Steel picked her way through the minefield of supermarket bouquets and teddy bears to the front gate.

The crowd turned to stare as she clacked the latch and pushed on through.

A uniformed constable sat on the top step, reading a copy of the *Aberdeen Examiner*, the bald patch on top of his head going beetroot in the evening sun. He glanced up as Steel and Logan tramped up the path. 'Hoy, I'm not telling you again: get back on the other side of the sodding. . .' He scrambled to his feet, hiding the newspaper behind him. Then ducked back down to retrieve his peaked cap and ram it on his head. 'Sorry, Boss. Thought you were another one of them journalists. Rotten sods have been trying to get past us all week.' He hooked a thumb over his shoulder. 'You want inside?'

'No, Gardner, I want to stand about out here like a pillock for a couple of hours. Open the bloody door!'

Constable Gardner's cheeks flushed bright pink. 'Yes, Boss.'

'Divot.' Steel waited for him to haul open the door, then barged past. 'And we're no' paying you to sit on your arse reading the paper. At least *try* to look like a bloody police officer!'

'Sorry, Boss. . .'

Logan waited till they were both inside, and the door had clunked shut again. 'Was that not a bit harsh?'

'Laz, what do you think's going to happen if he's still sitting there when that bunch of gits from Channel Four turn on their TV cameras? *"Bobbies skive off during hunt for Jenny's killer."* Finnie'll *love* that.' She hitched her trousers up. 'Besides, Gardner's the prick who delivered a death message to the wrong house, couple of weeks ago. Deserves all he gets.'

The hall looked much the same as it had in the video, only a little more depressing. It had that slightly fusty smell that the Identification Bureau always left behind. A mix of fingerprint powder, emptied Hoover bags, and sneaky Pot Noodles.

Logan took a pair of blue nitrile gloves from his jacket pocket, pulled them on and opened the door to the lounge. TV in the corner on a wooden stand, a Freeview box on the top, some sort of DVD recorder/player underneath. A stack of celebrity gossip magazines. A sofa well past its sell-by date, a colourful throw doing its best to disguise the faded brown corduroy. Three drawings were framed above the mantelpiece, bright crayon renditions of a man and a woman holding hands beneath a smiley yellow sun; a vague black-and-green blob with the word 'sooty' printed beside it in scruffy lower-case; a happy family outside a square house with a blue roof and smoke coming out of the chimney – 'MUMMY, DADDY, ME, DOGGY.'

A square-jawed young man in a black glengarry – with a silver stag's head cap badge on the side and a wee blue bobble on the top – stared out from a silver picture frame, blue eyes not-quite hiding the beginnings of a smile. There was a black ribbon tied around one corner of the frame, a little sprig of dried heather held in place by the bow.

Steel stuck her hands in her pockets and rocked back and forth on her heels. 'Doesn't look like much, for someone who's on the telly. . .'

The kitchen was stocked with tins of soup, diet ready meals, the kind of children's breakfast cereals that came laden with E numbers and sugar. An open bottle of white wine in the fridge.

'Shame to let it go to waste.' Steel dragged the bottle out, found a glass on the draining board, rinsed off the fingerprint powder, and poured herself a hefty measure. 'Don't look at me like that – you're driving remember?'

Then she followed him from room to room, glass in one hand, bottle in the other, watching as Logan worked his way through the bathroom medicine cabinet. Then the master bedroom.

Steel settled on the edge of the bed, bounced a couple of times. 'No' bad. Could have a decent shag on this.'

The room was festooned with photographs. Half a dozen wedding pictures sat on the wall by the bed – Alison McGregor dressed in a huge white dress that made her look a bit like a pregnant shuttlecock. Then a couple of her on holiday somewhere sunny with the dead man from the picture downstairs. Then another version of the photo the media department had used on all the posters. Alison and

100

Jenny on Aberdeen Beach, the sea in the background, only this time James McGregor was standing beside them. A happy family, beaming away for the camera.

One of Jenny with a huge microphone clutched in her hand, front two teeth missing, singing her little heart out. She looked more like her mum than her dad – long blonde curls, a long straight nose she'd never get the chance to grow into, apple cheeks. . .

Steel knocked back the last of her wine, then emptied the bottle into the glass, 'Have a wee rummage in the bedside cabinets.'

'Why?'

'Humour me.'

Logan pulled out the top drawer. Some jewellery – nothing expensive, amber mostly – a stack of ironed hankies, a couple of scarves. Next drawer down: pants – frilly skimpy ones and huge industrial passion-killers, all mixed up together. The bottom drawer looked as if it was full of socks. Logan scraped the top layer to one side, then pulled out a big stack of envelopes, held together with a red elastic band.

He held them up. 'This what you were after?'

Steel's face drooped slightly. 'Try under the bed.'

Logan tossed the envelopes onto the duvet and hunkered down on his hands and knees, peering into the shadows. 'Nothing.'

'*Nothing?*'

'Not so much as a ball of fluff.' The whole house was like that. If it wasn't for the Scottish Police Services Authority looking for forensics, covering everything in fingerprint powder, the place would have been spotless.

'Hmm. . . Must've been a fiddler.' Steel delved into one of the envelopes, coming out with a letter – pale-blue paper, dark-blue biro.

'What?'

'Think about it, Laz: widow, stuck here on her own with a wee kid and a dead husband. What's she going to do for a bit of bedtime fun? I was expecting a dirty big dildo . . . vibrator at the very least.'

'Oh for goodness' sake—'

'I've got one that lights up, bloody weird, but saves buying a torch when there's a power cut. But Alison was clearly a devotee of the two-finger fidget.' Steel held out the letter. 'Read.'

'You know she's probably lying dead in a shallow grave somewhere?'

'Just 'cos she's dead doesn't mean she was never *alive*, Laz. Now read.'

It was a love letter, addressed to Alison McGregor. Logan skimmed it: love of my life – blah, blah, blah – the moon and stars pale compared to the light that shines in your eyes – blah, blah, blah – I can barely sleep when the ghost of your touch haunts me. . . Who *wrote* this dribble? Logan flicked to the last page, it was signed 'MY ETERNAL LOVE, SERGEANT JAMES GEORGE MCGREGOR.'

He frowned. '*Sergeant*? Thought Doddy was just a squaddie?'

'Come on, read it out.'

'Get your eyes tested and you can read it yourself.' Logan dropped the sheets of paper back on the bed. 'What sort of person signs a love letter with their full name and a fake rank?'

'Ah, you're no fun.' She slumped back until she was lying flat out on the bed, staring up at the ceiling.

Logan abandoned her, going across the hall to Jenny's bedroom instead. The window was coated in that familiar film of Amido Black, making the back garden look dim and grey.

Pink wallpaper. Fluffy animals piled up on the toy box. Every breeze-block-sized book in the Harry Potter series.

The horse on the duvet cover was actually a unicorn. . . He stopped. Frowned. Tried to remember the video footage. There'd been something on the end of the bed. A teddy bear? It wasn't there any more. Wasn't lying on the bedroom floor either.

Maybe they'd let her take it with her? Maybe it'd offered a bit of comfort while they shot her full of morphine and thiopental sodium, so they could hack off her toe.

Maybe they'd even buried it with her. Out in the middle of nowhere, wrapped in a black plastic bag. Mouldering away in a shallow grave. Keeping her company as she rotted.

Christ, there was a cheery thought.

'You look like you've eaten a cold jobbie.' Steel: standing in the doorway.

Logan turned his back on the room. 'There's nothing here.'

Just a dead girl's bedroom in an empty house.

A thin slice of sunlight lies on the bare wooden floorboards, little binks of dust glittering like fairies just above it. Everything's blurry. And it smells. She wipes her pyjama sleeve across her eyes. Shifts her bum along the floor a bit so she's sitting closer to the sun.

It smells of old people in here. Old people like Mrs McInnes next door, with her hairy mole and thick glasses, and breath like a sausage that's been left in the fridge too long.

She wipes the sleeve across her face again, getting Winnie the Pooh all soggy with tears. Tries to wriggle closer, but the chain around her chest and neck pulls tight. They used to keep Sooty on a chain in the back garden, fixed to a big metal spike so he could run round and round. Till he had to go to heaven.

Only she's not a dog, chained to a spike in the back garden. She's a little girl, chained to a bed in a dark, dusty old house.

She reaches out a pale little foot, and wiggles her toes in that tiny line of sunshine. Not making any noise.

The monsters will come back if she does.

A groan behind her.

She turns, the chain cold against her chin. Mummy's talking in her sleep again.

'No. . . You can't. . . I don't want to. . .' Then her mouth twitches, opens and closes with little smacking noises. Mummy turns over onto her side. The chain around her ankle rattles against the metal bed. 'No. . .' Then her breathing goes in and out slow and steady.

Teddy Gordon's eyes sparkle in the gloomy room. He's lying on the bed, on his side like Mummy, staring.

She snaps her head back to the front. Not looking at him. Not looking into those shiny eyes. One time, she'd watched a crow eating a squished rabbit in a lay-by, while Daddy was having a wee behind a tree. The crow had eyes like Teddy Gordon's: black and shiny and horrible.

Look straight ahead. Don't move. Don't make any noise. Be a Good Little Girl.

There's a clunk and she flinches, a tiny squeak pops out between her lips.

A thump.

Coming from the shadows where the door's hiding.

A rattle.

Eyes front. No moving. Biting her lip hard enough to make it sting and taste of shiny new pennies.

Clump. Clump. Clump.

A shadow blocks out the little slice of sunlight, killing the sparkly fairies.

The monster's voice is all metal and buzzy, like a robot. 'Hey sweetcheeks. . .'

She closes her eyes.

15

'—*memorial service tomorrow at noon. Sarah Williamson is at the church now. Any change, Sarah?*'

The TV picture jumped to a woman in a black overcoat. '*So far, all we know is that the memorial service* will *be open for the public to come and show their respects for Jenny. I* can *tell you that Robbie Williams will be attending, along with Katie Melua and a host of other celebrities, before heading back down to London for a special live tribute episode of Britain's Next Big Star.*'

'Ooh. . .' Samantha sat forward on the couch. 'Have to set the recorder.'

Logan took another mouthful of wine, washing down the last of the pasta they'd had for tea. 'Why do we have to clog the machine up with that shite?'

There was a small pause. 'You're such a bloody telly snob.'

'I'm *not* a snob.'

'Just because you don't like it, doesn't mean it's shite.'

'—*special guests performing the songs that Jenny and her mother*—'

'It *is* shite. It's just more cheap reality TV bollocks where halfwits humiliate themselves just so they can get on the bloody telly.'

'Here we go again.' She pulled her knees up to her chest, black leather jeans squeaking against the couch. 'Like what *you* watch is so damn intellectual.'

'—*charity single tipped to hit number one, we spoke to Gordon Maguire, chairman of Blue-Fish-Two-Fish Productions*—'

'At least I—'

'*The Simpsons* isn't bloody Panorama, is it?'

A middle-aged man in a T-shirt and suit jacket appeared on the screen. He had trendy sideburns with bits cut out of them, a soul patch, a Dundee accent, and a bald head. '—*bear in mind that the kidnappers still have Alison and we all have to make sure*—'

'I'm just saying it's exploitative, OK? It's—'

'Have you even watched it?'

'—*have to keep raising money while there's still a chance we can bring her home safely.*'

'What? I don't *need* to watch—'

'See!' She poked the arm of the couch with a black-painted fingernail. 'You have sod-all idea what you're talking about!'

'—*thank you. And now over to Gail with the weather.*'

Logan slumped further into the couch. 'Can we not—'

'Apart from anything else, this is *why* Jenny and Alison got kidnapped. If they weren't on TV, they wouldn't be famous. And if they weren't famous, they wouldn't have been grabbed.' Samantha stopped poking the couch's arm, and poked Logan's instead. 'So you've got no business being a snobby cock, this is directly related to your case.'

'—*mass of Arctic air coming in will hit the north east of Scotland, so we can expect some unseasonably cold weather over the next couple of days*—'

Logan finished his wine in a single gulp. 'OK, OK: fine. I'll set the machine.'

She didn't look around, just stared straight at the TV,

where the map of Scotland was a mess of blue and grey. 'Thank you.' Clipped.

He levered himself to his feet. Tried to force a smile into his voice. 'You want some more wine?'

Silence.

'Sam?'

'How's your arm?'

Logan looked down at the sleeve of his shirt, all bulked out by the bandages. 'It's OK.' No it wasn't. It throbbed and stung every time he brushed against anything. Bloody Steel punching it hadn't helped.

Sam sneaked a glance at him. 'You're a terrible liar.' Then back to the telly. 'And we're watching *Britain's Next Big Star* tomorrow, whether you like it or not.'

'Fffff?' Logan sat straight up in bed, blinked a couple of times, then breathed out again. Squinted at the alarm clock. Quarter past two.

He collapsed back into the pillow. Who the hell called at quarter past *two*?

Lying next to him, Samantha made mumbling noises.

The phone kept ringing.

Logan rolled out of bed, grabbed his mobile, and hit the button. 'This better be important!'

'*Hullo? Hullo?*' A broad Doric accent, not one he recognized. '*That DS McRae?*'

'Who's this?' Rubbing his eyes with the heel of one hand.

'*PC Gilbert, doon the station? Anyway, got a wifie in here screamin' blue murder. Keeps sayin' she's been raped.*'

Another yawn.

'*Hello? Sarge?*'

'Gilbert, I'm going to call you a very rude name, then I'm going to hang up. Then you can go get someone who's on bloody duty to deal with it! I'm on day-shift, you—'

'*Hud oan, DI Bell wants a word. . .*'

The constable's voice disappeared, there was some muffled talk, then DI Bell's voice grated in Logan's ear. '*McRae? Get your arse up here.*'

'It's quarter past two in the—'

'*I don't care if it's the second coming, I've got a mental cow up here trying to castrate people, and she's got your name on her.*'

'No offence, sir, but—'

'*I mean literally. She's literally got your name on her. In black marker pen. And if you're not wanting a visit from Professional Standards first bloody thing, you'll do as you're sodding well told!*'

Half-two on a Saturday morning and the streets were in their usual post-pub haze. By now most of the chucking-out-time violence had settled down. It would only flare up again when the nightclubs kicked their crop of boozed-up idiots out onto the streets. Men and women, barely dressed, bashing the crap out of each other for a place in the taxi rank, or kebab shop queue. 'Are you lookin' at my bird?' 'Leave it, Tracy, she's not worth it. . .'

Logan paused halfway across Union Street, waiting for a battered Toyota with a taxi sign bolted to the roof to grumble past. There were two blokes just inside the entrance to Lodge Walk: the usual short-cut to the back of FHQ. One was keeping himself upright with a hand against the wall, peeing on his own shoes, the other making retching noises.

He took the scenic route instead, round the council buildings and down Queen Street.

Stopped outside the Sheriff and JP Court.

The crowd gathered on the forecourt outside Force Headquarters was a lot smaller – just forty, fifty people? All linking arms and swaying back and forth. They had makeshift lanterns: tea lights in old jam and pickle jars, the captive flames flickering a warm waxy glow that made shadows writhe as they sang.

It took a while for Logan to recognize the tune: *Wind Beneath My Wings*. Of course it was. Only someone had changed the lyrics so it was all about Jenny and Alison McGregor. Christ that was quick.

And touching. . .? Or creepy. It was hard to decide.

A few uniformed officers hovered on the periphery, some watching the crowd, the rest watching the small knot of drunken idiots lurching about and trying to sing along.

Logan wandered over to the nearest officer – a wee man with thick hairy eyebrows and a baggy face. 'What's this?'

Constable Baggy sniffed, then nodded towards the crowd. 'Candle-lit vigil, Guv. Don't know what possible bloody good they think it'll do. Outside the house, or the church where they're doing that memorial thing, *maybe*, but here?' He sucked on his teeth for a moment. 'Whole city's gone fuckin' mental.'

The Police Custody and Security Officer puffed out her cheeks and scowled at Logan. A red mark covered half of her chin, slowly purpling itself into a bruise. She pointed along the corridor, mouth barely moving, teeth clamped together. 'Down there.'

DI Bell was limping up and down outside the little row of cells reserved for female prisoners. He walked like a bear that hadn't quite got the hang of it yet, thick rounded shoulders rocking from side to side. He stopped, gave Logan his second scowl of the night, then waved him over with a big hairy paw. 'Where have you been?' Voice not much louder than a whisper.

'Thought you were meant to be on back shift? How'd you get on with Steel's sex offenders, anything—'

'Want to explain this?' Bell pointed at the cell in front of him.

Logan checked the name scrawled on the little board beside the door: name, alleged offence, and last time checked. 'TRISHA BROWN ~ O.A.M.H.O. ~ 02:30' Which meant she'd probably been done for taking a swing at some poor PC.

'So?'

DI Bell hauled open the hatch, and Logan peered into the little cell.

Trisha Brown was lying on the blue plastic mattress, with her knees drawn up against her hollow ribs. She was wearing a skimpy halter-neck top, exposing a swathe of sickly-pale skin that almost glowed in the harsh strip-lighting, a couple of bruises, and a tattoo. Bare feet with long toes, like an extra set of fingers.

Logan shrugged. 'She working tonight?'

The inspector closed the hatch again. 'Says you raped her.'

'She. . .?' Logan backed off a step. 'Are you kidding me? I wouldn't touch her with fucking *Bob's* never mind mine! She's lying!'

Bell grabbed him by the sleeve and dragged him away to the stairwell. 'She better be. . . But soon as she makes the complaint official, you *know* what happens: Professional Standards explore your colon with a searchlight. Something like this, you're probably looking at gardening leave while they investigate.'

'But it's—'

'It doesn't *matter* if it's a load of old shite or not – it goes down on your record.'

'No. Fuck this.' Logan turned and marched back to the cell, slammed the flat of his hand against the metal door. Bang, bang, bang. He hauled the hatch open. 'Trisha Brown! WAKEY WAKEY!'

The figure on the mattress stirred, rolled over onto her back, one arm flopping across her eyes. Her hip bones stood proud beneath her sallow skin, sores on her forearms, ribs on show. How the hell could *anyone* think he'd get naked with her?

Bang, bang, bang. 'TRISHA!'

A muffled voice came from the next cell. 'Fuckin' shut it! Some of us trying to sleep here. . .'

Bang, bang, bang. 'TRISHA BROWN!'

Another disembodied voice. 'Christ's sake, don't wake her up – daft bitch only just stopped screaming.'

The figure on the bed, moved her legs, sat up. Blinked. Then twisted sideways and sprayed yellow vomit all over the dark-red terrazzo floor, chunks of orange and pink splattering everywhere. She heaved a couple more times, then wiped a trembling hand across her chapped lips. 'Thirsty. . .'

Logan banged his hand on the door again. 'Do you know who I am?'

She squinted at him. 'Fuck off.' Then collapsed back on the mattress. 'Not well. . .'

Bang. 'Who the fuck am I?'

'Leave us alone!'

Logan turned to DI Bell. 'See? She hasn't got a bloody clue.'

The inspector pushed Logan out of the way and shouted through the hatch. 'Trisha? Remember when we brought you in? What were you saying?'

A loud sigh. Then she dragged herself up off the thin mattress, bare feet splatching through the puddle of sick as she made for the door. The bitter, eye-tightening stench of vomit wafted out of the hatch. 'I was raped. RAPED!' A dull thunk, as she rested her head on the metal. 'I was raped.'

Logan banged his hand on the door again and she flinched back. 'Who?'

Trisha pulled her halter top up, exposing tiny wrinkled breasts covered in penny-sized bruises. 'DS LOGAN MCRAE' was written on the bony expanse of chest below her clavicles in black ink block capitals. Trisha frowned at it, a drip of spittle dangling from the tip of her chin.

'Him. He raped me. . .'

Logan stared at his own name. Lying cow. He slammed the hatch closed again, then turned on DI Bell. 'She hasn't got a bloody clue. Did you do a rape kit?'

'I told you, it doesn't matter if—'

'Did you or didn't you?'

Bell threw his hands in the air. 'We couldn't, OK? She was tearing the place up. Nearly ripped my balls off!'

'Get her in an interview room and we'll get her to retract the—'

'No, no, no, no, no. That's not the way it works, and you know it. No way in hell you can be in on an interview of a rape victim *you're* supposed to have raped!'

Logan paced down to the end of the little cell block and back again. 'Fine, you do it.'

Bell ran a furry hand through his hair. Looked away. 'I can't.'

'Yes you bloody can. Stick her in number three and find out who put her up to it.'

'Why would anyone—'

'She's got my name written on her! What, did the graffiti fairies break into her house and have a go with a black marker pen?'

Bell shrugged. 'Maybe she wrote it herself?'

Moron.

'If she wrote it herself it'd be upside down, wouldn't it?'

'Well, maybe. . . I dunno, a mirror?' He must have caught the expression on Logan's face, because he took a sudden interest in examining his own hands. 'OK, OK, someone else wrote it on her. Fuck.' The inspector worried at a hangnail. 'I'll speak to her. But you know, if Professional Standards find out I did a sneak-around, I'm blaming you, understand?'

16

On the little screen, DI Bell pushed a sheet of paper across the scarred interview room table. *'I'm showing Ms Brown a selection of photographs reference: one five zero five zero one. Can you identify the man you say raped you?'*

'No she bloody can't.' Logan took another swig of coffee. Bitter and dark, which was pretty sodding appropriate. The caffeine fizzed through his arteries, making his eyeballs itch.

Sitting on the other side of the table, Trisha Brown rocked back and forth, then chewed on the side of her thumb. They'd chucked the ID sheet together using a bunch of random faces from the database – local criminals: a couple of rapists, some burglars, a paedophile – Logan, George Clooney, and the current head of the BNP. Nine faces for Trisha Brown to pick from.

'Trisha? Can you pick him out?'

Logan leaned forward until his nose was just inches from the TV screen. It was mounted on a rickety old table in what was laughingly referred to as the Downstream Observation Suite. It'd been a broom closet before the last refit, and still had that pine and bleach smell.

'Trisha?'

She took her thumb out of her mouth, held it above the ID sheet, then turned it down, like a Roman emperor, and jabbed it into one of the faces.

DI Bell scratched his hairy head. *'OK. . . I see. Are you sure?'*

A nod.

'You have to say it out loud for the tape.'

'Aye, it was him. Number Five.'

A silent pause. Then the inspector scraped his chair back from the table. *'Right, well, interview terminated at. . .'* He checked his watch. *'Three thirty nine AM. Constable Gray will take you downstairs to the duty doctor for a wee examination, OK?'*

Logan watched them filter out of the interview room, then clicked off the set.

A minute later DI Bell clunked open the door and slumped back against the wall. He folded his arms, tufts of hair sticking out from the ends of his shirt cuffs. He wasn't smiling.

'Well?'

'Bad news.'

Oh . . . fuck. She'd picked him out. Nine faces to choose from, and Trisha Brown had chosen his. She only recognized him because he was the idiot shouting in through the hatch of her cell. Stupid. Stupid. Fucking. Idiot.

'Come on, Ding-Dong, you know it's not—'

'We've got to go arrest George Clooney. His fans are going to be gutted.'

'Sarge? Sarge, you awake?'

Logan jolted upright in his seat, grabbing the desk for support. He sat there, staring at the blurry screensaver on his computer monitor for a moment. 'What time is it?'

A lanky young lad with a streaky-bacon complexion, watery eyes, and a PC's uniform fidgeted with the Airwave handset clipped to his stab-proof vest. The numbers on his epaulettes marked him out as one of the year's new recruits.

God knew how he'd ended up on nights, he looked as if a strong fart would blow him over. 'DI Bell says that's the duty doc done with your junkie. Says you can sod off home if you like?'

Logan yawned, stretched out in the seat, shuddered, then slumped. 'Where is he?'

'Had to go out on a shout – some tadger's taken a scaffolding pole to Vicious Vikki's Ford Fiesta.'

'He say what the result was?'

The constable nodded. 'Car's completely buggered.'

'Not the window, you idiot, the rape kit.'

'Don't know, Sarge.'

Logan creaked his way out of his swivel chair, stuck his palms against the small of his back and tried to straighten the knots out of his spine. Then let out a big hissing breath.

Constable Streaky-Bacon was still standing there.

'Anything else?'

Shrug.

'Get back to sodding work then.'

Dr Donna Delaney looked up from the copy of the *Aberdeen Examiner* open on the desk in front of her, covering the keyboard of a battered laptop. 'LOCAL PSYCHIC'S PLEA TO POLICE'. A white porcelain teapot – with matching cup and saucer – trailed the lemon-washing-up-liquid smell of Earl Grey into the tiny office set aside for the on-call duty doctor.

She peered at Logan over the top of her trendy glasses, then smiled. 'How's the stomach?'

'You did a rape kit on Trisha Brown?'

'Yes. . . *Lovely* young lady. Apparently I tried to, now how did she put it, "Lez her up". Let me see your hands.'

He held them both out, and she scooted her chair closer on squeaky castors, took hold of his left hand and peered

115

at it. Two little scars marked the middle of the palm, about half an inch apart, the skin all pink and shiny. She turned it over and peered at the back. Two more scars.

'Still giving you gyp?'

Shrug. 'Depends on the weather.'

'Well, let me know if they start to throb, or you get swelling, or stiffness moving your fingers. Don't want to end up with cysts.'

'Rape kit?'

'Hmm? Oh, yes. Well, there's vaginal bruising consistent with forced intercourse, some tearing to the anus as well, more bruising on the breasts and inner thighs.'

'Semen?'

Dr Delaney bit her top lip. 'Some.'

'But?'

'Well, you see, someone like Trisha, with her habit, has to get money somewhere. So while it *does* look like she's been raped, it wasn't today, and the semen I've got to send off to the labs is probably going to be from her last bunch of punters. She's not big on using protection.'

'She say anything?'

'Other than, "get your hands off me you dirty lesbian bitch"? Not really, no.' The duty doc scooted her chair back to the desk. 'It'd be nice to think that she'll get herself some help – kick the drugs, settle down somewhere nice with her wee boy. But I get the feeling we all know where she's going to end up.'

'Yeah.' Sooner or later, Trisha Brown would go from being Dr Delaney's patient to Doc Fraser's corpse.

'Shh. . . It's going to be OK, sweetheart. It's going to be OK. . .'

Mummy's voice sounds like something sticky, caught on broken glass. Arms wrapped around her Good Little Girl, rocking her from side to side in her lap. Sometimes, when you're scared, Mummy is the warmest place you can be. . .

Sometimes.

She sniffs and wipes her sleeve across her eyes. Then only just stops herself from sucking her thumb. Sucking your thumb is naughty, it makes your teeth all squint like a nasty rat.

Teddy Gordon watches her from the foot of the bed, plastic eyes glittering and black.

He has eyes like a rat.

Like a crow tearing chunks out of a squished rabbit.

Like the lens of a video camera.

'Shhhhhhh. . . Shhhhhh. . .' Mummy shudders.

Something lands in her hair, then trickles down to her scalp – warm and wet. Mummy never cries. Not since they put Daddy in a box in the ground so he could be with the angels.

Mummy strokes her hair. 'I'm sorry, sweetheart, I'm so sorry. . . It'll only hurt for a little bit, I promise.'

When the monsters come back to take her toes.

17

Trisha Brown sniffed. Her eyes were Barbie-pink, her pupils two tiny black dots as she peered out through the hatch in her cell door. The shakes had come early, bringing a sheen of sweat with them. The hard-edged stench of BO and stale vomit radiated off her in waves.

Logan tried again. 'Who wrote "DS Logan McRae" on your chest?'

'I'm not well. . .'

'Trisha, it's quarter to five in the morning, my shift starts in two and a bit hours, and I've been up all bastarding night because of you. Now who wrote my name on your bloody chest?' Trying hard not to shout.

She blinked. Then a frown made little wrinkles in her shiny forehead. 'You're him?'

'Who wrote it?'

She placed a bony hand against her chest, rubbing the halter-top where it hid Logan's name. 'You're the one did that raid on Billy's house, yeah? Took Ricky round to stay with mum?'

'What about it?'

She licked her pale, chapped lips. 'You seized all that gear, right?'

'We—'

'You've still got it, right? You know, where you can get at it?'

'Trisha – focus. Who wrote my name on you?'

''Cos you've got to give it all back to me. Everything you've got.'

'No chance.' Logan slammed the hatch shut.

'No, you *have* to! The guys Shuggie got it off want paid – if we haven't sold it we gotta give it back!'

Logan opened the hatch again. 'You got six bricks of heroin and a suitcase full of mephedrone on *sale or return*?'

'They're gonna fuck him over if we can't get the money. . .' She stepped closer to the hatch, sour breath washing over Logan. 'What if they come after me and Ricky again? He's only a wee kid.'

'Here's the deal: you give up your suppliers, Shuggie turns himself in and coughs to the drugs charges, and I'll get you and your little boy into protective custody.'

Trisha looked away for a moment. And when she came back she was pouting. She licked a finger, then stuck her hand up inside her halter-top and rubbed at a shrunken breast. 'How about you let us have the gear and you get *anything* you want. Yeah? I do it *all*. Rough as you like. You can bring your mates too, if you like?'

Logan shrank back from the hatch. 'Don't think so.'

'Bet a big guy like you could make me come and come and come. Mmmmmm. . . Oh yeah. I'd be a dirty bitch for—'

Logan slammed the hatch shut, before Trisha wasn't the only one smelling of sick.

*　　*　　*

119

Davey 'English' Robertson, AKA: Daniel Roberts (69) – Rape, Indecent Assault, Attempted Murder

'. . . so you see, it wasnae my fault, was it? Fucker came at me in the shower wi' a fuckin' hard-on, what was I supposed ta dae? Bend ower and spread ma arse cheeks? Fuck that.' Davey Robertson squared his shoulders inside the threadbare suit jacket. Grey-stubbled chin coming up. 'Poof bastard was askin' for it.'

Logan stifled a yawn. God it was hot. Even with the window open, the hotel room was like a microwave. He rubbed at his eyes. 'Can we just stick to the—'

'And anither thing, fit wye do you think I've got nithin' better ta dae than ponce about in here wi' you lot? Saturday mornin': should be gettin' ready for the match.'

'Alison and Jenny McGregor, Mr Robertson. Did you—'

'I seen her man oan the telly, after that rag-head cock-pirate blew him up. Fuckin' disgrace. IEDs. . . Every retard's makin' bombs out of washin' up liquid and Blu-Tack these days. What's the point of spendin' millions on tanks when you can blow holes in the fuckers with crap you find under your sink? Should nuke all them Muslim bastards and have done with it.'

Logan slammed his palm down on the arm of the chair. 'Did you, or did you not know Alison and Jenny McGregor?'

Robertson's chin came up again. 'I'm no' a young mannie, loon, but I could still kick yer arse from here tae Rhynie and back.'

Logan rubbed at the palm of his hand – both scars stung and throbbed like cuts laced with Tabasco. He gritted his teeth. 'Just answer the question, Mr Robertson, and we can all get out of here.'

'Seen the pair of them at that civic thing the cooncil hud for those visiting French bastards. Even got tae say, "fit like" tae the pair of them. Ken this: Alison wis nice tae everyone.

No' like these stuck-up cows you see on the telly. Hud the common touch like.'

Logan nodded. 'And what did you talk about?'

Davey Robertson grinned. 'Asked me back tae her place for a tin of Special and a blowjob.'

Silence.

'What the fuck d'you think we talked aboot? The weather, her bein' oan the TV, my lumbago. The usual.'

'Not much better than yesterday. You?' Logan squeezed himself a cup of coffee from the pump-dispenser thermos in the hotel meeting room. The rest of the team were slumped around the tables, speaking in low voices while DI Steel grumbled her way through the interview notes DI Bell's team had filled in yesterday evening. Trying to find out if any were worth watching on video.

DS Doreen Taylor pulled a face. 'A nice young man offered to "bang the living shit" out of me.' She'd abandoned her usual twinset-and-pearls for a pair of jeans and a fuchsia hoodie with 'ANGEL' picked out in sequins across the back. Like someone's mum trying to convince herself she was still down with the cool kids. 'I swear, after a morning questioning rapists and other assorted sexual degenerates, DI Steel's life-style is becoming a lot more appealing. You men are disgusting.'

Steel didn't look up from her paperwork. 'I heard that.'

'No one connected to any hospitals or vets?'

'One dentist done for molesting his sister's little girl, but he's not allowed to practise any more.' Doreen took a sip of coffee. 'Have you spoken to Mark recently?'

Logan grimaced. '*Acting* DI MacDonald? Yeah.'

Another sip. 'The first fortnight, I went home and cried my eyes out – every night. Dealing with Finnie was the worst. You think he's bad when you're a DS? Wait until it's your turn in September.'

'Yeah, I got the same motivational speech from Mark.'

A bee buzz-bumped against the widow, braining itself, retreating in dazed loops, then smacking its head into the glass again. So at least they weren't the only ones.

Logan's phone went off in his pocket. 'McRae.'

'Hello? Logan, is that you?' Doc Fraser. *'Hello?'*

'Doc, what can—'

'Remind me again: why did I let you talk me into coming out of retirement?'

'It—'

'We just got the DNA results back on the toe you brought in.'

There was a long pause.

'Doc?'

'BBC One.'

Logan stuck the phone against his chest. 'Who's got the remote?'

Shrugs. Then Rennie stuck up a hand. 'Found it.'

'BBC One.'

The flatscreen TV mounted on the far wall bloomed into life. Some sort of kids' programme. A click. And the picture switched to the media briefing room – DCI Finnie, DCS Bain, that prick Green from SOCA, and the Media Liaison Officer – all sitting behind a desk topped with microphones.

The news ticker along the bottom of the screen read, 'BREAKING NEWS: TESTS SHOW SEVERED TOE DOES NOT BELONG TO JENNY MCGREGOR.'

Steel scrambled up from her seat, interview reports going everywhere. 'Shite. . .'

'Why did I let you talk me into it?' Doc Fraser made rummaging noises. *'Must've been mad.'*

On the screen DCS Bain gritted his teeth. *'I'm not saying that, I'm saying DNA evidence has confirmed the toe belongs to an unknown individual.'*

'What the hell happened?'

'I told Sheila to run the usual tests – she sent samples off to the lab for toxicology, and DNA. It's standard practice.'

A weedy-looking reporter with frizzy brown hair stuck up her hand. 'Chief Superintendent? Why did Grampian Police claim the toe was Jenny's yesterday?'

Doc Fraser: 'We didn't get the sodding DNA back till today. Whoever sent the blood on the note off for testing didn't bother sending a tissue sample to go with it.' A long sigh sounded in Logan's ear. 'The blood was Jenny's, but the toe isn't.'

'Oh, buggering hell.'

Rennie waved the remote at the screen. 'But this is good, isn't it? Means Jenny's not dead – she's still alive.'

'Chief Superintendent, will the memorial service for Jenny still go ahead?'

'I really can't comment on that.'

Doc Fraser sniffed. 'Logan: your boss is storming about like a shortarsed Godzilla, and if he calls me an idiot once more, I'm not going to be responsible for my actions, understand?'

'I know Finnie can be a bit—'

'I retired to get away from crap like this!' The pathologist hung up.

'Now I really can't answer any further questions—'

'Michael Larson: Edinburgh Evening Post. Are you now prepared to admit that this has all been a hoax perpetrated by the production company behind Britain's Next Big Star?'

'—briefing to an end.'

'Answer the question, Chief Superintendent!'

The three people on the stage got up and marched off, led by a trembling Finnie.

'Chief Superintendent!'

'Wow. . .' Rennie rubbed at the back of his neck, a faint bloom of skin-flakes glowing in the sunshine. 'Finnie looks really *pissed*.'

Logan watched the door at the back of the briefing room

swing shut, then the journalists and TV cameras jostled into position to do their pieces to camera. A doughy-faced man with a comb-over appeared on screen, clutching a microphone. *'So there you have it. Grampian Police admit that the severed toe, found earlier this week, doesn't belong—'*

The screen went black.

DI Steel dropped the remote control onto the table. 'Right, you bunch of jessies. Back to work. This changes sod all – we've still got a little girl's killer to find.'

The two-person teams bustled out of the meeting room, all of them talking about Jenny McGregor's return from the dead.

'No' you, Laz.'

Logan froze on the threshold.

'Rennie!'

The constable stuck his head back into the room. 'You rang?'

'Get Laz's share of paedos and rapists divvied up between the other teams, we're going to pay our respects.'

18

'No, it's definitely getting colder.' Rennie shifted from foot to foot, tilted his head back and let out a long, huffing breath. A faint plume of white drifted up from his mouth. 'See! Told you.'

'Aye, very clever.' Steel screwed up her face, peering into the line of dignitaries in through the front doors of the Kirk of St Nicholas, mobile phone clamped to her ear. 'No' you, sir. . . Aye. . . I think so too. . .'

A sea of faces filled the graveyard – everyone, packed in shoulder-to-shoulder all the way from the church to the ornate columned frontage that separated the grounds from Union Street. A row of orange traffic cones and 'POLICE' tape kept the crowd off the wide path to the church. There had to be at least a thousand people in here, probably more. Camera crews and photographers clumped together into little islands, training their lenses on the shuffling masses.

Rennie popped up onto his tiptoes. 'See anyone famous yet?'

Logan ignored him. Almost everyone was wearing black, some clutching garish teddy bears, others floral tributes with the price stickers still on from Asda, Tesco, or the nearest petrol station.

'Think they didn't have time to go home and change?' Rennie nodded, agreeing with himself. 'Bet half of them are really disappointed Jenny's not dead any more. Can't mourn a wee girl if she's still alive.'

'Cynical bugger.' Steel held her phone against her chest. 'Ooh, is that no' thingie off the telly? What is it, *EastEnders*?'

'Where?' Rennie bounced up and down. 'God, it is! Wow. How cool is that? Look, he's got Melanie from *Corrie* with him! MELANIE! MELANIE, YOU'RE BRILLIANT!'

'Oh for God's sake.' Logan slapped him on the arm. 'Will you grow up? Supposed to be a police officer.'

Rennie grinned. 'Think we'll get to meet them after the service?'

Steel stuck a finger in her ear, back on the phone again. 'Aye, sorry, sir, bit noisy here – got the telly on for the memorial service. . . Who's looking into where the toe came from?. . . Oh.' She drooped slightly. 'No, no, I'm sure you know what you're doing. . .' She snapped her phone shut.

'Surprised they're still going through with it.' Logan leant back against a lichen-covered headstone, the name barely legible on the weather-beaten granite. 'What's the point of having a memorial service when she's not even dead?'

'Too late to back out now. Look at it. . .' Steel waved a hand, indicated the milling throng packing the graveyard, the TV crews, the huge screens and speakers. 'Celebration of a wee girl's life and all these famous buggers actually setting foot in Aberdeen for a change. They're here anyway, what else they going to do, go down Codonas and play on the dodgems?'

'Ooh, ooh! Look, it's Robbie Williams!' The only thing Rennie didn't do was clap his hands as he jumped up and down. 'ROBBIE!'

'Next time, I'm not going to thump you, I'm going to knee you in the balls.'

Rennie's face fell. 'Inspector. . .?'

'Don't be such a jobbie, Laz. Rennie, you scurry off and wet your wee star-struck panties if you like.'

'Thanks, Guv!' Rennie pushed his way through the crowd, making for the progression of VIPs. 'God, there's the bloke off *Cash In The Attic*!'

Logan watched him go. 'Next time we're at the vet, I'm getting him fixed.'

'Let the wee loon have some fun.' She pulled out her fake cigarette, switched it on, and took a puff. 'Finnie's got a team going through all the missing kid reports, see if we can get a match on the toe. Bastards must've got it from somewhere.'

Logan shifted, the tombstone's cold leaching through his suit jacket. 'If it *is* a paedophile ring they might've had her for years. . .' There was a comforting thought. 'Might not even be local – they could've bought her off the Eastern Europeans.' In which case they'd probably never know who she was. 'Who's SIO?'

Steel pulled her mouth down at the edges and took a long hard sook on the plastic cigarette. 'McPherson.'

'You're *kidding* – they made McPherson Senior Investigating Officer? DI Disaster?'

'All he's got to do is go through the misper reports and get DNA samples. No' even McPherson can screw that up.' Another sook. 'I hope. . .'

Rennie had shoved his way to the front of the crowd lining the path, waving his hands at someone Logan vaguely recognized from the TV.

'I can't believe they put *McPherson* in charge of a murder inquiry.'

'Give it a rest, eh?' DI Steel went for a dig in her armpit.

'With any luck we'll catch the bugger long before McPherson ruins. . .' She pursed her lips. 'There he is.'

'Who?'

She pointed at a bald bloke with ridiculous sideburns and a pedestal-matt-style soul patch. Gordon Maguire – MD of Blue-Fish-Two-Fish Productions. Fancy black suit and expensive-looking T-shirt with a skull and crossbones on it. Sunglasses. Big cheesy grin.

He was waving to people as he strolled towards the church. Signing the occasional autograph.

'You want to question him?'

'Alternative line of enquiry, Laz. Watch and learn.'

'You think he. . .' Logan stared. Someone had ducked under the blue-and-white tape and out onto the path: a rumpled, chinless sack of skin with a big hooked nose. Michael Larson. The git from the *Edinburgh Evening Post*.

A photographer stumbled onto the path behind him. Click, flash, whirr, click. . .

'Mr Maguire, is it true you obtained a dead girl's toe in order to con people into buying your so-called "charity record", when—'

'Complete rubbish, we're here to celebrate the fact that Jenny's still alive.' Maguire turned and pumped his fists in the air. 'JENNY'S STILL ALIVE!'

A huge cheer.

'Mr Maguire, your company—'

'I think it's disgusting that you're exploiting this terrible tragedy to sell your sleazy newspaper. You should be *ashamed* of yourself. THE REST OF US ARE GOING TO FOCUS ON GETTING JENNY AND HER MUM BACK ALIVE! AREN'T WE?'

Another huge cheer.

The reporter glanced at his photographer – still snapping away – and back. 'I put it to you, that you're a heartless—'

'NOTHING MATTERS MORE TO ME THAN JENNY AND ALISON'S SAFETY!'

Cheer.

Someone reached out and shoved Michael Larson, sending him lurching to the other side of the walkway, knocking over a traffic cone, where someone else shoved him back.

'Get off me!'

Gordon Maguire stuck a hand in the middle of the reporter's chest and pushed past. 'WE DON'T HAVE TIME FOR SLEAZY JOURNALISTS, DO WE?'

A resounding 'NO!' echoed back from the headstones.

Logan shifted his feet, feeling for the little canister of pepper-spray in his pocket. 'Inspector?'

'Meh, not like Larson needs all his teeth anyway. A wee spanking might do the boy some good.'

The reporter was shoved again, this time hard enough to make him clatter to the ground. Then a grunt, as someone's boot thumped into his ribs. Then another. Then a blister of people burst out onto the path, buckling the line of tape, hauling the reporter back between the graves, punches raining down onto his head and chest.

'BASTARD!'

'PEOPLE LIKE YOU MAKE ME SICK!'

'FUCKIN' HIT HIM!'

Steel sighed, then twisted the filter on her e-cigarette. 'Suppose we better go do something.' Stuck her hands in her pockets. Stared up at the clouds.

'Fine. . .' Logan dragged out his pepper-spray and shoved his way through the crowd. 'POLICE! MOVE IT!'

By the time he'd fought his way to the path, Gordon Maguire was on his way again, smiling and waving at the crowd.

Logan pushed into the crowd on the other side. 'BREAK IT UP!'

Feet thumped down on the reporter's chest and head. He was curled on his side, arms covering his face, shrieking. 'HELP ME!'

'I SAID BREAK IT UP!' People parted in front of Logan. Black suits, jeans, skirts, cargo-pants, forming a little ring around the groaning, bloody figure on the ground. Blood trickled from Larson's ear, poured from his nose. His face was already beginning to swell.

'Bunch of bastards. . .' Logan squatted over the reporter. 'You OK?'

A groan. A cough. A spatter of blood on trampled grass, a tooth glistening pink in a puddle of dark red.

That would be a no then.

'You're all under arrest. . .' He looked up, but the faces around him had changed. They'd melted away into the crowd, blending in with everyone else dressed in funereal black. 'All right, who did this?' Logan stared at the wall of people surrounding Michael Larson. They stared at the ground, or the big display screens. Shuffled their feet. Not one of them looking at him or the battered reporter.

A clatter of heavy boots on paving stones and a uniformed officer appeared at Logan's shoulder. 'Jesus, he all right?'

'Don't just stand there – call a bloody ambulance.'

'Oh my *GOD*!' An oversized woman in a black miniskirt, clutched her chest. 'Is that Ewan McGregor? EWAN! WE LOVE YOU!' Jumping up and down like an ecstatic Labrador, while a man lay bleeding at her Doc-Martened feet.

By the time Larson was wheeled away on a stretcher the service was well underway.

The organizers had set up four huge screens in the St Nicholas Kirkyard, each one showing the action inside: a nondescript man in full Church of Scotland regalia, going on about peace and understanding, when all anyone outside seemed interested in was ogling the celebrity guests.

Logan elbowed his way through the crowds, back to the monument where he'd left DI Steel. She was leaning against the lichened granite, smoking her fake cigarette.

'Aye, aye, save the day did you?'

Logan looked back over his shoulder. 'Paramedics say he'll probably be OK: concussion, fractured jaw, broken ribs. Maybe a dislocated shoulder.'

'Couldn't happen to a nicer guy.' She blew a little puff of vapour towards the heavens where grey clouds were spreading across the sky, like ink dropped on wet paper.

'Where's Rennie?'

She waved a hand in the general direction of the church. 'Off worshipping at the altar of whatsherface from Girls Aloud.'

'Skiving little—'

'Oh, lighten up.' She turned to face the nearest screen, where the minister was giving up the stage. 'How often you get this in Aberdeen, eh?'

'Ladies and gentlemen, Mr Robbie Williams, and Ms Katie Melua are going to sing for us. . .'

The speakers crackled and the church organ rang out through the speakers: the opening bars to *Wind Beneath My Wings*.

'Oh Christ, not again!'

Close-up on Mr Williams and Ms Melua, microphones in hand.

Everyone in the graveyard was silent. The crowd seemed to be holding its breath for the first two verses, but as soon as the chorus started, they joined in.

Logan watched the woman who'd bellowed her love to Ewan McGregor, hands clutched over her massive bosom in full opera singer pose, warbling along with tears streaming down her cheeks. She wasn't the only one. Half the crowd seemed to be wetting itself with emotion.

Then someone started in on the alternative lyrics and it spread like a cancer through the throng.

'Can you believe. . .' Logan turned to Steel, but she was singing along too.

What the hell was *wrong* with everyone?

When the service was over, Steel shoved her way to the front, warrant card out. 'Come on, shift it: police business.'

As soon as Gordon Maguire appeared from the church, she dug Logan in the ribs. 'Heads up.'

The producer was swaggering down the path, arms up over his head, giving everyone the victory Vs. Like a bald Richard Nixon. 'YEAH! COME ON ABERDEEN!'

Cheers.

Logan pulled up the 'POLICE' tape and Steel ducked under, right in front of Maguire. He raised his hands. 'Sorry, love, I can't—'

'We'd like a word.' She stuck her warrant card under his nose.

'Ah, right. . .' He backed off a couple of paces. 'Can it wait? I'm kinda in the middle of—'

'*Now*, Mr Maguire.'

'But I've got a plane to catch, it—'

'Shall we?' Logan took hold of Maguire's elbow and steered him back inside, commandeering a small room just off the main entrance, lined with dark wood. It smelled of old wax and older cigarettes, light coming from a bare strip-light in the ceiling. Cardboard boxes were stacked in one corner, a display cabinet full of spider webs and dusty silver things opposite the door.

'Look, is this going to take long? Only, like I said, I've got a plane—'

'You're no' going anywhere till I say you are.' Steel smiled at him. 'You must be raking it in: all this publicity?'

Maguire shrugged. 'I do OK.'

'Aye, I'll bet you do. What's the fund up to now?'

He pulled out a packet of Silk Cut. 'I don't see how—'

'No smoking.' Logan took the cigarettes from him. 'Answer the question.'

Maguire scowled. 'Two-and-a-bit. Million. But it's not like I get to see any of that, OK? It's all downloads. Every penny goes into a marked account, and it's for the *ransom*. I don't even have access to it.'

Steel pursed her lips. 'So what happens if we turn up Jenny and her mum, all safe and sound? What happens to your two-and-a-bit million then?'

Maguire cleared his throat, ran a hand across the back of his neck. 'I *suppose* it'd go to charity . . . or something. . . After administrative deductions.'

'Aye, I'll bet it will.'

'You can't just—'

'Is this all just a big PR stunt?' Logan tossed the packet of Silk Cut from one hand to the other. 'Did you set the whole thing up?'

Maguire took off his trendy glasses, pinched the bridge of his nose. 'Listen, OK? Yeah, the pre-orders for the album are huge, but if I don't have Alison and Jenny, I can't finish recording the bloody thing. We've got about half the tracks in the can and I've only got three weeks to get it done.'

'Don't—'

'*Three weeks* – after that the bank call in my overdraft. We've sunk everything we've got into making *Britain's Next Big Star*. Orchestras, backing choirs, classical scores, performance rights payments, cameras, crew, sets. . . The costs are suffocating. But we can't cut corners because we're up against *The X Factor* and *Britain's Got Talent*, and the *Search for Andrew*

Lloyd Webber's Next Whateverthefuck. If we pull it off, we make a sodding mint, but right now the whole production company's sliding down a razorblade into liquidation using its ball-sack as a brake.'

Maguire ran a hand across his bald head. 'And you'd think my investors would be rubbing their hands at all the publicity, wouldn't you? But *no*, the thieving wankers are waiting for us to go under so they can step in and take a hundred percent, get some cheap-arsed Lithuanian company in to make the next series, and pocket the difference. You lot are lucky – there's honour amongst thieves. TV companies are all bastards.'

Steel fiddled with her e-cigarette. 'So you're no' the one who sent us a severed toe?'

He closed his eyes. 'No. I didn't send you a toe. Where the fuck would I get a *toe* from?'

'You've done worse for a wee bit of publicity: like them tampons—'

'It wasn't even real blood! We dipped them in some fake stuff we got off the internet, OK? We're a small company, we do everything we can to create a buzz. Alison and Jenny don't *need* it – they're going to win *Britain's Next Big Star*. . . They *were* going to win. Fuck knows what's going to happen now.' He pinched his nose again. 'Look, I want them back. If they come back, the ratings go through the roof, we finish the record, Blue-Fish-Two-Fish doesn't have to go into receivership, everyone makes a shit-pile of money, and we all live happily ever after.'

Steel scowled at him. 'Aye, well, you know what I think? I think—'

The door banged open.

DCI Finnie stepped into the little room. Behind him, Logan could see Superintendent Green and *Acting* DI Mark MacDonald filling the corridor.

'Inspector Steel,' Finnie's rubbery face pulled itself into something that wasn't quite a smile, 'I thought you were supposed to be tracking down a paedophile ring. Did I *imagine* that? Or have you somehow managed to *miraculously* work your way through every sex offender in Grampian in time for a jolly into town? Hmmm?'

19

'Afternoon, Guv. If you're here for Kylie Minogue's autograph you're too late – she's buggered off home. Took the hump when I wouldn't give her a seeing to.'

'Do I *really* have to remind you, *Inspector*, that one little girl is already dead, and we've only got five more days to stop Alison and Jenny McGregor *joining* her?'

They stood staring at one another.

Steel sniffed, then stuck the e-cigarette back in her pocket. 'I'm done with Mr Maguire anyway.'

'*Acting* DI MacDonald.' Finnie turned his fake smile in Mark's direction. 'Why don't you do me a favour and *escort* Mr Maguire back to the station?'

'Oh, come on!' The producer threw his hands in the air. 'I've got a bloody plane to catch! We're shooting a live TV tribute in—'

'After all, I'm *sure* he wouldn't like anyone to think he wasn't cooperating with the police at this delicate time. Would you, Mr Maguire?'

'Bloody. . . OK, OK.' He barged past into the corridor. 'Let's get this over with.'

'Excellent.' Finnie gave Logan the once over, top lip curled.

'If you *don't* mind, Sergeant, I'd like to speak to DI Steel in *private*. Perhaps you could use the time to pop past Professional Standards? I hear they'd love a little chat with you about some rape allegations.'

Shite. So much for plan A.

'Yes, right.' Logan squeezed out of the room, and Finnie closed the door.

A muffled argument.

Standing out in the corridor, Superintendent Green nodded: as if they'd just agreed on something. 'So, Detective Sergeant. . .?'

'McRae. Logan. Sir.'

Another nod. 'I see.' He tilted his head on one side, staring, a little crease between his eyebrows. 'Rape?'

'Just a junkie making stuff up. Thinks she can blackmail me into giving back the drugs we seized off her boyfriend.'

'I see. . . And have you ever investigated a kidnapping before, Sergeant? I mean a *real* one, not just drug dealers grabbing each other off the street: ransom notes, body parts in the post, that kind of thing?'

No, but you have, haven't you, you smug bastard. 'Not really, sir. Kidnapping's not that common in the north-east.'

More nodding. Then Green patted him on the shoulder. 'Walk with me, Sergeant.'

The Superintendent turned and marched out into the afternoon. The graveyard was slowly emptying – now the TV cameras were turned off and all the celebrities had gone, the crowd would all be scurrying away home to check their DVD recorders. See if they'd managed to get on the telly.

Green looked down at his feet as they walked along the path from the church – big grey slabs laid in a wide, meandering walkway. He stopped just in front of a large rectangle of granite. It was a gravestone laid on its back in the middle of the path, the name nearly worn into obscurity by generations of scuffing feet. 'When I was small, my father would take me to church every Sunday, after Mother. . .' Frown. 'Well, anyway, one day he said, "You see that? That name beneath your feet? We're walking on dead people." And I nearly wet myself. I was about five, I think. Had nightmares for months.' Green took a step, so he was standing right on top of the headstone. 'Why does the inspector call you "Laz"?'

'Private joke.'

Green raised his chin, shoulders back, staring out across the emptying graveyard. 'We're going to need to pull out all the stops on this one, Sergeant. It's vital we get Jenny back before anything happens to her.'

Well, *duh*. 'Yes, sir.'

'Normally I'd expect the kidnappers to grab some rich kid, send a ransom note to the parents telling them not to get in touch with the police or the kid dies. A demand for money to be handed over at a clandestine location. All done in complete secrecy.' His eyes narrowed. 'But this. . .'

He looked as if he expected stirring theme music to swell up at any minute.

'They grab two people in the public eye – people without *any* family – and instead of conducting their seedy business in the shadows, they send their ransom demands to the newspapers. They *want* the police involved.'

Go on, say it. . .

'We're not dealing with ordinary kidnappers here, Logan.'

Dun, dun, daaaaaaaaa!

'No, sir.'

As if they hadn't worked that little gem out for themselves.

NO! NO! NO! NO! She tries to wriggle free, but the monster in white holds her tight, wraps his papery arms around her, lifting her up off the ground.

'Hold still, you little bitch!' His voice is all weird: hard and metal like a robot, like the silver monsters on Doctor Who, like a Cyberman.

Her heel smashes into something soft and squishy.

A buzz, a crackle. 'Oh, fuck. . .' And the arms let go.

She tumbles to the bare floorboards. The monster staggers against the wall, one hand on the paint-sprayed wallpaper, the other grabbing his willy.

She scrambles to her feet and runs for the door. Get back through to Mummy, where the bed is, where—

Ulp. . .

Her feet fly out in front of her as the chain around her neck snaps tight.

'Come back here, you little cow.'

Mummy's voice, shouting in the other room: 'Don't hurt her! You promised you wouldn't hurt her!'

'Kicked me in the bloody balls!'

She's dragged backwards across the floorboards, arms and legs thrashing.

'MUMMY!'

'YOU PROMISED!'

Thump. She's lying on her front, with a heavy weight on her back – warm and rustling. The monster grabs her wrist, wraps something around it and pulls. It makes a Vzzzzwip noise. Then the other wrist, and both her arms are stuck behind her back.

'MUMMY! MUMMY, THEY'RE—'

A purple hand covers her mouth. It smells like bicycle tyres on a hot day.

'Tom: don't just bloody stand there!'

More weight, pinning her legs to the floor.

Vzzzzwip. Vzzzzwip. And now her ankles are stuck together. A scritchy, ripping noise, then the hand lets go of her mouth and a strip of something sticky is jammed into

139

place. She can't even open her lips. All she can do is hiss and mumble and cry.

Then the monsters let go.

She wriggles as hard as she can, flopping about like a goldfish on the bathroom floor. That's what happens to Bad Little Girls. . .

'Bloody hell. Looks like she's having a fit.'

Wriggle. Thrash. Flop . . . struggle . . . twitch. Lie panting on the floorboards, tears dripping from her nose.

Another monster steps into the room and clunks the door shut behind it. 'Will you two stop pricking about?' A lady monster – it's difficult to tell from the Cyberman voice, but she has boobies. She has a name badge stuck to her white crinkly chest, with 'HELLO MY NAME IS' at the top, and 'WILLIAM' underneath.

All the monsters are wearing them. 'TOM' and 'SYLVESTER' stand back, staring down at Jenny.

WILLIAM crosses her arms. Every move makes a rustling sound. It's not skin, not like she thought in her bedroom when they came for her – it's that stuff the police wear on the television when something bad happens. Sticky purple gloves, blue shower-caps on their feet. Plasticy masks that hide their faces and make them look like robots. It goes with the horrible metal voices. 'Where's Colin?'

TOM shrugs. Then SYLVESTER points over his shoulder. 'Throwing up.'

'Oh for Christ's sake.' She nods. 'Get him.'

'But—'

'Now!'

Robots, arguing.

'OK, OK. . .' SYLVESTER hurries out, feet scuffing on the floor.

'Get her on the table.'

TOM grabs her by the collar and waistband of her jammies

and hauls her off the ground. 'Wriggle and I'll bloody drop you on your head, understand?'

She stays very still.

'Good girl.'

Good Little Girl.

Thump – TOM dumps her on the table. Holds her there with a heavy hand in the middle of her back.

WILLIAM, the lady monster, stands over her. 'Stop crying. If you behave yourself it'll all be over soon.'

The door clunks.

Jenny blinks away the tears. It's SYLVESTER, back with another monster. This one has 'COLIN' written on his chest. He's carrying a little plastic box.

WILLIAM doesn't look at him. 'Get on with it.'

COLIN clears his throat. 'I. . . Erm. . . Look, it's just. . . I mean, do we have to? Can we not just send the papers another photo or something?'

'You saw what they're saying on the news.'

'But I've never done. . . She's just a little girl.'

'I *know* what she is. Now do your bloody job. Or do you want me to tell David you won't? Is that really what you want?'

'But I—'

WILLIAM grabs him by the front of his crumply white suit. 'What fucking good are you if you can't do a simple bloody procedure?'

'But amputating isn't just. . . There's the risk of infection, MRSA, septicaemia, blood clots, shock, what if—'

'Pull – your – fucking – weight.'

She lets go and he steps back. Stares down at his blue feet. Then nods.

'You need to roll up her sleeve.'

Fire bites her shoulders as TOM twists her arm, dragging her jammie sleeve up to her armpit.

Please no. Please no. Please no.

COLIN puts the plastic box down on the table. Opens it. She can see shiny sharp things sparkling inside. Then he takes out a tiny jar and a jaggy needle. He goes back in for a little foil packet, tears it open and pulls out a little tissue. Wipes it against the inside of her elbow, it makes the skin go all cold.

Then he fills up the jaggy needle.

'I'm sorry. . .'

A hard scratchy feeling, then a stabbing pain, like being stung by a bee.

Another wipe.

'We need to give it a minute.'

She blinks.

The bee sting doesn't hurt any more.

'I still don't think—'

'No one's asking you to *think*, Colin.'

Blink. Blink.

She's in the playground on the roundabout, spinning faster and faster, round and round, trees and houses and monsters whooshing past. Blurry plastic faces, muzzy booming Cybermen voices. Fuzzy warmth spreading between her ears.

She blinks, but her eyes won't open again.

20

'So why *did* she have your name written on her?' Chief Inspector Young sat back in his seat and surveyed Logan over the expanse of his desk. The Professional Standards office was empty, except for the two of them: three desks; framed diplomas and handshake photos on the walls; a case of legal textbooks and policing manuals; and the clinging reek of spearmint.

Young had rolled up his sleeves, exposing a pair of huge hairy arms. But then he was big all over, like a rugby player or a professional boxer. Or a mob enforcer. Pale scar tissue made ripples across his knuckles. Definitely not the sort of man you'd want to fuck with.

Logan puffed out his cheeks. 'Best guess? Someone thought she wouldn't remember who to ask for otherwise. But the idiots didn't even write it upside down so she could read it. Mind you, given how off her face she was. . .'

The Chief Inspector drummed his fingertips on the desktop, the tendons and muscles dancing beneath the fur of his forearms. 'And tell me, Sergeant, why did she think you'd hand the drugs over to her?'

'Because she's an idiot too?' Logan shrugged. 'She's

convinced the people her boyfriend bought the stuff from are going to hurt him if he doesn't come up with the money. What else is she going to do?'

'Hmm. . .' Young stopped making thumpitta-thumpitta noises on the desktop. 'And have you put anything in place?'

'Well, Shuggie's wanted on drugs charges from the Thursday morning raid, and it's pretty obvious he's still in contact with Trisha. So I've advised DI McPherson to put her under surveillance.' Another shrug. 'It's his case.'

'I suppose . . . there's always hope.' Young started drumming again. 'We've not seen you up here for a while, Logan. I think Superintendent Napier's missing you.'

'Really, sir?' He glanced over his shoulder at the Arch Bastard's desk. All neat and tidy, everything carefully arranged in straight lines.

The Chief Inspector looked off into the middle distance. 'Tell me . . . how's Acting Detective Inspector MacDonald getting on?'

Silence.

Logan shifted in his seat. 'In what way, sir?'

'Is he settling in all right? Getting on with his colleagues? Can be very stressful, suddenly moving up from DS to DI like that.' Young wouldn't make eye contact.

'I'm sure he's coping fine.'

'Good. Good.' A pause. 'What with the McGregor case and everything. . .?'

'Fine. Couldn't be better. Doing a great job.'

Another pause.

'Well, then I'll let you get back to your sex offenders.'

Dodgy Pete's wasn't exactly what you'd call a watering hole for the bright young things. More a hospice: palliative care for alcoholics on their way to a booze-soaked oblivion.

But it was a two-minute walk from the Munro House Hotel, and that was good enough for Steel.

The scuffed linoleum made sticky noises, trying to hold onto the soles of Logan's shoes as he followed her over to the bar. It was busy in here for a change: a dozen people scattered in pairs about the low room, staring up at a wide-screen TV mounted on the wall. The Aberdeen versus VfB Stuttgart live from Germany: two–nil to the home team.

The barman was huddled at the far end of the long hard-wood bar, holding a muttered conversation with a thin girl in cargo pants and a camouflage hoodie. There was something laid out on the surface between them, but Logan didn't have time to see what it was before she snatched it up and stuffed it into the black rucksack at her feet.

Steel thumped her hand down on the bar and clambered onto a stool – the red vinyl held together with grey duct tape. 'Hoy, Pete, stop perving up that young sex-pot and make with the drinkies.'

The huge man sniffed. Then turned and lumbered over, a red Aberdeen University sweatshirt stretched to ripping point over his belly. Pete ran a hand through his Santa-on-an-off-day beard, and squinted at the three of them. 'Usual?'

Steel nodded. 'And a couple brace of Grouse too.'

'You paying for these?'

The inspector stuck out her bottom lip. 'Pete, I'm shocked. Are you suggesting Grampian's finest come in here looking for freebies?'

'Bloody right I am.' He grabbed a couple of pint glasses from under the counter, stuck one under the Stella tap, the other under the Deuchar's IPA. Then sniffed in Rennie's direction. 'What about the sunburnt wee loon?'

The constable stuck out his chest. 'I'll have a pint of—'

'He'll have a Diet Coke.' Steel pulled out her fake cigarette. 'Driving, remember?'

'But Guv—'

'Give him a packet of prawn cocktail too.'

Dodgy Pete stuck the pint of IPA onto a curling cardboard coaster, then picked up a couple of short glasses and clunked a double shot in each from the Grouse whisky optic, making a great show of waiting till the little plastic container filled all the way up each time. 'Anything else?'

The girl in the camouflage hoodie grabbed her rucksack and slipped quietly out of the pub.

Steel turned and stared after her. 'You're no' up to anything dodgy, are you, Pete?'

'My daughter. Not that it's any of *your* business.' He rapped a knuckle on the sticky bar. 'Now are you paying for these or not?'

'Lighten up, eh, Pete? No' my fault the Shop Cops did you for serving short measures, is it?'

They took their drinks through to the snug – pretty much a walk-in cupboard with two bench seats and a table wedged into it. Steel crumpled down, sighed, then took a huge gulp out of her pint. 'Can't hang about tonight, boys, I'm on a promise.'

Logan pulled the reports out of his pocket and stuck them on the table. 'Ninety-six RSOs interviewed today. . . So far we've got three with possible access to veterinary surgeries. No hospitals – turns out the NHS frowns on registered sex offenders creeping about the wards.'

Steel had a scratch. 'Who's doing the vets?'

The whisky tasted like a peat fire, burning its way across Logan's tongue, making his gums tingle. Dodgy Pete must've stopped watering the booze down too. 'DI Evans. No one's reported any thiopental sodium missing.'

Rennie crammed in a mouthful of crisps. 'What if they bought it off the internet?'

Steel stared at him. 'Drink your Diet Coke. Things are

sodding complicated enough as it is.' Then back to Logan. 'You sure about the hospitals?'

'McPherson says—'

'God's sake, he's no' doing that as well is he? Talk about abandon-bloody-ship. I'll have a word with Finnie, see if we can't get someone else to. . .' She creased her face up. 'Marmite-flavoured arseholes. He's no' speaking to me any more.'

Logan frowned. 'Yeah, about that – why *were* we winding Maguire up? He's not on the register, I checked.'

'Because. . .' She turned and looked at Rennie. Then dug out a handful of change. 'Here, go get yourself some more crisps.'

'But I don't—'

'Then go play on the bandit, something.' Pause. 'Bugger off for five minutes.'

Rennie picked a couple of pound coins from the pile, then scooped up his crisps and drink. 'Be like that, then.'

She waited till he'd left the little room. 'We gave Mr Baldy a hard time because Acting DI MacDonald was in charge of that bit of the investigation. And I don't trust him. OK?' She held up a hand. 'It's no' that he's dodgy, it's just that he's completely fucking hopelessly out of his depth. And I know Finnie thinks the same, or he'd no' have been there holding his hand at the church.'

'I see. . .'

'Laz, I know you lot in the Wee Hoose are thick as thieves, but there's a wee girl's life at stake. I'm no sodding about with this one.'

Fair point. 'So what about McPherson?'

Steel pulled a face, then took a swig of whisky. 'You leave Disaster to me, we'll—'

The rest was drowned out by cheering coming through from the main bar. 'GO ON MY SON!', 'RUN YOU WEE BUGGER!', 'GO ON, GO ON!'

The volume on the telly was cranked up – the roar of the crowd booming out of the speakers. *'And it's Hansson to Paton. Up the outside . . . and he crosses to Gibson . . . Gibson shoots and—'*

Sudden silence.

'AWWW! FUCK'S SAKE! NO' NOW!', 'PETE! FIX THE FUCKING TELLY!', 'DID HE SCORE?'

Logan's phone rang – he dragged it out and checked the caller display: Colin Miller.

'Colin?'

The TV blared into life again: *'Interrupt your programming to bring you a news bulletin. . .'*

DI Steel's phone was ringing too. 'Can a girl no' have a wee drinkie in peace?'

'. . . believe that?' Colin's voice was almost inaudible over all the racket.

Logan stuck his finger in his other ear. 'Hello? Colin?'

'I said, they've sent another package, aye: to the BBC! Mate of mine works there, he's just called.'

Crap.

'What is it? What did they send?'

'I mean, why didn't they send it here? They always send stuff here first.'

'Colin: what – did – they – send?'

Steel was on her feet. 'Shite. . .' She stuck her phone against her chest. 'They've sent more toes to the BBC.'

Rennie crashed back into the snug. 'You got to come see what's on the telly!'

'Have I no' done everythin' they've asked for? How's that fair?'

Everyone in Dodgy Pete's stared up at the big TV, where a straight-backed reporter was doing a bit to camera. *'. . . just five minutes ago.'* There was a perfectly framed shot of two tiny toes in high-definition. Pale pink digits with swollen ends, the edges of the cut dark and discoloured. Unlike the big toe sitting on ice in the mortuary, these had *definitely* been cut from a living person.

Colin: *'Laz? Laz, you still there?'*

'Shut up a minute.'

'The toes were delivered to BBC Scotland offices in Aberdeen, along with a DVD and instructions to play it on air. The following footage contains graphic scenes and may distress some viewers. . .'

Steel had her phone to her ear again. 'Aye, we're watching it.'

The screen went black, then faded up on a graffiti-covered room, bare floorboards, sunlight streaming in through the chinks in a pair of boarded up windows. The whole image swung around, the autofocus taking a moment to catch up. A pair of tiny feet, stained orange-brown around the sides. Chipped pink nail varnish.

The two little toes were missing, the stumps where they should have been puffy and red, the skin stitched together over the holes with black thread. The knots looked like spiders, bursting out of the angry flesh.

'Holy fuck. . .' Someone in the bar dropped their pint. A crash of splintered glass.

The camera swung upwards. There was no mistaking the wee girl lying on her back, on what looked like a swathe of white plastic sheeting. Blonde curls, that long straight nose, the apple cheeks. Eyes half shut, a sheen of drool streaking down from the corner of her open mouth. An IV line was taped to the inside of her left wrist.

She groaned and twitched.

A purple-gloved hand moved into shot, holding a copy of the *Edinburgh Evening Post*. 'TOE NOT JENNY'S BUT POLICE *STILL* DENY HOAX'. The camera zoomed in on the date. It was today's edition.

The picture faded to black, then the familiar artificial voice burst out into the silent bar.

'*This is not a hoax. You have four days left. If you raise enough money, they will live. If you do not, they will die. Do not let Jenny and Alison down.*'

A pause, then the newsreader appeared back on the screen. '*Harrowing footage there. We go live now to Grampian Police Headquarters and our correspondent Sarah Williamson. Sarah, what can you tell us?*'

21

'. . . man's a complete prick.' Biohazard Bob wrinkled his nose. The Wee Hoose's door was closed, muting the noise from the main CID room: phones ringing; constables and support staff running about, trying to cope with the sudden barrage of calls from people who'd seen the broadcast. 'You'll never believe what he said to me yesterday: gave me this big monologue about the McGregor case and then—'

'"One thing's for certain",' Rennie struck a pose, '"we're dealing with no ordinary kidnappers!" Like he thinks he's on TV.'

Bob raised his big hairy eyebrow. 'You too?'

Logan nodded. 'And me.'

DS Doreen Taylor sighed. 'And there I was, thinking I was special.'

The sound of phones and borderline panic got louder as the door swung open. DI Steel slouched into the room. 'Right, listen up, 'cos I can't be arsed saying this twice.' She nudged the door shut with her heel, then stared at Rennie. 'Well? Move it!'

The constable stood, and perched himself on the edge of Bob's desk instead.

151

Steel groaned her way into the vacated chair. 'In light of recent developments we're having a wee reorganization. McPherson's trying to track down the dead kid the first toe came from; Acting DI MacDonald's taking over the hospital enquiries; Evans has the vets, and I'm sticking with the sex offenders.'

Rennie held up his hand. 'Does this mean—'

'I'm no' telling you again.'

He put his hand down.

'The media's going mental. The Chief Constable's arse is knitting buttons. SOCA's rubbing its grubby wee hands. And Bain's decided to give Superintendent Green a "more active role in the investigation".'

Here we go.

'Apparently he's got *experience* with kidnap cases.'

Every bloody time.

'So,' Steel dug a hand into her armpit and rummaged, 'we need someone to "facilitate" Green's "interactions", whatever the hell that means. Logan—'

'Why? Why does it *always* have to be me? Why do I have to babysit every tosser that comes up to Aberdeen?'

'If you'd shut up moaning for ten sodding seconds and let me *finish*. . . Logan: you're excused from Mongtown – with Bell doing the back shift we're nearly through them anyway. As of now you're on arse-covering duty. Go over everything we've done so far: victim profile, door-to-doors, everything, make sure there's nothing a public enquiry can do us for screwing up. Get yourself a minion.' She gave up on the armpit and started hauling at her bra instead. 'Doreen: Superintendent Green has chosen you to hold his hand. Try an' no' get carried away, eh? We know what you horny divorcees are like.'

Bob reached over and patted Doreen on the shoulder. 'See, you *are* "special" after all.' Then he grinned at the Inspector. 'What about me, Guv?'

Steel sniffed. 'You found Stinky Tam yet?'

'Well. . . Not as such. . .'

'Then you'd better get your finger out, hadn't you?'

Logan paused the video. Swore. Hauled out his ringing phone and cut *Lydia The Tattooed Lady* off short. 'Sam?'

Her voice nipped from the earpiece. *'Forget something did we?'*

'No, I didn't. I'm coming home in a minute.'

'Where are you, like I need to ask?'

He looked around the gloomy room. It was a scruffy admin office on the fourth floor, one of the ones slated for refurbishment, which was the only reason he'd been able to commandeer it. Half the ceiling tiles were missing, loops of grey cabling snaking between the concrete supports for the floor above. A little oasis of dirty green carpet tiles clung to one patch of grey floor, and that was where Logan had set up the desk he'd conned from Building Services.

One desk. One chair. One laptop. And two heavy brown cardboard boxes full of files.

'I'll be home soon, OK?'

'Half-seven, McRae – I'm holding you to it. Oh, and I've got a box of Stella and a couple of Markies' lasagnes in. We can make a night of it.'

'Soon, I promise.' Pause. 'Look, I've got to go.'

'Half-seven, remember?'

And she was gone.

Logan pressed play again.

On the laptop screen, Alison McGregor was being bundled down the stairs, kicking and struggling, trying to head-butt the guy in the SOC suit carrying her. Through the hallway into the kitchen. The guy was wearing one of those stick-on name badges they handed out at conventions. It was nearly impossible to read, but the BBC's *Crimewatch* had chucked a pile of licence-fee-payers' money at a digital imaging house to pull out the word, 'TOM'.

A little girl in Winnie the Pooh pyjamas was huddled in the corner by the fridge – a pillowcase or something over her head. Hands fastened in front of her. Trembling.

Alison McGregor froze, then exploded. Legs flying, kicking out at random, bucking, writhing. Eyes bugging out above her duct-tape gag.

The guy holding her finally gave up: slammed her into the fridge, then bent her over the working surface and fastened her ankles together with thick black cable-ties. A bag over her head. Then someone stepped into frame and brained her with a cosh, or something similar.

Alison went limp.

All done in total silence.

Whoever hit her, bent and hauled her up into a fireman's carry. For a whole two frames his name badge was perfectly clear: 'DAVID'. Fifteen seconds later they were out through the kitchen door and into the darkness of the back garden.

Fade to black.

Then the artificial voice:

'You will raise money for the safe return of Alison and Jenny McGregor. You have fourteen days, or they will be killed. You will tell the police. You will tell the television stations. You will tell the public. Or they will be killed. If you raise enough money within fourteen days, Jenny and Alison will be released. If not, they will be killed.'

'You still here?'

Logan turned. DI Bell stood in the doorway, a slice of toast in one hand, a mug of something in the other. A warm, meaty smell drifting out of it. 'Just heading off, Guv.'

154

Bell stepped into the room, wandered over to the window, stuck the toast in his mouth – like a rectangular duck's beak – and peeked through the blinds.

Logan powered down the laptop. 'Thought you were in charge of back shift interviews?'

The inspector let go of the blind, took the toast from his mouth. Chewed. 'Got a call from Trisha Brown's mum – nine, nine, nine. Completely off her face: says someone was round there with a cricket bat smashing her prized heirlooms to smithereens.' Another bite of toast. 'Wasn't you, was it?'

'Very funny, sir.'

'Who says I'm being funny?'

Logan just stared at him.

DI Bell shrugged. 'Anyway, when McHardy and Butler got there the place was even more of a craphole than normal. She'd been given a going over too.'

'Drugs?' Logan clunked the laptop shut and slipped it into its carrying case.

'Poor old Helen probably tried to buy them off with a freebie, but being clean-living and sensible sorts, they beat the shite out of her instead. And the answer to your next question is no: your girlfriend Trisha wasn't there.'

He hefted the laptop bag over his shoulder. 'Anyone found Shuggie yet?'

'If the bugger's got any brains he'll be lying low in Dundee or Glasgow by now. Blending in with the scheemie smackheads till the heat dies down.'

Logan stood. 'That's me off.'

'Right. . . Right.' Bell finished off the last chunk of toast, washing it down with whatever was in the mug. 'I'm not going to have to give you another call at three in the morning, am I?'

'Christ, I hope not.'

*   *   *

Logan stuck his head through the open door to the main incident room. It was a bit swankier than the one he'd commandeered on the fourth floor: Finnie had a complete set of carpet tiles for a start. It was lined with whiteboards and flipcharts, full of desks – seating for about thirty officers – its own photocopier, and a small glass-walled office in one corner so the Chief Inspector could keep an eye on his troops.

They'd set up a screen on the wall furthest from the door, a roof-mounted projector flickering away in the darkened room. Playing the latest video from Jenny and Alison's kidnappers.

Finnie, Superintendent Green, Doreen, and a handful of officers were watching as the camera panned across to Jenny's feet.

Green held up a hand. 'Stop it there. Go back a bit. . .'

The picture lurched into reverse.

'OK, freeze.' He stood and walked to the screen, took a chunky pen out of his pocket and pointed at the image. Click, and a little red dot appeared on the wall of the graffiti-covered squat, tracing around the timestamp in the bottom right corner. 'Eleven thirty-two. Now look at the patterns of light on the floor.'

The little red dot traced the shadows and highlights that fell across the bare floorboards. 'I have some *very* clever boffins in Edinburgh who can work out the position of the sun at eleven thirty-two this morning, relative to Aberdeen. We combine that with the angle of incidence on the shadows and that'll give us a good idea of where this was filmed.'

One of the uniformed officers whistled. 'Fucking hell. . .'

Green turned, a smile on his face, one eyebrow raised. 'I know: impressive, isn't it? It won't give us an exact address, but it'll let us know roughly which part of the city we should be looking at. Then we search every derelict property in that area.'

Logan frowned.

Finnie nodded. 'Excellent.'

Green's chest came out a notch. 'I'll get them onto it.'

'Erm, sir?' Logan shifted the laptop bag on his shoulder. 'Are you sure?'

The head of CID turned in his seat and gave him a rubbery scowl. 'Tell me, Sergeant McRae, do you have a *better* idea?'

'It's just that—'

'You've been going through the files for an hour and. . .' He checked his watch. 'Ten minutes, and you've *already* solved the case, *all* on your own?'

Logan could feel the heat rushing up his cheeks. 'No, sir. I just think we should take another look at the footage before we go running off to SOCA's technical services.'

'Really?' Superintendent Green leaned back against a desk, that TV smile of his slipping into a frown. 'And why is *that*? Exactly.'

'The kidnappers always take a lot of trouble to make sure we never get any forensic evidence. Why wouldn't they do the same with the video?'

Green pinched the bridge of his nose between thumb and forefinger. Sighed. Shook his head. 'It's a *video*, Sergeant – they can't control the angle and position of the *sun*. Now, if we can get back to the footage?'

'But they *can* control the timestamp on the camera.'

Green froze, half-turned back to the screen. 'What?'

'You have to set the time manually every time you change the battery.' He pointed at the little digital readout. 'Eleven thirty-two: the media briefing didn't even *start* till eleven. And what about the newspaper?'

'It's today's, so I don't—'

'The *Edinburgh Evening Post* headline was about the toe not being Jenny's. How did they manage to write the article, print the newspaper, get it up to Aberdeen, and sell it in a

157

shop, all in under thirty-two minutes? The paper doesn't even go to press till mid-day. I checked.'

'Ah. . .' Green nodded. 'I see. Well, that's a very valid point.' He turned back to face the screen. 'Thank you, Sergeant.'

'Anyway,' Logan pointed at the graffiti-covered room, projected on the back wall, 'just wanted to grab a copy of the video, if there's one going spare?'

'There's one here.' Doreen dug a CD in a clear plastic case from a folder on the desk beside her, then handed it over. Whispering. 'You've made him look like a complete idiot.' She gave Logan's hand a squeeze. 'Thanks.'

It was raining, pea-sized drops of lukewarm water that turned the pavement dark grey.

There was no point going out the front – the crowd was back in force, even with the horrible weather, huddling under thrumming umbrellas, being outraged for all the camera crews. The Lodge Walk entrance was just as bad, full of journos sheltering from the downpour while they waited to pounce on anyone leaving FHQ. So Logan hid the laptop bag under his jacket, trying to keep the thing dry as he hurried down the ramp from the Rear Podium and nipped through the little bit at the back of the Arts Centre.

Tonight the billboard sign outside the newsagent on King Street read, '*Evening Express*: Jenny's Torture – Can We Raise Enough To Save Her?' the white paper insert going nearly transparent as it soaked up the rain.

The other side had, '*Aberdeen Examiner*: Toe Terror Of Brave Jenny – Kidnappers Prove It's No Hoax'. He stopped off and bought a copy of both, then hurried down Marischal Street.

It was getting colder, the rain leaching the heat from the city. His breath steamed around his head as he unlocked the building's front door and dripped up the stairs to the flat.

'You in?'

Samantha's voice came from the lounge. 'Hurry up, it's just about to start.'

Oh joy.

Logan draped his jacket over a chair in the kitchen, moved the chair in front of the hot oven, grabbed a cold tin of Stella from the fridge, and made it back to the lounge in time to catch the opening titles.

Alison and Jenny McGregor
BRITAIN'S NEXT BIG STAR! – TRIBUTE SPECIAL
With Special Guests. . .

He sank into the sofa next to Samantha. 'Chucking it down out there.'

'You're cutting it a bit fine, aren't you?'

Logan fought with his soggy laces, then kicked his shoes off. 'Lasagne in?'

She raised her tin of lager. 'Bottoms up.'

Cheering burst from the television speakers as the camera swooped in over an excited audience to a big black triangular stage, polished to a mirror sheen, surrounded by hoops of red, green, and blue neon. Above the stage, three screens flashed from a red skull and crossbones to a green tick, the words, 'MARTINE', 'CHRIS', and 'SOPHIE' picked out in glowing white Perspex beneath them.

Logan pulled off his damp socks as the camera came to rest on two youngish looking blokes in black suits and black ties. 'Who the hell are they?'

'One on the left used to present *Blue Peter*, one on the right does a comedy thing on Channel Four.'

'So what, they're some kind of bargain basement "Ant and Dec"?'

'Shhhhhh. . . They're doing the intro.'

It was a bizarre concept – a TV talent show doing a tribute

to two of its contestants, by getting celebrities to come on and do cover versions of the cover versions Alison and Jenny McGregor did in order to get on the show and become the kind of celebrity that got asked to do tribute shows. . .

The first couple of acts were OK. But after every one the camera would zoom in on the row of judges for their comments.

Logan took another slurp of Stella. 'What's the point? Not like they can say anything nasty, is it?'

And then a familiar figure bounded onto the stage. Gordon Maguire, head of Blue-Fish-Two-Fish Productions, dressed in the same *Reservoir Dogs* get-up as not-Ant-and-Dec. He waited for the applause to die down. *'Thanks, guys. This has been one* hell *of a rollercoaster. First we thought Jenny was dead. Then the police told us they'd made a mistake, and she was still alive after all!'*

A cheer went up.

'And then, we all saw that horrible video this afternoon.'

That didn't get a cheer.

The record producer nodded. *'I know, I know. They told us we had fourteen days to raise enough money to save Jenny and Alison's lives . . . well we've only got four days left. I want to remind everyone that the charity single is on iTunes, Amazon, and BritainsNextBigStar.com, or you can buy it at HMV. All proceeds are going to pay the ransom. . .'*

Samantha shifted on the couch, a little line puckering the skin between her neatly-trimmed eyebrows. 'He's a greasy little shite, isn't he?'

'Hmmm. . .' Logan crumpled the empty tin.

'Oh, I saw the Reverend today. He's got a new dog collar – black leather with silver studs. I quite fancy one if you're feeling flush.'

On screen, Maguire finished his rousing speech to a standing ovation. Then there were comments of support from the judges. And then Lily Allen doing the McGregors' version of *Sergeant Pepper's Lonely Hearts Club Band.*

'*And viewers, tonight you can vote for which of our celebrities will perform* Wind Beneath My Wings *at the end of the show.*'

'*Yes, and don't forget: every phone call you make contributes towards the Alison and Jenny Freedom Fund. . .*'

Samantha turned the volume up. 'He wants to know if you're using the lotion.'

'What is this, *Silence of the Lambs*?'

'You have to use the lotion. Do you *want* it to get infected?'

'I'm using the lotion.' Logan stood. 'You want another beer?'

She raised her tin. 'Check on the lasagne when you're there?'

It looked like pretty much every ready-meal vegetarian lasagne he'd ever seen, bubbling away in its little oven-proof plastic tray. Smelled good, though. He pulled another two tins from the fridge.

The Alison and Jenny Freedom Fund – who the hell came up with that one? Made them sound like terrorists. . .

He popped open the cupboard above the fridge, hunting for crisps. Then groaned: his mobile was ringing, deep in the pocket of his steaming jacket. Logan shifted the chair and went rummaging until he found it. The number was withheld.

Sod it then. They could wait till he was on duty.

Unless it was something important.

Maybe Superintendent Green was calling to say he was sorry for being such a cock. That he didn't realize what a deductive *genius* Logan was. That he wished he hadn't picked Doreen to be his babysitter.

Not that Logan was jealous. The man *was* a prick after all. But what did Doreen have that he didn't? Other than boobs. And an ex-husband who'd run away with a social worker called Steve?

He hit the pick-up button. 'McRae.'

A pause. Then a fuzzy, vague voice sounded in his ear. *'Gotta give us them back, yeah?'*

It took a moment to place her. 'Trisha? Trisha Brown? That you?'

'They came to my mum's house and everything. Broke her leg and that.'

'Deal still stands, Trisha: tell me who they were, and we'll get them locked up. Don't want them to get away with battering your mum, do you?'

There was a big bag of Bacon Frazzles lurking behind a tub of Twiglets from last Christmas. Logan pulled them out and clunked the cupboard door shut again.

'Trisha?'

'Shuggie says they'll kill us if they find us.'

'All the more reason to dob them in then, isn't it?'

Silence.

Logan tucked the phone between his shoulder and his ear, picked up the tins of beer and the crisps. 'I'm going to hang up now, Trisha.'

'He says you gotta give them back, or next time he's gonna use a Stanley knife, you know?'

'On your mum?'

'To write your name on my chest. . .'

Samantha appeared in the kitchen doorway. 'What, are you brewing the beer yourself?' Arms folded across her 'ONE OF THE BEAUTIFUL PEOPLE' T-shirt, left hip jutting out. That line back between her eyebrows.

He held up a hand, mouthed, 'One minute. . .'

'I'm going for a pee – you've got till the end of the adverts.'

'Trisha, you have to tell me where you are.'

'You gotta give them back.'

'Who is it? Who's going to cut you?'

But she'd hung up.

22

An old man wheezed his way up the stairs, one hand on the black balustrade, the other clutching a rolled up, bright-pink *Hello Kitty* umbrella.

'Morning, Doc.' Logan leaned against the wall. 'Back again?'

Doc Fraser scowled from beneath hairy eyebrows. Water dripped from the point of his brolly. 'This is all *your* fault. I could've stayed retired, at home, chasing Mildred around the conservatory in my pants, but nooooo. . .' The pathologist shook his shoulders, sending a little downpour pattering to the stairs at his feet. 'Your mate Hudson's called in sick again. So it's either muggins here, or no one.'

'Toes?'

'Yes, *toes*. It's always bloody toes these days.'

'Erm. . .' Logan glanced up the stairs, then down. No one around. 'Fancy a coffee?'

Logan clicked the button and set the video playing again.

Doc Fraser leant forward in his seat until his nose was almost touching the screen.

Dr Dave Goulding had the room's only other chair. He'd turned it the wrong way around, straddling it and leaning

163

his arms on the back. Head tilted to one side, watching the pathologist watching the video. Goulding had on his little rectangular glasses, and a brand-new 1960s-Beatles-style moustache to go with his pelt-like hair. He ran a finger along the bridge of his hooked nose. 'It's an interesting choice, don't you think?' The voice was pure Liverpool.

Doc Fraser shrugged. 'They obviously know what they're doing. The stitching's good – not *wonderful*, but good. . . Which button pauses it again?'

Logan clicked it with the mouse.

'Thanks. Well, they've definitely got access to proper medical supplies. The brown stuff they've painted her feet with is Videne – it's an iodine-based disinfectant used to prep people for surgery. She's on an IV drip, so I'm assuming they don't have access to a PCA system—'

'PCA?' Logan opened his notepad.

'Patient Controlled Analgesia. You know, one of those machines where you press a button and it gives you more morphine? Well, until it thinks you've had enough, then it cuts you off so you can't overdose.'

'I see.' Goulding pointed at the screen. 'So they don't want to cause Jenny pain.'

Logan tried not to laugh. 'They cut off her *toes*, Dave.' So much for a psychology degree.

That got him a shrug. 'But that doesn't mean they want her to suffer. First they try to fob everyone off with a surrogate big toe from another child – it doesn't work, so they've got no choice, they have to amputate. It shows they're serious about killing her.'

Doc Fraser nodded. 'Aye.'

'And I think, if they *do* end up killing her, they'll do it so she doesn't have to suffer.'

Logan settled back against the windowsill. 'Kidnappers with a conscience.'

'Make it play again.'

He clicked the button.

'*This is not a hoax. You have four days left. If you raise enough money, they will live. If you do not, they will die. Do not let Jenny and Alison down.*'

A mobile phone rang.

Doc Fraser sighed. 'That'll be Finnie. Probably having a wee strop because the post mortem was supposed to start. . .' Quick check. 'Ten minutes ago.' The pathologist gave a big, pantomime stretch. 'Any more biscuits?'

Logan pushed the packet over.

'Now what I find interesting,' Goulding opened a pale blue folder and pulled out a half-dozen sheets of paper, placing them on the desk, 'is the language used. The voice on the videos is precise – no contractions, no colloquialisms – but the notes. . .' He read the latest one out. '"The police isn't taking this seriously. We gave them simple, clear, instructions, but they still was late. So we got no other choice: we had to cut off the wee girl's toe. She got nine more. No more fucking about."'

Goulding let his fingertips drift across the surface of the note. '"The police *isn't*.", "But they still *was*.", "So we *got* no other choice.", "She *got* nine more."'

'Different people?' Doc Fraser helped himself to another Jammie Dodger.

Goulding shook his head. 'No . . . different media. If they were slapdash, they'd use a voice-changer – like you get in toy Iron Man or Dalek helmets – but they don't. They know if we can get hold of the conversion algorithm we can decode their voice; and the pattern and rhythm of your speech stay the same anyway. So when they write the notes, they're typing in a fake accent. Trying to put us off.'

The psychologist held the note up. 'But even then they

165

still use a colon to delineate two parts of the compound sentence, and all the apostrophes are in the right place – given the idiom. Even the commas are correct.'

Doc Fraser's phone went again. 'Oh . . . bloody hell.' He gave a long sigh. 'I suppose I should really get down there and start the post mortem.' But he didn't move.

'I do wonder about the toes. . .' Goulding fiddled with the mouse, setting the video playing again.

Doc Fraser's phone stopped ringing. Then started again almost immediately. 'All right, all right. Some people.' He levered himself to his feet and stuck his hands in the pockets of his beige cardigan, pulling it all out of shape. 'Well, if you need me I'll be downstairs discovering traces of morphine, thiopental sodium, and Barbie-pink nail polish.'

'Thanks, Doc.' The door clunked shut and Logan stood in front of the window, looking out at the grey city.

Rain hammered the glass, gusts of wind shivering the few straggly trees planted between FHQ and Marischal College, tiny green buds whipping back and forth. He couldn't see the crowd gathered outside the front doors from here, but he had a perfect view of the outside broadcast units, parked illegally on the other side of the road.

The media must be loving this – the chance to whip up moral outrage, the chance to broadcast and print the most salacious and disturbing images and stories, all with the excuse that the kidnappers would kill Alison and Jenny McGregor if they didn't. . . 'What *about* the toes?'

'How you getting on?'

He looked around, saw the psychologist staring at him, then turned back to the window. 'I'm fine.'

'You've not turned up for a session for five weeks, Logan.'

Someone hurried across the road, passing in front of a grey Transit van with a satellite antenna on top of it, struggling to control an umbrella that looked hell bent on making a break for freedom.

'Do you think it's important they're sending toes, not fingers?'

Goulding sighed. 'The big toe – that's a huge loss to a foot, isn't it? It's the point of balance – cut it off and you're facing months and months of physical therapy learning to walk again. But the little toe. . .' A pause. 'Not just one, but both little toes. . .'

The umbrella broke free, tumbling end-over-end away down Queen Street. Its owner lumbered after it, right out into the path of a taxi. A blare of horn. Flashing lights. Probably a few choice swearwords as well.

'Logan, therapy isn't a quick fix. You have—'

'I had meat yesterday.'

'You did? *Really*?'

'Lasagne. Not vegetarian: proper beef sauce.' Well, if you couldn't lie to your therapist, who *could* you lie to?

The umbrella buried itself in a bush.

'And how did that make you feel?'

'Can we stick to the toes?'

'This is quite a breakthrough, Logan. Seriously, well done – I'm proud of you.'

And there was the guilt.

'Toes?'

'I don't think they're going to go through with it. I think however much money they get, they won't kill her.'

'Why would they kill her when she's worth a fortune on the paedophile livestock exchange?'

'Ah. . . You think she'd be better off dead than being passed around, sold on, abused?'

Logan didn't look around. 'Don't you?'

That artificial voice crackled out of the laptop's speakers again.

'This is not a hoax. You have four days left. If you raise enough money, they will live. If you do not, they will die. Do not let Jenny and Alison down.'

The umbrella's owner dragged it out of the bush and struggled with the mechanism. It stayed resolutely inside-out. He jammed the broken brolly back into the bush, stuck two fingers up to it, then marched off into the downpour.

Logan turned his back on the rain.

'The other trouble is: we're setting a precedent here.' Goulding sat back, arms crossed. 'They snatched two people everyone will recognize. They demand money from the public, but don't say how much it'll take to keep their victims alive. Everyone chips in, and they walk away with what: four, five million by the time Thursday morning comes around?'

'I know, what's to stop someone else from doing the same thing next week?'

'How did your lasagne taste?'

'Yeah. . .' Logan bit his bottom lip. 'Good. Meaty. Like I remembered it.'

'Not like human flesh?'

Warm saliva filled his mouth. Stomach lurching two steps to the right. A warm dizzy fog behind his eyes. Logan swallowed hard. Looked away. 'No. Nothing like human flesh.'

Furry. Warm and furry. She's lying on her back, looking up at the ceiling, watching it twist to the left a bit, then jump back to where it was and twist again, and again, and again, and again. . .

Jenny McGregor blinks. It just sets the room spinning faster.

Mummy's face appears, big and pink above her. Nose all red at the end, like a cherry, eyes all pink. Mouth a wobbly line. 'There, there, shhhh. . . It'll be all right, I promise. . . Shhhh. . .'

A cool hand strokes her head.

'Thirsty. . .'

A plastic bottle presses against her lips and wet dribbles down her chin. Jenny swallows. Some of it goes down the wrong way. Splutter. Choke. Cough. Barbed wire in her throat.

Mummy helps her sit up.

'Are you OK?'

She can see the bandages wrapped around each foot. Big lumps of white, with faint yellow-and-pink stains. Pins and needles stab and jab and tickle her little toes. . . Which is silly, because she doesn't have little toes any more. She saw them go into the envelope with the shiny CD circle.

This little piggy went to market,

This little piggy stayed at home,

This little piggy had roast beef,

This little piggy had none.

And these little piggies are gone. . .

The monsters are back. They're standing in the corner of the swirly room, with their names stuck to their chests and their metal voices. Maybe they've come for more toes?

'I'm just saying, OK? I don't see why I have to be "Sylvester".'

'Jesus, not again. . .' The one called TOM shakes his smooth plastic face from side to side.

'I want to be "Tom".'

'Tough: *I'm* Tom.' He settles back against the wall and crosses his white papery arms. 'Anyway, could be worse: you could be "Christopher", that's like being "Mr Shit".'

'Hey!' COLIN hits him in the arm. 'He was a great Doctor!'

'My arse. Doing a runner after only one series. Only *seems* better cos they threw all that money into special effects.'

169

'Yeah.' SYLVESTER nods. 'Sylvester McCoy would've been a great Doctor if they'd given him a decent bloody budget.'

Silence.

'You are *so* fucking *gay*!'

'Yeah, more *Gaylord* than Timelord.'

'Fuck the pair of you. . .'

The door opens and everyone stops talking. They stand up straight like pale white soldiers. DAVID walks into the room.

He looks around, breath hissing in and out. Then the same, dead, robot voice as all the other monsters. 'Has she been given her antibiotic yet?'

COLIN looks at the other two, then takes a step back. 'I was . . . erm . . . just about to start—'

'Well get on with it.' He steps up so close that Jenny can almost see the horns under his crime-person suit. But she *can* see his tail: long and red, with a forky bit on the end, swishing back and forward – like an angry cat.

COLIN picks up his little plastic box and hurries over. Opens it up. Pulls out another needle. Fills it with milk. 'I. . .' He glances at DAVID, then kneels down at the side of the bed.

Mummy flinches back. 'Don't hurt her!'

COLIN reaches out and strokes Jenny's hair with his rubbery purple fingers. 'It's OK. I just. . . I have to give you a little injection to stop you getting sick. Is that all right? I can't give you tablets in case you throw them back up.'

Jenny looks at him. His face looks like a dead person. Like Daddy in the box. Like the goldfish on the bathroom floor.

She reaches for him, little fingers grasping his sleeve. 'Please, don't . . . don't take my toes away. . .'

'Fuck. . .' COLIN rests his head against the stripy mattress.

'I won't, OK? You're going to be fine. It's just a little scratch.' He holds it against her skin. 'Sorry. . .'

She barely feels the jaggy needle as it goes in. Doesn't feel the bee's sting. 'I want to go home. . .'

'I know you do, sweetheart. I know you do.' COLIN stares at the floor for a bit, then stands. Makes himself look bigger by putting his shoulders back, bringing his head up. He turns, and walks across the swirling room to DAVID. Then slumps. 'I can't do this any more.'

Mummy strokes her forehead. 'Shhhh. . . It'll all be over soon, and we'll go home. Don't be scared.'

'You know fine what you signed up for, Colin.'

'It. . . It's *different*, OK?'

'Don't be an arsehole, we—'

'You're not the one had to cut off a little girl's toes!'

'Here, look, it's Teddy Gordon.' Mummy holds that horrible stitched-on smile in front of her. Twitches his head left and right, like he's having a fit. Like that girl in primary three they have to watch in case she bites off her tongue.

'So what, you're chickening out?' DAVID pokes COLIN in the chest.

'I'm. . .' He looks at his feet. 'You know what? Yeah, I'm chickening out. I've had it. I've had it with this whole fucked up—'

DAVID moves fast as a tiger. Grabs COLIN and thumps him into the scribbly wall. BANG – the room goes left to right for a couple of twists.

'You listen to me, you rancid little wanker: you don't *get* to chicken out. You do what you're fucking told, understand?'

'You can't make me—'

DAVID slams him into the wall again. And again. Then punches him in the tummy.

'DO YOU FUCKING UNDERSTAND?' DAVID's robot voice fizzes and crackles.

He lets go, and COLIN falls to his knees, crying. Holding his head in his purple hands.

DAVID backs away. 'Do your bit.'

TOM twitches, then walks over and puts his arm around COLIN. 'Come on, you just need a bit of air, yeah? Yeah, course. We'll go outside, get you a can of Coke, or something, OK?'

He helps COLIN to his feet and out the door. It slams shut like a fist.

DAVID rolls his shoulders back, then walks over, till he's standing over Mummy, looking down at them both. Breath hissing in and out.

Mummy's voice wobbles. 'Please, she's not feeling—'

'The antibiotics will take down her fever. She'll be fine.' DAVID tilts his head to one side. 'As long as you both do as you're told.'

'But she—'

'Misbehave, and I'll execute the pair of you. Do you understand?'

'We—'

'Do we need to have another fucking talk about how this works?' Silence. 'Well, do we?'

He throws an arm out, it leaves oily trails in the air. 'Sylvester: key.'

SYLVESTER shuffles his feet. 'Are you—'

'Give me the fucking key!'

SYLVESTER holds out a little bit of metal and DAVID snatches it, then grabs Mummy's ankle and unlocks the padlock that holds the chain around her ankle.

'I didn't mean any—'

'You're not on TV now.' He grabs her arm and hauls her off the bed. 'This is *my* house, and in my house you do what you're fucking told.'

The rooms spins.

Teddy Gordon smiles his horrible smile.

Jenny's missing toes throb.

'Oh yeah.' DAVID drags Mummy away. 'I'm going to *enjoy* this.'

'Please! I don't—'

The door bangs shut. Like the lid on Daddy's box.

Jenny feels warm tears rolling down her cheeks.

SYLVESTER's chin drops against his chest. 'Fuck. . .'

The room lurches like a drunk man.

23

'Well?' Finnie folded his arms and stared around the room.

Logan tore another sliver of Sellotape from the roll and fixed up the last sheet of A3. 'That wall over there,' he waved a hand at the dusty plastic sheeting covering the exposed breeze-blocks and cabling, 'is all the notes and transcripts of the videos. That wall,' he pointed at the corkboards he'd managed to salvage from the builder's skip out the back, 'is all the door-to-doors. Next to it you've got the interviews with Alison's friends, colleagues, and the people on her university course. Then it's the TV people. . .'

He took two steps back, arms held out wide. 'And *this* is the timeline. Well, as much of it as we can piece together. Starts over there – underneath the window – three weeks before the kidnapping and ends with the toes being delivered to the BBC yesterday.'

Superintendent Green pointed at the whiteboard propped up by the door. 'And this?'

'Kidnappers. We know there's at least three of them because of the first video – one to hold the camera, one to haul Alison McGregor down the stairs, one to hit her over the back of the head. I'm assuming there's one more to drive the getaway car. We'll need to go through every report of a stolen vehicle for the last week: I don't see them being stupid enough to use their own car or van. We might get lucky.'

Logan nodded at the whiteboard, split into four vertical columns headed: 'DAVID', 'TOM', '#3', '#4' with a small list of bullet points below each. 'One of them has medical training and access to a hospital or veterinary pharmacy. One's probably a hacker, or an IT security specialist – that's how they can send the emails and post footage to YouTube without leaving a trail. One's highly forensically aware, which is why we've got no DNA, fingerprints, or trace evidence.'

Green folded his arms across his broad chest, the fingertips of his right hand stroking the dimple in his chin staring at the list of bullet points under the #4 heading. 'Who's "Ralph"?'

Logan tapped the whiteboard. 'Not who, what. "Ralph" is one of the text-to-speech voices that come bundled with the Macintosh operating system. It's the voice they use on the videos.'

'I see. . .' Green sniffed. 'And is this all you've done?'

Logan gritted his teeth. 'Next I'm going to cross-reference the individual skills with every registered sex offender in—'

'You see, that's the trouble with never having investigated a kidnapping before. All this unfocused energy, flailing out in all directions.'

He stared at Finnie, but the head of CID just rolled his eyes. Play nice. Don't rock the boat. Don't tell Superintendent Green to go ram a filing cabinet up his arse.

Logan cleared his throat. 'And what would *you* do, sir? With your *wealth* of experience?'

Either Green wasn't very good at sarcasm, or he just didn't care. 'I'd go back to the start.'

What?

'With all due respect,' – you posing tosser – 'that's what I've been doing.'

A smile. 'No, Sergeant, not the start of the investigation, the start of the *crime*. Dig into similar events: not just in Aberdeen, but Glasgow, Edinburgh, Newcastle. Put it into context – where did Alison and Jenny's kidnappers get their inspiration from? Did they have a practice run? Is that where the first toe came from?'

Silence.

'Search the archives.' He patted Logan on the shoulder. 'Ten years or so should do it.'

Bastard. This was just Green's revenge for making him look like an idiot last night.

Logan turned to Finnie again. 'You can't be serious, this is a complete—'

'In the meantime, I hear you have three sex offenders with access to veterinary practices. I take it you're planning on doing due diligence to make sure they've been thoroughly checked out?'

'But DI Steel's already doing—'

'Now, now.' Finnie held up a finger. 'Superintendent, would you excuse us for a moment? There's something I need to *discuss* with Sergeant McRae.'

'. . . because he's a prick, *that's* why. Hold on.' Logan jammed his Airwave handset into the gap between the steering wheel and the instrument panel, changed down, and swung the pool car around the roundabout onto Mugiemoss Road. Windscreen wipers going full pelt. 'You still hear me?'

DS Doreen Taylor's voice crackled out of the handset's speaker, the volume turned up full, distorting the words. *'I'm not sure I want to.'*

'How can re-interviewing everyone be anything other than a *complete* waste of time? Never mind how pissed off Steel's going to be when she finds out we're double-dipping on her perverts. Like I'm checking her sodding homework.'

Rain hammered against the bonnet of the car, drumming on the roof, misting the space between Logan and the dirty big truck he was following. The River Don coiled grey and dark in the middle distance, like a slug. The streetlights glowing. Wasn't even mid-morning yet.

And his left palm ached, as if someone was grinding a hot needle into the flesh. So the weather was definitely going to get worse. Scar-tissue: the gift that keeps on giving.

'Well, you've got no one to blame but yourself. You didn't have to poke holes in his sunshine theory yesterday. Anyway, if you're looking for sympathy you've dialled the wrong number. While you're out gallivanting, I'm stuck in here listening to his posturing egotistical monologues.'

Another roundabout. Grove Cemetery on one side, the little caravan park where Samantha kept her huge static Portakabin thing on the other. Not that there was any point in keeping it: she hadn't been back in months.

Heavy grey clouds blanketed out the sky, thudding ever more water down on the city.

'And do you know what Finnie said?'

'Logan, did you just phone me for a moan? Because—'

'He said we've got to keep Green sweet, so he doesn't bring in all his SOCA tosser mates and take over the investigation.' Logan put on his best DCI Finnie impersonation – stretching his mouth out and down, like a disappointed frog. '"Can you *imagine* what would happen if Grampian Police had the case taken *off* them? Would the *media* write stirring articles about how *clever* and *special* we all are? Hmmm?"' He changed down and followed the huge filthy truck across the bridge and past the sewage treatment plant. 'And another thing—'

'I'm going to hang up now, Logan.'

'—explain to me why I always end up—'

'Goodbye.'

He frowned at the Airwave handset. 'Doreen? Doreen, can you hear me?'

The windscreen wipers groaned and clunked.

'Hello?'

She'd hung up on him. Unbelievable.

He took the Parkway, around Danestone and into the Bridge of Don. According to DI Ingram's notes, Frank Baker – the floppy-haired neat-freak they'd interviewed on Friday morning, the one who looked like a swimming pool attendant – worked in a fabrication yard in the Bridge of Don Industrial Estate. He was the first sex offender on Green's list.

Logan put his foot down, trying to get past the truck on the way up the hill, slithering back behind it as a Range Rover coming the other way flashed its lights at him.

And then his phone went – the brief chirrup signifying a text message. He flicked the windscreen wipers onto their highest setting, then pulled the mobile out of his pocket, thumbing the little envelope icon. Holding the phone against the steering wheel, so he could read and drive at the same time.

> 'I no where they is — jenny and her
> mum. If U want 2 C them alive, wee
> should meat.'

Not exactly the most appealing of messages.

Logan fiddled with the phone's screen, trying to get the sender's number up—

A horn blared.

Shite!

He swerved the pool car back into the right lane. The bus driver coming the other way gave him the finger on the way past.

Logan pulled over in the driveway of a little grey house, heart hammering in his chest. Jesus, that was close.

He fiddled with the phone some more, got the caller's number. It wasn't one he recognized. He hit reply, and tapped out 'Where?' on the screen.

'Ware R U?'

Fine, if that was the way they wanted to play it. Why should he go traipsing halfway across Aberdeen to meet up with some time-wasting weirdo? He picked out the reply: 'Danestone. That Toby Pub Place On The Parkway. Half an hour.'

Screw Superintendent Green and his 'due diligence'.

Half an hour later he was onto his second coffee and first sticky bun. The Buckie Farm was one of those chain pubs where you could get a carvery lunch for a couple of quid. Nice enough, even if it was a little soulless.

Logan checked his watch again, then peered out of the window at the car park. No sign of the mysterious texter. He pulled out his Airwave handset and called Rennie.

'Hey, Guv. You'll never guess what that cock Green said—'

'I need you to do a reverse look-up for me. Mobile telephone. . .' He went back to the message on his phone and read the number out. Then waited as Rennie punched it into the computer.

'Anyway, he was on this big speech about how kidnappers feed off fear, just like terrorists, when—'

'Have you got a name yet?'

'. . . Yeah. It's a T-Mobile phone registered to Mr Liam Weller, Gordon Terrace, Dyce.'

'Never heard of him. He on the sex offenders' register?'

'Erm. . .' A pause. *'No. But according to this he reported his phone stolen last week. Anyway, so Green's giving this big spiel, when in marches Steel and. . .'*

Logan's phone trembled in his hand, then gave that little chirrup again.

'Chanhe of plan. Meet me @ Fairview
Street were the uni playing feilds.
Im wating.'

*'. . . so Green says, "We can never underestimate the lengths that
desperate people will go to." And Steel says—'*

'Got to go.' Logan stabbed the disconnect button, paid for
his coffee, stuck his sticky bun in his mouth, and hurried
out into the rain.

Fairview Street was less than two hundred yards away. Barely
worth taking the car . . . except for the pouring rain. The
university playing fields lay on one side of the road – a
swathe of dark-green grass, partially hidden by a screen of
trees. Fluorescent green leaves, pink-and-white blossom
shuddering in the downpour.

The other side was taken up by a sprawling housing
development of beige boxes with brown pantile roofs. A line
of huge metal pylons marched through the middle, making
for the other side of the river, their tops brushing the low
grey clouds.

Logan peered out through the windscreen, looking for
someone hanging about.

No one.

The road took a ninety degree turn to the right, heading
into the housing estate.

Logan pulled the pool car into the kerb and his phone
bleeped up another text message.

'I see U.'

A small grass embankment ran along the side of the road,
then a bumpy lane, then a chain-link fence, then the playing
fields. A shape, on the other side of the fence, peered out
between the trees, waving at him.

Logan killed the engine and climbed out. Rain hammered
against his face and ears, soaking straight through his hair.

180

He plipped the locks on the pool car, stuck the keys in his pocket and flexed his aching left hand. Fist. Open. Fist. Open. Bloody thing was getting worse.

He clambered over the grassy hump, crunched across the lane, then waded through soggy, knee-high grass towards—

FUCK.

A huge black dog launched itself at him, gaping mouth snapping and snarling. It crashed against the chain-link; the fence buckled outwards. . .

Logan backed away a couple of paces.

Jesus that was a big dog.

'Uzi, fuckin' cool it.' The guy holding its lead gave a yank, and the massive Rottweiler stood for a second glaring at Logan, then settled onto its haunches. 'Sorry 'bout that. He's only a puppy. Gets excited.' The man sniffed, wiped a bandaged hand across his squint nose, two fingers and a thumb poking out from the filthy fabric. His eyes were hidden in the shadow of an NYY baseball cap worn under a grey hoodie. A leather jacket on over the top, glistening in the rain.

'Shuggie?' Logan took a step forward, and Uzi growled. Might be a better idea to just stay *exactly* where he was. He dug his aching hand into his pocket. 'Shuggie Webster?'

'You gonna give us them drugs back, or what?'

'Pin back your ears and listen: I'm – not – giving – you – any – drugs. OK? No drugs.'

The big man hung his head, chewed on the ragged tip of a finger. A pair of handcuffs dangled from his wrist, the metal shiny against the grubby bandage. 'Fuck.'

'What do you expect; I'm a police officer.'

'You've *got* to. They're gonna hurt Trisha again. They beat the shite out her mum, trashed the house. . . And what if they go after her kid?'

'Come on, Shuggie: it's over. You're still under arrest

181

from Thursday. Come down the station, make a statement, and we'll get whoever's threatening you off the streets.'

He raised his chin, and Logan finally got a look at his face: a black eye, a crust of blood around both nostrils, a beige sticking plaster across the bridge of his squint nose. 'I'm no' fuckin' daft, OK? What's gonna happen when you bang me up, eh? Fuckin' eight-inch chib in the guts. No thank you.' Shuggie Webster straightened up. 'How'd you like it: some cunt comes round your crib, threatens your missus? Would you hand yourself in?'

'Well, I'd—'

'Would you fuck.' He turned away from the fence. 'Come on, Uzi.'

'You're still under arrest, Shuggie!'

He stuck up a pair of fingers. There was blood seeping through the bandage.

'Shuggie!' Logan pulled out his pepper-spray and yanked the lid off. There was a hole in the fence, less than a dozen feet away. All he had to do was nip through and make the arrest.

Pepper-spray worked on dogs . . . didn't it?

He watched the muscles bunch and roll beneath the Rottweiler's shiny black hide.

Swallowed.

OK, it was all about appearing confident and in control of the situation.

Logan marched through the soggy grass to the hole in the fence, ducked through, and hurried after Shuggie. 'I'm not telling you again: you're under arrest.'

Confident and in control.

Shuggie stopped where he was. Turned. 'Get fucked. Told you: I'm no' goin' nowhere.'

'I'm serious, Shuggie. You're coming with me.'

'Oh aye?' He smiled, showing a gap where a tooth used to be. Then he let go of the lead. 'Uzi – BACON!'

The dog looked up at him, then followed the line of the pointing finger to Logan. Bared his teeth.

'Oh . . . bugger. . .' Pepper-spray. He had the pepper-spray! Perfectly safe. Confident and in control. Confident and—

The dog lurched forward.

Sod 'confident and in control', Logan turned and ran.

Barking behind him, snarling, the sound of huge paws splashing through puddles.

Closer.

Make for the fence, get back through the hole and. . . No way in hell he could outrun a Rottweiler. He glanced over his shoulder.

Right behind him, mouth open, red and slavering, like the jaws of hell. . .

FUCK!

Logan jinked right, and Uzi flashed past, tried to turn – powerful back legs skidding across the waterlogged grass, sending up a wall of spray.

Jesus, the bloody thing was the size of a bear.

Tree! Logan jumped for the nearest one, wrapped his arms around a branch, hauled himself up. Or tried to. A sudden jerk back, knives slashing across his ankle, then a ripping sound as his trouser leg gave way. 'AAAAAghhh. . .'

The ground slammed into his back, ripping the breath from his lungs; and then the huge dog was on top of him, teeth flashing inches from Logan's face.

Fuck – he'd dropped the pepper-spray.

Shuggie's voice cut through the snarls. 'UZI – hold!'

A low growl.

The dog's weight pushed Logan into the sodden grass, soaking through his jacket and shirt, cold and wet and oh God he was going to die. . .

Thunder boomed out across the slate-grey sky, but the Rottweiler didn't even flinch, just stood there with his front paws on Logan's chest, snarling, teeth bared. Its breath stank of rotting meat and bitter onion, drool spattering against Logan's cheeks and forehead, slimy and warm compared to the rain.

A shape loomed in his peripheral vision. Shuggie, standing over the snarling dog, cradling the bandaged hand against his chest. 'Hold real fuckin' still, or he'll rip your throat out.'

Logan flicked his eyes to the side and back again. The dog barked, teeth glinting, speckling his face with drool. 'Gah. . . Call him off!'

'Gonnae give us my drugs back now? Before them Yardie bastards hack my hands off with a machete?'

'I'm. . . I *can't*. I'm a police officer. . . I can't. Now call the dog off!'

Sniff. 'Nah, he can have you.'

Uzi barked again.

A drop of spittle landed in Logan's eye. He flinched, blinked. 'Fuck's sake, Shuggie – I *can't*!' Voice high pitched and trembling.

The only sound was the rain, drumming down all around them.

'Give us your car keys.'

'I'm not—'

'Uzi. . .'

Another roar of thunder, closer, almost overhead. The massive Rottweiler roared back. Teeth flashing in the thickening rain.

Oh Christing fuck. . .

Logan squealed.

'Now give us your keys.'

He dug his fingers into his pocket and pulled the Vauxhall's keys out. 'Take them!'

Shuggie snatched them out of his hand.

'Now call the bloody dog off!'

Shuggie turned and limped back towards the fence.

Logan tore his eyes away from the dog's teeth, and watched him squeeze through the hole in the chainlink. He crossed the rutted track, climbed the grass verge, and onto Fairview Street.

The dog tilted its head to the side, nose all creased and wrinkled, black rubbery lips pulled back from those butcher-knife teeth.

Logan blinked the rain out of his eyes. 'Please. . .'

The Vauxhall's headlights snapped through the gloom, the roar of the engine audible for a second, before another peal of thunder drowned it out.

Another bark, front paws digging into Logan's chest.

Hailstones battered down, stinging his hands and face, knocking blossom from the tree above, showering them with slow-motion pink.

Then the sound of a car door creaking open. 'UZI! UZI!'

The huge dog froze, head swinging around to face the car, both ears pricked.

'UZI! GET OVER HERE YOU DAFT BASTARD!'

It had one last snarl at Logan, then scraped its back paws through the muddy grass, before loping off.

Oh thank God. . .

Logan lay flat on his back, arms covering his head as he heard the Vauxhall's door clunk shut again, then the engine faded away into the downpour as Shuggie drove off in Logan's pool car.

How the hell was he going to explain this one?

24

'About bloody time.' Logan thumped his mug of coffee down as DC Rennie ambled in through the pub's front door, paused just inside, looked around, then waved.

Idiot.

Logan pressed send on his phone – 'Shuggie, I'm Fucking Warning You: Bring My Bloody Car Back!'

'Morning, Sarge. Been swimming?' Rennie's pearl-white grin flashed out from his fake tan.

Logan stuffed his phone back in his pocket. 'Are you really *that* desperate for a boot up the arse?'

'OK. . . Not in a great mood then.' He pointed over his shoulder. 'Got the car out front. You want a lift back to the station, or—'

'Where is it?'

Frown. 'Er. . . Out front. By the disabled spaces.'

Logan scrunched his eyes shut. Gritted his teeth. 'Not your car, *my* bastarding car!'

A shuffle of feet. 'You weren't serious about that, were you?'

A young woman appeared at the table, clutching a pot of coffee. She smiled a train-track smile, light sparkling off her braces. 'Would you like some more ice? Or a refill or something?'

Logan forced a smile. 'No, I'm fine, just on our way.' He reached down and unwrapped the soggy tea-towel from his left ankle. A few chunks of half-melted ice fell to the carpet. The skin was angry pink and swollen, four parallel dark-red lines burning and stinging where Uzi's teeth had ripped through his trouser leg and slashed across the ankle. At least it wasn't bleeding any more.

He handed the towel over. 'Thanks.'

Rennie watched until she disappeared through the door marked, 'STAFF ONLY'. He ran a hand through his spiky blond hair. 'Nice arse.'

'I told you to run a bloody GPS trace!'

'I thought you were joking. I mean, you know, why would you want a trace on your own car? How can you not know where your car is?'

'Surrounded by idiots. . .' Logan limped out of the front door, shoes squelching with every step, Rennie scurrying along behind.

'What happened to your leg?'

It wasn't difficult to spot the constable's CID pool car outside the pub – it was the manky Vauxhall with the dashboard overflowing with burger wrappers and empty crisp packets. Hailstones battered off the dirty paintwork, making a little drift of white across the windscreen wipers.

Inside it smelled much the same as every other CID vehicle – that mix of stale sweat, cigarette smoke, and something going mouldy under one of the seats.

Rennie got in behind the wheel. 'Where to?'

'Make the sodding call.'

There was a brief pause, then the constable pulled out his Airwave handset and punched in the number for Control. 'Yeah, Jimmy, I need a GPS trace on Charlie Delta

Seven?. . . Er. . . no. He's not answering his mobile. . . Or his Airwave.' Rennie glanced over at Logan, clocked the glower, and faced front again. 'Look just do us a GPS trace, OK?. . . *What*?' The constable sat up straight in his seat. 'No: Jimmy, don't you bloody dare put him—' A cough. 'Chief Inspector Finnie, yeah, I was just. . . DS McRae? Er. . .' Rennie stared at Logan, eyes bugging, mouth making a squiggly line across his face.

Logan mouthed, 'No!' waved both hands, palm out, shaking his head.

'Hold on. . .' Rennie held the handset out. 'It's for you.'

Bastard.

Logan took the Airwave. 'Sir?'

'Tell me, Detective Sergeant, did I accidentally *give you the day off and forget all about it?'*

'Well, no, but—'

'Then perhaps *you'd like to explain why you're not currently interviewing Frank Baker like I told you?'*

Logan peered out through the hail-flecked windscreen. How the hell did Finnie know he wasn't—

'Superintendent Green tells me he's been waiting for you to appear for the last fifteen minutes.'

'He's *what*? Look it's bad enough we've—'

'It would be nice, *Sergeant, if for once I thought I could* actually *depend on a member of my team to act like a professional. I don't care if you think it's a waste of time or not – get round there, interview Baker, and try not to behave like a petulant bloody child!'*

And then there was silence.

Logan held out the handset and read the little grey-and-black LCD screen: 'CALL TERMINATED'.

Perfect.

Just. Bloody. Perfect.

*   *   *

Logan rapped his knuckles on the car's passenger window.

Superintendent Green looked up from the laptop he was poking away at, and stared at Logan for a moment, then a smile crawled across the lower half of his face, going nowhere near his eyes. *Bzzzzzz* – the window slid down a couple of inches. 'Been on our holidays, have we, Sergeant?'

Warm air curled out into the cold morning. The hail had died off, replaced by a frigid drizzle.

Logan forced a smile of his own. 'Pursuing other avenues of enquiry, *sir*.'

'Yes. . .' Green turned to the uniformed constable sitting in the driver's seat. 'Wait for me.' He snapped the laptop closed and slipped it into an oversized leather satchel. Stepped out into the horrible morning. Looked Logan up and down. Raised an eyebrow. 'Is your suit meant to look like that?'

Logan glanced at his left trouser leg. The fabric was torn and tattered, stained dark-grey with blood, rain, and dirt. Muddy paw prints on his chest. 'I thought you were in a hurry?'

'After you.'

The fabrication yard where Frank Baker worked was a small industrial unit bolted onto a large warehouse, cut off from the road by a high chain-link fence topped with barbed wire. As if anyone was going to break in and make off with a two tonne chunk of drilling pipe. They lay stacked up around the building, held in place with wooden chucks and ratchet straps.

Green marched towards the door marked, 'ALL VISITORS MUST REPORT TO RECEPTION!'.

'Punctuality is the sign of an effective police officer, Sergeant.'

Tosser. How could Logan be late for an unscheduled meeting?

'Really, sir? I always thought it was catching criminals and preventing crimes.'

Green paused for a moment, then pushed through into a small room that smelled of industrial grease and coffee. A large woman with a bowl haircut looked up from a stack of forms and stared at them over the top of her glasses. No, 'Hello?' No, 'Can I help you?'

The superintendent glanced around the room – Health and Safety posters, framed photo of an oil rig, calendar with kittens on it, shelves groaning with lever-arch files. 'I want to speak to Frank Baker.'

She puckered her lips. 'He's working.'

Green thrust his warrant card under her nose. 'Now.'

Inside, the warehouse was vast: filled with machinery, forklift trucks, and more pipes. A radio boomed out something poppy, competing with the bangs, clangs, and thrum of heavy equipment. The machine-gun pops of welding.

Frank Baker didn't look the same without his nice clean suit. Instead he was wearing a pair of grubby orange overalls with a padded green jacket on top, the chest and shoulders covered with pinhole burns. Big leather gloves, steel toecap boots. A thick red line across his forehead from the welding mask he'd just thumped down on a length of rust-flecked pipe. 'I don't appreciate you *bastards* coming here every day.'

'Then answer the bloody question!' Green crossed his arms, legs shoulder-width apart, chin up.

Baker scowled at Logan. 'I've been through all this: with you, with the wrinkly old woman, so—'

'It's just a couple of follow-up—'

'And you're going to go through it all again for *us*.' Green stepped closer and Baker flinched.

'I have to work here.'

'Oh. Oh, I *see*.' The superintendent winked. 'They don't

know you're a pervert. That you like to interfere with little boys—'

'Keep your voice down!'

'A filthy kiddie-fiddling paedophile, who—'

'SHUT UP! SHUT YOUR DIRTY MOUTH!' Baker grabbed the handle of his arc welder.

Green leaned in close. 'Or *what*, Frank?'

Tears sparked in the corner of Baker's eyes.

A huge man in filthy overalls wandered over, a baseball cap turned the wrong way around on his massive head, face creased with dirt around a clear patch where his safety goggles must have sat. 'Everything OK, Frankie?'

Baker bit his lip. 'Yeah. . . Thanks, Spike.'

Spike stared at them for a bit. 'Any trouble, give us a shout.' Then he turned and lumbered away.

Baker waited till he was well out of earshot. 'I *told* them: I volunteer at a vets in town every Saturday. It's not illegal, OK? It's not against my SOPPO. I've not done anything wrong. So go away and leave me *alone*!'

'No, no, no, Frank – that's not how it works.' Green smiled. 'You tell me everything I want to know, or I'll make sure every sweaty-arsed bastard in this place knows your grubby little secret.'

'Sir?' Logan cleared his throat. 'That's not really—'

'You want that, Frank? You want them all to find out what you do to little boys?'

'This isn't fair!'

'You think what's happening to Alison and Jenny is fair?'

Baker closed his eyes and sagged. 'Please, I just want to be left alone. . .'

25

Green leaned on the roof of Rennie's pool car. Staring off into the middle distance, chin up. Posing. Again. 'Well, that was . . . interesting.'

Logan hauled open the door and threw his notebook onto the driver's seat. 'That is *not* the way we do things.'

It had stopped raining, though from the look of the deep-grey layer of cloud blanketing the city that probably wouldn't last. Still freezing as well.

Superintendent Green curled his top lip. 'Really? What a shock: something else Grampian Police *doesn't* do. Tell me, Sergeant, what *do* you do?'

'Frank Baker is a registered sex offender – do you have any idea what'll happen to him if his workmates find out?'

'That's hardly my—'

'They'll beat the shit out of him; he'll get fired; and he'll *disappear*! How are we supposed to manage him if we don't know where he is?'

Green's eyes narrowed. 'Sergeant McRae, are you always this resistant to the chain of command?'

'You had no business storming in there like something off the bloody *Sweeney*!'

The superintendent drummed his fingers on the roof. 'When Chief Inspector Finnie told me you were "wilful" I wasn't expecting full-on insubordination.'

Logan gritted his teeth. 'I thought we were meant to be on the same side.'

'Did you now?'

'Yes, *sir*.' Logan glanced towards the huge warehouse. Spike, Baker's huge friend was standing in the doorway, staring back at him. Then he turned and melted away into the shadows. 'Anything else?'

There was a pause. A cold smile. 'Well, I'd better get back and check on the team. We need a strategy for Thursday – hostage exchange tends to be where you end up with dead bodies.' Green stepped back from the car. 'I'll be seeing you.'

Logan clambered into the passenger seat and slammed the door shut. 'Not if I fucking see you first.'

Rennie looked up from his book. 'Sarge?'

'Nothing.' He hauled on his seatbelt. 'I want that GPS fix on Charlie Delta Seven *now*.'

'Already doing it.' He stuck the book on the dashboard and dug out his Airwave handset.

Logan tilted his head sideways, frowning at the title. '*The Accidental Sodomist*?'

'It's literature: shortlisted for the Booker this year. Emma says I need to broaden my horizons, and— Hold on. Aye, Jimmy, how you getting on finding Charlie Delta Seven for me?. . . Uh-huh. . . No. Still no sign of him. . . Yeah, if you can. . .' Rennie put a hand over the mouthpiece and nodded at the book in Logan's hands. 'You can borrow it when I'm finished. It's about this concert pianist from Orkney who moves to Edinburgh 'cos he's in love with his cousin, and ends up shagging a bunch of mental. . . Yeah? It is? Cheers, thanks, Jimmy.'

'Well?'

Rennie cranked the key in the ignition. 'We have a winner.'

'There . . . over by the trees.'

Logan squinted through the rain-flecked windscreen. 'Where? It's all bloody trees.'

Gairnhill Woods lay three-and-a-bit miles west of the city, part of a little conjoined network of Forestry Commission land. Quiet and secluded.

Pale grey cloud curled around the tops of Scots pines and spruce, the light flat and lifeless as a thin drizzle made the undergrowth shine.

The windscreen wipers squealed their way across the glass again.

'There.' Rennie poked a finger at a little car park off to the right of the road. Charlie Delta Seven, AKA: Logan's crappy blue Vauxhall, sat in the far corner, under a drooping branch.

No other car to be seen.

Rennie smiled. 'This where you left it?'

'You're an idiot, you know that, don't you?' Logan undid his seatbelt. 'Block it in, then we'll go take a look.'

The constable licked his lip. Looked from Logan to the abandoned pool car. 'You want to tell me what's going on? Just in case?'

'Shuggie Webster; dirty big dog. If you see him, arrest the bastard. Try not to get bitten.'

'OK. . .' Rennie eased his car up the dirt track and parked directly across the back of Charlie Delta Seven.

Logan opened the door and climbed out into the rain. It misted on his face, making his breath steam out around his head. Got to love summer in Aberdeen.

He pulled out his pepper-spray and inched his way around to Charlie Delta Seven's driver's door. Peered in through the window.

Empty.

'Think he's done a runner?' Rennie appeared on the other side. 'Might have nipped into the woods for a slash?'

'If he hasn't taken a dump in the driver's seat. . .' Logan hunkered down and peered up at the space behind the door handle. Then took a pen from his pocket and clacked it about in there.

A faint shadow fell across him. Then Rennie sniffed. 'No offence, Sarge, but you look like a spaz.'

'When I joined CID there was a DI: right bastard, always storming about shouting at everyone. Had to deliver a death message to this drug dealer's family – their son managed to choke on his own vomit in custody.' Logan stood. 'So while DI Cole's inside breaking the bad news, their other kid nips outside and jams a wodge of chewing gum right up under the door handle where you can't see it.'

The constable shrugged. 'Could be worse, dog shite would—'

'Then he stuck a dirty razorblade in the chewing gum. DI Cole swapped the tips of two fingers for a dose of Hepatitis C.' Logan clunked the car door open. 'Never hurts to check.'

Inside, Charlie Delta Seven looked every bit as crappy as it had when Shuggie nicked it. Only now it stank of wet dog.

'So, you think he's still about somewhere?' Rennie clacked open his extendable baton. 'SHUGGIE! SHUGGIE WEBSTER: COME OUT WITH YOUR HANDS UP!'

Logan stood. Laid a hand on the bonnet. It was cold. 'Car's been here at least an hour.' He turned around, looking out at the damp brown earth of the car park. 'Must have had a back-up vehicle here. . . Or maybe someone was off having a walk in the woods, and he nicked theirs instead. Or he was meeting someone. . .'

Rennie collapsed his truncheon again. 'Want me to call it in?'

'What, and let everyone know Shuggie Webster stole my pool car? No thanks. What Professional Standards don't know, won't hurt them.' Logan stepped out from under the canopy of green needles. The rain was getting heavier again, pitter-pattering against the undergrowth. 'Can you smell something?'

'What if Shuggie's knocked down some old dear, or something?'

He held a finger to his lips. 'Shh. . .' The car park was surrounded with dense green ferns, their long fractal fronds waving in the thickening rain. Someone had forced a path into them, at thirty degrees to the official trail that led off into the woods.

Logan picked his way around a puddle. Dark stains turned the mud black around the trampled ferns. He stepped to the side, making sure he wasn't treading on anything that looked important as he crept closer.

'Sarge?'

He waved Rennie back. 'Give us a second.'

Standing on his tiptoes, he could just see into a little flattened clearing at the end of the path. It couldn't have been much more than five-foot across, the undergrowth trampled, ferns and grass stained a shiny black.

Something lay off to one side: a dark mound, torn open, chunks of red, purple and white poking out. A curl of grey tubes, glistening on the darkened grass.

'What?' Rennie appeared at his shoulder. 'What have you. . . Fuck me. Is that a dog?'

It was. A huge Rottweiler, by the look of what was left of its head.

Someone had hacked Shuggie Webster's dog to death.

* * *

196

The Wildlife Crime Officer sat back on his haunches and shook his head. 'What a bastard. . .' A slow, steady rain beat a tattoo on the hood of his white SOC suit; a pair of purple gloves on his hands, blue plastic over-booties on his feet. 'Who'd do this to a wee dog?'

The bright glare of a camera flash froze raindrops in mid-air. An IB technician shifted around for another shot. Logan nodded at the remains. 'What do you think?'

'I think someone needs taking out and shot, *that's* what I think. Beautiful dog like that.' The WCO reached out and stroked the dark fur on the back of the massive animal. 'Lot of people think Rottweilers are these horrible aggressive dogs, but they're big softies really. . .'

Yeah.

That's *exactly* what Uzi was when he was trying to rip Logan's throat out. 'I meant: any idea what killed it?'

A long sigh, making the white paper oversuit rustle. 'Well, I'm no pathologist, but looking at the size of the cuts . . . most of them to the dog's back and shoulders. . .' Another sigh. 'A sword? There's a lot of wee toerags buying those samurai swords off the internet these days. Or maybe a huge knife? Proper Rambo job. It'd have to be at least, what?' He looked over at the IB technician he'd brought with him. 'Eighteen inches long?'

The IB tech lowered his massive digital camera. 'Give or take.'

About the same size as a machete.

Which explained where Shuggie Webster had gone, and why he'd left the CID pool car behind. Sodding hell. Now Logan *had* to call it in.

'What about prints, fibres, that kind of thing?'

The IB tech slung the camera strap over his shoulder. 'You want the full CSI treatment?'

Logan looked back at the hacked-up Rottweiler. There

was no way Shuggie Webster would've gone quietly, not after someone did that to his dog. Chances were his mutilated corpse would be turning up soon enough. Any trace evidence they could find would help. As if today *needed* to get any shittier. 'As much as you can give me, without Finnie throwing a wobbly about the cost.'

'You'll be lucky – all this rain, outdoors, public place. . . Can't promise anything.' He patted the WCO on the shoulder. 'It's OK, Dunc, you can take him away if you like. I'm done.'

They left him stuffing chunks of butchered Rottweiler into a white child-sized body-bag.

The IB tech dumped his sample kit next to a couple of Tesco carrier bags, lying flattened on the muddy ground, weighed down with stones. He removed one of the rocks, and peeled back the plastic. There was a perfectly rectangular puddle of plaster-of-Paris underneath. Pure white in the middle, greying at the edges. He poked it with a finger. Sighed. Then wiped the digit on his oversuit. 'Still not convinced we're going to get anything. . .'

'What about fingerprints?'

'I mean, the footwear marks weren't exactly in the best of shape to start with, were they? Doesn't help it's pishing with rain.'

'You could dust the car while you're waiting for it to set? Maybe they touched the paintwork?'

He flopped the bag back into place, and weighed it down again. 'I mean, mud's great for *taking* footprints, but soon as it starts to rain again, they go all mooshy—'

'Ernie: the car.'

'Don't be daft.' He pulled off his facemask, exposing a little ginger goatee beard and a smile full of squint teeth. 'What do you think fingerprint powder's going to do on wet metal?'

'Ah. . .' Bugger.

'Exactly.' Ernie peeled back the hood of his SOC suit, exposing a high forehead barely holding onto a crown of yet more ginger. 'Have to get it back to the ranch. Stick it somewhere dry for a couple of hours.'

'Right. . .'

Rennie was sitting in his pool car, head stuck in *The Accidental Sodomist* again.

Logan knocked on the window.

A pause while the intellectual marked his place with a lottery ticket, then the window buzzed down. 'Guv?'

'Steel says I'm supposed to pick a minion: you're it.'

Rennie grinned. Then hunched up one shoulder, scrunched up his face, and put on a ridiculous voice. 'Yeth Maaaaathhhhhter. . .?'

'Get your lopsided arse back to FHQ – I want a break-down of every kidnapping in the country for the last ten years.'

The constable paused, biro hovering over his notebook. 'Ten *years*?'

'You heard.' Logan watched the Wildlife Crime Officer waddling backwards into the car park, dragging the white body-bag. 'Find out who's running the drug gang investigations this week – I'm looking for Yardies with a thing for machetes.'

Rennie scribbled it all down. 'Ten years. . .'

'And,' Logan pointed at his abandoned pool car, 'you're taking that back to the station. Wear gloves. *Don't* sign it back in, don't let anyone else touch it. Park it in the garage and let it dry off till Ernie can dust it for prints. If Big Gary gives you a hard time, tell him it's evidence.'

'Anything else?'

'Yeah, if anyone asks. . .' What? How the hell was he going to explain this one? Stolen car; dead dog; probable abduction: possible murder. '. . . if anyone asks, tell them I've been acting all concussed since you picked me up.'

Rennie nodded. 'Thank God for that: thought you were going to ask me to lie for a minute. . .'

26

'Yes, yes, I know that. . .' Logan slumped sideways until his head clunked against the driver's window.

Finnie's voice boomed out of the Airwave handset. *'Then what* exactly *were you thinking, Sergeant? That the* magic La-La fairies *would turn up and hand your pool car back to you?'*

'I didn't. . . It. . . I was being attacked by a dog at the time. Then you said—'

'You'll be lucky if that's the only savaging you get today. Professional Standards: half-three.'

He thumped his head against the glass again. 'Yes, sir.'

'Where are you?'

Logan peered out through the rain-ribboned windscreen at a grubby house with a boarded-up window, 'GELLOUS BITCH!!!' scrawled in dripping purple spray-paint across the wall and front door.

A bashed and battered Ford Fiesta sat at the kerb, the windows shattered or empty, the bodywork a collection of huge dents and scratches.

'Outside Victoria Murray's house.'

'I see. . .' A pause. *'Tell me, Sergeant, do you* actually *think "Vicious Vikki" is going to give you information that'll have you*

scurrying off to solve the case? Meaning you can get out of your meeting with Professional Standards? Because if you do, *I've got some bad news for you: you* will *be back at headquarters by half-three. And after you've spoken to Superintendent Napier, you and I are going to have a little chat.'*

Oh joy. Logan closed his eyes. Superintendent Napier, the Ginger Ninja.

'Because I think *we've got a bit of a communication problem, don't you, Sergeant? You see, I thought I said, "Don't* piss off the *man from SOCA." And yet, for some* unfathomable *reason, you seem to have heard, "Insult Superintendent Green and call him a moron." Isn't that strange?'*

Something smelled of shit. Logan checked the soles of his shoes: they were clean. He sniffed again. The stink got worse the closer he got to Victoria Murray's front door. There was no way he was touching the bell.

He knocked on the wood instead, next to the purple letter 'B' in 'BITCH!!!'

Waited for a minute.

Did it again.

Maybe she wasn't in? Maybe she'd had enough of all the vandalism and hate mail, and gone into hiding?

One more, then he was heading back to the car.

A voice on the other side of the door: 'Fuck off, I'm not in.'

'Mrs Murray?'

'If you don't fuck off, I'm calling the police! I know my rights.'

Logan pulled out his warrant card and lifted the flap on the letterbox. 'Detective Sergeant— What the. . .?' There was something sticky on his fingers. He let the flap clack back into place.

Brown.

There was sticky brown muck all over his fingertips. 'Oh. . . Jesus. . .'

Filthy *bastards*.

He wiped them on the door, leaving a chocolate-coloured rainbow. 'I *am* the bloody police!'

There was a clunk. Then the door opened a crack, and a bloodshot eye peered out through the gap. 'Prove it.'

Logan shoved his warrant card at her. 'There's *shite* in your letterbox.'

She nodded. 'Stopped the bastards from peering in, trying to take photos of me in my bloody pants, didn't it?' The door thumped shut, then what sounded like a chain being removed, and it opened again. 'Serves them right.'

Victoria Murray folded her arms underneath the sagging parcel shelf of her bosom. According to the article in last week's *Aberdeen Examiner*, 'ex-exotic dancer and call girl "Vicious" Vikki (22) had a threesome with two city councillors'.

God, they must have been desperate. A cigarette smouldered in the corner of her mouth, curling smoke around her narrowed eyes. Her chin disappeared into her neck, the pale skin speckled with spots around her nose and mouth. Making her head look like a used condom full of milk.

She hoicked her boobs up. 'What do you want?'

'I need to wash my hands.'

'That it?'

'You're lucky I'm not arresting you. Putting shite in your letterbox is—'

'Aw, like *they* never did it. What the hell do you think happened to my carpet?' She nodded at the floor.

A mat of newspaper was laid out across the bare floorboards. 'Piss, shite, rotting vegetables, fucking . . . roadkill. I've had the lot. So don't tell me I'm not allowed to get my own back, OK?' She jerked her head to the left. 'Toilet's down there, first door on the left.'

He squeezed past and she thumped the door shut, rattled the chain back in place, turned the key in the lock. There was a plastic bag taped over the inside of the letterbox, bulging with something dark.

She was waiting for him in the kitchen when he'd finished. His fingers didn't smell of shite any more, they reeked of lavender, washed again and again under the hot tap until his hands were pink and swollen. Victoria Murray had a Chunky Kit Kat in one hand and a mug in the other. 'If you want tea you can make it yourself.'

'I need to talk to you about Alison and Jenny McGregor.'

Her face curdled. 'Of course you do. Christ forbid you're here to tell me you've caught the bastards who wrecked my car. Or the ones who smashed my window. Or painted lies all over my house!' She slammed her mug down on the working surface, black coffee slopping over the edge. 'I was spat at yesterday. Spat at. Some OAP cow howched up a mouthful of snot and spat it right in my face! Fucking papers.'

Logan filled the kettle from the cold tap. 'They've not been very nice—'

'Didn't even tell them *half* of what that snooty bitch got up to when we were kids. But *no*: how *dare* I suggest the sainted Alison McGregor used to get pissed and stoned after school. Aye, and that was primary seven – she was giving blowjobs for cigarettes when she was eleven!'

The last chunk of Kit Kat disappeared, washed down with a gulp of coffee. 'There was this family moved in down the street, and they had this mongol kid. You know, Down's Syndrome and that, and Alison would rip the piss out of the poor bastard every – fucking – day. One night, right, we sank this bottle of vodka she nicked from the Paki shop on the corner, and she went round and panned in all their windows.' A sniff. 'Course, I *tried* to stop her, but she wouldn't

204

listen, would she? And I'm the one they call "Vicious Fucking Vikki"?'

Victoria pulled a packet of cigarettes from a kitchen drawer and lit one. Shook the packet at Logan.

'Given up.'

Shrug. 'Suit yourself.' She sent a plume of smoke crashing against the extractor hood. 'Course, we used to be real tight. . . Best friends. Used to tell me everything. We were something *special* back then; sixteen years old, sexy as hell, men throwing themselves at us.' A smile oozed across Victoria's face, then disappeared. 'Now look at me.'

The kettle rumbled to a boil. Logan filled a mug. Fished the teabag out with the handle of a fork. 'So what happened?'

A long smoky sigh. 'Doddy McGregor happened. She thought he was just this big stupid lump of muscle, but he knew a good thing when he saw it.' Victoria rubbed two fingers up and down the side of her face, pushing the skin into folds. 'Walked in and caught us at it, didn't she? Doddy says he's just getting it out of his system, before the wedding. Invites her to join in, says it'd be hot. And she's standing there: six months pregnant. Fuck, I thought she was going to kill him.' Victoria laughed. 'Thought she was going to kill me too. Never spoke after that.'

Logan poured the last dribble of semi-skimmed into his mug. 'So you haven't seen them recently?'

'Course I have.' She curled back her top lip, exposing little brown teeth. 'They're fucking *everywhere*: on the telly, in the papers, can't turn on the radio and they're playing that bloody song. She gets a tribute show with Robbie Williams, what do I get? Fucking diabetes.'

Quarter to three. Forty-five minutes to go. Logan drummed his fingers on the steering wheel. One sex offender due diligence interview down, two to go. Should really go visit the vets Frank Baker volunteered at, make sure DI Steel had followed it up properly. Be a good little boy.

He rode the clutch down to the roundabout, joining the queue waiting to get over the King George VI Bridge.

Superintendent Napier. . . Why did it have to be him? At least with Chief Inspector Young you got a decent chance to explain your side of things.

Forward another couple of car-lengths. A huge eighteen-wheeler with the Baxters' logo down the side hissed and juddered around onto Great Southern Road. A taxi blared its horn at a massive four-by-four, then it was Logan's turn on the roundabout.

He accelerated out, turned right . . . and kept on going, right around the roundabout and back the way he'd come. Sod Superintendent Sodding Green and his sodding due diligence.

Five minutes later Logan was standing outside the house where they'd dropped off Trisha Brown's wee boy so he could spend the night with his drug addict granny. It was worth a try.

The front door was scuffed, the wood dented, as if it'd been given a bit of a kicking. It wasn't a bad neighbourhood, just a bunch of bland granite houses a few streets over from where Alison and Jenny McGregor lived. Logan tried the doorbell. No answer. Then he tried the handle, and the door swung open.

The Browns' hallway was a minefield of broken furniture. A ratty purple sofa was twisted onto its side, half in and half out of the living room door. A glass-topped coffee table made glittering mosaic shards on the carpet.

When Shuggie said his Yardie mates had trashed the place, he wasn't kidding. . .

'Hello?' Logan pressed the bell again, and a dull clunking buzz sounded somewhere down the hall. 'Anyone home?'

Glass scrunched under his shoes. 'Anyone?'

He peered into the lounge. More damage: TV smashed, armchairs broken, the floor littered with CDs. Fleetwood Mac lying by the door, the cover cracked.

Shattered jars and bottles littered the kitchen floor, covering the dirty linoleum with glass and sticky liquid. Pickled onions amongst a shattered jar of beetroot, like tiny eyes swimming in a sea of blood. Cupboard doors ripped from the units, the fridge dented and buckled.

It wasn't random destruction, it was systematic.

The stairs creaked as he climbed.

Bathroom: toilet smashed, grey-pink pedestal mat soaking wet. Sink cracked. The bath's front panel kicked in, the mixer shower ripped from the wall.

Bedroom one: mattress gutted, its innards burst across the bare chipboard floor. Ripped clothes. A chest of drawers turned into a Picasso sculpture. A wardrobe lurching drunkenly against the headboard. Curtains torn down.

The second bedroom wasn't so bad. It actually looked as if someone had tidied up in here. A small pile of clothes sat in the corner: other than that, the floor was relatively clean. OK, so the wardrobe was living testimony to the miraculous powers of silver duct tape, and the mattress lay on the floor instead of a bed, but it had sheets and an almost-clean duvet cover. . . About four drawers were stacked, one on top of the other, by the window, overflowing with bras, socks, and pants.

Logan walked over to the room's cracked window and looked out across the road at the houses on the other side. The neighbours must *love* it here. You save hard, buy your very own council house, and then Helen Brown moves in. Next thing you know you've got three generations of drug users living next door. Breaking into your house, shed, garage, car, anywhere they can nick something to sell and feed their habit.

And then a pair of Yardies turn up and wreck the place. Do a bloody good job of it too.

Ah well. . .

It'd been a long shot. Shuggie Webster wasn't lying low at his girlfriend's mum's house. He was probably off licking his wounds in a squat somewhere. If the Yardies hadn't killed him.

Logan checked his watch again. Twenty-five minutes to get back to the station in time for his bollocking. He turned and . . . stopped. Frowned.

The wardrobe – a cheap-looking flatpack job, all veneer-covered chipboard, papered with tatty photos cut from the pages of *Hello!* and *Heat* and *Bella* – was creaking. It was moving too. Not much, just a little trembling back and forth motion, but it was definitely moving.

A smile crawled across Logan's face. Shuggie Webster, you predictable little shite. . .

Time to come out of the closet.

27

Logan pulled out his pepper-spray, and popped the top off. He crept over to the rocking wardrobe. Grabbed the wooden handle. Threw it wide open. 'You enjoying Narnia then, Shug—'

Something slammed into Logan's stomach and he went staggering backwards. Then over, the room flipping through ninety degrees, and then *thump*. Flat on his back. Cold, sharp pain, as if six-inch metal screws were being twisted into his guts.

A small bare foot flashed past Logan's nose. A hand, a blue sleeve. The rancid piddly smell of stale clothes, left too long in the washing machine. Scrabbling, swearing, then the slapping sound of naked feet on floorboards.

Logan shot a hand out, groping. . . Not finding anything. He rolled over onto his side, forced himself upright and lurched to the bedroom door. It sounded as if there were snakes in the hallway below – hissing and writhing. He stood at the top of the stairs, one hand on the wallpaper for support.

There was a little boy sitting on the bottom step, wearing grubby Ben 10 pyjamas, clutching his feet in both hands.

'Ricky?'

The kid stood, limped, collapsed against the battered sofa poking out from the lounge door. A set of bloody footprints followed him across the glass-strewn carpet.

'There you go.' Logan clunked a tin of Irn-Bru down on the bare floorboards at the side of the mattress.

Ricky Brown wrapped his arms around his knees, face set in a line much harder than the two crusted streaks beneath his nose. He turned his head away.

'How's the feet?'

The response was too mumbled to make out.

Logan pulled up his tatty left trouser leg, showing off three parallel lines of scabs. 'See, you're not the only one.'

Ricky picked at a loose thread on the ribbons of towel Logan had wrapped around the little boy's feet. The soles slowly soaking through in shiny red patches.

'Where's your mum, Ricky?'

A shrug. 'Went out.'

Aha, so he could speak after all. 'You know where she went?'

He shook his head, little more than a twitch. 'Said someone killed Dad's dog.'

'Shuggie Webster's your dad?'

'This week.' Another thread unravelled from the impro-vised bandage.

'Do you know where he is?'

'Mum went to get food and that.' Pause. 'You going to arrest me?'

Logan forced a laugh. 'Why would I do that?'

'Gran says it's what you pig bastards do. You arrest people what haven't done nothing wrong.'

'No, Ricky, I'm not going to arrest you.' He held out

the Irn-Bru. 'Did your mum say when she's going to be back?'

'Gran says you arrest people and you shag them up the arse. 'Cos you're all paedos and poofs.'

'Yeah, your granny sounds like a bundle of laughs.' Logan cracked the ringpull off the tin, and helped himself to a swig. 'Your mum and dad are messed up with some very bad people, Ricky. Now, I can help, but I need to know where they are.'

Silence.

'Don't you want your mum and dad to be safe?'

Ricky shifted his feet, leaving a red smear on the duvet cover.

'OK, well, if you're sure.' Logan knocked back another gulp, then set the tin down back on the floor. 'Right, I know a nice doctor who'll fix you up, then we'll see if we can find someone to look after you.'

'She's coming back for me.'

'Never said she wasn't.'

'She told me last night.'

'Yeah, well we'll. . .' Frown. 'Last night? You've been on your own since last night? In the wardrobe?'

'Said she'd come back soon as it was safe.'

And the nominees for 'Mother of the Year' are. . .

Logan stood. 'You think you can walk, or do you want me to give you a piggy back?'

Ricky looked up at him, then away again. He gripped a handful of duvet cover. 'Are you going to shag *me* up the arse?'

'Wasn't top of my agenda, no.'

A nod. 'Can you carry me then?'

Logan knocked on the doorframe. The paintwork was chipped and peeling, a thick grey line halfway up marking where countless trolleys had bashed their way through. 'Shop?'

The mortuary was nearly twice the size of the one in the basement of FHQ, done in sparkling white-and-blue tiles, like a swimming pool. A little speaker system sat on a shelf by the refrigerated drawers, Dr Hook's *Sexy Eyes* echoing slightly in the antiseptic space.

'Hello?' A head appeared from a door at the back of the room – ginger curls bobbing as she wheeled a mop and bucket into the cutting room, white mortuary clogs squeaking on the floor. She smiled. 'Sergeant McRae, we've not had you here for a while. Picking up, or dropping off?'

'They got you mopping up now? You not a bit overqualified for that?'

'Fred's off sick, so we're all chipping in.' The Anatomical Pathology Technician hauled the mop out of the bucket and slopped it across the tiles, making little streams rush along the grout. 'How's Sheila? She still channelling Vincent Price?'

'Three weeks to go.' He limped into the room. 'Wanted to ask you a question.'

'What happened to your leg?'

'Rottweiler. Look, I've only got a minute – have you had any dead children in recently? Girls. Between four and eight years old?'

'I had a neighbour with a Rottweiler, lovely big lump it was. Broke her heart when it got cancer.' The APT dumped the mop back in the mangle bit of the bucket and hauled the handle down, squeezing out the dirty water. 'Hop up on the table and I'll take a look.'

Logan looked at the stainless-steel table, the one with guttering around the edges, and a water supply to rinse away the blood. 'I'm. . . Nah, it's OK. I'm fine.'

'Oh come on.' She smiled. 'Never lost a patient yet.'

212

'Ever saved one?'

A sigh. 'That's a good point.' She leant the mop against the wall, then crossed to a laptop sitting on its own on an expanse of shining worktop. 'Little girls between four and eight. . .' Her fingers clicked across the keys. 'Am I allowed to ask why?'

There's no need to sound so dramatic, *Sergeant. Where do you think the kidnappers got the thing from, Toes R Us?*

'Was sitting upstairs, waiting for them to put a dozen stitches in a wee boy's feet, and I thought – where would you get a dead little girl's toe from?'

'Lovely.' She shook her head, Irn-Bru curls swaying. 'So when you think of dead little girls: I'm the one who springs to mind?'

'Have you had any? Over the last two or three weeks? They'd have been given morphine and thiopental sodium.'

She leant her head closer to the laptop's screen. 'That narrows it down a bit. . . Here we go: female, five-year-old, brought in suffering from abdominal pains. Died on the operating table.' A sigh. 'Poor wee soul.'

The song on the stereo changed to *All the Time in the World*.

Logan limped over. 'Could we do a DNA test? See if the toe they sent us was hers?'

'I remember her now. Such a pretty little girl. When we opened her up she was riddled with cysts and cancer. . . Five years old.'

'You'd have tissue samples though, right? We could—'

'It's not her.'

'But if we check—'

'It's not her.' The APT stepped back and pointed at the screen.

A photograph filled the right-hand side next to a list of post mortem notes: a little girl, lying on the cutting table, eyes taped closed, the breathing tube still in her mouth. Her skin was the colour of dusty slate, all the blood and life leached out of it.

The APT closed the laptop with a click. 'There's no way they could pass a toe from her off as coming from a little white girl.'

'That's not what I meant.' Deep breaths. Stay calm.

'Then what *did* you mean, Sergeant?' Superintendent Napier steepled his fingers, then rested his chin on the point. He smiled, dark eyes wide behind his glasses. His desk was arranged so that his back was to the window, meaning the chair reserved for visitors, supplicants, and sacrificial offerings, faced into the sun. The light made a fiery halo of Napier's ginger hair, his black dress uniform a solid silhouette against the bright blue sky.

Logan squinted. 'There just didn't seem to be an opportunity to call it in. After I banged my head. . .' He reached up and rubbed a spot behind his ear, just to sell the lie.

'Ah yes. Of course. Detective Constable Rennie mentioned . . . where are we?' The superintendent picked a sheet of paper from his in-tray and peered at it down his long pointy nose. '"He was acting all confused and had difficulty remembering the end of sentences, when I collected him. I believe he may have been concussed."' The paper went back in the tray. 'A more cynical man might think you'd cooked that up between you to deflect the blame, don't you think, Sergeant?'

'When was the last time you were attacked by a Rottweiler?' Or battered to death with your own office chair?

'And I suppose it was this alleged "concussion" that made you twenty minutes late for our appointment?' Napier swivelled from side to side, sunlight flaring in Logan's eyes: shadow, bright, shadow, bright. 'We've not had to deal with you for several months, Sergeant, but I see from Chief Inspector Young's notes that you were in here only yesterday. Twice in two days. Are you embarking upon some kind of record attempt?'

'They were trumped up charges by—'

'Someone allegedly trying to extort drugs from you. Yes, I do actually read the case files of the officers I deal with, Sergeant. And a little birdie tells me that you're having interpersonal difficulties with Chief Inspector Green from SOCA?'

Did the bastard hire a publicist? 'We had a frank exchange of views, yes.'

'Did you now?' Napier swivelled again.

'We disagreed about what was and wasn't acceptable behaviour when interviewing sex offenders. Green thinks it's OK to put the fear of God in them and threaten to tell their colleagues.'

'I see. . .' He sat forward, blocking out the sun. 'So, would you say that Superintendent Green was less than receptive to Grampian Police's thorough and rigorous approach to offender management? That he disregarded best working practice? Was contemptuous of it?' There was that smile again, the one that made him look like a shark, about to tear into a paddling pool full of orphans.

'Er. . .' Logan was getting set up for something. 'It was . . . a non-standard situation that . . . *may* have caused some confusion on his part.'

Napier raised an eyebrow. 'I shall, of course, attempt to smooth out any difficulties in understanding. It's important that we all get on with our colleagues from the Serious Organized Crime Agency, don't you think?'

'. . . Yes?'

The superintendent picked a silver pen from his desktop, rolled it back and forth between his fingers as if it were a shiny joint. Then returned it to its rightful place, lining it up perfectly with the edge of a desk calendar. 'Well,' he stuck out a hand for Logan to shake, 'thank you for coming in, Sergeant. It's been most . . . informative.'

That's it – he was screwed.

It would just take a while to find out why, and exactly how badly.

'Well, if you'd hold still for two minutes I wouldn't have to, would I?' Dr Delaney shifted her grip on Logan's ankle. She had fingers like pliers, digging into the skin and muscle, the purple nitrile gloves pulling out leg hairs every time she moved.

'Ow!'

'Oh don't be such a baby.' She wiped a disinfectant-soaked pad across the dark-red teeth-marks again, rubbing away the scabs. Setting them bleeding again. 'When was your last tetanus shot?'

'No idea.'

'You're a silly sod. Lucky we don't get a lot of rabies in Scotland – the needles are massive.'

Sharp, stinging pain tore up his leg. He gritted his teeth, tried not to flinch.

'If you don't hold still, you're going to get gangrene and your foot'll fall off. Is that what you want?' She rubbed more disinfectant into the wounds.

'Did you do a check-up on Ricky Brown?'

'Pass me the pack of gauze.' She tore the plastic packet open with her teeth. 'He wasn't exactly the most cooperative of patients.'

Dr Delaney laid a square of gauze across the huge gouges in Logan's ankle. 'Barely a scratch, I don't know why you're being such a whinge about it.'

216

'He going to be OK?'

'Nothing a decent meal and a bath wouldn't sort out. Hospital did an excellent job on his stitches. I've got suits with worse needlework in them.' She wrapped a bandage around the ankle, securing it with a claw-toothed metal thing on the end of a bit of elastic. 'And I bet he made a lot less fuss than you did.'

'Thanks, Doc.' Logan hopped down from the desk, then picked up his bloodstained sock and soggy shoe.

'One more thing.' She took off her glasses and pinched the bridge of her nose. 'I'm recommending they take him into permanent care. A family full of drug users is bad enough, but if his mum and . . . this Shuggie person are involved with Yardies. . .'

Logan limped back to his desk, popped open the top drawer and stuck his newly-washed coffee mug and teaspoon inside, then locked them away. That was the trouble with working in a police station – all the thieving bastards.

Biohazard Bob swivelled his seat around until he was facing the middle of the room. 'Beer o'clock?'

'Can't.' Doreen stayed hunched over her desk. 'Superintendent Green wants details on every kidnapping in the area, going back five years.'

'Logie the Bogie?'

Logan switched off his computer. 'Green needs taking out and shot. He's got me digging out the same info for the last *ten*. I've got Rennie doing it now.'

Doreen hunched her shoulders, grinding out the words, 'Why – didn't – you – say – that – three – hours – ago?'

Biohazard poked the power button on his computer. 'Well, another day spent hunting the elusive Stinky Tam has left me gasping for a pint.' He picked up the slew of paperwork covering his desk, ruffled it into something approaching order, and jammed it in his pending-tray. 'Anyone seen my stapler?'

He hauled open his top desk drawer. 'The hell's this?' Bob pulled out the pair of knickers Logan had stuffed in there last week – the ones he'd found clothespegged to his lamp along with all the socks.

Bob turned them back and forth, flashing the brown streaks that covered the gusset. 'Aye, aye, someone's been a bittie manky.'

Doreen straightened her back, pink rushing up her cheeks. 'Well, don't look at me!'

The door banged open and DI Steel grumbled into the Wee Hoose. 'Sergeant Marshall, why aren't. . .' She frowned. 'What are you doing?'

He twirled the skidmarked panties around his finger. 'Just discussing personal hygiene with DS Taylor, here. Superintendent Green's never going to want to jump in her pants if she's left filthy bumscrapes—'

Doreen hit him. 'Detective Sergeant Robert Marshall, I'm warning you!'

'Behave, the pair of you.' Steel chucked a manila folder at Bob. 'General Enquiry Division just turned up a body on Gairn Terrace.'

'Yeah?' He pulled out the paperwork, flipped through it. 'I'll get on it first thing tomorrow, Guv, it'll. . .' A sigh. 'Shite.' He held up a photograph – a man's face: nose bloated like a pockmarked golf ball, scraggly beard full of bits, unkempt hair, dirty red Aberdeen Football Club bobble hat. 'Stinky Tam.'

'Aye, so get your filthy panty-whirling arse out there and bring the poor bastard in.'

Bob went pink. 'Yes, Guv.' He hurried out the door, taking the folder with him.

'And as for you,' she turned and poked Logan with a finger, 'what the hell were you thinking?'

Doreen stood. 'Well, I guess I should really be off—'

'No' so fast.' Steel slammed her hand into the doorframe, blocking the way. 'You tell your new boyfriend Green, I don't need somebody running around checking my work like I'm a bloody probationer. And if I catch him spreading shite around about anyone on my team again, I'm going to jam my fist so far up his arse I'll be working him like a fucking Muppet. Understand?'

Doreen nodded. Steel lowered her hand and the DS crept out.

Steel closed the door, slowly and quietly. Now it was just her and Logan.

'If you're planning on shouting at me, don't bother.' Logan picked his jacket off the back of his seat and pulled it on. 'I got enough of that from Napier and Finnie. I thought I could get the car back before anyone found out.'

She poked him again. 'If you'd bloody well called it in we could've tracked the car and grabbed Shuggie Webster before the Yardies got him! Probably hacked into a million pieces by now!'

'It's not like I handed him the keys to the bloody car and said, "Nah, you go ahead and borrow it, mate; I'll just lie here in the pissing rain!" His dog nearly ripped my face off.'

'See, you've got to keep your eye on wee shites like Shuggie. Got to keep them under control. Can't bury your head in the clouds and expect them to behave themselves. That's just common sense.' She picked up her mug again, took a slurp. 'You try a GSM trace?'

'Of course I did. He's only turning his mobile on for a couple of minutes at a time, then moving.'

'No' as daft as he looks.' She sucked at her teeth for a bit, staring off into the middle distance. 'Get a car organized.'

'But the shift finished—'

'We're going to sort out your cock-up before it gets any worse.'

28

Logan hauled on the handbrake. 'How many more?'

'Till we find him. And don't be so sodding ungrateful.'

Logan groaned. 'Shift finished two and a half hours ago, and I've not had a day off in weeks. What happened to the Working Time Directive?'

'Pfff, Working Time Directive's for poofs.' Steel crumpled up the map and stuffed it into the already overflowing glove compartment. 'Don't see me complaining, do you?' She climbed out into the evening light. Fiddled with her fake cigarette. 'Anyway, you think Jenny and Alison McGregor don't want a day off?'

'Thought you said Susan was up for sex again – how come you're not off—'

Steel scowled. 'Don't be so fucking personal.' She turned and stomped towards the building.

It was a tenement in Hayton, a long row of four-storey apartment blocks: bland, grey-frontage with a stripe of red or blue paintwork marking out the stairwells. As if that was going to make the place look any better. A handful of tower blocks loomed over the buildings, rusty-oatmeal monoliths with balconies and satellite-dish acne. Someone was having a party in the nearest block, the music thumping out from an upper floor. A red balloon drifting away into the misty drizzle.

Typical: when he was in with Napier, or getting a bollocking from Finnie, it was blazing sunshine, but the minute he stepped outside FHQ – sodding raining again.

'You just going to stand there looking gormless?' She pushed through the brown front door. 'Chop bloody chop.'

The smell of frying onions filled the stairwell, making Logan's stomach growl as he followed Steel up the stairs. 'I interviewed Victoria Murray today.'

'Oh aye, and what was Vicious Vikki saying to it?'

'Sounds like Alison McGregor isn't the paragon of virtue everyone thinks. Turns out she—'

'Used to vandalize stuff? Drink? Shagged about when she was still at school?'

'Oh.' Logan paused on the landing, but Steel kept climbing. 'You interviewed her too, didn't you?'

'Nope.'

Logan hurried after her. 'You must have. It's—'

'Don't be a prick, Laz: it was in all the papers. How'd you think Vicious Vikki got her nickname: embezzling the house-keeping? She sold their dirty wee childhood stories to the *Daily Mail*. Big cries of outrage. Then *OK!* magazine did a spread – "Alison's secret schoolgirl shame: 'I was a teenage tearaway', admits BNBS semi-finalist." Or some shite like that. Can you no' at least *try* and keep up with popular culture?'

Steel stopped on the third floor and puffed on her e-cigarette for a bit. 'Right, same as last time. Only try no' to look like your arse is eating your face, eh?'

'It's not my fault Susan won't shag you.'

'Just knock on the bloody door.'

Logan pulled a little nub of Blu-Tack from his pocket and

222

squidged it over the peephole, stepped to the side, then knocked.

Nothing.

Logan banged the flat of his hand against the wood, making it shudder.

Pause.

'Maybe they're not. . .'

A voice from inside. 'OK, OK, calm your fucking monkeys.' There was a shuffly silence. That would be them peering through the peephole and seeing sod all. 'Who is it?'

Logan put a tremble in his voice. 'Dave. . . Dave says you can . . . you know? Set us up and that?'

Another pause.

'How much?'

It didn't matter who they were, they *always* knew a Dave. 'Fifty quid?'

The clunk and rattle of deadbolts and chains. Then the door opened, and a short hairy man appeared with baggy jeans hanging down around his thighs, exposing his Calvin Klein's, a muscle top stretched over a pot belly, fur sprouting out across his shoulders. Gold chains dangling around his neck. White powder dusting his thick moustache. 'What's your poison? We've got. . .' His eyes went wide. 'Fuck.'

DI Steel jammed her foot in the opening. 'Evening, Willy, how's the wife and kids?'

The smell of onions got stronger.

'Fucking, fuck.' Willy rubbed a hand under his nose, scrubbing the powder away. 'It's not what it looks like, I was just . . . baking a cake, well, a quiche, and. . . Erm. . .'

'It's your lucky day, Willy: I don't give a toss about you violating your parole, *or* your dealing; just want a word with Shuggie. Know where he is?'

The wee man's eyes darted left. 'I . . . haven't seen him. For ages.'

Steel smiled. 'Then I take it back: it's no' your lucky day after all.'

Logan pulled out his handcuffs. 'William Cunningham, I'm arresting you on suspicion—'

'He's a mate, I can't just—'

Steel nodded. 'I understand, Willy, very noble of you. Sergeant?'

'Of possession of a controlled substance with intent to supply—'

'Come on, Inspector, Molly'll kill us: be reasonable.'

'Willy, Willy, Willy – when have you ever known me to be reasonable?'

He stared at the ground. 'Shuggie's in the kitchen. Look, could you at least barge in or something? Make it look . . . you know?'

'Nope.' Steel patted him on the furry shoulder. 'Lead on, eh?'

It was a nice flat. Not huge, but well laid out and tidy, painted in comforting shades with photos and prints on the walls. As they walked down the hall, Willy pulled the living room door shut, but not before Logan had seen a little kid dressed in a Spiderman costume and pink sparkly fairy wings, stomping about on stiff, chubby legs.

Willy stopped with one hand on the kitchen door handle. 'Give us a second, OK?'

Steel gave him a shove. 'In we go.'

He staggered into the room, hands up. 'Shuggie, I'm sorry. Didn't have any choice. . .'

Shuggie Webster was hunched over a small table, jammed into the space between the sink and the wall. A frying pan on the stove filled the room with the sweet meaty smell of caramelizing onions.

It seemed to take Shuggie a while to drag his head up

and around. His eyes looked like two black buttons sewn onto his pasty face. Bruising on his cheek and chin. His right hand was wrapped in stained bandages, speckled with red and yellow, only the thumb protruding from its grubby prison. There was a splash of dried blood on his hooded top.

He blinked. Frowned. Blinked again. Then shook his head.

Willy sidled over to the frying pan and stirred his onions. 'Can't let them burn.' A pale pastry case sat on a chopping board next to him.

Logan stepped into the little room. It was getting crowded. 'Come on, Shuggie. Time to go down the station.'

The kitchen was uncomfortably warm, but Shuggie shivered. 'They killed my dog. . .'

'That's why you've got to tell us where they are.'

Shuggie cradled his bloodied hand against his chest. 'Poor wee Uzi. . .'

Willy tipped his onions into the pastry case, then stuck the frying pan in the sink. 'He's a bit out of it. Took something for the pain, you know?'

'Shuggie, they'll keep coming after you. Look what happened to Trisha's mum.'

'Trisha. . .' A frown. He rocked back and forwards, as if he was on one of those children's rides outside a supermarket. 'What if they hurt her again, or her kid?'

'Don't worry about Ricky, he's safe, OK? Now you just have to—'

'What about Trisha?' He stopped rocking. 'She safe?'

'Well. . .' Logan looked back at DI Steel. No help there. 'Yeah, she's fine.'

Willy broke eggs into a Pyrex jug.

Shuggie forced himself to his feet. 'Lying fuck.'

'See, you've got to get the mix of eggs and cream right, or—'

He slammed his unbandaged hand down on the kitchen

table, sending a tin of Special Brew spiralling to the lino. A spurt of foam. 'Is – she – fucking – safe?'

'Aww, Shuggie! It's all over the floor.'

Logan backed up a pace. 'She's probably fine—'

'Where is she?'

'At least put a tea-towel down or something.'

'She left Ricky at her mum's house yesterday. She's not been back yet, but I'm—'

Another slam. 'They fucking raped her!'

'*Hey*, come on, man,' Willy held up the fork he'd been beating the eggs with, 'cool the beans, eh? My wee girl's through the house.'

Shuggie nodded, buried his face in his cupped hand. 'Sorry, it's just. . .' His shoulders shook. Silence. Then a deep breath.

OK, so at least this was going to be a lot easier than last time.

Logan stepped forward and placed a hand on Shuggie's arm, gave it a little squeeze. 'It's going to be OK.'

The big man looked up, tears dripping from his pink eyes. 'Will it FUCK!'

A shove, and Logan went staggering back. Then Shuggie grabbed a carton of milk from the working surface and hurled it. It went wide, crashing against the tiles, spurting out across the fridge.

'God's sake, Shuggie, calm the—' A fist battered into Willy's face, cracking him back into the cooker.

A carton of double cream flew across the room.

Logan ducked: it sailed over his head.

A chair followed it.

He scrabbled in his pocket for the pepper-spray.

Too slow.

Shuggie took hold of the table in his good hand and flipped it, slamming the Formica into Logan's chest, sending him sprawling against the units. Something crunched under

226

his foot – the beer can – and he went down, elbow bashing into the linoleum as he hit the floor.

Jagged pain rushed up his arm, like cramp and pins-and-needles all at the same time. 'Bastard!'

Shuggie dived on top of him . . . or on top of the upturned table. The bottom edge cracked into Logan's shin, the upper edge hard across his chest. Shuggie drew back a massive fist and swung.

Logan wrapped his arms around his head, ducking down behind his forearms like a boxer, eyes screwed shut as the punch hammered into his right bicep. Then another one, catching him in the right armpit.

'Aaaagh, get off, you—'

One more on his right elbow, thumping his head back into the kitchen units.

'This is all your fault!' Another punch. 'I want them fucking drugs back!'

The next one slammed into Logan's arm again.

Always on the right side – Shuggie was using his left fist, saving his right. . .

Logan's head bounced off the units, but this time he dropped his guard and grabbed the bloody bandage, wrapped his fingers around Shuggie's right hand and squeezed hard.

29

'AAAAAAAAAAAAAAA!' Shuggie's face went pale.

Logan jerked the hand to the side, digging his nails in.

'FUCK!' The big man slapped at Logan's wrist, scrabbled backwards. Out of reach. 'FUCK!' Eyes wide, a string of spittle spiralling down from his open mouth. And then he lurched forward and stomped on the table, sending Logan crashing back to the linoleum.

'Fuck. . .' Shuggie lurched out of the room, clutching his bloody hand to his chest.

Logan could hear him staggering down the hall, bumping into the wall, the crash and tinkle of framed pictures hitting the floor. Then the front door slammed.

So much for everything going easier than last time.

Get up. Get up and charge after him. Tackle him on the stairs and crack the bastard's head off the concrete walls. Slap the cuffs on. Then kick him in the balls. . .

Logan slumped back against the soggy lino.

Sod that.

Just lie here a minute. Catch his breath.

His right arm throbbed.

Willy Cunningham's hairy face appeared above him, one

eye already heading from lurid pink to post-box red, the skin around it swelling and darkening. 'You OK?'

'No.' He shoved the table away, and struggled to his feet. Then stood for a minute, holding onto the working surface.

'Bloody hell. . .' Willy turned on the spot, arms held out from his sides. '*Look* at the place. Molly's going to kill me!'

DI Steel's gravelly voice came from the hallway. 'Little help?'

Logan cradled his battered arm, scowling. 'Where the hell were you?'

A single black-shoed foot appeared in the doorway, about two-feet off the ground, toe pointing upward, followed by a short length of crumpled sock, a flash of bare ankle, then a wrinkled grey trouser leg. 'Argh.'

He picked his way across the beer-and-milk-slicked linoleum to the door.

She was lying on her back, tangled up in the chair Shuggie had tried to take Logan's head off with. The battered carton of cream lay beside her, its contents splattered all over her.

Steel wiped her eyes, flicking droplets of thick white against the walls. 'Sodding hell. . . Pfffffffp. . . Ack. . .' She stared at her hands, her arms, her chest – all dripping with double cream. Smeared another handful from her cheeks and chin. 'Now I know what it feels like to star in a porn film. . .'

Logan hauled her to her feet. 'You were a lot of bloody good.'

She scowled. 'He threw a chair at me! What was I supposed to do?'

'What happened to, "You've got to keep an eye on people like Shuggie", "Can't bury your head in the sand and expect them to behave", "That's just common sense"?'

'Oh . . . shut up.'

*   *   *

229

'And an orange-and-soda for the big girl's blouse.' Big Gary clunked the pint glass down on the coffee table in front of Rennie.

'I'm driving, OK?' The constable took a sip.

The Athenaeum was relatively quiet for a Sunday night, meaning they'd managed to bag two of the big saggy sofas, with a view out onto the Castlegate: a couple trying to conceive in the bus stop, some drunken singing, a lone idiot marching up and down with a placard proclaiming 'JESUS WILL SAVE ALISON AND JENNY IF YOU BELIEVE!'

Logan reached for his pint of Stella, winced, then tried with his left hand instead. His whole right arm was seizing up, probably covered in thick black bruises. Sodding Shuggie Webster. . .

Big Gary levered his huge arse down into a creaking sofa. Raised his Guinness. 'To Superintendent Green – our man from SOCA – may his life be long . . . and plagued with piles.'

Doreen clinked her white wine against Gary's glass. 'And verrucas.'

Steel joined in. 'Impotence.'

Logan: 'Anal leakage.'

Rennie: 'Premature ejaculation!'

Steel hit him. 'How can he have premature ejaculation if he's impotent, you tit?'

'Ow! Just means if he ever *does* get it up, it's going to be sod all use to him.'

Big Gary nodded. 'The loon's got a point.'

'Meh.' Steel tried her whisky, following it down with a big glug of IPA. 'Right, before we all get irredeemably blootered, how do we find Alison and Jenny McGregor?'

Doreen groaned, let her head fall back until she was staring at the ceiling. 'I've been doing this all bloody day!'

'Tell that to a wee girl who's no' got her little toes any more.'

Rennie popped open a packet of cheese and onion. 'What about the forensic thing? I mean, they don't leave a single trace – that's not normal, is it?'

'*And*?'

Shrug. 'Maybe we should, you know, be looking at police officers? Or the IB? Maybe someone retired, or fired, or something?'

Doreen nodded. 'Would make sense. They'd have motive for making the rest of us look like idiots.'

Steel's mouth fell open, eyes wide. She snapped her fingers. 'That's *brilliant*! Rennie, you're a *genius*!'

The constable sat up straight. 'Well, sometimes it's—'

'Why did *no one* think of that earlier? A whole squad of highly experienced officers, and no one thought to look at the forensics angle. You're some sort of deductive *god*!'

Rennie's shoulders sagged a bit. 'What?'

'We *certainly* haven't had a team looking into that for the last week and a bit!'

'Oh. . .'

Steel hit him again. 'Twit.'

Logan helped himself to one of Rennie's crisps. 'What about the students in her psychology class?'

Steel sucked her teeth for a moment. '. . . McPherson's looking into it, I think. Well, him or Evans. Don't see a bunch of spotty layabouts managing to pull this off though, do you? They'd have to get up in the morning. Be too busy analysing each other's bumholes.'

'No, I'm going home.' Logan stood. His shins bumped the low table, setting the graveyard of empty glasses clinking against each other. 'Samantha's waiting.'

231

The pub had got busier, the noise level rising with the alcohol consumption.

A group of middle-aged women, dressed in clothes far too young for them, were singing 'Happy Birthday to You' for about the sixth time, complete with shrieks of laughter. Rennie had been sent over to complain, and returned with a paper plate heaped with slices of chocolate cake and a cheek smeared with bright-red lipstick.

'Aw, go on.' The constable waggled his third pint of Tennent's at Logan. 'One more for the road!'

'Thought you were driving?'

Rennie shook his head. 'Emma says she'll come get me.' Grin. 'Isn't she great?'

Doreen tipped the last of the white wine into her glass, and sagged. 'Everyone's got someone to go home to, but me. . .'

DS Bob Marshall appeared through the throng, carrying a fresh pint of something dark. 'You can come home with us, if you like, Doors? You me and Deborah can re-enact the Swinging Sixties.' He gave her a big leering wink.

'Urgh. . .' Doreen shuddered. 'I think I just threw up a little.'

'Charming.' He dragged a seat over. Paused, wrinkled his top lip and sniffed. 'Why can I smell cheese?'

Logan pulled on his stained jacket. 'Don't worry, I'm leaving.'

Bob hump-shuffled his chair closer to the table. 'Surprised I can smell anything at all: Stinky Tam was like. . . Actually, you don't want to know. But *Jesus*, what a stench. Found him in the bushes at the side of the road, all bloated and leaky and bits falling off. Pretty sure the rats had been at him too.'

Doreen scowled. 'You were right, we *didn't* want to know.'

'How can someone drop dead in the middle of the city,

and no bastard notices, eh?' A slurp of beer. 'I'd've been here ages ago, but those GED bastards dragged me off to some poor sod who'd topped himself. General Enquiries Division my arse – Gormless Evil Dickheads more like.' Another slurp. 'Anyway, so come on then: who's the bird with Steel?'

'With the dark hair?' Big Gary peered over Doreen's head towards the bar.

Logan turned and did the same. DI Steel was just visible through the throng, her hand on the small of some woman's back. Curly dark hair shot through with grey; jeans and a tight silk shirt; glasses perched on the top of her head; party hat set at a jaunty angle.

Steel leaned in and said something. The woman laughed, setting an impressive set of bosoms jiggling.

Logan edged his way out from the table and made for the door. Stopped. Then turned and waded through the crowd to the bar. He tapped Steel on the shoulder. 'That's me away.'

She turned, her eyes narrowing for a moment. 'Good for you.' Then back to whispering something in her new friend's ear.

The woman threw her head back and gave another cleavage-wobbling laugh. 'Oh, Honey, you are *priceless*.' American accent.

Logan forced a smile and grabbed hold of Steel's arm. 'Excuse us a minute.' He pulled her away to the nearest alcove. 'What are you doing?'

Steel shook herself free. 'Fuck does it look like I'm doing? I'm talking to—'

'You're *married*, remember?'

The inspector's mouth became a hard thin line. 'Since when is it any of your bloody business what—'

'You *really* need me to answer that?'

Pink flushed up her cheeks. Then she looked away. 'I'm just having a bit of fun, OK? It's no' like I'm going to shag her or anything.' Steel stuck both hands against her forehead, pulling the wrinkles away. Sighed. 'Susan says she *still* no' ready. Been nearly a year. A *year*, and she still won't. . . I'm only fucking human, Laz.'

'Just. . . Just don't do something you're going to regret.'

'Aye.' She patted him on the arm. 'Thanks.'

Logan stepped out into the bustle of Union Street: the rumble of buses, the wailing screech of seagulls, that idiot with the 'JESUS!' sign singing some sort of hymn in a broken falsetto. The streets were still wet from the last downpour, shining in the evening light.

He sidestepped a teenager with a cigarette dangling out the corner of her mouth, a mobile phone clamped to her ear, and a wee kid strapped into a buggy.

'Yeah. . . Yeah, I know, but he's a total wanker, so what can you do?' Click-clacking on too-high heels.

Logan glanced back through the Athenaeum's windows, and there was DI Steel, back at the bar, with her arm around the buxom party girl.

Christ's sake. . .

You know what: he wasn't her mother. If she wanted to screw everything up, she was on her own.

'You're a big baby, there's nothing to see.' Samantha settled back on the couch.

'You sure?' Logan peered at his right arm. . . 'There, that's a bruise.'

'That's dirt.' She clapped her hands, once. 'Come on then, let's see the other one.'

He slipped the shirt all the way off and turned around. The little square of wadding was frayed, the surgical sticky tape peeling and dirty around the edges. 'Should it not stay—'

'Can't believe you're still wearing that.' She bounced off the couch, grabbed the wadding and tore it off.

A sudden sting of ripped out hair. 'Ow!'

'There.' She nodded. 'Looks good – told you the Reverend was an artist. You happy with it?'

'Steel says they're investigating the IB, in case any of you lot kidnapped Alison and Jenny?'

'It suits you. Very minimalist.'

'Can't see it myself. Criminal masterminds? Half your team couldn't tie their shoelaces without adult supervision.'

'Let it breathe a bit: the redness will go down quicker. And for your *information*, we could run rings round you CID carpet-shaggers.'

He sat on the arm of the sofa. 'Did you know Alison McGregor was a horror when she was young?'

'Well . . . *duh*. Everyone knows. Then she met Doddy, and he swept her off her feet and she got pregnant, and vowed to put her life back on track for her husband and her little girl. Très romantic.'

'Found a big pile of love letters when we searched her house on Friday.' Logan picked at a tuft of thread, sticking up from one of the sofa's seams. 'Does it bother you?'

'What?'

'That I've . . . well, I've never written *you* any?'

'Oh dear Jesus, no. I read the bloody things when Bruce brought them back to the lab last week.'

'You *read* them?'

'Who do you think put them back in the bottom drawer? Someone had to check her mail for threats, or secret lovers.' She clasped her hands to her chest. '"Oh how the embers of my heart burn with the heat of a *million suns*!" Pffff. . . "Million suns." I'd have more respect for the man if he'd said he burned with the heat of a summer's day in Banchory. Or a bag of chips.' Samantha tilted her head on one side, and stared at him. 'If you *ever* write something like that at me, I'm going to kick you in the nuts and leave. Understand?'

'Yeah, well, I wasn't planning—'

'Anyway,' she pointed at his arm, 'that means a hell of a lot more to me than some cheesy moon-in-June bollocks.'

She unfastened the thick leather belt from her jeans, popped the top button, unzipped the zip, then pulled her T-shirt up. 'So. . .' There was a little patch of wadding, not much bigger than a beer mat, stuck to her stomach, just beside her bellybutton. She peeled the sticky tape off. 'What do you think?'

It was the number twenty-three, reversed out of a circle made up of squiggles. The ink was black, the skin slightly swollen, angry red fading to pasty-Scottish-white. It sat not far from the topmost spines of the tribal spider thing that reached all the way down to her knee; equidistant from a teddy bear with an axe in its chest, and a sort of bramble-twined rose.

'Twenty-three?'

'Yup. Call it a reply to the love note on your arm. See,' she pointed at the squiggles, 'now I've got twenty-three little scars. Just like you.'

Logan put a hand against his own stomach. Squinched up one side of his face. 'Thanks. . . I think.'

She pulled her T-shirt back down again. 'You don't like it.'

'No, it's not that. . . I. . .' He frowned. 'I just . . . can't decide if it's a really sweet gesture, or a little creepy.'

Samantha grinned. 'Can't a girl be both?'

'Dunno, she's no' looking that good.'

'Course she's not – she's got a fever, you idiot.'

Hot. Far too hot. Jenny forces her eyes open. Cold. And

236

Hot. And the light stabs her head like a sharpened pencil. The room starts to twirl. Dirty ceiling, scribbled-on walls, a bare light bulb that swims across a dirty sky. . .

So thirsty.

'Well? What the hell are we supposed to do?'

The monsters are in the corner, all crinkly and white. Like ghosts made of paper.

'So, do we call a doctor, or what?'

Her lips crack and burn. 'Mummy. . .'

'Don't be a dick, Tom.'

'Who're you calling a dick, *Sylvester*?'

'Mummy. . .?' Her head thumps and whumps.

'It's OK, darling, Mummy's here. Shhh. . .'

A cool hand strokes Jenny's forehead. 'Thirsty.'

'Use your heads.' This monster isn't like the other ones. He has pointy horns and a red swishy tail. And when he steps on the floorboards little circles of fire sprout into life. 'How the fuck are we supposed to explain this to a doctor? "Oh, you know those two off the telly who've been kidnapped? Well, guess what we found. . ."'

'Where's bloody Colin when you need him?'

Mummy raises her voice. 'She needs water.'

The monsters stop arguing. 'Yeah, right. Sylvester, get her a bottle or something. . .'

'He's not answering his phone. Why isn't he answering his bloody phone? I said he was fucking unreliable, didn't I, David? Didn't I say he was a big fat fucking liability?'

'Here, it's pretty cold. You maybe shouldn't let her drink it all at once, or she'll puke.'

Mummy's face ripples into view. Her eyes are pink, so is her nose. She sniffs, wipes a drip away with the back of her hand. 'Here, sweetie, try and take little sips. . .'

The hard plastic shape presses against Jenny's lips and she gulps. Cold, wet, soothing – spreading out inside her.

A frozen octopus reaching all the way from her elbows to her knees.

'We got to do something, what if she dies?'

'She's not going to fucking die.' DAVID leaves a trail of fiery feet across the floor. 'Here: the useless tosser's left his medical bag. She just needs more antibiotics or something.'

The water goes away. Jenny reaches for it, but her hands wobble and flap. Two balloons filled with sausages. . .

'Shhh. . . It'll be OK, sweetie, it'll be OK. Mummy promises.'

'Found some Fluc. . . Fluc-lox-acillin,' sounding it out, 'that's right, isn't it?'

'How much do we give her?'

'I dunno. Can you overdose on antibiotics?'

'God's sake, Tom.' DAVID sighs, his shoulders hunching. 'You've got an iPhone, Google it.'

'Right. . . OK. Yeah. Here we go – got it. Flucloxacillin. . . How much does she weigh?'

'The fuck does that matter?'

'Dose depends on how much she weighs: thirty milligrams per kilo. She's about, what – nineteen, twenty kilos?' He fiddles with a needle and a little glass bottle, then squirts a little arc into the air, just like on the television. 'Right . . . who's going to do it?'

SYLVESTER backs away. 'Nah, that's Colin's job.'

'Yeah, but Colin's no' here, is he?'

'Give me the bloody thing.' DAVID holds out a hand. 'Does it go into a vein or muscle?'

'Erm. . .' He looks at the shiny flat thing again. 'Either.'

Mummy's voice wobbles. 'Please don't hurt her. . .'

'You want another fucking lesson?'

She flinches back.

'Didn't think so. Hold the kid's arm still.'

Jenny watches the shiny needle. It glints and sparkles in the sunshine. Out on the beach. A picnic with egg sandwiches, sausage rolls and Daddy. He lifts her up onto his shoulders and charges into the sea, laughing. Mummy waves from the sand.

The scratchy bee stings.

30

The bear crinkled its top lip. 'What? Do I look like your fuckin' mother?' Its face was half fur, half scar tissue, the skin twisted into a permanent sneer.

Logan sneaked a look at the fridge. 'I don't know where it is.'

A smile. Not a *nice* smile, an I'm-going-to-bite-your-fucking-face-off smile. . . 'You better hope that's—'

The bear's tummy started singing. 'Shite. . .'

'Jenny's toe has to go back in the fridge.' Logan blinked. Darkness. Blink. The pale green glow of the alarm-clock-radio turned the bedroom monochrome. The room had a funky, spice-garlic-and-bleach post-coital smell, socks and pants thrown about the place like a Roman orgy.

'Urgh. . .' Did the Romans wear pants under their togas?

His mobile was ringing.

'Bloody. . .' It took two goes to grab the thing.

Samantha grumbled and shifted in her sleep, mouth open just enough to expose the tip of her tongue and her top teeth. A snort. Smack, smack. Mumble.

Logan stabbed the button. *'What?'*

Yawn. He ground his right fist into his eye socket.

Silence.

Typical – that's what he got for handing out his CID business card to every smack-head junkie tosspot in the north-east of Scotland.

'I'm not running a sex line for mimes here. You either say something, or I'm hanging up in: five, four, three, two—'

'Fuckin' gave you the chance. . .'

Logan held the phone out and squinted at the little screen. 'UNKNOWN NUMBER'.

'Who is this?'

'Consequences. . . You know? Everything has fuckin' consequences.'

'Yeah, very funny. Now who the hell is. . .' He frowned. 'Shuggie Webster. It's *you*, isn't it? Next time I—'

The line went dead.

'Please. . .' Trisha Brown slumps back against the radiator. 'Please. . .'

Just that little movement sends sharp flashes of pain racing up her left leg, like some fucker's twisting screws into the broken bone.

Don't look at it.

But it's like a car crash, you know? Gotta look. Gotta see the blood and that.

Oh Jesus. . . The bit between her knee and her ankle is one huge fuck-off bruise, a lump, big as a scotch egg, sticking out the side. She wants to reach out and touch it, or pick at the scabbed bite marks on her ghost-white thighs. But she can't, not with both hands cuffed above her head. Naked and shackled, on display like meat in a butcher's shop.

She looks away.

It's a basement, or a garage, something like that. Boiler for the central heating, big chest freezer. Washing machine.

241

Shelves with tins and shit on them. No windows, just that fucking buzzing strip-light that he never turns off.

Her whole body *aches* and *stings* and *burns*. Cold and hot at the same time. Something deep inside her, torn and bleeding. Dirty.

She blinks back a tear. All that time down Shore Lane, making a bit of cash to keep herself in gear – and her little boy in them wee frozen pizzas he likes so much – and she never felt dirty before. Not like this.

How's Ricky supposed to manage now? Stuck with his bloody smack-head grandmother. Trisha thumps her head back against the radiator. The cool metal sounds like a muffled bell or something. She does it again. Harder. Grits her teeth. Slamming her head into the thing – at least if she knocks herself out it won't hurt any more.

It doesn't work.

'Maybe I should go off on the sick?' DS Doreen Taylor stared into her coffee, spreading out the red-and-silver foil wrapper from her Tunnock's Teacake on the canteen table, smoothing it to a shine with the back of her finger.

'Ah. . .' Bob nodded. 'Women's problems, eh?'

She didn't look up. '*No*. I just don't know if I can take another day with that sanctimonious git-bag Superintendent Green.' She sat up straight. 'There, I said it.'

Logan smiled. '"Git-bag"?'

'Well, he is.' The foil square was perfectly mirror smooth. She scrumpled it up into a ball. 'You know that Finnie and Bain are worried SOCA are going to take over the McGregor investigation?'

Bob nodded. 'They'll be all over us like Gary Glitter in an orphanage.'

'Don't be disgusting.' She dropped the foil ball in his empty mug. 'And they've no intention of taking over. I heard Green talking on his mobile last night – they won't touch this case with a bargepole. We've got nothing to go on: no leads, no witnesses, no forensics. If they move in they'll be just as stuck as we are.'

'Ah. . .' Logan stuck his mug back on the table. Winced slightly. His right arm ached – one huge mess of blue and purple and green where Shuggie Webster had pounded his fist into it. 'So when the deadline comes round on Thursday morning, and we've got no choice but to hand over the ransom money, they don't want to be the ones in charge.'

Doreen slumped over her coffee. 'Exactly: they point the finger at us for messing everything up, we get the blame, and they take over as soon as we get Alison and Jenny back.'

'Dirty bastards.' Bob stabbed the table with a finger. 'We do all the sodding about, and they swoop in and interview the only witnesses we're likely to get.' He raised one cheek off his seat, squinted an eye shut, then sighed. 'Right, I'm off.'

Bob disappeared, giggling.

The smell, when it hit, was like being battered around the head with a mouldy colostomy bag.

Rennie was waiting for Logan in the little makeshift office, sitting at the borrowed desk peering at the laptop's screen, his fingers rattling across the keys.

'You better not be messing about on some porn chat site.' Logan placed a wax-paper cup next to the mouse. 'Coffee. For not dumping me in it with Professional Standards.'

'Ooh, thanks, Sarge.' He creaked the plastic lid off and nodded at a small stack of paper. 'Been looking up kidnappings – got seven years' worth so far.'

Logan picked up the PNC printouts and leafed through them. 'Anything?'

'Nothing even *vaguely* like the McGregors. There's not as many legit kidnappings as you'd think – with proper ransom notes and stuff – most are drug dealers getting nabbed by rivals, a couple of silly sods kidnapping themselves for the attention, and about a dozen tigers.' He raised an eyebrow. Probably waiting to be asked what a 'tiger' was.

Tough.

Logan dumped the pile on the desk. 'What about older cases?'

'You know: when you abduct someone's family, 'cos you want them to help you rob their bank or something?'

'You want me to take that coffee back?'

'Just trying to—'

'Rennie!'

A sigh. 'I've got an appointment with the force historian at ten. She's got a bunch of stuff booked out for an exhibition she's putting on.'

'Good. While you're there, see if you can't go back another ten years, just to be on the safe side.' Whatever shite-storm Napier was whipping up with SOCA, no one was going to accuse Logan of not being thorough.

The constable groaned. 'Can we not stick this stuff on the back burner for a bit? I mean, I could help you interview Alison's student mates instead? Maybe we can crack the case: get Alison and Jenny back before Superintendent Soapy-Tit-Wank takes it off us?' He struck a pose, one hand on his chest, the other reaching out towards the manky ceiling tiles. 'Rennie and McRae save the day!' A grin. 'Hey, that rhymes.'

Logan chewed on the inside of his lip. 'You want to help interview everyone on Alison McGregor's course?'

Nod.

'OK, you can.'

'Woot!' Rennie punched the air. 'Thanks, Sarge!'

'Just as soon as you've finished digging stuff out of the archives.'

'Nope.' Sergeant Eric Mitchell looked up from his computer screen, then ran a finger through his oversized moustache, sunlight glinting off his bald head. 'Everything's booked out.'

'How can everything be booked out?' Logan tried to peer at the screen, but Eric twisted it away.

'Finnie's got everyone off interviewing doctors and vets again, *that's* why. Take a bus like normal people. Or get a taxi.'

'Right. A taxi. You ever tried to claim one of those back on expenses?'

'So walk.'

'To Hillhead?'

'Ahem. . .' The voice came from just over Logan's shoulder. 'Perchance I can be of assistance, young Logie? I happen to be going that way myself.'

Logan closed his eyes. 'I'm not sharing a car with you, Bob.'

'I'll let you drive?' Bob jangled a set of keys at him. 'Come on, what's the worst that could happen?'

Logan climbed out into the cool morning and slammed the pool car's door shut. Hauled in a lungful of clean air.

Bob got out of the other side. 'What? I opened the window, didn't I?'

'You need medical help. Or a bloody cork.'

'Better out than in, as my granny always said.' He stood and stared up at the soulless collection of Stalin-style concrete apartment blocks, then bit at his top lip. 'Don't fancy coming in with me, do you? I fucking hate suicides.'

'Thought you took the body in yesterday?'

'Yeah, but. . .' He shuffled his shoulders beneath his shiny grey suit jacket. 'Murder's different: something horrible happened and we catch whatever sick bastard did it. Make sure the victim gets justice. With suicide, they're the same person.' He sniffed. 'Don't tell me it's not creepy. Bloody depressing too.'

The room wasn't huge, just enough space for a single bed, a built-in wardrobe, a little table and one chair. A pair of bookshelves sat above the desk, full of dog-eared medical textbooks. The obligatory Monet, Klimt, and *Star Wars* posters. A copy of *FHM* lay on the floor by the bed. 'KAREN GETS THEM OUT! IS THERE A DOCTOR IN THE HOUSE?'

The little window looked out onto yet another block of student accommodation. Pale and drab and lifeless.

'Bruce Sangster, twenty-one. Got pissed on Highland Park, then shot himself full of morphine, tied a plastic bag over his head, never woke up again.' Bob tucked his hands into his armpits. 'Twenty-one and you go do that to yourself. What a fucking waste.'

Whisky, opiates, and suffocation. It wasn't a cry for help: whatever Bruce Sangster was running away from he'd made bloody sure it wasn't going to catch him. How could anyone's life be *so* bad they'd just throw it all away?

Bob shuddered. 'Was going to be a doctor. . .'

Medical textbooks and lads' mags weren't the only reading material in the place. There was a little pile of *Heat*, *Hello!*, *Now* and *OK!*: 'ALISON'S SECRET SCHOOLGIRL SHAME: "I WAS A TEENAGE TEARAWAY", ADMITS BNBS SEMI-FINALIST.'

DI Steel had got it word perfect. Which was worrying.

Logan picked the magazine up and skimmed through all the cheesy smiles, fake tan, flock wallpaper and chandeliers, until he got to Alison McGregor's photo. She was sitting in her living room, looking off into the middle distance, holding that framed portrait of Doddy in his uniform. Hair:

immaculate, make-up: perfect, dressed in a silky top that managed to be respectable and revealing at the same time.

No doubt about it, she was a very attractive woman. Very, *very* attractive.

The article seemed to be about her admitting she'd done everything Vicious Vikki accused her of. And more. Acting out because her foster parents couldn't relate to her on an emotional level, whatever the hell that meant. Then she'd met Doddy and discovered she wasn't a horrible person after all and there was more to life than drinking, smoking, and vandalizing bus shelters. Along came the little miracle that was Jenny growing inside her, then the tragedy of losing Doddy's parents, a fairytale wedding, the birth. . .

Tearaway turns her life around, becomes a loving wife and a devoted mum, Doddy dies in Iraq, Alison gets on *Britain's Next Big Star* to honour his memory, and the rest is history.

More shots of Alison and Jenny at home, then. . . Logan frowned. The next two pages were stuck together. They came apart with a ripping sound, and there was a photo of Alison at the beach, wearing a yellow bikini, smiling at the camera, one hand behind her head, Jenny building a sandcastle at her feet. There were bits of the opposite page stuck to Alison's stomach chest and face.

Bob appeared at his shoulder. 'Someone got a bit excited. . .'

Logan dumped the magazine in the bin. 'What the hell's wrong with people?'

'Give the kid a break. Like you've never entertained a five-fingered shuffle over a photo of some half-naked bird.'

'There was a wee girl in the pic, Bob.'

He curled his top lip. 'Aye, I'll give you that.'

Maybe that's what he'd been running away from?

'Sangster leave a note?'

'Yeah, the usual. I'm sorry, I couldn't take it any more, I've let everyone down. . .' Bob shook his head, then settled on the edge of the bed. 'Do you have any idea how often people write *exactly* the same thing? Their last words on earth, and they're sorry they let everyone down. How fucked up is that?' He ran a hand through his hair, until he got to the bald patch at the back. 'At least I'm not doing the death notice this time, some poor sod in York can tell Bruce's parents he couldn't live up to their expectations. . . I fucking hate suicides.'

Logan looked around the room. 'So, come on then – why *are* you here? We've got no suspicious circumstances: why aren't the GED dealing with it?'

'They are. I'm not here because Bruce's dead – apparently Finnie doesn't care about that. What Finnie *does* care about is where Bruce got the morphine from. Controlled substance. Must be someone dealing on campus.' Bob raised his chin. 'So now I've got to go tell all of Bruce's mates he's dead, and ask them, "Are you a drug dealer?"' He pulled a sheet of paper from his jacket pocket and passed it over. 'Got them off his phone and laptop contacts. Don't fancy helping do you?'

Fat chance.

Logan skimmed the names. 'Think I did Liam Christie for stealing shop mannequins last year. Silly sod said he was building a plastic army to overthrow our reptilian overlords. Bloody medical students are always the worst. . .' He stopped, then pulled a list from his own pocket. Double checked the names and addresses. 'You're in luck, Bob – I'm speaking to some of these guys today anyway.'

'Do us a favour: ask them if they're doing a bit of dealing to pay their way through university, eh?'

Logan threw Bob's list back at him. 'We can sort out what it's going to cost you later.'

31

'It's just, like, can the world *get* any worse?' Another poky little room – this time plastered with *Twilight* posters and featuring a life-sized cardboard cut-out of the vampire bloke with the greasy hair. Tanya Marsden dabbed at her pink eyes, sniffed, then worried the paper hanky into tiny scraps with bony fingers. 'I mean, first Alison, and now poor Bruce. It's like, the whole university's been placed under some evil curse. . .' She stared at Logan from the depths of a dark, floppy fringe.

'How well did you know Bruce, Miss Marsden?'

'Please, call me Tiggy. We used to role play together: AD&D, a bunch of us, you know, got a group together in first year. Most of them just drifted away. . . But Bruce hung in till last Christmas – too much studying to do. I like Bruce. He was a good friend, you know?'

'And did he ever speak to you about drugs?'

'For real? No *way*. Bruce is going to be a doctor. . .' She looked down at the shredded paper in her hands. '*Was* going to be a doctor. He was super smart, there's no way he'd risk getting kicked out of uni.'

'Did he say anything to you in the last couple of weeks? Anything that might explain why he did it?'

Her shoulders quivered. 'I should've done something. I mean, what's the point of doing psychology if you can't even help a friend? He was always working, you know? Always had his head in a textbook, never went to the pub. . .' She bit her bottom lip, blinked, then rubbed a hand across her eyes. 'I'm sorry. . .'

Logan sat back in the plastic chair and watched her sniff. That was the trouble with psychology students, the little sods were being *taught* how to manipulate other people. Of course, they didn't call it that, they called it Neuro-Linguistic Programming, and things like that. The kind of thing Rennie was trying to pull with the sex offenders.

'So, you knew Alison McGregor, eh? Must've been hard for her – single mum, studying, raising a little girl, rehearsing, being on the telly?'

She rolled her eyes and laughed, a short, brittle sound. 'Oh God, yes. But she was terrific, seriously, like a *total* inspiration. We were thick as thieves, Alison and me, complete BFFs. Used to crib each other's lecture notes, if one of us couldn't make it and that.'

'Uh-huh.' Logan wrote the word 'Liar' next to Tanya Marsden's name in his notebook. Every single student he'd talked to had sworn they were Alison McGregor's bestest friend. Jumping on the D-lebrity bandwagon and fighting over the seats: look at me, I know the kidnapped woman and her tortured daughter!

'I can't believe this happened. . .' The tears were back. 'They'll let them go, right? Alison and Jenny? I mean, there's got to be millions in the fund by now – that's got to be enough.'

'She was just the best person I'd ever met.' Jade Shepley sighed. 'Wow. To just, I mean, *imagine* what she must be going through.' She furrowed her brow. Barely nineteen and she was already wearing a twinset-and-pearls, hair cut into a sensible bob, Velma-from-Scooby-Doo glasses.

Her room was decorated with yet another collection of posters: Audrey Hepburn – *Breakfast at Tiffany's*; a kitten in a tree – 'SOMETIMES MONDAY LASTS ALL WEEK'; and a couple advertising am-dram musical productions.

'It's such a horrible thing to happen. Poor Alison. . .' Jade lent closer and lowered her voice to a whisper. 'We were best of friends, you know.'

'Oh no, I can't think of *anyone* who'd want to hurt her.' Phillipa McEwan blinked, bit her bottom lip, stared at her hands. 'Alison was just the *loveliest* person in the whole world. She was always popping past to talk about how her day went, or borrow a book or something.' Posters: *Harry Potter and the Order of the Phoenix*; Zebedee from the *Magic Roundabout*; Einstein sticking his tongue out. 'There's not a day I don't pray for her.'

'Actually, she was a complete bitch.' Stephen Clayton sprawled in the room's only seat, leaving Logan to stand. Posters: Coldplay; Yoda; U2; David Tennant getting his sonic screwdriver out, with the TARDIS in the background – signed; and the classic *Jurassic Park* logo. A remote-control Dalek sat on the floor, next to a wastepaper basket overflowing with scrunched up empty Cheesy Wotsits packets.

Clayton cracked open a tin of Red Bull and gulped at it. Belched. Skull-and-crossbones earring, T-shirt with cannabis leaf motif, stud in the nose, blond hair down to the middle of his back.

Ooh, look at me, I'm such a rebel.

'And why was that?'

Clayton curled his top lip. 'Why do you think? Always swanning about like she was fucking royalty.' His voice jumped an octave. '"Oh, I'm on TV, I'm so *special*, so much *better* than the rest of you ordinary little plebs." Bitch.' He brushed the hair from his face. 'Stuck up, holier than thou, lying, two-faced bitch.'

So predictable.

'She turned you down.' Logan tried not to smile.

'Like *she* was such a fucking catch with a wee kid in tow. Who wants lumbered with that?' Another scoof of caffeinated sugar. 'Was doing her a favour.'

Yeah, you and your grow-your-own-moustache kit.

'So, this kidnapping thing: you think she deserved what she got?'

Clayton's face soured. 'You're kidding, right? When they let her go she's going to be worse than ever. Everyone'll be falling over themselves to lick her arse, like she's Richard Hammond and Princess Fucking Di all rolled into one. Getting kidnapped was the best thing that ever happened to that manipulative cow.'

'No, I didn't know Bruce had killed himself. That's. . . That's just terrible.' Craig Peterson sat on the end of the bed and stroked the little tuft of beard that clung onto his chin. Throw in the big nose, floppy curly brown hair and furrowed eyebrows, and he looked like a vaguely disappointed goat. Posters: *Reservoir Dogs*; Hitchcock's *North by Northwest*; *War of the Worlds* – the Orson Welles version, not the Tom Cruise one; Marc Caro and Jean-Pierre Jeunet's *La Cité des Enfants Perdus*. 'I mean, I knew he'd been a bit stressed recently – what with trying to catch up with his coursework and Tanya dumping him – but *suicide*? Why wouldn't he come speak to me? He must've known I could have helped him.'

'Tanya?' Logan flipped a few pages back in his notebook. 'Tanya Marsden?'

More beard stroking. 'Likes to call herself "Tiggy" for some reason. I tried to tell Bruce she wasn't his type, but *"l'oeil de l'amoureux est aveugle à tout défaut".'*

Oh, to be young and pretentious.

So Tanya Marsden and Bruce Sangster had been an item – she'd kept that quiet.

'I see. . .' Logan underlined the word 'LIAR' next to her name a few more times.

'Molière – it means "the lover's eye is blind to all fault."'

'Does it now.' He moved on a couple of pages and wrote 'PATRONIZING PRICK' next to Peterson's. 'Did he ever say anything to you about drugs?'

'Well. . . Off the record?'

Logan smiled. 'No.'

'I wouldn't want his parents to get the wrong idea, they had very high hopes for him.'

'But?'

'Where do you stand on the subject of cannabis, Sergeant?'

Logan just stared at him, letting the silence stretch.

A big sigh. 'Look, Bruce might have said something about hooking up with a woman when he was down in Dundee at one of those Dungeons and Dragons conventions last year. This person – Bruce always called her "Stumpy the Dwarven Queen" – was getting him cannabis, amyl nitrate – poppers, maybe some speed if it was coming up to exam time and Bruce needed to cram. And Bruce always needed to cram.'

'Stumpy the *Dwarven Queen*?'

Peterson folded his arms, then crossed his legs. 'Look, I'm really not comfortable talking about a dead friend behind his back, so if you'd like to save the sarcastic tones until you get back to the station, Sergeant, that'd be fine with me.'

'Sarcastic tone, Mr Peterson? I *think* you'll find I'm just trying to get to the bottom of a suspicious death. Surely that's worth treading on a few sensibilities?'

The student's nose came up. 'You can't "tread" on sensibilities, you have to "offend" them.'

Logan smiled. 'If you insist: where were you yesterday afternoon between the hours of twelve and five?'

'What?' His eyes went wide. 'My God, you're actually serious. You think Bruce was *murdered*?'

'And if you can give me the names and addresses of anyone who can confirm your whereabouts, that'll be a great help.' You arrogant little prick.

There was a bit of bluster, some self-righteous indignation, but eventually Peterson handed over the details of two friends who were with him most of the day watching DVDs and being pretentious. Logan took down the details. 'Now: tell me about Alison McGregor.'

Peterson opened his mouth, puckered his forehead, then clamped his lips together. 'Sorry?'

'You were in the same psychology class as her.'

'Well, yes. . . I mean, I went over all this with an Inspector McPherson—'

'And now you're going to go over it again.' Logan shifted forward in the seat, getting close enough to make Peterson edge back, until his back was up against the wall.

'I never really knew her. I mean, I knew who she was – well it'd be difficult not to when there's paparazzi hanging about outside the lecture theatre – but we never really talked. I tend to be very campus orientated, and she lived on the other side of town, so I didn't really see that much of her. Outside lectures and tutorials. Maybe a couple of times in the library.' He rubbed a hand at the side of his neck. 'It's terrible, what's happened, but I didn't really know her. She seemed really popular. . .?'

Logan just sat there and stared at him.

'Lots of friends? Especially when there were photographers about. I think some of the girls had a pool running on who could get their faces in the papers the most. You know, by talking to her while she was being snapped. . .'

More silence.

'Erm. . .' He licked his lips. 'Look, I never really knew her, OK?'

'I see.' Logan didn't move.

'And I've got studying to do. So if there's nothing—'

The *Danse macabre* blared out from Logan's pocket. He pulled it out and hit the button. 'McRae.'

'Sarge?' Rennie. *'Where are you? I'm in the car park.'*

Logan glanced up at Peterson. It wouldn't hurt to take the patronizing little sod down a notch or two. 'Yes, I'm speaking to him now.'

'Eh? You in the pub already?'

'No, he claims he,' Logan checked his notebook, smothered a smile, '"never really knew her."'

'Knew. . .? Ah – I get it. OK.'

'That's right. Says he has an alibi for the Bruce Sangster death too.'

Peterson shifted from cheek to cheek.

'I got everything you wanted from the archives, so I'm out at Hillhead, ready to crack the McGregor case!'

Logan stared at Craig Peterson until the student looked away. 'No, I think I'll take care of it personally.'

'Where do you want me to start?'

'Stay where you are.' Logan hung up and slid the phone back in his pocket. Then stood. 'We'll be in touch, Mr Peterson.' He leant forward, looming, and the student shrank back again. 'Don't leave town; remember I'll be watching you.'

Rennie leant back against a filthy Vauxhall, pink face raised to the sun, hands in his pockets, little white cables dangling from his ears, eyes closed.

Logan poked him in the shoulder. 'How did you get a pool car?'

'Eh?' He took out his earbuds. 'Oh, hi, Sarge. Did he cough? Whoever you were noising up?'

'Bloody Eric told me all the cars were booked!'

'Really? He was fine with me. Maybe—'

'What happened with the archives?'

'Not a lot. Couple of idiots kidnapped a jeweller's daughter; animal rights activists dug up someone's mum and demanded an end to animal testing at the Rowett; gang grabbed the wife and kids of a bank manager in Ellon so he'd let them in to loot the place. . .' Rennie stared off into the middle distance. 'Oh-ho, hold your breath, here comes Biohazard.'

Bob was shambling out of the block of student accommodation opposite, jacket over his shoulder, shirtsleeves rolled up to expose two forearms so hairy it looked as if he was wearing a furry pullover. He waved, then ambled over.

Logan turned, looking up at the block behind them. The one where, with any luck, Craig Peterson was currently crapping himself. 'Waste of time then.'

'Sorry, Sarge.' Rennie rubbed his hands together. 'So, come on – who were you winding up?'

'Jesus, I bloody hate students. Bunch of animals. . .' Bob had a scratch at his pelt, then nodded at Rennie. 'Constable, what a happy coincidence! I've got a big list of tosspots who need interviewed.'

Rennie shook his head. 'Sorry, Guv, but I'm officially DS McRae's minion till Friday. We're grilling Alison McGregor's classmates. McRae and Rennie, at the ready!'

Bob raised his arms to the sky, then let them fall back to his sides with a theatrical groan. 'Logie, you'll let me borrow the loon, won't you?'

'Nope. Soon as we're done here we have a nationwide search on historic kidnappings to wade through.'

'Aw, come on – we could divvy up Bruce's mates. Three of us, we'd get through them in no time.'

'Goodbye, Bob. . .' Logan took a step away, then stopped, turned, and went back to the car. 'You might want to keep an eye on one Tanya "Tiggy" Marsden. According to Craig Peterson she was Bruce's girlfriend, but she says they were just friends.'

Bob raised one side of his monobrow. 'Oh aye, trying to distance herself after the fact? Think she's his dealer?'

'Doubt it.' Logan told him about Stumpy the Dwarven Queen.

A grimace. 'That's sod all use. . .' The grimace turned into a smile. 'Still, at least it takes the source off our patch – I can fob it off on Tayside. I was going to renege on buying you that pint, but I've changed my mind. Now lend us the wee loon here, and I'll throw in a packet of crisps.'

Logan looked back up at the block of student flats. Someone was staring back down at them. Craig Peterson, stroking his billy-goat beard. Logan made a gun from his thumb and forefinger, pointed it at Peterson, then shot him in the face.

32

Logan made a special point of checking up on Peterson's alibi. Adrian Kerr: MSc E-Commerce Technology; posters of *The Muppet Show*, *China Town*, a football team composed of half-naked women. Nicholas Tawse: Psychology; *Citizen Kane*, Che Guevara, Monty Python's Flying Circus.

They both backed up Peterson's story – of course – but it was still fun to make the stuck-up little sods squirm. Petty, but fun.

Logan met up with Rennie back in the car park.

'Anything?'

'Thought a couple were a bit dodgy – one was trying to hide a home-made bong, the other got all gooey-eyed every time I mentioned Alison and Jenny's names. Swear to God, she had a shrine to them above her bed. Newspaper clippings, magazine articles, signed photos, the lot. I think there was a lock of hair too.'

'Hair?'

'Not, like a scalp or anything.'

'Nobody else?'

'Nah, mostly they're just students. Bit of weed, bit of

booze, bit of studying, bit of pining away in their rooms wondering why nobody wants to shag them.'

'Right, let's go pay Alison and Jenny's biggest fan a visit.'

Good God. . . Rennie hadn't been kidding – there really *was* a shrine above Beatrice Eastbrook's bed. Right in the middle of the wall was an amateurish watercolour portrait of Alison McGregor, Jenny sitting on her knee. Alison had a tinfoil halo that glimmered in the light of two big church candles, arranged either side of a lock of curly blonde hair in a little glass box, tied with a black ribbon and a sprig of heather. Just like the one on Alison's photo of her dead husband.

Around the icon, a sea of newsprint and magazine articles spread out like a tumour. 'MY SECRET FEARS FOR JENNY – WILL FAME DESTROY HER CHILDHOOD?', 'NORTH-EAST MUM THROUGH TO BNBS SEMI-FINAL', 'ALISON'S SECRET SCHOOLGIRL SHAME: "I WAS A TEENAGE TEARAWAY", ADMITS BNBS SEMI-FINALIST', 'SHE'S NO ANGEL – THE SKELETONS LURKING IN ALISON MCG'S CLOSET'. . .

That last one had a photo of Victoria Murray, AKA Vicious Vikki, on it, her face scrubbed out with angry red biro, until the paper was tattered and sliced through, the word 'LIAR!!!' scrawled across the article over and over again.

And around the edge, a series of glossy photos – the kind you could get printed at pretty much any supermarket these days.

No posters: there wasn't room.

Beatrice Eastbrook would probably have looked like a perfectly normal person a year ago. But. . . She'd dyed her hair blonde, and had it curled to look exactly like Alison McGregor's. Her make-up was exactly like Alison McGregor's. Her clothes were exactly like Alison McGregor's, right down to the shoes.

259

Probably had a tinfoil-lined hat lying about the place somewhere too.

She twirled the hair behind her ear. 'Of course I didn't hurt them, why would I hurt them? I love them.' The accent was hard to place, a weird mix of Birmingham and Aberdeen – as if it wasn't enough to look like Alison McGregor, she was trying to sound like her too. 'Alison was . . . is – fantastic. A superstar. I mean, can you imagine it, someone like that living in Aberdeen, and I *know* her. She *talked* to me, like a real person.'

'And you've no idea who might have taken her?'

Beatrice's eyes narrowed. 'If I did, I'd kill them. I'm not joking – I'd *literally* kill them. Strangle them with my own hands. They cut off Jenny's toes! What kind of bastard cuts off a little girl's toes?' She sank back onto the bed and shuffled back, feet on the duvet, knees against her chest. 'You know what, when you catch them, you should cut off *their* toes, like in the Bible. Cut them all off and see how *they* like it.'

'Did you see anyone strange hanging around her, before she went missing? Trying to talk to her?' Other than yourself, of course, you card-carrying nutjob.

'I don't remember. Not that I noticed. Well, you know it was always pretty busy, with the photographers hounding her all the time and those bitches pretending to be her friend, just so they could get in the papers. *I* never did that. . .'

Logan nodded. 'What did she think of your new look?'

A frown. 'Well, she was flattered, obviously. Said I looked lovely. She's a very generous and giving person.'

'And she didn't mind when you followed her home?'

Standing at the door, Rennie opened his mouth, but Logan held up a hand.

'I. . .' Beatrice blushed. 'I don't know what you—'

'The photos around the outside of your mural.' He pointed at the glossy pics. 'That's Alison's and Jenny's house in Kincorth. Look, there's Alison putting the recycling out.'

'I. . . It was only once.'

'And there she is taking Jenny to school. And in that one Jenny's wearing a tutu. Off to dance classes?'

Beatrice rested her head on her knees, speaking into the little hidden gap between them and her chest. 'I wasn't hurting anyone.'

Logan put his notebook down on the desk. 'Did you see who took Alison and Jenny?'

When she looked up, her eyes glittered with tears. 'I just wanted to be her *friend*. A real friend, not like those two-faced bitches.'

'Did you see who took them, Beatrice?'

'She's someone special. She's famous – she'll leave a mark on the earth that says she was here. I'm *never* going to be famous. Don't matter if I live or die, does it? Don't matter if I was never even born. I just thought, if she could see we had so much in common, we could be friends. I just wanted her to like me. . .'

'It's OK, Beatrice, I understand.' Logan picked up his notebook and stood. 'Now, if it's all right with you, we'd like to search your room. Is that OK?'

She wiped her eyes, then looked up at the lock of hair in its little glass box. Licked her lips. 'What do you think they'll do with Jenny's toes?'

'Of course, I spotted those photos the first time,' Rennie hauled the pool car's boot open and dumped a handful of evidence bags inside, each one filled, dated, labelled and signed for, 'just didn't want to prejudice your first impressions.' He clunked the boot closed again.

'Don't be a dick.' Logan climbed into the passenger seat.

'Fair enough.' Rennie got behind the wheel. 'Worth a try though.' Grin. 'Back to the ranch?'

'Yeah, then I want you to go through every photo on that camera and laptop. We're looking for someone watching Alison McGregor's house.'

'Other than Beatrice McFruitloop, you mean.' He started the engine. 'How the hell did she manage to get into university? Psychology degree? Talk about "physician heal thy-bloody-self".'

'Maybe she's good at exams. Just make sure— buggering hell.' Logan's phone was ringing. He pulled it out. 'McRae.'

'Told you there'd be consequences.' Shuggie Webster, sounding stoned out of his box. *'You happy now? You fucking happy?'*

'Shuggie, you've got to turn yourself in. Turn yourself in and we'll talk about it.'

'It's your fault!'

Logan checked the display – not the same number as before. 'Where are you?'

'Consequences.' And then Shuggie hung up.

Rennie was looking at him. 'Sarge?'

'Back to the ranch.' Logan dragged out his Airwave handset, dialled Control and told them to get a GSM trace set up on Shuggie's new mobile. If Sheriff McNab gave them a warrant, and the phone company didn't drag its heels, they'd know where Mr Consequences was before clocking off time.

He stuck the handset back in his pocket and watched the halls of residence fade in the rearview mirror. Consequences. . . Then his mobile started ringing again. It was Colin Miller from the *Aberdeen Examiner*. *'Got another note.'*

Logan clutched at the grab handle as Rennie juddered the pool car out of the junction and onto King Street. 'Are you *trying* to shake the fillings out of my head?'

262

'Laz?'

'Yeah, sorry, Colin. What are they saying? Let me guess: you have two days left or Jenny will die?'

'No, it's no' from them. Look, we've been gettin' in dozens of fake ransom demands every day since this kicked off, right? All fuckin' mentalists wantin' us tae drop off a few hundred thou in a bin bag in Torry, that kinda shite. Well today we got one that wasnae all about Jenny and Alison.'

Silence.

'Are you waiting for me to guess what it says, Colin?'

'OK, OK. It says, "Trisha Brown has a little boy called Ricky. If you ever want him to see his mummy alive, you'll start raisin' money now. If you can do it for that showbiz bitch, you can do it for me." That last bit's in italics, with three exclamation points, but.'

Oh . . . fuck. 'Did they say how much and where?'

'Aye: "I want a hundred and fifty thousand. Pocket money compared to how much that bitch is gettin' – take it out of her pot if you like. I don't care. Five days. Or she dies." Note's got blood on it.'

Logan tapped his knuckles against the car window.

'You still there?'

'What are you doing about it? You printing it?'

'That's kinda where you come in. The Examiner doesnae want tarred with that "encouraging copycat crimes" brush your guvnor likes slappin' about. Last thing we need's another run-in with them pricks on the Press Complaints Commission after the whole Bondage-gate fiasco.'

Consequences.

Shuggie Webster, you silly, silly bastard. Did he actually think they were going to fall for that one? Kidnap his own girlfriend, send a note to the papers, ransom her for enough to pay off their drug debt and set the pair of them up on the Costa del Sol for the next couple of years.

'Laz?'

'I'll get someone over to pick up the note.'

'Aye, but should we print—'

Logan hung up.

'Boss?'

Logan looked up from the stack of interview forms. PC Guthrie was standing in the doorway of the little office, one hand behind his back, the other stroking his trouser leg as if it was nervous and needed comforting. Logan went back to his paperwork. 'You'll go blind if you don't stop doing that.'

'Got that note from the *Aberdeen Examiner*, you want it?' Guthrie held up a clear evidence bag.

Logan closed his eyes. 'No, I don't *want* it. I want you to take it up to the third floor and get the IB to—'

'Already done it. They lifted prints off the envelope and the note: Bill's running them now. Blood's off to the lab, for analysis.'

'Already?'

A nod. 'Rennie said you needed it urgently, so. . .?'

'They got prints?'

'Three partials and one beauty from the note, Bill says it's a near-perfect right thumb.'

See, that was the difference between professionals – like the ones who snatched Alison and Jenny – and idiot copycats like Shuggie Webster and Trisha Brown.

'Good, thanks Allan. Do me a favour, go chase up the GSM trace on Shuggie Webster's phone. Who knows, we might actually get a result for a change.'

Soon as Guthrie waddled off like a happy penguin, Logan finished typing up his interview notes. Then checked them against the ones DI McPherson had done. From the look of things McPherson had taken over the campus canteen and arranged for a team of DCs to go through all of Alison's classmates in alphabetical order. Which meant whoever interviewed Beatrice 'Single White Female' Eastbrook had no idea about the stalker's shrine on her bedroom wall.

The one thing McPherson's team *had* done well was to get information from the university on each of the students' performance, along with some comment from the department head and a couple of the lecturers. Apparently Beatrice was reasonably dedicated, if a little prone to daydreaming, and not the most original thinker in the world. A mediocre student who could perhaps scrape a 2.2 if she really applied herself.

Logan read to the end, then flipped the form over again. McPherson's team didn't seem to have checked for criminal records.

Logan logged onto the PNC and ran a search against her name. Just in case.

Three warnings for vandalism, one for sending threatening letters. According to West Midlands Police, Beatrice had taken exception to a mother of two asking her to stop bothering her family. There was talk of a restraining order and that seemed to put an end to it. So Beatrice wasn't new to the creepy stalker game.

Maybe she'd decided it would be a lot less effort to kidnap Alison and Jenny than follow them about the whole time? And Alison was going to be more famous than ever when she finally got released. . . Maybe it was all some twisted attempt to help her?

Beatrice Eastbrook wasn't really the gang-leader-criminal-mastermind type, but Logan picked up the phone and got a patrol car organized to bring her in to 'help with their enquiries' anyway. Maybe get Goulding to sit in on the questioning? A bit of steamy psychologist-on-psychologist action.

Then he went back to the list of Alison McGregor's classmates.

The PNC check on Tanya 'Tiggy' Marsden came back clean, even if she had lied about being Bruce's girlfriend.

According to his lecturers, Stephen Clayton was a straight A student, but his name returned a list of petty crimes from when he was eight all the way up to the age of fourteen. Nothing serious, probably just enough to give mummy and daddy 'look-at-me!' palpitations. Which would explain the carefully-crafted rebellious cliché appearance and attitude.

Logan ran PNC checks on everyone in Alison's class, then added the results to his interview notes.

Rennie grunted and dumped a file box on top of the pile. 'And that's the lot. . .' Frown. 'Oh poo.' He wiped at the dust greying his shirt and trousers. 'Emma's going to kill me.'

Their little makeshift office was starting to look a lot more professional – if you ignored the dusty plastic sheeting covering the bare walls, pipes, and conduits. They now had three desks and a trestle table, the latter beginning to sag under the weight of Rennie's file boxes. Three phones, two laptops, and a printer that sounded like a creaky floorboard every time they sent a file to it.

Logan swivelled his seat around. 'Kidnappings?'

'Five years ago.' He pointed at a small stack of pristine files. 'Ten years ago, fifteen, and these dirty old sods are twenty. But that's just the north-east – be months before we get stuff that old from everywhere else.'

'Probably more than we need anyway. Now go see if they've got that GSM trace done yet.'

The constable flounced over to his desk, sank into his chair, and grabbed the phone.

'Sergeant?'

Logan looked up from his screen. Finnie was standing in the open doorway, his rubbery lips turned down at the edges, eyes narrowed. He looked like a constipated frog.

Green must have been moaning again.

'Afternoon, sir – I was just about to go looking for you, we—'

'I understand there's another ransom note come in.'

'Trisha Brown, she's the one involved with Shuggie Webster. Looks like—'

'And may I *enquire* why you didn't see fit to inform me?'

'I did.'

Finnie frowned. 'I think I would've noticed if—'

'Emailed you as soon as we got back to the station. I think you were in with Superintendent Green at the time. The kidnapping's probably a hoax – Shuggie and Trisha's way of wriggling out of a drug debt.'

'Oh.' Finnie swapped the folder under his arm from one side to the other. 'Yes, well, in that case,' he held the folder out. 'I was going to give the investigation to Acting DI MacDonald, but you can keep it.'

'Thank you, sir.' Logan took the folder and peered inside. It was the fingerprint report. 'I've requested a firearms team. If you can approve it, we'll get Shuggie Webster picked up as soon as the GSM trace comes in. He isn't exactly—'

'Just make sure I have a complete risk analysis on my desk before you do anything. And by the book, understand? The last thing we need is Green getting the idea we can't do *anything* right.'

'Already working on it, sir.'

'And speaking of Superintendent Green. . .'

Here we go.

Finnie pursed his lips, looking over Logan's left shoulder. 'Professional Standards tell me Green's been throwing his weight around with some sex offenders? That you're thinking of putting in an official complaint.'

'I am?' Logan backed away a step. 'Sir, I didn't—'

'I think it would be wise to put it all in writing, Sergeant.'

'Actually, sir, I was going to drop—'

'I think it would be *wise* to put it all in *writing*, Sergeant.'

He cleared his throat. 'Yes, sir.'

A smile. 'Now, how are you getting on with your due diligence?'

'Actually, it—'

'And the sooner you put it in writing the better.'

Rennie took the phone from his ear and clamped a hand over the mouthpiece. 'Sarge? Got a result on the GSM trace. Webster's in Tillydrone.'

'Excellent.' Finnie headed for the door. 'Tell you what: this time, Sergeant, just for fun, let's *try* not to let him escape. OK?'

Oh ha-bloody-ha.

Logan waited till the door shut before pulling the report from the folder: whorls, deltas, points of correlation, right thumb. . .

That wasn't right.

He turned the sheet over, then back over again. 'This is definitely the print off the ransom note?'

Rennie shrugged.

According to the database the thumb didn't belong to Shuggie Webster, it belonged to someone called Edward Buchan.

33

'Any questions?' Sweat trickled down Logan's ribs. The unmarked van was unbelievably warm inside, packed full of firearms-trained officers dressed in the traditional ninja ensemble of black trousers, boots, jackets, bulletproof vests, helmets, goggles, gloves, and scarves.

Rennie stuck his hand up. 'Are we allowed to shoot him?'

'No. You're not.' Logan pointed a finger, swept it around the muggy van. 'No shooting anyone, understand? This is going to be a clean operation – we go in, we subdue Edward Buchan, we rescue Trisha Brown, and we go home. Got it?'

Everyone nodded.

'Good. Teams One and Two: in the front. Teams Three and Four: back door. One and Three stay downstairs, Two and Four take the first floor. Weapons check.'

The harsh click and clack of slides being drawn back and released filled the van's interior. Logan ejected the magazine of his Heckler & Koch MP5, checked that all the rounds he'd signed for were still there, stuck it back in, then did the same with the small chunky Glock.

He looked up. 'We good to go?'

More nods.

'Doors.'

The two ninjas sitting at the back popped them open and they all swarmed out into the evening sunlight. Half-five and the sky was delicate sapphire blue, a white slash of cloud following an aeroplane on its way west.

A little kid on a scooter stopped at the end of the pavement, mouth hanging open, watching as the firearms team scurried into position. Edward Buchan's house was in the middle of a terrace of six two-storey buildings: grey harling on the ground floor, weatherboard cladding above that. The roof and first floor stretched from one end of the tenement to the other, but little passageways punched through between every other building, leading to the back gardens.

Teams Three and Four lumbered up the stairs and disappeared into the passageway: the sound of their heavy boots thumped back a distorted echo. Logan led Team One and Team Two up to the front door, motioning them to flatten out along the wall on either side.

It was less than two minutes' walk away from where Trisha Brown's mum lived.

Rennie's voice sounded in his earpiece. *'Sarge? You sure we shouldn't, you know, seal off the street and evacuate everyone?'*

Logan glanced back at the kid on the scooter. 'Element of surprise, remember? Don't want this turning into a hostage situation.'

He waved a large black-clad figure forward.

PC Caldwell slipped the holdall from her shoulder. 'Big Red Door Key?'

'In five.'

'Ferguson,' Logan pointed at the constable second in line, 'have you got the hoolie bar with you this time?'

The constable raised it above his head. 'Right here, Sarge.'

Wonders would never cease.

270

Logan clicked the button that transmitted to everyone in all four teams. 'And we're live in: five, four—'

PC Caldwell rested the tip of the battering ram against the front door, directly across from the lock. Glanced back over her shoulder. 'Watch and learn, Greg.'

'—one. GO!'

BOOM – the Big Red Door Key battered into the UPVC. The whole thing shook and juddered. The second blow landed two thirds of the way up, and this time the top half parted with the doorframe. The third blow was at ankle height and the whole thing crashed open – the hinges hanging broken, bent and twisted.

'We're in.'

Logan charged through into the hallway, the rest of Team One and Team Two swarming in behind him. 'POLICE: ARMED OFFICERS! ON THE GROUND NOW!' Stairs on the left, open door to the right, closed door at the far end through to what was probably the kitchen. No sign of anyone.

The sound of hammering came from the back of the house, then a crash and, 'POLICE! NOBODY MOVE!'

Logan burst through the open doorway, PC Caldwell right behind him. Living room: red carpet, two red sofas, yellow walls. Sort of a rhubarb and custard theme.

A man was sitting on the couch in front of the television, with a plate balanced on his lap, cutlery in his hands, staring at them. A baked bean dripped from the chunk of toast on the end of the fork, leaving a little bloodstain on his white T-shirt.

The rumble of boots came from the hallway, as Constables Ferguson and Moore charged up the stairs.

PC Caldwell pointed her submachine gun right between Mr Beans-On-Toast's eyes. 'DROP THE KNIFE!'

'Eek. . .' He dropped the knife. It bounced off the edge of his plate and went twirling to the carpet. He swallowed, sending a huge Adam's apple bobbing up and down his scrawny neck. 'I. . . I. . .'

'THE FORK TOO!'

Edward Buchan had aged a bit since his mugshot was taken – drink driving in the company Mondeo seven years ago. His dark hair was receding, hints of grey flecking the temples, the stubble on his pointy chin almost white beneath his long nose.

From upstairs came the sound of a scuffle. *'OW! FUCK. . .'* Then, *'ON THE BLOODY FLOOR!'*

Buchan glanced up towards the sound. 'We didn't—'

Logan hauled him off the couch, the plate of beans bouncing off the floor, sending them everywhere. 'ON YOUR KNEES, HANDS BEHIND YOUR HEAD!'

He assumed the position, trembling. 'Oh God, oh God, oh God. . .'

Caldwell grabbed Buchan's left wrist, twisted it around, slapped the handcuffs on, then did the same with his right, fastening them behind his back.

Logan towered over him. 'Where is she?'

'Oh God. . .'

'TRISHA BROWN! WHERE IS SHE?'

Buchan stared up at him, a drip forming on the end of his nose. 'I. . . I don't. . . Oh God. . .'

Rennie appeared in the doorway. 'House is clear, Sarge. We've got his missus upstairs: kneed Henderson right in the hairy-funbags. Searched the attic and the garden shed too. No sign of the victim.'

'I said, where – is – she?'

'I don't know, I really don't know.' He bit his bottom lip. 'Please.'

'You sent a ransom note to the *Aberdeen Examiner* – and don't pretend you didn't, the thing's covered in your fingerprints.'

272

Buchan stared at the bean-stained carpet. 'I didn't mean anything by it.'

'Didn't mean. . .? You wanted a hundred and fifty thousand pounds!' Logan poked him in the shoulder with the barrel of his H&K. 'Where is she?'

'I don't know! Someone took her.'

'Who? Who took her?'

'I was in the garden and she was staggering down the road and there was this car. And it pulled up and maybe they pretended they were asking for directions or something, but she goes over and the guy driving opens the passenger door and she gets in. I don't know, maybe she knew him?'

Buchan hunched his shoulders. 'And she's there for about a minute, then they argue or something. Then suddenly, for no reason, he punches her in the face, really hard, you know? She tried to get out of the car, but he dragged her back in. Hit her a couple more times. Then drove off. . .'

Logan stared at him. 'And you didn't *report* it?'

He sniffed. 'Linda thought we could, you know, if we sent in a ransom demand before anyone else did. . . I got made redundant last year, and ever since—'

'The note had blood on it.'

'It was on the road, after he drove off. Must've been when she tried to get out of the car. I . . . sort of rubbed the paper in it.'

'You saw a woman being assaulted and abducted, and instead of trying to *help* her, or calling the police, you sat down and figured out a way to make money out of it?' Logan curled his top lip. You nasty, opportunistic, crappy excuse for a human being. 'What did he look like?'

'I can't really—'

'What kind of car did he drive?'

'It was a sort of blue saloon thing, but I don't—'

'WHEN DID IT HAPPEN!'

Buchan flinched. 'It wasn't my fault, OK? She was a nightmare – her and her bloody mother, always nicking things so they could buy drugs. Lurching about pissed or stoned out of their brains. Shouting at people, swearing. They shouldn't be allowed to live near decent people!'

PC Caldwell grabbed the handcuffs and hauled Buchan to his feet. 'You're *not* decent people. Because of you her wee boy had to sleep on his own in a bloody wardrobe, in an empty house! She might be dead!' Caldwell gave the handcuffs another haul. 'Now answer the bloody question: when?'

'Ow! You're hurting me! Saturday, it was Saturday evening, after that tribute show for Alison and Jenny.' He stared at the carpet and its bloodspatter of beans. 'That's. . . That's sort of where we got the idea from.'

Logan couldn't look at him any more. 'Get him out of here.'

PC Caldwell shoved the trembling man towards the living room door. 'Edward Albert Buchan, I'm arresting you for attempting to pervert the course of justice. . .'

'Sarge?' Rennie let his MP5 dangle on the end of its strap. 'Might still be Shuggie, then? Maybe she wasn't cool with the plan so he smacked her about a bit. Wouldn't be the first time.' He paused, head on one side. 'Or *maybe* it was all staged, you know? Make sure there's a couple of witnesses and put on a show. They call the police, and that way when the papers get the ransom note it all looks legit!'

Logan looked down at the mess on the living room floor. Alison McGregor's face stared back at him from the cover of a glossy magazine. 'WHY I'M BACKING THE "HOPE FOR HEROES" CAMPAIGN.'

'There hasn't *been* a ransom note, remember? It was all that tosser Buchan.'

'Oh . . . right.'

'Saddle the troops. One body stays to watch the house, one takes the Buchans back to the station – I want an e-fit of whoever grabbed Trisha Brown. Everyone else back in the van. Let's go see what Shuggie Webster has to say for himself.'

The unmarked van shuddered to a halt. Then a thump came from the thin metal wall dividing the driver's compartment from the rows of seats hidden in the back. They'd arrived.

'OK,' Logan checked his MP5 again – all the bullets were still there, 'same drill as last time: no shooting anyone, no getting shot. Webster used to have a huge Rottweiler, but that's dead. This doesn't mean he doesn't have another dog – so be *careful*. If you fancy a few days' holiday resting up in A&E do me a favour and slip in the shower tomorrow morning.'

PC Ferguson stuck his hand up. 'We sure this is the right address, Sarge? I mean, I thought those GSM traces only gave you a hundred-foot radius?'

'We went over this already, Greg.' Logan fastened the Velcro on his bulletproof vest. 'We've got a known associate of Shuggie's bang in the middle of the area they traced his phone to. *Try* and pay attention.'

Silence.

'Sorry, Sarge.'

'We ready?'

Nods.

'Then let's do it.'

Tillydrone baked in the light of the evening sun. The housing block was a huge U-shaped canyon made up of harled concrete – four storeys tall on all three sides, arranged around some yellowy grass and a car park: the tarmac bleached to a pockmarked grey. A handful of trees tried to make the barren space look a bit more presentable, their branches groaning with blossom.

Rennie took point, scuttling across to a brown door, ducked inside, then held it open for everyone else to charge through. A gloomy corridor, the window at the far end blocked off with cardboard and brown parcel tape. Rennie charged up the stairs, Logan doing his best to keep up – the scabs on his ankle complaining with every step. First floor. Second floor. . .

'Here, watch where you're going!' An old lady stooped on the landing, a squeegee mop making dark wet streaks on the concrete. 'I just cleaned that!'

Rennie pulled the black scarf down away from his mouth. 'Sorry.'

'So you bloody should be! Do you think I've got nothing better to do than clean up after your size nine jackboots?'

'Sorry, sorry. . .' He crept past on tiptoes, then ran up the next flight of stairs.

Behind him, Logan shrugged. 'We'll try to be quick, but maybe you should go get yourself a cup of tea or something?'

She shook the mop at him, sending droplets of pine-scented water spattering over his bulletproof vest. 'Don't you tell me what to do, you bloody fascist! I'm eighty-three. . . You come back here!'

Logan hurried up the stairs after Rennie, hearing a procession of 'Sorry,' and 'Excuse me,' and 'You're doing a lovely job,' behind him.

Third floor. Rennie was flattened against the wall outside a blue door with a brass number five on it. The constable shifted his submachine gun into position. 'Big Red Door Key?'

'It's a third floor flat, where's he going to go?' Logan reached out and pressed the doorbell.

A dull buzz came from inside.

A minute later, someone shouted, *'Hold on, I'm naked. . .'*

Finally the door clunked open and a man stood in the gloomy hallway, a short, threadbare green dressing gown clutched about his middle. He ran a hand over the stubble covering his lopsided head, looked Logan up and down, then stuck his head out into the corridor. Saw the rest of the firearms team. Grunted. 'Suppose you'd better come in then.'

Zack Aitken slumped back in his seat, knees twitching open and closed, as if he was working a set of bellows between them. The room had the unmistakable funky-sweat odour of cannabis and dirty bong water.

PC Caldwell grimaced. 'Any chance you can sit with your knees together or something? Or at least put on some under-wear. It's like watching two mangy hamsters fighting over a cocktail sausage.'

'All right, enough.' Logan unfastened his helmet and dropped it on the couch. 'Where is he, Zack?'

'Who?'

'You *know* who – Shuggie Webster. We tracked his mobile here.'

'Wee bastard. . .' A pained smile. 'Well, you see, he kinda asked if he could borrow my phone to make a call, and I thought, yeah, why not – what are friends for, right?'

'Where is it?'

'Wh—'

'If you say "what" I swear to God I'm going to drag you down the station and get a doctor with the biggest hands I can find to give you a full body cavity search.'

'Aye, OK. On top of the telly. And before you ask, I got the receipt somewhere.'

Rennie picked it up and threw it across. Logan went through the menus till he got to the call log. And there it was – a two-minute call made at two forty-five that morning to Logan's mobile.

277

'Where is he?'

A huge shrug, his arms coming level with his shoulders which made his dressing gown ride up even further. 'No idea. Shuggie wanted to borrow a phone and a bit of folding, you know? I didn't ask any questions.' Aitken's smile was full of squint little teeth. 'Like I said, I'm a good mate.'

Logan peeled off his gloves and dumped them in the upturned helmet. 'You know he's screwed, don't you?'

The smile narrowed. 'He's got some problems, yeah.'

'Witness says Trisha Brown was snatched off the streets Saturday evening. Someone beat the crap out of her. Blue saloon car.'

The smile disappeared completely. 'Fuck.'

'Yes, "fuck". Fuck is exactly right. Shuggie Webster is well and truly fucked. Now, if you're really such a "good mate" you'll help *me* help *him*.'

'Seriously, I have no sodding idea. He turned up at my door last night, looking like shite and wanting a place to crash. Made a couple of phone calls, got stoned, ate all the Coco Pops, fell asleep, woke up, ate all the bread, left with five hundred quid in his pocket.'

Logan stared at him. 'That it?'

'That, and I know he seriously hates the shite out of you.'

Shock, horror.

PC Ferguson knocked on the doorframe. 'Sorry, Sarge: been through the whole place, no sign of Shuggie. Even took the front panel off the bath like you said.'

'Attic?'

'Communal; access off the next floor up – nothing but cardboard boxes, some wine-making kit, and spiders.'

'Well, sorry I couldn't be more help, officers, but I really need to jump in the shower.' Zack gave PC Caldwell a wink. 'You want to stay and shampoo my back? I like a big girl when she's all soapy.'

'You manky little—'

Rennie and Ferguson grabbed Caldwell and dragged her away before she could kill him.

Logan picked his helmet off the couch. 'One more thing. These dealers he's in trouble with?'

'Ah . . . yeah. Robert and Jacob. Yardies. Now normally I've got no trouble with our proud Jamaican brothers, but these two are a right pair of cunts. You see what they did to Shuggie's hand?' A shudder. 'He was fucking *mental* to get involved with that pair. And you know what?' Zack pointed towards the front door. 'I'm not going to make the same mistake.'

34

'Pub?' Rennie waggled his hand in the universal sign-language for pint.

Caldwell nodded. 'Pub.'

Ferguson: 'Pub.'

Then everyone was at it, all seven members of the firearms team: 'Pub.'

'*After* you've written up your incident reports.' Logan smiled. 'And as no one got shot, it's my round.'

It was like watching small children discover there *was* a Father Christmas after all.

'Right,' Caldwell sniffed her own armpit, 'quick shower, then Archies?'

'Not *again*!'

'Last time I was in, so were three blokes I did for nicking cars. Kept spitting in my pint when I wasn't looking.'

'How about the Athenaeum?'

'Illicit Still?'

That was the thing about Aberdeen – you were never more than five minutes from at least half a dozen pubs.

Logan pushed through the door to the locker room. 'What about Blackfriars? We could. . .'

Sergeant Big Gary McCormack was standing right in front of him, blocking most of the room. Mug of coffee in one hand, Tunnock's Caramel Wafer in the other. 'The sainted Sergeant McRae, as I live and breathe. How *gracious* of you to bless us with your exalted presence. Where's my pool car?'

'It's evidence, you can have it back when the IB are finished with it.' Logan pushed past him. 'We're off to the pub in about half an hour, if you're—'

'Oh, no, no, no!' Big Gary jammed the last chunk of chocolate into his mouth and masticated it to death. 'You're not going anywhere. You have *guests*.'

Logan opened his mouth, but the huge sergeant held up a hand.

'Reception: soon as you're ready.'

'Hmm. . .' Dr 'Call me Dave' Goulding peered at the little TV monitor in the Downstream Observation Suite. On the screen, a young woman – little more than a girl, really – was sitting at the interview room table, in the chair that was bolted to the floor. Both hands clasped in front of her, thumbnails worrying at the skin on her right forefinger.

'I can't say I remember her at all.' The psychologist frowned. 'But then, I only lecture final year students, so. . .' He flipped through the file Logan had given him – all the interview transcripts, the university's comments, the stuff from the PNC. 'Hmm. . . A history of stalking, *and* a shrine in her room to Alison and Jenny McGregor—'

'No, just Alison.' Logan passed over the photographs of her room, taken by the constables who'd gone to pick her up: Beatrice Eastbrook's bedroom wall, in all its *Silence of the Lambs* glory. 'Well, Jenny's in the painting, and a couple of the photos, but mostly it's just Alison. She's the only one who gets a halo.'

'Now that *is* interesting. . .' A small smile. 'The religious iconography isn't what I'd have expected, given her background. Normally your stalker types are more fetishistic in their devotions.' He stroked the screen with his fingertip, tracing the outline of Beatrice's face. 'Is she under arrest?'

'She's in on a volly. It's not illegal to be a bit creepy.'

'Well, in that case. . .' He handed the file back. 'Let's not keep the young lady waiting.'

It took about five minutes for Logan to become completely and utterly lost.

Beatrice leant forward. 'Actually, my thesis is going to be investigating the role of sublimation and suppression in the intimacy-versus-isolation phase of psychosocial development, with direct reference to the role played by the media's celebrity bias.'

Goulding nodded. 'Erikson and Freud, I like it. Have you considered including Kohlberg's ideas of self-focused morality?'

She smiled. 'Yes, that would make sense. Celebrity culture often portrays examples running contrary to the negative consequences of transgressing the perceived moral law.'

'Glad I could help.'

The one thing Logan *did* understand was that the longer Beatrice spoke to Goulding, the more her true Birmingham accent came out in response to his Liverpudlian one. And the less she sounded like the bunny-boiling fruitloop they'd interviewed that afternoon.

Goulding opened the folder, and pulled out the photos of her room. 'Now that we've established a rapport, Beatrice, I'd like to ask you about these. . .' He laid them out on the scarred tabletop.

She picked at the skin around her finger again. 'I know you're probably thinking I'm being obsessive, but it. . . I think

282

she's an inspiration. A loving mother, a single, independent woman, and she's a super-talented singer, and she's doing a degree. . .' Beatrice reached for one of the photographs, a close-up of the watercolour with the tinfoil halo. 'People believe in the strangest things, don't you think? Some tribes worship a tree, Scientologists think we're all descended from aliens. Mormons, Anglicans, Catholics, Hindus, Muslims, Buddhists – all have their own little quirks.' A shrug. 'I chose to invest my faith in something human. Does that sound strange, compared to believing there's an invisible magic man who watches everything we do and can damn us for all eternity?'

'Do you feel it's a normal response?'

'You think I might be displacing my need for a maternal role model?'

Goulding smiled. 'Is that what *you* think you're doing?'

On and on and on and on. Psychologist and psychology student, sounding like a self-help seminar for Martians.

Logan rapped his knuckles on the table. 'What did Alison think about you having a shrine to her on your bedroom wall?'

Beatrice shifted in her seat, hands flattening out the photo on the table in front of her.

'Did she know about it?'

'She . . . came round this one time to borrow some lecture notes. There was a knock at the door, and I opened it, and there she was. I mean right there – at *my* door.' Beatrice nodded, up and down, and up and down, curly bleached blonde hair falling over her eyes like a curtain. 'I mean, *God*, can you imagine it? Right there in front of me. And I couldn't speak. I mean, literally couldn't speak. And she said, "Hi Beatrice, can I come in?"'

The student looked up, a huge smile stretching her mouth wide, eyes glittering. 'She knew my name. Alison McGregor

283

knew *my* name. And I asked her in and she saw the wall. . . And she said, and I'll never forget it, she said, "Wow. That's a lovely painting, did you do that?"'

A tear broke free, running down through the foundation on her cheeks. 'She loved it. She said it was nice to know that someone loved her, like I loved her. That other people didn't understand. And I ran down to the shop and got us a bottle of Chardonnay and we sat and she told me about Jenny's mumps and I told her about my mum and it was the best night of my whole entire life.' Beatrice stroked the photograph. 'She was just perfect.'

And the bunny-boiling fruitloop was back.

'I was worried about her – all those photographers and crazed fans pestering her all the time. So I followed her home on the bus a few times. Just to, you know, make sure she was safe. She never even knew I was there. . . But I kept her safe.'

Tell that to Jenny and her missing toes.

'Did you follow her on Wednesday night – the night she went missing?'

Beatrice wrapped her arms around herself, as if she was trying to stop herself bursting apart. 'No. . . The one time it mattered, and I let her down.' She stared straight into Logan's eyes, tears running down her cheeks. 'It wasn't my fault. I tried, but she didn't take the bus, someone pulled up outside the lecture theatre and she got in his car. And they drove away. And I never saw her again.'

Why did no one *ever* think about calling the police? Logan sat forward. 'Did you get a photo of the car? Do you know who was driving? Did she mention meeting anyone?'

'No, I mean yes. . . I saw him.'

Silence.

For God's sake. Logan pinched the bridge of his nose. 'What did he look like?'

284

'Bald. And he had a silly little patch of hair on his chin, sideburns with a sort of zigzag cut into them.' She wrapped her arms even tighter. 'It was that Gordon Maguire: the TV producer guy who owns the record company.'

Logan stifled a yawn. Shuddered. Then put the phone back on the hook. Stretched in his seat. Sagged. 'Christ. . .' He ran a hand over his face. 'What do you think?'

Goulding raised an eyebrow. 'Could Beatrice have hurt them? Oh yes, definitely. She seems to have compartmentalized her life – the dedicated student, the obsessive fan, the dutiful friend, the loyal protector. . . If she thought Alison McGregor had rejected her, I wouldn't be surprised to see her falling back into her old behaviour patterns. Mummy has spurned me again, I will punish her. I will—'

The door banged open and there was DCI Finnie in all his rubber-faced glory. 'Well?'

'The Met are on their way to the studio.' Logan pointed at the phone. 'Maguire's still broadcasting the round-up of tonight's semi-final.'

'Excellent, excellent.' The head of CID rubbed his hands together. 'Are they flying him up to Aberdeen?'

'Can't. The CPS say we don't have enough to arrest him. I've asked for a video-conference thing when they talk to him, so at least we'll get to sit in.'

Finnie's smile slipped. 'Oh, well, I suppose we shouldn't lose sight that it's a result. And this all came from interviewing the Eastbrook woman? The Eastbrook woman McPherson was supposed to have interviewed?'

'Ah. . .' Logan shifted in his seat. 'Yes, well—'

'I think I might have to have a few words with Detective Inspector McPherson, don't you agree? I might start with, "idiot" and see how it goes from there.' A nod. He reached out and patted Logan on the shoulder, keeping his body stiff, as if he'd heard about this kind of thing, but had never done it before. 'Good work, Sergeant.' A pause. 'Now, have you written up that formal complaint yet?'

'No, I don't. . .' Logan sighed. 'I know, but what am I supposed to do?'

The silence on the other end of the phone kept on getting colder.

He took a sip of tea, watching as the macaroni cheese and chips congealed on his plate. Killing time with Goulding, waiting for the Metropolitan Police to call and say they were ready to question Gordon Maguire.

The canteen was quiet, just a couple of the back shift in for bacon rolls and strong coffee.

'Sam, it's the only break we've had in nearly two weeks, I can't—'

'It's half nine! We were supposed to book a holiday tonight, remember?'

'Yes, but you know what the job's like, I—'

'Don't you dare play the "job" card with me, Logan McRae. Every time there's a big case on you disappear up there and never come home. Well, if you'd rather hang out with that wrinkly lesbian mother-substitute of yours than come home to me, you—'

'She's not even here! It's just me and Finnie and Goulding. We're waiting—'

'It wouldn't be so bad if it was just now and then, but it's all the sodding time.'

'—Gordon Maguire, because he lied and—'

'And I know there's a little girl and her mum missing, but killing yourself isn't going to change—'

'—video conference. I'll be home as soon as I—'

'And you can pick up a bottle of wine as well.'

'It's. . .'

She'd hung up.

Wonderful. Logan stuck the phone back in his pocket.

Goulding leaned forward. 'So, do you fancy Aberdeen's chances against Toulouse this weekend?'

'Don't even pretend.' He stabbed a chip and dragged it through the wrinkly cheese sauce. 'And before you start: I know she's right, OK? I'm knackered, I've not had a day off in ages, and Big Gary keeps moaning about the overtime bill.' The chip was cold, the sauce lukewarm. 'But what am I supposed to do: sod off home and miss Gordon Maguire's interview?'

'Well,' the psychologist dabbed the napkin at the corners of his mouth, 'I suppose that depends on what you feel's more important. Doesn't it?'

Guilt – even better. 'I'm not. . .' His phone was ringing again. He pulled it out and hit the button. 'Sam, I've been thinking: how about—'

'*All your fucking fault.*' Shuggie Webster. '*It's all your fucking fault!*'

Not again. 'It's getting old, Shuggie. We know about Trisha, OK? If your mates Jacob and Robert have got her we can help. But you've got to stop—'

'*I want them fucking drugs back, and if you won't give us them. . .*'

'Stop sodding around and turn yourself in. OK?'

'*I warned you. I fucking warned you.*'

'Shuggie—'

'*Consequences. . .*'

Consequences? Silly bugger. This wasn't the bloody *Godfather*, and Shuggie Webster was no Al Pacino. Logan hung up on him.

'You know what?' He pushed his plate away. 'I'm getting sick and tired of. . .'

His phone. *Again.*

He stabbed the button. 'God's sake: *what*?'

287

'*Logan?*' Samantha. '*Look, I'm sorry . . . it's been a crappy day. I didn't mean to be a nag.*'

'Sam, I—'

'*If you've got someone for the McGregor thing, nail the bastard to the wall by the balls.*'

Pause. 'You sure?'

'*Spent the whole day scraping bits of brain and skull off the roof of some poor sod's bedroom. I hate suicides.*'

Logan smiled. 'Well, at least you've finally got something in common with Biohazard.'

'*Urgh. . . Great: now I feel dirty* and *depressed.*'

'How about I take you out to dinner tomorrow night? And I'll be home as soon as I can. Promise.'

'*Love you.*'

'Love you too.'

'Well *I* sodding hate you!' DI Steel stood at the end of the table, arms folded, face creased into a scarecrow scowl.

'Sam? I've got to go. . .' He put the phone back in his pocket.

'What the *hell* were you thinking?'

Dr Goulding pulled on a smile. 'Good evening, Inspector.'

'Fuck off, Ringo.' She stabbed a finger at Logan. 'He's gone. Done a runner.'

'Who's—'

'Frank Sodding Baker, *that's* who. Didn't turn up for work this morning – the Diddymen went round tonight and his flat's a tip. Packed his clothes, his toothbrush, and sodded off!'

Logan stared at her. 'That's not my fault. How's that my fault?'

'You and that cock-burger Green! Charging about like—'

'Oh, no you don't.' He stood, chest out, shoulders back.

Goulding groaned. 'Logan, maybe now's not the best time to—'

288

'One: Green was the one doing all the shouting. Two: I tried to stop him! The bastard wouldn't listen—'

'Oh, don't give me that, you—'

'I put in a formal complaint about it. In *writing*!'

The psychologist held up his hands. 'I really think you should both—'

'Shut up.' Steel ran a hand across her eyes. 'Are you telling me you put in a formal, *written* complaint about Stupidintendent Green?'

'*Yes*. I had nothing to do with—'

'Are you *mental*? Never go on the record moaning about a superior officer, no matter how much of a tosser they are!' She clenched her fists at the ceiling. 'What's *wrong* with you?'

'I—'

'The minute you made it official, you gave that arsehole Green a target.'

Goulding stood. 'I really think—'

Steel glared at him. 'What part of "shut the fuck up" do you no' understand?'

The psychologist just pointed over her shoulder.

Oh. . . bollocks. Logan turned.

Superintendent Green was standing in the canteen doorway with DCI Finnie. The man from SOCA stuck his nose in the air, turned, and stormed from the room.

35

'Well, that could have gone *better*, don't you think?' Finnie settled into the chair on the other side of the boardroom table, then shuffled around until he was facing the screen.

Logan doodled a little skull and crossbones in the corner of his notepad. 'I didn't know he was there.'

'I hardly think that's relevant. Do you, Doctor?'

Goulding shrugged. 'Sometimes it's better to get inter-personal issues out in the open. If we never let people know how we feel, how can we expect them to change?'

The TV flickered, then settled on a view of a small room. A round table with a chair behind it – facing the camera, two more on this side, facing away.

A voice boomed out of the speakers. *'How's that? Any better?'* Then a figure bent into frame and waved at them. He was too close for the camera to focus properly.

Logan clicked the button on the conference phone. 'We can see you now.'

'I bloody hate IT.' He sat with his back to the camera, just the edge of his shoulder visible on the screen.

Logan let go of the button. 'That's DI Broddur, he's the one's been looking into Maguire for Mark.'

Finnie shifted in his seat. 'Can they see us?'

'Video link's one way. The inspector can hear us, but only if you press the "talk" button. He's got an earpiece so no one else in the room knows what you've said.'

Finnie drummed his fingers on the boardroom table. 'You do realize that Superintendent Green is probably going to demand an apology?'

'I *told* him threatening Frank Baker would just make him run.'

Broddur's voice crackled across the room. *'We ready?'*

Logan pressed the button. 'Whenever you are, Inspector.'

A blurry hand waved across the screen. *'Bring him in, Charlie.'*

Gordon Maguire looked very shiny over a video link, his bald head flaring in the overhead light. He took the chair facing the camera and scowled. *'You do know we've got a live update on the voting in fifteen minutes, don't you? Not to mention half a million other things that have to be—'*

Broddur: *'You've not been entirely honest with us, have you, Mr Maguire?'*

The producer licked his lips. *'This is all a big misunderstanding. Like I told those Aberdonian idiots: I can't afford to have Alison and Jenny out of circulation. If I don't get that album out soon I'm going to lose everything.'*

Logan pressed the 'TALK' button again. 'Then why did our witness see Alison McGregor getting into his car the—'

'Yes, I was actually getting to that.' Broddur leant forward, showing more of his back to the camera. *'Then why do we have a witness that saw Alison McGregor getting into your car the night she went missing?'*

'Ah. . .' Maguire looked off to the left. *'Well, yes, but you see . . . we had to discuss some business. So I gave her a lift home.'*

'And you conveniently *forgot to mention that fact, even though you've been questioned three times?'*

291

'Look, it's. . . God.' Maguire scrubbed a hand across his face. 'We were . . . seeing each other. We went back to my hotel, had a few glasses of wine, and. . .' He cleared his throat. 'Look, do I really have to spell it out for you?'

'Some of my colleagues north of the border can be a bit dim when it comes to the social niceties, Mr Maguire. Better make it nice and clear.'

He sighed. 'We met last year during the auditions for Britain's Next Big Star. We got chatting, ended up having coffee, then dinner. We got on, liked each other.' He rubbed a hand across his bald scalp. 'If anyone found out I was . . . involved with one of the contestants there'd be people shouting, "fix" and it's not true: I didn't influence the judges. I didn't have to. She was brilliant.'

He shifted in his seat, scooting back and forward. 'On Wednesday night we went to my room, and afterwards I gave her a lift home, then went back to the hotel to pack. Had to get the redeye back to London. That's it, I swear: I know nothing about her going missing.'

He fidgeted in silence for a minute.

'You won't tell anyone about me and her will you? You know how the media like to blow stuff like this out of all proportion.'

'Hey kiddo, how you doing?' A robot voice in the darkness.

Eyes are all crusty. . . Jenny wipes the eye-bogies away and blinks, screwing her face up against the light. 'Sleeping.'

'I know, but it's time for another shot, OK?' SYLVESTER pulls up her sleeve, his white suit all rustly. 'Should be getting good at this by now, shouldn't we?'

The scratchy bee stings. Jenny bites her bottom lip and doesn't cry. She is a Brave Little Girl.

'OK, perfect, we'll just give that a wee swab. . .' He rubs a little cloth across the sting. 'And a plaster. . .' Small, round, and pale as Barbie's skin. 'And we're done.' He holds a lollipop in his purple-gloved hand.

Jenny takes the lollipop. Unwraps it. Sniffs it.

'It's cola-flavoured. Chewy in the middle too. Just don't tell your mum.'

Never take sweeties from strange men. She puts the lollipop on the mattress, next to the chain around her neck.

The other monsters are in the corner of the room, DAVID, TOM, and another one – a woman. Jenny can't read the name badge from here, but the new monster has a huge camera slung around her neck all wrapped up in clear plastic.

SYLVESTER reaches down and strokes Jenny's hair, but she doesn't even flinch. Brave. 'It's going to be OK. It'll all be over in a couple of days, and you can go home with your mum. That'll be good, won't it?'

The other monsters are arguing.

DAVID: '. . . fucking police.'

TOM: 'I know. But what are we supposed to do about it?'

The new monster gives herself a hug. 'Poor Colin. I can't believe he'd *do* something like that. . .' She sounds the same as the others.

DAVID shakes his head, that horrible shiny plastic face all dead and glinty. 'Get a grip, Patrick, fuck's sake. He was a moron, OK? It's his fault the police are sniffing round.'

TOM shrugs one shoulder. 'Come on, the guy's dead, it's no' like—'

'Everything we've done, everything we've achieved,' DAVID pokes him in the chest with a purple finger, 'only matters if no bastard ever finds out.' Another poke. 'You got any idea what they'll do to us if they catch us? Any idea what we'll get in prison? The bastards that cut off Jenny McGregor's toes?'

TOM backs off a step. 'I'm just saying, OK? He killed himself.'

SYLVESTER strokes Jenny's hair again. 'Don't worry about them, they're just upset. It's going to be OK. No one's going to hurt you. . .'

PATRICK shifts her feet. 'What if he left a note? What if he told them what we've done?'

'Don't be fucking stupid. If he did that we'd all be in a cell by now. He didn't say anything about us.'

Silence. Then PATRICK tilts her head to one side. 'How do *you* know?'

There's a clunk, then Mummy comes out of the poopy room, and closes the door behind her. It's not a toilet, not like in a proper house, it's a cupboard with a bucket in it and it smells like nappies left in the bin for too long.

The chain around Mummy's leg clanks and rattles as she shuffles across the bare floorboards. Then it pulls tight and she has to wait until SYLVESTER undoes the padlock holding it to the radiator, and fastens it to the bed again. She sinks onto the mattress next to Jenny, curls up on her side with her back to the room.

SYLVESTER stands over Jenny for a moment. Looking down at her. Then he goes to be with the other monsters.

Jenny watches him shuffling on the outside of the group, like a fat boy in the playground. Then someone's pocket makes the Doctor Who music.

DAVID pulls out a shiny phone. 'What?. . . Yes, I know, they spoke to us too. . . No, I don't know. . . Because I'm not fucking psychic, that's why!'

Jenny closes her eyes, grits her teeth, and struggles onto her side. The holes where her little toes used to be throb and sting. But she doesn't make a sound. Brave Little Girl.

36

Someone was in the house. Someone was in the house, with a knife, standing over the bed and he couldn't move, and—

Logan jerked awake. Lay on his back staring at the ceiling, heartbeat pounding in his ears. He held his breath, listening.

Nothing, just the faint-raspy sound of Samantha sleeping beside him.

A dim orange glow oozed in around the edges of the curtains, not enough to light the room, just enough to make the wardrobe and chest of drawers look like monsters looming in the shadows. Big rectangular wooden monsters. Full of socks.

The alarm clock radio glowed 03:00.

He let the breath out in one long hiss. Sodding hell . . . Why couldn't he dream about a bouncy castle full of naked Page 3 girls for a change?

Logan settled back into the pillow and frowned at the ceiling. Gordon Maguire – what a dodgy baldy little sod, sleeping with one of the contestants on his show. Jammy too. What the hell did Alison McGregor see in him? Other than a TV company, of course.

And all that stuff about bankruptcy and evil investors: they only had his word for it. Might be an idea to call up someone in the Met's fraud division first thing tomorrow morning, see if they couldn't give Blue-Fish-Two-Fish Production's accounts a going-over. Find out if Maguire was telling the truth.

A clack.

Then there was creepy stalker Beatrice 'Mummy Issues' Eastbrook. . .

Probably should get someone to look into Edward Buchan's property arrangements too, just in case the pathetic excuse for a human being had a lock-up or an old relative's house he was looking after. Somewhere to stash Trisha Brown where no one would hear her screaming for help.

If the Yardies didn't have her.

Thump.

And assuming Superintendent Green didn't get him fired first. . .

Logan frowned. Did he need to pee? Possibly. But that meant getting out of bed.

A huge, jaw-cracking yawn.

Unless Shuggie and Trisha really *were* trying to pull off a scam?

Logan rolled out of bed and stood, naked and pale, in the green glow of the clock radio. Like a scrawny version of the Incredible Hulk. He flexed his right arm a couple of times, trying to work the stiffness out of it, aggravating the bruises, then creaked open the bedroom door.

Pale light seeped through the glass pane above the front door, picking out just enough detail in the dark hallway to make the path from the bedroom to the bathroom reasonably safe. Nothing worse than standing on something sharp in the dead of. . .

His letterbox was open. He could see a vague glow around

the edges. And then it went dark. Logan glanced up. The light still shone through the glass above the door.

He started forward.

There was something sticking through the opening – a pale shape that swelled and drooped as he watched.

'What the hell?'

It was a condom. A big, ribbed condom. It was getting bigger. Why was there a—

He froze as the familiar sour-sweet pear-and-vinegar smell of petrol hit him. 'Don't you bloody dare!'

The condom gave one last droop, then fell. It hit the hall floor and bounced, petrol squirting from the open end, up the walls, across the carpet, into the coats. Logan snatched his hands over his eyes as a jet slashed across his naked chest.

'Fuck!'

The letterbox creaked open again and a book of matches poked through.

Logan backed up. Backed up some more. Nearly fell over the unit they kept their keys on. 'SAMANTHA!

A scratching noise.

The bastard was trying to light a match.

Scratch.

'SAMANTHA! WAKE UP!'

Scratch.

The smell of petrol was getting stronger, the liquid starting to evaporate in the warmth.

Run into the kitchen, grab a bucket of water. . . He was covered in bloody petrol. When the hall went up, he'd go up with it.

'SAMANTHA!'

Scratch.

Logan hauled open the bedroom door and nearly fell inside. Slammed the door shut again.

'God's sake . . . do you know what time it is?' She was sitting up in bed, one eye scrunched shut, the other squinting at him. 'What's so—'

'Someone's trying to burn—'

A loud crumping WHOOOMP. The bedroom door shoved hard against Logan's back. Blinding yellow light. Heat. Darkness.

Cough. There was something rough, scratching at his cheek. Logan blinked. Tried to shake the ringing sound out of his head. It thumped into a solid wall of wood. Ow. . .

Someone tugged at his arm, the motion scrubbing his face against the carpet. Pressure on his back.

'LOGAN, GET UP!'

Orange light flickered across the skirting board. Why was he lying on the floor?

'LOGAN!'

The pressure on his back eased.

Samantha knelt next to him, tattoos dancing across her pale skin in the shifting light. He looked up and she was naked, struggling to lift the bedroom door off him. He forced his arms under himself and shoved, fighting his way to his knees.

'Don't just sit there!' She shoved at the slab of wood. 'Help me!'

He shook his head again, but the ringing wouldn't go away. Poland – it was just like Poland, huddled in a junkyard flat, the flames the rubble the death and destruct—

A sharp, stinging pain flashed out across his cheek.

'Logan!' She slapped him again.

'Ow! Cut it out: I hear you.'

'Then *help*!'

The room was filling with smoke, thick greasy clouds of grey-black, lit with that horrible crackling glow. It was roasting in here, literally, sweat beading on his arms and petrol-soaked chest. . .

He glanced around the side of the detached door. It was like sticking his head in an oven, a wall of hot air that made his skin tighten. The paint on the back of the door was blistered and steaming. Flames filled the hallway outside, the carpet crisping and popping, sending out gouts of choking smoke. The coat-rack crashed to the floor, burning jackets and scarves flashing like fireworks.

'Jesus. . .'

Samantha shook his shoulder. 'Do you want another slap?'

'What? I was just—'

'Then help me get the door back in place!'

Easier said than done. The blistered paint on the other side was too hot to touch, so all they had was the handle and the little rack Logan had bought from B&Q to take dressing gowns. He took hold of it, dragged in a deep breath, and stood. Smoke closed around his head, the heat making his skin itch. Like instant sunburn. He kept his shoulder to the warm wood, inching his way forward with his eyes closed.

Clunk. It hit the wall.

Shuffle sideways, breath screaming in his chest, ears nipping and painful as he forced the thing back into the empty doorway.

Logan ducked down again, still leaning against the door. Gasped in a breath. A cough rattled through him, deep heaving barks that made spots swim past his eyes.

'Move!'

He staggered back and Samantha shoved the chest of drawers against the door, pinning it in place. She backed off a step, staring. 'What the fuck happened? Bomb?'

Logan sank onto the carpet and coughed till he gagged. '. . . petrol . . . through the . . . the letter—' More coughing.

A pair of jeans smacked into his chest. 'What are . . . are you. . .' The rest of his clothes rained down on him.

'We're naked and the bloody building's on fire: get dressed.'

Logan hauled on a stripy jumper. No point bothering with socks and pants. He wriggled into the jeans. 'Where's my shoes?'

Samantha hauled on a Sisters of Mercy T-shirt. 'What did you do?'

'It's not my fault, OK?' He crawled across the floor to the bedside cabinet and wrenched out the top drawer, sending all the garbage he'd stuffed in there over the last God-knew-how-many years spilling out across the smouldering carpet and grabbed his phone from the mess.

Something crashed against the wall behind him.

Logan spun around. The wardrobe was tipped forward, its top edge had taken a gouge out of the wallpaper, and Samantha was hauling one of the doors off.

'What the hell are you doing?'

'This shite was expensive. . .' She dragged out a black leather jacket, then the corset she'd bought online, then three pairs of thigh-length leather boots, then a black ball gown.

'Everyone's gone bloody mental.' The phone bleeped at him. No signal. 'Fucking thing!' He switched it off, then on again . . . this time he got a single bar. Dialled.

'Hello?'

He could barely hear the woman on the other end. *'Emergency Services, which—'*

'Fire brigade!' He rattled off the address, then made her repeat it back to him.

'Right, you need to stay calm. I want you to get some wet towels and use them to block any gaps between your door and the floor.'

'We're trapped in the bloody bedroom – where are we supposed to get wet towels from?'

'Well. . . You could get some jumpers or bedding or something and use that instead?'

'Brilliant. What do you want me to do for water? Pee on them?'

'I'm only trying to help.'

Samantha poked his shoulder. 'Time to go.'

He looked at her. 'Fire engine's on its way.'

'Do the math – how long's it going to take them to get here?'

'Five, ten minutes maybe?'

'And set up the ladders, and get everything sorted. And we're round the back – how are they going to get a fire engine anywhere near us?'

He risked another glance at the steadily lowering layer of smoke. Three feet from the floor and still falling. 'We're fucked, aren't we?'

'Probably.' Samantha crawled over to their makeshift barricade and pulled three of the drawers out. Then dragged them over to her pile of clothes by the window.

Logan hung up on the emergency services woman. Then scrabbled over.

A loud bang and a crash sounded from somewhere on the other side of the bedroom door. The TV exploding, or something like that.

She grabbed him by the neck, hauled him close and kissed him. She tasted of charred plastic and ozone. 'You still owe me dinner – so no getting killed, understand?'

'You ready?'

'No. You?'

'Nope.' He grabbed the windowsill and hauled himself up to a crouch. Reached through the smoke for the security catch and snibbed it open. Then hauled. The window creaked, then juddered open. Ancient wood and layers of paint squealing in protest.

It was like switching on a vacuum cleaner – the difference in air temperature hurling smoke out into the night. Outside the bedroom door, the crackle of flames built to a roar: the updraught feeding the blaze.

Samantha popped up beside him and stared down. 'Oh. . . shite.'

That was the trouble with living in a top-floor flat, the ground was a long, long way down. Three storeys of vertical granite, and then the flat roof of the building behind.

She ducked back down and hurled her ball gown and corsets out of the window.

Logan looked from side to side – maybe they could climb onto the roof? Haul themselves up on the guttering. He reached up and gave it a tug.

A chunk of rusty black came away in his hand.

Samantha's boots went spiralling to the flat roof far below, followed by the contents of all three drawers. Pants, bras, and stripy stockings, drifting down like lacy snow.

She coughed, wiped a hand across her soot-covered face, leaving a slightly cleaner patch. 'You want me to go first?'

'Where? There's nowhere *to* go.'

'Fine. You can follow me.' Samantha bit her bottom lip. Took a deep breath. Coughed. Then eased a leg out over the windowsill, keeping hunched down so she was beneath the level of the whirling smoke.

Logan grabbed her. 'What the fuck are you doing?'

'Downpipe. We get to the one from the kitchen and we can climb down.'

'You're fucking *mad*!'

She nodded back towards the bedroom door. Flames were licking through the gap around the eviscerated chest of drawers. 'You want to stay and take your chances?'

No he didn't. 'Hold on. . .'

Logan hauled the duvet off the bed. Sweat dripped from

his forehead, he could feel it trickling down his back as well. He wrestled the fitted sheet from the mattress's grip, then twisted it up into a loose rope. 'Tie this around you.'

'It's not long enough, how am I supposed to—'

'In case you slip on the way to the bloody pipe. Just do what you're sodding told for once.'

'Your face is a mess, by the way.' She took the end of the sheet and twisted it around her wrist.

'Right. . .' Samantha eased her bum from the windowsill, lowering herself down onto her elbows, then down again until her arms were wrapped around the granite ledge.

Logan braced himself against the wall, knotting both hands into the sheet, holding tight. It was crappy climbing technique, but the thing was too short for anything else.

The heat was getting worse, the air thick and choking.

She looked up at him. 'You let me go, and I'll kill you.' Then she started edging her way along, making for the cast-iron downpipe that ran from the kitchen down to . . . whatever the hell it drained into.

A siren wailed in the distance, getting closer. At least that was something.

'Fuck. . .' A lurch and Samantha let go of the ledge with her left hand, reaching out for the black pipe.

Please let it be in better condition than the guttering. . .

She grabbed it, wobbled for a moment, then stared up into his eyes. Licked her soot-blackened lips. 'Don't drop me.'

Logan tried for a smile. 'I won't.'

A nod, then she let go of the window ledge.

And didn't fall to her death. Oh thank God.

'Fuck this is high up.' Samantha eased herself down about a foot. Then another, until the fitted sheet was stretched tight. 'Let go.'

'No.'

'Don't be a dick, you have to let go, or I can't go any further.'

She was right.

He tossed the end out of the window. It dangled from her arm, stirring back and forward in the updraught – cool air dragged up the side of the building by the heat of the fire. Right. He could do this. No problem. Just ease out onto the ledge. No need to rush. All the time in the world.

This was stupid.

Stay in the flat. Stay put and wait for the fire brigade.

Logan glanced back over his shoulder. The smoke was even thicker, and flames weren't just licking around the edges of the chest of drawers, they were eating it. A groan, then the bedroom door shuddered as something crashed against it.

The ceiling was caving in.

Oh God. . .

He clutched at the edge of the window, swung his legs out over the void. Three storeys straight down to a flat roof. Fuck, fuck, fuck. He reached out with his left leg, feeling for the downpipe.

Above his head the smoke was shot through with shards of flame. The roar of the fire nearly deafening.

He lowered himself down, armpits level with the sill, battered right arm aching, the scars in his left palm throbbing, the ones across his stomach stretched and taut. Where the hell was the bloody pipe?

Samantha had managed it, and she was a good six inches shorter than he was!

Her voice blared through the fire's din. 'Left, you idiot!'

Clunk. His shoe touched something. OK – good, fine – he could do this.

No he couldn't. 'WHAT THE FUCK DO I DO?'

'There's a wee ledge, about six inches below your left foot.'

Jesus, fuck, Jesus, fuck, Jesus, fuck. . .

He could feel it. Little more than an inch wide. A minimalist decorative feature on the backside of a tenement building. Now all he had to do was let go with his left hand, and grab the pipe. Just like Samantha had. No problem. Easy.

'Don't just bloody hang there!'

OK, deep breath. Three storeys wasn't that high. Not really. Just about forty, maybe fifty feet. Shite.

He shoogled over as far as he could and reached out with his left hand. Arm flailing about in the air. And then he grabbed the pipe.

Oh thank God.

Now all he had to do was let go with his other hand. Five, four, three—

A crash sounded in the room, the smoke swirling above him.

Logan let go of the ledge and snatched at the downpipe, holding on tight, face ground into the rough granite surface of the wall.

Not dead.

Something went BOOM and the kitchen window exploded outwards, showering him with shards of glass. A gout of flame billowed out into the night.

He looked down. Samantha was about four feet below him, edging her way down, using the brackets that fixed the pipe to the wall as hand and footholds. It was all OK. They'd made it. Just a bit of a clamber and they'd be safe.

Logan's vision clouded. He blinked, feeling warm tears seeping down his cheeks.

Don't let go.

He inched down a little, feeling for the next bracket.

Everything was OK.

He looked down. Just in time to see Samantha looking

up at him. She smiled, her filthy face streaked with clear trails. At least he wasn't the only one.

'You all right?'

Samantha's smile became a grin. 'Told you.' She eased down another foot. 'This dinner you owe me, it better be a—'

Creak. The pipe juddered. Her eyes went wide. 'Oh. . .'

A clang, a little tearing noise, just audible through the flames.

The section of downpipe she was holding on to lurched to the right, the bracket fell, disappearing into the darkness. She scrabbled for the length of pipe still attached to the wall, but her fingers grabbed empty air.

37

'Logan. . .?'

It happened in slow motion: her fingers scrabbled at nothing as the section of pipe she was climbing burst free of its rusting support brackets. Then she was falling, arms pin-wheeling, legs running on an invisible treadmill. Mouth open in a perfect 'O', the whites of her eyes shining from her soot-streaked face.

Bits of broken pipe tumbled end over end around her. The tail of the fitted sheet fluttering from her arm like a pennant.

Then back to full speed again.

She slammed into the flat roof, three storeys below, and went straight through it. A cloud of orange-grey dust burst into the air, hung there, then drifted up the granite wall, pulled by the temperature gradient.

'SAMANTHA!' Logan tried to flatten himself to the building, feet dug into the last bracket before the pipe came to an abrupt end. 'SAMANTHA!'

The fire engine's siren was getting closer, its wail joined by the familiar *weeeeeeow* of a patrol car's siren.

'SAMANTHA!'

*   *   *

Sick spatters into a pink plastic bowl. Jenny hunches her back and retches again, adding to the mess. Happy Meals don't look so happy after they've been eaten.

The room's all gloomy, just a nightlight plugged into the wall socket so the monsters can keep an eye on them.

She spits, closes her eyes, and rests her thumping head on the rim of the bowl. Her tummy feels as if it's been punched. Much worse than when she had to lose weight for the television people.

No one wants to see a Fat Little Girl on their TV screens, darling...

She reaches for the bottle of water lying on the floor beside her, pulls the little nipply top up with trembling fingers, and takes a gulp. It tastes sweeter than strawberries.

Mummy's lying on the mattress, flat on her back.

Jenny knows she's not asleep. She can tell because of her breathing. Mummy's lying there, staring at the roof and wishing Daddy was here.

Daddy would make everything better.

Jenny rubs a hand across her mouth and wipes the slimy mess on her jammies. Rinses her mouth out with water and spits it into the bowl. Puts the lid on to keep in the smell. Then closes her eyes, grits her teeth, and pulls herself upright using the bed as a climbing frame. Wobbles on her burning feet. Bites her top lip and squeezes back the tears.

Brave Little Girls don't cry.

But she *wants* to. She wants to so much it hurts more than her missing toes.

Jenny climbs up onto the mattress and cuddles in next to Mummy, one arm wrapped around Mummy's tummy, her head resting in the soft crook of her arm.

A cool hand strokes her forehead. 'Hey you. Feeling better?'

Brave Little Girls don't cry. 'Uh-huh. The andy-bionics make my tummy angry.'

Mummy leans in and kisses her on the top of her head. 'I know, sweetie, I know. But they make you better.'

Jenny blinks back the tears. 'Are we going to be dead?'

'Shhh. . . Only two more days and the bad men will let us go home. You, me, and Teddy Gordon.'

Jenny raises her head and scowls at the bottom of the bed, where those nasty dead-fish-greedy-crow eyes glint in the dark. Teddy Gordon doesn't want to go home. Teddy Gordon is right where he wanted to be from the start. Where he can watch them suffer.

'Samantha? Samantha, can you hear me? I need you to squeeze my hand, OK?'

The ambulance tore through the streets, lights blazing, siren screaming, a patrol car leading the way. Logan sat on the little fold-down seat, one hand wrapped around the seatbelt, the other holding the oxygen mask in place. The vehicle rocked as they swung around the outskirts of Mounthooly Roundabout onto Hutcheon Street.

'Come on, Samantha, squeeze my hand.'

The bag, attached to the drip, attached to Samantha's wrist, swung back and forth. Heart monitor pinging. Paramedics bent over her, as if they were praying.

Maybe. . . Maybe that wasn't such a bad idea.

'Female, late twenties, impact trauma and smoke inhalation.' The doctor hurried along beside the trolley, reading from a clipboard as they charged through Accident and Emergency.

Unhappy people stared at them from the waiting area as they rushed past, Logan limping, trying to keep up. Breath tight in his chest. Like something heavy was sitting on it.

The doctor flipped the page. 'I don't like the look of her BP.'

Bang, and they were through a set of double doors – into a scuffed corridor painted in cracked spearmint green. The smell of boiling cabbage and bleach, strong enough to over-power the stench of burning that clung to Logan's clothes and skin.

Samantha's face was horribly pale and filthy at the same time.

'Sir?'

A hand on his arm.

Logan kept going.

'Sir, you need to come with me, OK?'

He tried to jerk his arm free, but the grip was firm – fingers digging into his bruised skin. 'I have to—'

'I know, but she's in good hands. You need to let them do their jobs.'

He sat on an examination table, a knackered-looking doctor with a name Logan couldn't remember tapping his chest and back. 'Well, you've probably inhaled enough smoke to do you for the next five years, but other than that. . .'

'How is she?'

A sigh. A shrug. A stifled yawn. 'It's going to be a while. You should go home. Try to get some rest.'

Go home – how the hell was he supposed to do that?

Logan glanced up from the creaky plastic seat as a nurse hurried by. The soles of her trainers made little screams with every step, breaking the humming stillness of the hospital. 'Is there anyone—'

'Sorry, I really don't know.' She didn't even slow down.

'But—'

'Sorry.' And she was gone.

* * *

310

Logan blinked. Shook himself. The corridor was empty, just the purr of the air conditioning and the distant sound of someone coughing.

It was the middle of the night, but you couldn't tell from the lighting. It was the same twenty-four hours a day, that horrible institutional twilight that went with the sickly-green walls and the cracked terrazzo floor. A gloomy fluorescent-lit world that never let you go. You were born here, you got ill here, you died here.

Bears. Rubble. Suicide. Fire—

'Dude, you still here?'

Logan shivered. Shifted in his plastic prison. 'Sorry. . .'

'Dude, you should, you know, sleep or something.' He didn't look a day over twenty: long hair, piercings in his nose, ears, eyebrow, and lip, a grey overall with a name-badge. He pulled one white earbud out and leant on the handle of the big, scissor-shaped-mop-brush-thing he'd been pushing across the floor. 'I know it's a hospital and all, but there's no *way* it's healthy just hanging out here.'

Logan didn't bother hiding the yawn. 'What time is it?'

'Half-five. Seriously: go home, get some sleep.'

Yeah, right. 'I can't.'

'They give you sleeping pills?'

Logan sat back. 'What? No. . .'

'Cutbacks are a bitch.' He glanced up and down the corridor, then lowered his voice. 'Dude, if you're worried about nightmares and that, I've got the perfect thing for you.' He dug into an inside pocket of his overalls, and came out with a little foil blister-pack of pills. Held them out. 'I've got a mate who's a medical student, fixes me up now and then. Two of these and you'll be out like a light.'

'I can't take—'

311

'Nah, seriously, no charge. Call it a karmic down-payment. Doesn't hurt to help a fellow human being now and then, know what I'm saying?'

'Laz?'

The world rocked forward and backwards a couple of times.

'Laz? You in there?'

Frown. Logan screwed up his face, then mashed his fists into his eye sockets. 'How is she?'

'You look like a bowl of shite soup. With crap croutons.' Steel creaked her way into the seat next to him, making it groan. Her hair stuck out in random directions on one side, flat as a pancake on the other. Wearing a turtleneck jumper and a pair of jeans. She reached over and squeezed his shoulder. 'You OK?'

'Samantha. . .'

A sigh. 'Aye, I know. Look, you're no' doing her any good hanging about here like a bad smell. . .' Steel sniffed. 'And that's no' a euphemism, you *really* sodding honk.'

'Staying here.'

'No, you're no'.' She stood. 'Come on, Susan's making up the spare bed.'

'I'm not—'

'Don't make me drag your blackened arse out of here. Be undignified. Home. Shower. A decent sleep. I'll give you a bell soon as we hear anything. OK?'

Logan looked up the corridor, towards the intensive care unit. 'I didn't. . .' What didn't he? Mean for it to happen? Keep Samantha safe? Want to panic? Behave like a man?

'Aye, I know. I know.' Steel gave his shoulder another squeeze. 'Come on. We'll crack open that bottle of Isle of Jura I got for my birthday. Give it a wee seeing-to. Finnie can manage the morning briefing without me.'

He hauled himself out of the plastic chair, it seemed to take forever. 'Can you give me a lift?'

''Course. I'm driving home anyway, so—'

'No. Somewhere else.'

Steel licked her lips, glanced up and down the corridor, swallowed. 'You're not going to do anything stupid, are you?'

38

'You're off your sodding head. This *is* stupid!'

Twenty past six and the sun was well on its way up a pale-blue sky. The trees were filled with birds, singing and chirping and crawing, as if everything was hunky-fucking-dory. As if this was just a day the same as any other.

'Come on, still no' too late to change your mind. Back to mine, couple of drams and. . .'

'I'm fine.' Didn't feel fine. Felt like someone had hollowed out his body, leaving a brittle shell behind. Logan clambered out of Steel's little sports car. 'Give me a call if you hear anything.' He closed the door, then stood there watching as she shook her head, put the MX-5 in gear, and drove off into the early morning.

As soon as she was gone, he let his face sag. Samantha's static caravan was part of a little park on the bank of the River Don, opposite the sewage treatment works. That wasn't the smell that pervaded everything though, it was the fatty, slightly sickening odour that came from the Grampian Country Chickens factory.

He lurched over to the door. Two gnomes, one on either side – one with horns and a forky tail, the other with halo

314

and wings. Logan picked the devil up, flipped it over, and shook. A metallic rattling sound. He tipped the key into his palm.

Sometimes people were more predictable than they thought.

He unlocked the front door and stepped inside. Locked himself in. The skylight in the hall was a mass of green algae and clumps of moss, filtering out most of the oblivious sunshine, leaving the place shrouded in gloom. The door to the living room was open, light seeping in through the closed curtains. He could smell her. Her scent was imprinted on the place, in the carpet and furniture. He could smell it even through the acrid stench of smoke that stuck to his clothes, hair and skin.

When was the last time they'd spent a night here? Or even a couple of hours? At least five months. Probably more.

He reached out and flicked on the hall light. It blinked and buzzed, then bloomed into cold fluorescent life. So at least the power was still on.

Logan shuffled through into the small kitchen and peeled off his stinking clothes, emptied the pockets of his jeans, then stuffed everything into the washer-dryer. Found some washing powder under the sink. Set the thing going to wash and tumble dry, then sank back against the fridge and cried.

Where the hell was. . . Logan frowned into the gloom. The bedroom had shrunk, and the duvet smelled of mildew. He blinked. Not home. Samantha's caravan. His mobile phone was ringing.

It took two goes to grab it off the stack of books acting as a bedside cabinet. 'McRae.'

'*Hello, is this. . .*' Some rustling. '*Er, Detective Sergeant Logan McRae? This is Dr Lewis, I'm calling about—*'

Logan sat bolt upright. 'Is she OK?'

Please let her be OK, please let her be OK.

'Well, she's had a very nasty fall. Samantha's condition is what we like to call serious, but stable. It was touch and go for a while, but she seems to be responding to treatment.'

He threw off the duvet and lurched to his feet. 'I'll be right up.'

There was a pause. *'Actually, that might not be such a good idea. We've had to put her in a medically-induced coma—'*

'Coma. . .'

'Just until the swelling in her brain comes down.'

Logan let his head rest against the cool wall of the caravan. 'I see.'

There was more – the list of broken bones, the internal injuries, the surgery.

'Basically, the next twenty-four hours are going to be critical, but she's getting the best care possible.'

Logan closed his eyes. 'Thank you, Doctor.' He hung up, then sank back onto the bed. Lay there staring at the ceiling.

Shuggie Webster and his fucking "consequences". Samantha slamming through the flat roof three floors below. Flames screaming through the smoke above his head. That moment when she looked up and said, *'Logan. . .?'* The smell of everything they had, burning. Samantha, lying in the ambulance, pale and broken. Shuggie Fucking Webster. . .

Logan thumped back into the musty pillow, eyes screwed shut. Then pounded his fists into his forehead. Stupid. Fucking. *Useless.* Moron.

Then lay there, breathing heavily.

He checked his phone again. Eleven o'clock. No way he could get back to sleep now. His head was stuffed with burning cotton wool. Everything stank of mould and smoke.

*   *   *

A huge spider scuttled at the sides of the bath, slipping down to the bottom, then trying to escape again. Logan turned on the shower. Watched it scrabble away from the water. Why shouldn't the little bugger drown? Everything died. Maybe it was Mr Spider's turn.

Sigh.

He pulled a couple of sheets of toilet paper from the roll, scooped the thing out of the bath and chucked it out into the hall.

By the time he got back to the bedroom there were three messages waiting for him on his phone. One from his mother, one from his brother, and one from Rennie. He listened to them all, then deleted the lot.

Logan dragged his clothes out of the washing machine and hauled them on. Still slightly damp. Everything he now owned was sitting on the dusty worktop: a handful of change, a packet of chewing gum that stank of smoke, his wallet, and his phone.

Shuggie Webster wanted *consequences*, did he? Well he was going to bloody well get them.

He stared at his mobile for a moment. Then picked it up and made a call.

'*You sure you're OK?*' Rennie's voice sounded as if he was trying to comfort the dying. '*I mean, you know, is there anything I can do?*'

Logan squinted out into the bright morning. 'Yeah, you can get another GSM trace authorized.' He read out the number Shuggie Webster had called from yesterday. 'Let me know soon as you get anything.' Keeping his voice flat, calm, and dead.

'*Er. . . Actually, Sarge, Finnie's kinda laying down the law on that one.*'

317

He locked the hire car's door and walked up to the big wrought iron gates. Leaves and sunshine made a writhing freckled pattern on the gravel driveway.

'Everyone's been told not to bother you with police stuff. You're meant to be on compassionate leave.'

That was news to him. 'Then pretend Steel told you to do it.'

'Yeah, that's cool. It's all her fault.'

There was one of those buzzer entry security things mounted on the high stone wall. Logan pressed the button.

'Listen, I was onto the fire brigade this morning – they're saying the flat's not safe for the IB to go into yet. But there's definitely signs of an accelerant.'

'No shit.'

'. . . Yeah. OK, so we're getting together a collection, for Sam. There anything you think we should buy? You know, something she'll like when she wakes up?'

If she wakes up.

'Hold on.' He jabbed the mute button. The security thing was buzzing at him.

Then a broad Aberdonian accent crackled out of the speaker. *'Fa is it?'*

'Logan McRae to see Mr Mowat.'

'Hud oan.' Silence.

Back to Rennie. 'I've got to go.'

'Erm, I was thinking – have you sorted out your insurance yet? You know, home and contents?'

Logan ground the heel of one hand into his eye. One more thing to add to the list. 'All the paperwork was in the flat. . .'

'You want me to do it for you? I can phone round, get stuff sorted? You know, if it helps?'

The gates gave a clunk, then swung open. Walk into my parlour, said the spider to the fly.

'*Sarge? You still there? I mean, it's not much, but—*'

'No, it's great. . . Thanks.' The gravel crunched under his smoke-blackened shoes. 'Really, I appreciate it.'

'*Hey, no probs – what are mates for, right?*' A cough. '*And. . . I'm really sorry about Sam.*'

'Yes. I'm sorry too.'

The gates swung shut behind him. Logan hung up.

'Will you take a wee dram, Logan?' Hamish Mowat, AKA Wee Hamish, waved a liver-spotted claw at a display cabinet. A set of crystal decanters and tumblers were lined up behind the glass. Midday and Wee Hamish was dressed for bed – tartan jammies, grey slippers, a fleecy robe.

'Not for me, thanks.'

'Ah, got to keep a clear head. I understand. You're a man on a mission: have to keep your wits sharp.' His voice was a raspy mix of Aberdonian and public school, not much louder than a whisper. 'I'll have one, if you don't mind?' He shuffled over to the window, wheeling a drip stand along for the ride. A clear bag swung on a hook at the top, the IV line disappearing into the plastic shunt taped to the back of his left hand.

Logan opened the cabinet. 'Glenmorangie, Dalwhinnie, Macallan, or Royal Lochnagar?'

'Surprise me.'

Logan picked a decanter at random, poured a decent measure, and added a splash of water. Carried it across to where Wee Hamish was surveying his domain.

'Thank you.' The old man took it in a trembling hand. '*Slainte mhar.*'

The house was huge, a rambling mansion on the south side of the River Dee, perched high enough on a hill to give a panoramic view over Aberdeen. Who said crime didn't pay? The large garden stretched away to a border of trees, and one of those black-and-yellow ride-on mowers hummed its way across the lawn, like a low-flying bee – a huge scowling man perched on the little seat. He was massive: not just fat, but tall and broad too, his face a web of scar tissue and patchy beard.

Wee Hamish sighed. 'It pains me to think of you two at each other's throats. I do wish the pair of you would bury the hatchet.'

Yes, well, there'd be no prizes for guessing where Reuben would want to bury it.

'I don't think he's the forgive and forget type.'

When the old man nodded, it set the saggy droop of skin beneath his chin wobbling. 'I suppose you're probably right. But I'm not going to be around forever, Logan, and if you two can't sort out your differences, it's only going to end one way. . .' He rested the tips of his fingers against the window. 'I've been thinking a lot about that kind of thing lately. What my legacy's going to be.'

Wee Hamish licked his pale purple lips. 'So I fund community projects, I set up bursaries so underprivileged children can go to university, I sponsor families in Africa. . .' He took another sip of whisky, not taking his eyes off the garden and its angry mechanical bee. 'You know, much though I love him, Reuben's apt to be a bit . . . impulsive. Don't get me wrong, he's ferociously loyal, a great man to have on your side, someone who'll do whatever it takes to get the job done, but a good leader has to weigh up his options. Make unpalatable decisions. Compromise sometimes. Not just go charging in with a sawn-off shotgun.'

Wee Hamish turned and tapped Logan on the forehead with a curved finger, the skin dry like parchment. 'Head first.' The finger prodded Logan in the chest. '*Then* heart.' The old man curled his fingers into a loose clump. 'And fists last of all.' He shook his head, sending that sag of skin wobbling again. 'Reuben, bless him, is all fists.'

'Mr Mowat, I—'

'Of course, that's the problem, isn't it? Who do I hand everything over to, when I go?' He touched the glass again. 'I had a son once. Lovely lad, but not . . . temperamentally suited to this line of work. It was a motorbike accident that took him, he was eighteen. And by then it was too late for Juliette and me to try again. Too old the pair of us. No heart left in it.'

'Actually, I—'

'I was sorry to hear about your young lady. I sent some flowers, I hope you don't mind. A hospital is such an ugly place, don't you think? It's a wonder anyone gets better at all.'

How the hell did Wee Hamish know about Samantha? It wasn't even in the papers yet.

'Thank you.'

'And if there's anything you need. . .' Wee Hamish chuckled, a wet, rattling sound. 'Of course there's something you need. You wouldn't be here otherwise. You want whoever set fire to your home. You want revenge.'

Logan looked away, cleared his throat.

Wee Hamish put a hand on his arm. 'Oh, don't worry, I'm not offended. Why else would you come to visit a sick old man, eh?'

'Shuggie Webster. I want to know where he is.'

'I see. Yes, well I dare say we can organize something along those lines for you.'

'I. . . I need you to understand something – if you do this, it doesn't mean you own me.'

Another chuckle. 'Logan, trust me when I say that I have no desire to "own" anyone. Oh, I keep a couple of your colleagues on the payroll, but I don't "own" them; they're valued members of the team. Simply think of this as a favour, and if you ever decide police work is no longer the career for you. . . Well, as I said, it would be nice to know that my legacy was in good hands.' He gave Logan's arm a squeeze. 'Now, when we deliver Mr Webster, would you like a gun as well?'

Logan swallowed. 'A gun?'

'Something Russian: clean, untraceable, never been used.'

'I. . .'

'Well, you don't have to decide right now.' He drained the last of the whisky. 'Tell me, are you any closer to catching the animals who kidnapped Alison and Jenny McGregor?'

'Not really. Well, we've got a couple of leads.' Shrug. 'Don't know if they'll come to anything.'

'The whole situation . . . discomforts me, Logan. The media crawling all over the city like flies on a dung pile, giving everyone the impression that we live in a horrible, dangerous place. It's not good for local businesses if people think our city's not safe.' He tilted his tumbler from side to side, rolling the last oily smear of whisky around the sides. 'I've made a few enquiries of my own, but no one seems to know anything about these people. That discomforts me too.'

'This thing with Shuggie Webster—'

'Oh, don't worry, we shall be very discreet. No one will even know that you have him. And if you need a hand disposing of him afterwards, I'm just a phone call away.'

39

A cordon of blue-and-white 'POLICE' tape stretched all the
way across Marischal Street. A patrol car was parked at
the side of the road, along with the Identification Bureau's
grubby Transit van, and a white Fiat with the Grampian Fire
Brigade crest on the side.

*'. . . only a day and a half to go before the kidnappers' deadline.
In other news, Grampian Police have issued a public appeal for a
Mr Frank Baker to come forward. . .'*

The lounge window was a black-ringed hole, smoke
staining the granite above, dirty water the granite below.
The street still had that charred-wood-and-molten-plastic
smell. The flat directly below had all its windows open, the
curtains flapping in the breeze. Probably trying to dry out
after the fire brigade pumped Christ-knew how many gallons
of water into the building. So it wouldn't just be Logan's
insurance getting a hammering.

*'. . . concerned for Mr Baker's safety following his disappearance
from his Mannofield flat on Sunday evening or Monday morning—'*

Logan pulled the keys out of the ignition. Stared up at
the place where he used to live. Then climbed into the sunny
afternoon. So what if he'd parked on double yellows? The

323

whole street was closed off anyway. If anyone wanted to make an issue of it . . . he'd quite happily ram their teeth down their throat.

He ducked under the cordon of tape.

'Oi, you!' A uniformed constable clambered out of the patrol car. 'Where do you think you're. . .' He stopped. 'Sorry, Sarge, thought you were another one of them journalists.' He looked at his feet for a moment. 'You OK? Finnie said—'

'Was anyone else hurt?'

'Only, we're not supposed to—'

'Sergeant McRae!' Someone in full SOC gear was waving at him from the doorway to his building.

Logan left the constable spluttering to himself, and marched over. The tech peeled back her hood then hauled off her facemask – Elaine Drever, Samantha's boss, head of the Identification Bureau, a thickset woman with greying curly hair.

She stuck out a gloved hand for Logan to shake. 'I want you to know we're doing everything we can.'

Logan stared up at the building. 'Thought you didn't do field work any more?'

'Sam's one of ours. Fire brigade just gave us the all-clear to start collecting evidence.'

'There won't be much. Condom through the letterbox, filled up with petrol, match dropped in after it.'

She smiled, showing off a gold crown on one of her front teeth. 'Ah, but he sodded about for too long, let the petrol evaporate.'

The scritching noise – Shuggie struggling to get the matches lit.

Elaine made a ball with both hands, then jerked them apart, fingers spread wide. 'The vapour ignited like a bomb, blew the front door clean off.'

'Did the same with the bedroom. Can I see?'

324

She raised an eyebrow. 'Of course you can't. Finnie read the riot act this morning: you're not allowed anywhere near the investigation.' She turned and marched back towards the stairwell door. 'There's spare suits in the back of the van, just make sure you've got a mask on so we can all pretend not to recognize you.'

They'd laid down a walkway of metal tea trays, each one on little metal legs, keeping Logan's blue plastic booties three inches off the charred, waterlogged carpet. Stopping any evidence from being destroyed.

'Bloody hell. . .'

He stared in through the open doorway. The hall was a blackened mess, chunks of ceiling lay on the floor, scorched beams exposed above his head. The roof was still in one piece, but all the things they'd stored up in the attic were gone, strings of vitrified plastic and a small metal half-tank, all that was left of the bread-maker he'd been given years ago and never used.

Logan paused. 'Is the floor safe?'

Someone – anonymous in a baggy SOC suit, mask, goggles, and gloves – nodded at him. 'Just don't go jumping up and down in the kitchen.'

What was left of the flat stank – the peppery reek of blackened wood; the bitter tang of roasted plastic; and the sour, cloying smell of burnt carpet.

He started in the lounge. No need for a crime scene walkway in here – everything that mattered had happened in the hall. The TV was a hollow skeleton of metal struts, the plastic casing melted away, the CRT screen shattered. CDs lay heaped in the corner where the shelving unit had collapsed, grimy silver disks glittering like discarded fish scales. The bay window was just a collection of empty, scorched frames, all the glass long missing.

The kitchen was a mess, all the units stained with soot, the fridge-freezer door cracked and part-melted.

But the bedroom was worse. The mattress was a pile of ash and springs in a sagging metal frame. Chunks of ceiling had come down, and only two sides of the tipped-over wardrobe remained.

Logan wiped a gloved hand across his eyes. Swallowed hard. Then stepped over to the shattered window.

Three floors down, the flat roof still had its dusting of underwear snow, Samantha's boots, ball gown, and corset lying twisted and empty.

He stood there, staring down at the hole she'd made with her falling body.

Fucking Shuggie Webster. . . No matter what happened, the doped-up junky bastard deserved everything he was going to get. Every single last fucking—

A hand on Logan's shoulder made him flinch.

'You OK? You've been standing there for about fifteen minutes.' It sounded like Elaine Drever, but with all the SOC gear on it was difficult to tell.

'Can you. . .' He pointed down at Samantha's things. 'I don't . . . want people. . .'

'I'll take care of it. Get it all bagged up for you.' The rumpled figure sighed. 'I know you don't want to hear it, but if you'd stayed in here, we'd be digging your bodies out of the rubble. It doesn't take a lot of smoke to kill someone. You did the right thing.'

Tell that to Samantha.

The head of the IB patted his shoulder. 'Got one bit of good news for you though – come see.'

She led him out and across the landing to the other top floor flat. Logan's front door was propped up against the wall, the paint on one side all blistered and peeling, pristine Saltire blue on the other. The little brass plaque engraved

326

with, 'LOGAN AND SAMANTHA'S SECRET HIDEOUT' shone in the sunlight, but the letterbox was covered with a thin film of fingerprint powder.

'Like I said, our arsonist waited too long to light the petrol. So he was standing right in front of the door when, boooooom!' She did the thing with her hands again. 'Right off its hinges. Must have hit him like a battering ram. Force of the blast threw him across the landing, slamming him back against your neighbour's door. Probably hurt like hell.'

'Good.'

'That's not the best bit.' She pointed at the exterior side of the door. 'When it hit him, it cracked his head against the paintwork. You see here?' She pointed with a purple-gloved finger at a small matt patch on the blue gloss surface. 'That was his cheek, and this. . .' She described an oval with her fingertip, just left of the smudge. 'Looks like we've got sputum, and maybe some tiny drops of blood. Incredibly lucky: normally when you get a big blaze like this the fire brigade sod-up all our evidence. All that water hits the flames, you get huge plumes of steam, and any DNA gets cooked to oblivion.'

Samantha's boss smiled. 'Because it got blown across the hallway – and the outside surface's facing away from the fire – it's been protected from the heat and the worst of the water. I think we're going to get DNA.'

Logan tried to force some enthusiasm into his voice. 'That's great.'

'Don't you worry: we'll catch them, whoever they are.'

'I know you will.'

But right now Shuggie Webster had better be praying Grampian Police got there before he did.

'What on *earth* do you think you're doing here?' DCI Finnie stood in the doorway to Logan's office/building site, fists on his hips. 'You should be home resting. . .' Pink rushed up

Finnie's jowly cheeks. 'I mean . . . not *home*, but. . . You know what I mean.'

He stepped into the gloomy room and closed the door behind him. 'Seriously, Logan, you shouldn't be here. You've had a horrible shock and—'

'I'm fine. Really. I appreciate the concern, but if I sit about for much longer—'

'You're on *compassionate* leave. And that's an order.'

'I don't want—'

'An *order*, do you hear me?' Finnie perched himself on the edge of the desk. 'Come on, Logan, be sensible. You *know* you can't have anything to do with the arson investigation. It's—'

'I'm not. Look,' Logan turned the monitor screen around, and pointed at the spreadsheet, 'I'm going over the Trisha Brown case. I'm not going anywhere near the fire. I want whoever did it caught and banged up; I'm not going to screw up the prosecution by giving the defence a conflict of interest to scream about. I just need. . .' He rubbed a hand across his forehead. 'I just need something to keep busy with. I can't sit about in the dark worrying about Samantha any more. It's driving me mental.'

Finnie sighed. 'Logan—'

'I can keep reviewing the McGregor case too. It's belt and braces stuff, nothing that's going to get in anyone's way.'

The head of CID pinched up his face. 'I understand your need to be doing something, but—'

The door banged open. 'Are you no' right in the sodding head?' Steel marched into the room, waving a rolled-up newspaper like it was a machete. 'You nearly died last night!'

'I didn't—'

'I was just telling Sergeant McRae he—'

'Oh no you bloody don't.' She turned on Finnie and poked him in the shoulder with her newspaper. 'I don't care how short staffed you are, he's going home. What the hell's wrong with you?'

Finnie bristled. 'I'm sorry, Inspector, did I *somehow* give you the impression I was running a democracy here? I don't need your permission to decide who can and can't come to work, understand?'

Wonderful. Logan scrubbed a hand across his eyes, rubbing them until little yellow dots sparked in the darkness. 'I'm fine, I just need—'

'Andy, for Christ sake, his girlfriend's lying up in intensive care. In a sodding *coma*!'

'I am well aware what the situation—'

'Then do something about it! Send him home! He can crash at my place, Susan'll look after him.' Another poke. 'Don't be a prick all your life!'

Finnie's eyes went wide, fists trembling at his sides. 'That's *enough*! If you *ever* speak to me like that again, you're going to be on a disciplinary charge, do you understand?'

'You're no' being—'

'DO YOU UNDERSTAND?' Spittle flying everywhere.

Steel's chin came up, pulling the wattle of skin beneath it taut. 'Yes, sir.'

'DS McRae,' Finnie shot a finger in Logan's direction, 'you will not go anywhere near the arson investigation. You will confine yourself to Trisha Brown's disappearance and reviewing the McGregor investigation, is that in any way too vague and fuzzy for you?'

Logan shook his head. 'No, sir.'

'If I find you even *thinking* about interfering: you're out of here.'

'Thank you, sir.'

Finnie glowered at Steel a moment longer, then turned and stormed from the room, slamming the door behind him.

Pause.

Steel let out a huge hissing breath, then sagged against the plastic covered wall. 'Oh thank God. . . Thought the rubber-faced bastard was going to fire me for a minute there.' She pulled out her e-cigarette and took a deep drag. 'You really sodding owe me one: this reverse psychology lark is no' as easy as you'd think.'

Logan stared at her. 'You called him a "prick" on *purpose*?'

'Like I'm no' stressed enough as it is.' She dumped the newspaper on the desk in front of him. The *Aberdeen Examiner*, evening edition. 'POLICE HUNT FOR MISSING SEX BEAST.'

The photo of Frank Baker wasn't recent – probably hauled out of DI Ingram's files and issued as a 'HAVE YOU SEEN THIS MAN' poster. A smaller picture showed a huge man with a draught-excluder moustache: Spike, Baker's friend from the fabrication yard. The one who'd marched over to defend him.

'"DON'T COME BACK!" PAEDO FRANKIE'S WORKMATES KEPT IN THE DARK ABOUT HIS FILTHY CRIMES.'

Steel flicked Spike in the face. 'So now we've got a nation-wide manhunt to deal with, because sodding Green had to go stirring things up. And he's all, "Look at me, I was right!". . . Wanker.'

Logan skimmed the article. 'You think Baker's in the frame for Alison and Jenny?'

There was a knock on the door, then Rennie stuck his head into the room. 'How'd it go?'

'Coffee, milk two sugars. And get something for Laz too.' Steel picked the stack of student interview forms off the desk and rifled through them. Then glanced back towards the door. 'You're still standing there, Constable.'

Rennie nodded at Logan, then held up a couple of bulging black plastic bin-bags, both sealed with a knot of yellow-and-black 'CRIME SCENE' tape – the stuff only the IB used. 'Elaine Drever says you wanted these?'

He dumped them on the floor.

'Thanks.'

The constable grinned. 'Did you hear about McPherson? Apparently, right, he was supposed to come in for a bollocking this morning, and halfway down Union Street he nips across the road, dodges a bus, overshoots and goes arse over tit down those stairs onto Correction Wynd. Broken leg and concussion. They got the whole thing on CCTV, if you fancy a laugh?'

'And some chocolate biscuits too.' Steel waved a hand at him. 'Run along, there's a good wee soul.'

As soon as Rennie was gone, Steel dumped the forms back on the desk. 'Here's the deal: you work till five, then we go home to my place and you let Susan fuss over you. You have a few drams, watch the telly, have tea, brush your teeth, and go to beddy-byes, all where I can keep an eye on you. You're no' going back to that manky wee caravan by the jobbie farm to mope, brood, and fester in the dark.'

'I. . .' Logan could feel the heat rushing up his cheeks. 'Thanks.'

'Should think so too. Meantime: who torched your flat?'

Don't look away. Keep eye contact. 'I've no idea. Been trying to figure it out all day, but. . .' Frown. Shrug. Nice and natural. 'Has to be someone I put away. Can't just be random.'

Steel rolled the fake cigarette around her mouth, the plastic end clicking off her teeth. 'IB's running DNA tests on some stuff they got off your front door. We'll get a match, and we'll catch the bastard, and I'll make sure he gets done for attempted murder.' She stood, rested a hand on his shoulder. 'You trust your Auntie Roberta: that wanker is going to pay.'

Logan's phone blared its drunken, sinister waltz. He hauled it out and checked the display: Steel.

'Thought we had a bastarding deal!'

Logan flattened himself against the two-tone green wall as a huge hospital bed was wheeled past – a pale old man in an oxygen mask staring at the ceiling, his face slack and greasy. A woman in blue scrubs and squeaky white trainers tutted at Logan as they went past. 'You're not allowed to use your mobile in the hospital!'

'Sorry.' He watched them disappear.

'I called Finnie a prick for you! I nearly got sodding fired: and soon as my back's turned—'

'I'm up at the hospital.' He started down the corridor again. 'Someone has to tell Trisha Brown's mother her wee girl's been abducted.'

'You could at least've taken Rennie!'

'I wanted. . . They say I can sit with Samantha for fifteen minutes.'

A pause. *'Fuck's sake, Laz, I would've come with you. You know that. Could've sat in the canteen ogling nurses while you were in with her.'*

'Look, I've got to go.' He hung up before she could say anything else.

The plump nurse eyed Logan up and down for the third time in as many minutes as she led him towards a curtained-off area at the far end of an eight-bed ward. It was oppressively hot in here, even though the windows were open, letting in the droning rumble of traffic and the occasional screeching wail of ambulances.

'Now, I need you to understand that Mrs Brown isn't to be excited.' The nurse ran a hand across her chest, just above the massive shelf of bosom. Then checked the watch pinned to her blue top like a medal. 'She's not due another dose of methadone for two hours and she's a bloody nightmare when she gets going.'

'I'll do my best.'

The nurse grabbed a handful of curtain and wheeched it back.

Helen Brown lay on top of the covers, head back, mouth hanging open, snoring gently. No teeth. A wad of gauze was taped over one eye, the rest of her face a patchwork of bruises and stitches. Her right arm was encased in a fibreglass cast from palm to elbow, her left leg from the ankle all the way to the thigh. But her right leg came to an abrupt end at the knee, the exposed thigh stained yellow and green.

Logan winced. The attack must have been horrific. 'They cut her leg off?'

'About three years ago. Gangrene.' The nurse checked the chart hanging on the end of the bed. 'That's the trouble with intravenous drug users. Don't know when to stop.' She looked up at Trisha's mum. 'Mrs Brown? Helen? There's a policeman here to see you.'

A mumble.

'Helen?'

Trisha's mum squinted with her good eye. 'Fuck off. . .'

'Come on, Helen. What have we talked about your language?'

She struggled over onto her side. 'Fuckin' fat bitch. Where'th my painkillerth?'

A sigh. 'You know you can't get anything more till five. Now there's a policeman here to see you; do you want a glass of water?'

'I need my fuckin' painkillerth! In fuckin' agony here. . .'

Logan settled into the seat beside the bed. 'Mrs Brown, my name's Detective Sergeant McRae. I need to speak to you about Trisha.'

The nurse nodded. 'Well, I leave you to it then.' She stepped away from the bed and pulled the curtains closed again, shutting Logan in.

Trisha's mum scowled at him. 'Fuckin' bitch never gives me anything for the pain.'

'She was seen getting into a car on Saturday evening—'

333

'Oh, here we go.' Helen curled back her lips, exposing a pair of bruised and battered gums. 'Just 'cos she sucks someone off in—'

'The person in the car attacked her. She was seen being beaten.'

'Oh. . .' Helen rolled over onto her back. 'Is she OK?'

'We don't know. He drove off with her still in the car.'

Silence. Helen rubbed the fingers of her good hand up and down the blanket. Then a tear rolled its way down her bruised cheek.

Logan looked away. 'I'm sorry.'

'You're sorry? You're fuckin' *sorry*?' An empty plastic tumbler bounced off Logan's shoulder. 'Why aren't you out there? Why aren't you looking for my little girl?'

'We're doing everything we—'

'SHE COULD BE FUCKIN' DEAD FOR ALL YOU KNOW! Dead. Raped in a fucking ditch! My wee Trisha. . .'

'If you can think of anyone who threatened, or—'

'And they send round a fuckin' *sergeant*? Alison McGregor gets the Chief Constable and half the pigs in Scotland, and all Trisha gets is a fuckin' sergeant! WHAT FUCKIN' GOOD ARE YOU?'

'Mrs Brown, I want to assure you that Grampian Police are taking this very seriously.'

The curtains burst open and the big nurse was back. 'What did I tell you about upsetting her?'

'I didn't—'

'TRISHA!'

'Come on, Helen, quieten down: you don't want to disturb the other patients, now do you?'

She grabbed a grey cardboard bedpan and threw it at the nurse. 'MY WEE GIRL'S MISSING! I DON'T GIVE A FUCK ABOUT YOUR FUCKIN' PATIENTS!'

'We're doing everything we can to find—'

'You bunch of bastards. You think she's just a junkie hoor, she's not worth anything. SHE'S MY LITTLE GIRL!' Helen Brown swung her fibreglass cast at Logan's head. 'I'LL FUCKIN' KILL YOU!'

He jerked back out of the way, the plastic visitor's chair tipping over, clattering to the floor, as he stood.

'Right, that's enough.' The nurse lunged, pinning Helen to the bed.

'GET OFF ME YOU FAT BITCH! AAAAAAGH!'

'I said that's *enough!*' The nurse scowled up at Logan, teeth gritted. 'I think you'd better go, don't you?'

'You're looking well. No really. . .' Logan squeezed Samantha's hand. 'Very goth.'

She didn't look ill, there was barely a scratch on her. At least, not on the bits he could see. They'd taped her eyelids shut. A breathing tube snaked in through the side of her mouth, a pulse monitor clipped to her right index finger, an IV line plugged into a shunt on her right wrist.

'I moved back into the caravan. Place smells worse than your dad. All mouldy. . .'

Wee Hamish's flowers were sitting in a large vase on the windowsill. A vast arrangement of roses and carnations and fuzzy-white-spray-stuff and leaves and twirls of bamboo. Extravagant, but tasteful.

'Elaine picked up all your clothes, by the way. The pants and boots and things.' He sank forward until his head was resting against her chest, rising and falling on the swell of her mechanically-assisted breathing. 'Fuck. . . I don't know if you can hear me or not. But it's going to be OK. I promise.'

Lying bastard.

'Starting to think you're stalking me.'

Logan scrubbed a hand across his eyes, kept his head facing

the corner. 'Sorry. . .' It took him a couple of beats to realize where he was – a subterranean corridor, deep within the bowels of the hospital. The thrum of the ventilation system, the smell of over-boiled cauliflower and industrial floor polish.

He sniffed. Wiped his eyes again. 'I used to wander the corridors . . . you know, after the stabbing. Must've worn out three pairs of trainers by the time they let me go home. Always ended up down here.' Staring at four watercolours framed on the scuffed cream walls. A single landscape split over the seasons, the colours so vibrant they were surreal.

The APT moved around, peering at him, her fiery-orange hair swinging like a pendulum. 'You OK?'

He almost laughed. 'Been a rough couple of days.'

Silence.

'You want a cup of tea, or something?'

'Milk, two sugars.' She placed a steaming mug on the desk in front of him.

Coffee. He could smell it over the bleach and formaldehyde. Over the smell of institutionalized death. 'Thanks.'

The Anatomical Pathology Technician glanced over her shoulder. 'Don't worry about Mrs Sawyer, it was very peaceful.' An old lady – laid out on the cutting table, just her head and bare feet sticking out from beneath the white plastic sheet. 'Are you sure you're OK?'

'No.'

A nod. 'Well, tell you what, I've got something that might cheer you up. . .' She was back a minute later, carrying the laptop from the other room. It went on the desk, next to Logan's coffee, then she fiddled with the touch-pad. 'Remember you were looking for dead girls who'd been given morphine and thiopental sodium?'

The screen was fuzzy, out of focus. He blinked. It was a little girl, her eyes half shut, face covered with scrapes and bruises, blood crusting around her nose. Bowl haircut and a razor-sharp fringe.

The APT poked the screen. 'Olivia Brook. Five and a half. Car accident. Riding her bike and got broadsided by a teenager in a VW Polo. I was going to email you after we'd seen to Mrs Sawyer.'

Logan stared at the photo. Poor little sod. . . 'I thought you searched—'

'Oh, she didn't *die*. They had to take her left leg off just above the knee. Was hanging by a thread anyway; blood supply was completely compromised; the bones were all crushed; nothing they could do.'

'Where's the leg?'

'We incinerate hospital waste.' She raised her hands to the ceiling tiles. Giving her head a little shake, one eyebrow raised. 'So. . .?'

'So no one would notice a missing toe.' Bastards.

'*But* we do have blood samples on file. I can send one over, if you want to try for a DNA match?'

'Yeah, could you make it—'

Logan's mobile rang, deep in his pocket – the generic tune marking the call as one from an unknown number. If it was Shuggie Bloody Webster calling to talk about consequences he was in for a fucking nasty shock. Logan dragged the phone out. 'What?'

A small, rustling pause, then, *'Logan?'* A man's voice, the accent a whispery, gravelly mix of Aberdonian and public school. Wee Hamish Mowat.

Logan licked his lips. Sat up straight. 'Hello?'

'I hope you don't mind me calling, but I thought you might like to know that we've managed to locate your missing . . . friend.'

40

A small warehouse in Dyce – not much bigger than a double garage, oil stains on the concrete floor, metal shelving around the bare breezeblock walls loaded down with dusty boxes.

A layer of thick, clear plastic sheeting was spread out on the floor, the corners held down with chunks of rusty machinery.

One of the roller doors was open, letting in the bang and clank of the industrial estate, the whumping roar of helicopters on their way to and from the rigs. A dented Transit van had been backed part way into the warehouse, its rear wheels sitting on the plastic sheet, its front end sticking out into the sunny afternoon. Engine idling.

The young man with the green hair sniffed, then picked up a metal attaché case, popped open the catches, and held the thing out to Logan, as if he was starring in a spy film. Jonny Urquhart – *From Mastrick With Malice*. He smiled, showing off a set of perfect teeth, his cheeks a moonscape of old acne pockmarks. 'Don't worry, totally clean, like.'

Logan looked into the case. It was a big semi-automatic pistol, wrapped in a clear plastic zip-lock food bag. Another bag had the clip. One more, a handful of snub-nosed 9mm bullets.

'Hollow point.' Urquhart winked. 'They'll fuck you up good.'

Logan's palms were suddenly damp. He wiped them on his jeans. 'No. Thanks, but no.'

'Ah, going hands-on, eh? Old school: like it.' He slammed the case shut again, twiddled with the combination lock. 'You got gloves? No? Don't worry, I'll sort you out.'

He hauled open the Transit's back doors and clambered inside, then backed out again, hauling a fully-grown man by the armpits.

Shuggie Webster: hands fastened behind his back, legs kicking out in random directions. THUMP, he hit the concrete floor . . . or rather, the plastic sheeting. A muffled grunt from behind a duct tape gag. He was still wearing the same filthy hoodie as before, but his shoes were gone, exposing a pair of socks with a hole in one toe. Urquhart dragged him into the middle of the sheeting, then let go.

Shuggie lay there, eyes wide, breath hissing out of his nose.

Logan swallowed.

'There we go, one tosspot, delivered as promised. Like FedEx for fuck-heads.' Urquhart dug another zip-lock bag from his pocket and tossed it across to Logan. 'Compliments of the house.'

Three pairs of gloves: one leather, two latex – the skin-tone ones you never saw on crime scenes any more.

'Now, you sure you don't want that gun?'

On the ground, Shuggie tried to shout something, bucking and writhing.

'No one fucking asked you.' Urquhart took two steps and slammed his boot into Shuggie's side.

That got him a muffled grunt.

'See? This is what happens when you buy your drugs off fucking foreigners.' Another kick. 'Support local businesses!' Urquhart clapped his hands together. 'Right, I'll leave you guys alone. Give us a knock when you want me to come help you get shot of what's left, OK?' He swaggered over to the back of the van, reached in and produced a portable stereo the size of a bulldog. Fiddled with it for a moment, then clicked a button.

Heavy metal boomed out of the speakers, loud enough to drown out any screams.

He popped it on the ground, creaked the van's doors shut again. It pulled forward four feet.

Urquhart turned, tugged his green forelock, stepped outside and hauled the roller door shut. Now it was just Logan, Shuggie, and Metallica.

Shuggie stopped wriggling, just lay there on his back, staring up at him.

Of course the right thing to do would be to look on all this as an object lesson. To accept that Shuggie Webster was just a screwed up little man who got in with the wrong people when he was young. Whose life had been blighted by drug use and a second-rate education. That he was a human being, as flawed and redeemable as anyone.

Logan slid the little plastic zip open and pulled out the latex gloves.

Revenge wasn't going to solve anything. It wasn't going to make Samantha's spleen and left kidney grow back. Make the swelling in her brain go down. Fix her busted ribs, broken shoulder, shattered left knee, or dislocated hip. Make her wake up.

It wasn't going to do a fucking thing.

He snapped one set of latex gloves on, then struggled the leather pair over the top. Give Shuggie a good scare, then haul him back to the station, hand him over to the

340

authorities, and make sure he goes down for eight-to-twelve years. Which means six-to-eight before he gets out on parole. Four-to-six with good behaviour. Less time-served while waiting for the case to come to court.

Logan pulled the last pair of latex gloves on over the leather.

Barely worth arresting him at all. Might as well give the little fuck a slap on the wrists and send him on his way with a stern talking to.

Save everyone a lot of bother.

'On your feet.'

Shuggie just stared at him.

'I said, "ON YOUR FUCKING FEET!"' Logan slammed a kick into his thigh.

Shuggie hissed behind the gag, then struggled to roll over onto his side. The bandage covering his right hand was almost black with dried blood and dirt. Logan grabbed his shoulders and hauled him up onto his knees.

'You wanted "consequences", Shuggie? Fine.' Logan grabbed the cable tie holding the big man's wrists together, and pulled. 'You're going to get your fucking "consequences".'

A muffled scream, but Shuggie got to his feet, socks slipping on the plastic.

Just a bit of a scare. . .

Logan slammed a fist into the big man's kidneys – he collapsed to his knees again.

'She's in a coma.' Logan took a step back and kicked Shuggie in the kidney again.

'MMMMMMMMPHHHHH!'

Shuggie narrowed his eyes above the duct tape gag, a growling hiss coming from his throat.

'A fucking coma!' Logan rammed his forearm into Shuggie's face, using the solid strip of bone just before the elbow to crack him right across the nose. Barely felt it. But

Shuggie went sprawling back across the plastic, moaning and whinging like a baby.

A swift boot in the nuts and he was folded over again, blood pouring from his ruined nose, jerking back and forward.

Logan stamped on his left ankle.

'Say you're sorry!' He kicked the big man over onto his back, then sat down hard on his chest. Rammed another elbow into his face. Shuggie's head bounced off the plastic sheeting with a dull *thunk*. Logan hauled the duct tape gag off and Shuggie dragged in a huge breath.

Logan hit him again, not bothering with the elbow, using his fist. 'Say—' punch, '—you're—' punch, '—fucking—' punch, '—SORRY!' Then sat back, breathing hard.

Shuggie's face was already beginning to swell up, one eye closing over, the other well on its way – the pupil adrift in a sea of bright red. Nose flattened, lips split. Probably a broken cheekbone.

'Urgh. . .' Bubbles of blood popped at the side of his battered mouth.

'Everything we do, all the shit we put up with, to keep bastards like you from hurting people. Stealing from them. Dealing drugs to their kids and ruining their fucking lives. . .' Logan hauled himself to his feet, flexed his right hand, feeling the layers of glove tight across his skin. He kicked him again, catching Shuggie on the side of the knee, where it would do the most damage.

The big man screamed.

'Say you're sorry.'

Shuggie just lay there, gurgling blood and crying.

'SAY IT.'

'I'm sorry! I'm sorry. . .' His voice was wet, strangled with sobs. 'Whatever . . . whatever I did – oh God – I'm sorry.'

Logan stared at him. '"Whatever you *did*"?' Piece of shit. He stamped on Shuggie's stomach, folding him up again.

'Aaaaaa! Please, I'm sorry!'

'YOU SET FIRE TO MY FLAT, YOU FUCKING WANKER!'

'I'm so. . . I'm so sorry. . .'

'You stuck a condom through my letterbox, filled it with petrol, and set fire to the fucking thing!' Another kick in the stomach. 'What, were you too stoned to remember? Samantha's in a fucking coma because of you!' One more for luck.

'Aaaaaaaaagh!' Shuggie lay there, trembling and panting. 'I didn't do it, please, I didn't set fire to anything!'

Logan backed off a couple of steps. 'How stupid do you think I am?'

The song on the stereo ended, replaced by another round of thumping drums and squealing guitars.

'I can't. . . My hand. How could . . . could I pour fuck-all through . . . through anything?' Shuggie curled up into a ball, battered forehead resting on his one good knee. 'Look at it. LOOK AT IT!'

Logan walked around to the other side and stared down at the filthy bandage completely covering Shuggie's right hand. 'Doesn't mean you can't still use it.'

'They skinned my . . . my fingers.' He coughed, spraying blood and chunks of tooth all over his jeans.

Logan knelt down behind him and yanked Shuggie's arms back. A safety pin held the tatty bandage end in place. Logan fumbled with it, the three layers of gloves making it nearly impossible. And then he got it, pulled the rust-flecked pin out, and unwound the bandage.

Shuggie screamed – the grubby fabric tugging at the raw flesh, coming away like strawberry jam, stinking of rancid meat.

'Jesus. . .' Only the thumb and forefinger were visible,

343

but they were a stomach-lurching mess of purple, red and black, the tendons just visible as grey strips. Logan backed away to the edge of the plastic sheeting. 'Why didn't you go to the hospital?'

'Every . . . every day I. . . I couldn't pay them back . . . they took . . . took another one. . .' Breath hissing out through bloody lips.

God almighty.

'I didn't. . . I didn't set fire . . . to anything.' He made a sound that almost sounded like a laugh. 'How could I?'

Logan's stomach lurched. Head full of burning coals, mouth full of saliva. He staggered back against the shelving.

It wasn't him. It wasn't Shuggie.

He swallowed, forced down the bitter taste of bile. Even if Shuggie *didn't* pour the petrol, it was still his fault. There had to be *consequences*.

'Where are they? Jacob and Robert – your Yardie mates? Did you tell them I wouldn't give you your fucking drugs back? Did you set those bastards on me?'

Logan's eyes stung, his vision blurring.

Blink. Swallow.

'Where the fuck are they?'

Lying, sobbing on the warehouse floor, Shuggie told him.

'Oh. . .' Jonny Urquhart stood looking down at Shuggie Webster's battered body. 'Cos it's no problem if you want me to . . . you know.' He made a gun with his thumb and forefinger.

'No.' Logan cleared his throat. 'He's under arrest.'

'You sure? Cos you've *really* kinda fucked him up. What's going to happen when he's served his time, eh? You want some junkie scroat bag coming after you?'

Silence.

That's what had caused this whole mess in the first place.

344

'Tell you what.' Urquhart hunkered down next to Shuggie. 'Listen up, fuckwit, and listen really good, cos if I have to repeat myself, you're screwed. You do anything to this nice police officer and we're gonna find you. You're gonna give yourself up, and you're gonna cough to whatever he says, and you're gonna go to prison and do your time like a good little boy. You so much as whisper "police brutality" and I'll get some huge bastard to rape your arse ragged, then cut your fucking throat. We clear?'

Shuggie coughed up a mouthful of dark red.

'I said, are we fucking clear?'

'Yeth. . .' It was little more than a whisper, borne on a bubble of blood.

Urquhart ran a hand through his green hair. 'Course he's a junkie, and you know what their word's worth. Sure you don't want me to—'

'No. Just. . .' What? Drop him off at the station looking as if he's been run over by a combine harvester? Take him to the hospital? Anything that ended up with Wee Hamish being connected to Shuggie Webster was eventually going to lead right back to him.

And maybe Logan deserved it.

He peeled off his three layers of gloves. His hands stank of elastic bands, the knuckles tainted deep pink, the skin puffy and tender. 'I'll deal with it.'

'OK.' Urquhart nudged Shuggie's crying body with the toe of his boot. 'You're a lucky fuck, Shugs. See if you'd set *my* house on fire?' A smile. 'You just remember what I said: one step out of line and. . .' he drew a finger across his throat.

41

Logan hauled on the handbrake outside Accident and Emergency, pulse rushing and booming in his ears. 'This is all your own fault. You should've turned yourself in when I gave you the sodding chance. You'd still have your fingers, and Samantha wouldn't. . .' He gritted his teeth. Then opened the car door and climbed out into the warm afternoon. 'Stay here.'

Shuggie sat in the passenger seat, cradling his skinned hand, his face a bubbling mass of raw meat. Tears making clean tracks on his bloody cheeks.

Past the small knot of smokers and in through the automatic doors to A&E. There was a herd of wheelchairs just inside – not proper ones, just brown vinyl seats with four little wheels at the end of their legs. Logan grabbed one and performed a seven point turn with the thing, fighting to get it facing the right way.

'Worse than a wobbly shopping trolley, eh?' It was the guy from last night: Mop Dude, pushing a buggy loaded with newspapers, crisps, bars of chocolate, and assorted sweeties. There was a little stack of the *Evening Express* next to the Curlywurlies, 'SICK COUPLE TRY TO CASH IN ON KIDNAP TRAGEDY'.

346

He nodded. 'Unbelievable, isn't it? Got to wonder what's wrong with some people, you know?'

He flicked a strand of long brown hair away from his face and grinned, the piercing in his nose sparkling in the hospital's dismal fluorescent lighting. 'How's your girlfriend? She doing better?'

Logan looked away. 'No change.'

'Aw, man, sorry to hear it. You got some sleep though, yeah?'

'A bit.'

'Yeah, those pills are the mutt's.' He stared at Logan for a bit, then shook his head. 'You're looking kinda pale, man.'

'Been a tough day.'

A laugh. 'Tell me about it. Doing double shifts so I can afford T in the Park. . . Mind you, maybe I should stick it all in that fund for Alison and Jenny. One day to go. Nightmare, eh?'

One of the uniformed officers stationed at the hospital marched out from the reception area, pulling his peaked cap on over his bald patch. 'Hoi, you with the chair!' He pointed out through the doors. 'That your car? You can't park in an ambulance bay. . .'

Officer Baldpatch went pink and lowered his hand. 'Sorry, Sarge; didn't know it was you.'

Logan gave the wheelie chair a nudge and sent it trundling off towards the car park. 'Shuggie Webster's in the passenger seat. He needs a doctor.'

'Yes, Sarge.' The constable hurried out after the chair.

Mop Dude cleared his throat. 'You're a cop?'

After today, that was debatable.

'Look . . . man . . . about those pills—'

'Pills? What pills?' Logan dug a handful of change from his pocket. Karma. 'Now how much for an *Evening Express* and a packet of Skittles?'

* * *

'Where've you been?' DI Steel settled onto the end of Logan's desk, her face creased into a scowl. 'Ten to six, should be home by now.'

Logan pulled the next sheet of paper from his in-tray and gave it a skim before dumping it in the bin. 'Hospital.'

'Aye, I heard. How the hell did you get your hands on Shuggie Webster?'

The next three sheets were e-fits, printed off from the identikit software with no indication of who it was meant to be, who'd done them, or who the witness was. They were part of a little stack of unlawful removal forms and other assorted random gubbins, as if someone had grabbed the lot off the printer without bothering to check what they'd picked up. All of it anonymous. 'I got a tip-off.'

'And you thought you'd go after him on your own?'

'Yup.' Logan stuck the printouts on his desk – they didn't even have case numbers. That was the trouble with people nowadays: no pride in their work, and no clue how to do it properly either. Not that he was in a position to hand out lectures on professionalism any more.

'Laz, you daft sod, you had a bloody firearms team trying to track Shuggie down yesterday. You're lucky he didn't beat the shite out of you.'

Yeah. . . Lucky.

'I got a tip-off, he came quietly. It was fine.' Next down were the results of the GSM trace on Shuggie's mobile phone. Apparently he was in Aberdeen Royal Infirmary.

Logan stuffed the next three reports in the bin. 'You know anything about a pair of Yardies calling themselves Jacob and Robert?'

'We had a deal, Laz. Five o'clock – you come home with me and let Susan spoil you.' Steel picked up the *Evening Express* he'd bought at the hospital and flicked through it. She sucked on her top lip for a minute, then dumped the open newspaper back on his desk. 'POLICE HERO IN HOUSE FIRE TRAGEDY.'

She tapped the story with a scarlet-painted nail. 'Susan's worried about you.'

Logan chucked a memo from Superintendent Napier in on top of the discarded reports. 'I'm fine.'

'No you're no'.' The inspector stood. 'Did you see Samantha?'

Fifteen minutes of sitting at her bedside. Just sitting there, holding her hand and listening to the machinery breathing for her. Somehow he couldn't bring himself to tell her what he'd done to Shuggie because of her.

She probably wouldn't have been impressed.

'. . . to Planet Laz, come in Planet Laz?'

He blinked. 'Sorry. Didn't get much sleep. Finnie about?'

Steel narrowed her eyes. 'Did you no' hear a single word I said?'

'Just got to get something sorted before we go.' Logan made for the door, but she was blocking the way.

'Laz, look, I understand it's—'

'You do?' He stared down at her. 'You *understand*?'

Sigh. 'Fuck's sake, we've all—'

'I just . . . just need to speak to Finnie.'

'. . . and all I'm saying is that we can't put anything in place until we know what the terms and location for handover are going to be.' Superintendent Green was leaning back against the windowsill in Finnie's office. He looked up as Logan entered, then back to the head of CID again. 'Any plans we make now will be irrelevant as soon as they get in touch.'

'And I say there are contingencies we should be planning for *now*.' Finnie swivelled his chair around and frowned at Logan. Then his face softened. 'I understand you brought Shuggie Webster in. Well done.'

'Thank you, sir, but I wanted to talk to you about—'

'The only things you can *realistically* do at this stage of a kidnapping are put the hospital on alert, get a duty doctor on call, and get the force helicopter on standby.' Green folded his arms. 'It's irrelevant in any case – we should be concentrating on finding Frank Baker. We do that and he'll lead us straight to the McGregors.'

Finnie didn't even look around. 'This isn't *Miami Vice*, Superintendent; Aberdeen doesn't have a helicopter.' He paused for a moment, then took a deep breath, eyes closed, letting it out slowly. 'Now, what can we do for you, Logan?'

'I need another firearms team. Two Yardies going by the names Jacob and Robert, it's possible they're the ones who've abducted Trisha Brown. They skinned most of Shuggie Webster's right hand when he couldn't pay off his drug debt.'

Green sniffed. 'I think we've got more important things to worry about than a couple of two-bit drug dealers, Sergeant.'

'Really, sir?' Logan pulled on an ill-fitting smile. 'Oh . . . Well, in that case, would you like me to nip back up the hospital and tell Trisha Brown's mother her little girl isn't as important as Alison and Jenny McGregor, because she's not on the television?'

Pink rushed up the superintendent's cheeks. 'That's not what I meant. By all means go pick up your little drug dealers, but let's not lose sight of the fact that the kidnappers have already killed one little girl and time's running out for Alison and Jenny!' He squared his shoulders. 'Frank Baker's the key.'

'Frank Baker isn't—'

'You just can't admit when you're *wrong*, can you, Sergeant? You're wrong and I was right. Baker's guilty – that's why he ran. The guilty ones *always* run. That's why I exerted so much pressure on him, not because I think I'm,'

Green raised his fingers and made finger-quotes, '"something off *The Sweeney*."'

Logan clenched his fist, feeling the skin pull tight over his swollen knuckles. 'Frank Baker ran because you threatened to tell the people he worked with he was a paedophile.'

'Exactly!' Green stepped forward, until he was standing at Finnie's side. 'He's a paedophile with access to a veterinarian's, his own transport, and—'

'He's into little *boys*, not girls!' Getting louder and louder. 'And the vets he volunteered at haven't lost any thiopental sodium. They've checked, *six times*. You just pulled his name out of your arse and decided he was guilty!'

Green stiffened. 'Do I need to remind you, *Sergeant*, that I am a superintendent with the Serious Organized Crime Agency?'

Finnie bit his top lip. Cleared his throat. Turned to Logan. 'And do you have an address for the Marley brothers?'

'Marley. . .?'

'Robert and Jacob. Bob Marley: reggae singer, Jacob Marley: Scrooge's dead partner from *A Christmas Carol*. Either your Yardies have a *twisted* sense of humour, or they've been visited by the coincidence fairy, don't you think?'

Logan gave Finnie the address he'd got from Shuggie: a semi-detached in Kittybrewster. An address beaten out of a crippled man with his hands cable-tied behind his back.

'Hmm. . .' Finnie sat back in his chair, swivelling slowly from side to side.

Green raised that manly, cleft chin of his and stared down his nose at Logan. 'I thought you were supposed to be on compassionate leave?'

Prick.

The head of CID tapped a finger on his desk. 'DS McRae is a valued member of my team, Superintendent. If he feels

351

he's better off helping us recover a missing girl and her mother than sitting at home brooding, I'm inclined to support him.' He gave Green a smile. 'Dedication, Superintendent – one of the cornerstones of policework, don't you think?'

'I *think*,' Green picked invisible lint from the sleeve of his suit jacket, 'that Grampian Police seem to have problems interfacing with the reality of the situation. Alison and Jenny McGregor's survival depends on a unified and concerted response to Frank Baker, and we need to do it now.'

Silence.

Finnie pursed his lips, both hands spread out on the desktop. '*Superintendent*, I can assure you Grampian Police are *well* aware of the situation. And while I *deeply* value your input, *if* you don't mind, I think I might just try to do my job and get a couple of drug-dealing scumbags off the streets.' He ruffled some papers on his desk. 'Detective Sergeant McRae – I understand you wanting to be involved,' he cast a sideways glance at Green, 'but I think it might be best if nightshift handled this.'

'Sir, if I can just—'

'You've done more than enough today. Go home; get some rest. We'll deal with the Marley Brothers.'

'But—'

Finnie held up a finger, 'We'll deal with it.'

Logan frowned at the screen. 'So the red banana thing—'

'The Ninky Nonk.' Steel topped up his whisky.

'Thanks.' The living room was warm, a large LCD television mounted above the fireplace filled with bright primary colours. 'So the Ninky Nonk is some kind of random bus service?'

'Yup.'

'And the porcupines—'

'*Pontipines*. They want to get on the Ninky Nonk so they

can go wherever it is Pontipines go. Dole office, most likely. Work-shy bastards.'

'Only every time they try, the Ninky Nonk drives off?'

She took a sip. 'Got it in one.'

Susan's voice floated through from the kitchen. 'Come on Stinkypants, time for bed.'

Steel patted Logan on the arm. 'It's OK, she's not talking about you.'

There was a sort of toddler jail set up in front of the couch – a big circular enclosure made of plastic and netting. A little girl in a skull-and-crossbones babygrow lay on her back in the middle of it, trying to suck her own feet in that disturbing double-jointed way very small children have.

'So why does it keep driving off?' The whisky was making the world go fuzzy at the edges. That or the lack of sleep.

'Best guess? The driver's a cunt.'

'Roberta!' Susan appeared, wiping her hands on a dish towel. 'What have I told you about that? What are they going to think when Jasmine starts nursery?'

'They'll think, "who's this beautiful wee monkey with the colourful vocabulary?"' She creaked up from the couch and broke Jasmine Catherine Cassandra Steel-Wallace out of Baby Barlinnie. 'Oh-ho, someone's made trouser truffles. . .'

Susan smiled. 'Are you OK, Logan? Do you want some more ice cream?'

'No, no, I'm fine thanks.' Just as long as he didn't think about Shuggie Webster. Or Samantha. Or not being in on the firearms team picking up the Marley brothers. Engineering a little accident for them. . .

'. . . Logan?'

Blink. 'Sorry?'

'I said, do you want to kiss your daughter good night?'

'Oh, er . . . yeah. Sure.' He stood and planted a little kiss on the top of her head. Steel was right – Jasmine smelt like she'd been rolling around in something brown and sticky. 'Sweet dreams.'

'Say nighty-night to Daddy, Jasmine.' Susan took hold of a little chubby wrist and waved it at Logan. 'He gave your mummies a little tub of wriggly sperm, so doctors could put you in my tummy.'

'Do you have to do that every single time I come round?'

Susan laughed. 'Could you *be* any more uncomfortable?'

He could feel the blush crawling up his neck. 'So. . .' He went back to the TV. 'Do you really watch this rubbish all the time?'

'I *know*.' Susan laughed, Jasmine cradled against her chest making big wet-mouthed yawns. 'You get used to it.'

'Whisky helps.' Steel finished her glass. 'Tell you, half the sodding licence fee must go on heroin and tequila.'

'*. . . movement out the back. Hang on. . .*' There was a pause, then the harsh whisper came from the Airwave handset again. '*Nah, you're OK – just a cat.*'

Logan propped the lumpy grey rectangle against the vase of daffodils on the breakfast bar, then turned the volume up.

'*Jesus, that's no' a cat, it's a fucking tiger! Did you see the size of its—*'

'*All right, settle down.*' DI Bell sounded as if he was eating something. '*Timecheck: oh two-fifty. We are live in ten. Teams Two and Three, take up positions.*'

Logan glanced at the clock on the cooker: nearly five minutes fast. The room was bathed in the pale orange glow of the overcast sky, the back garden a jungle of silhouettes and shadows through the window. He filled the kettle, then poured half of it out, before sticking it on to boil. The growing rumble drowned out the babble on his Airwave handset as DI Bell got his firearms team into place.

Mug. Teabag. Boiling water. Milk—

The kitchen burst into sudden brightness.

Logan screwed his eyes up, peering through the glare. Steel was standing in the doorway, wearing a pair of tartan pyjamas, clutching a brass poker like a baseball bat.

'Christ's sake, Laz, thought you were burglars.' Her hair looked as if she'd lent it out to a colony of howler monkeys. She flicked the light off again. 'Couldn't sleep?'

He fished the teabag out and dumped it in the bin. 'Kind of.'

DI Bell: *'And we're live in five. Everyone where they're meant to be?'*

Steel sighed. 'What's going on?'

'You want tea?'

'Peppermint. What's going on?'

'Team One, ready to rock.'

'Team Two, readiness: we has it.'

'Logan?'

'Team Three, good to go.'

'Team Four, hot to trot.'

He rinsed the teaspoon under the cold tap. 'Ding-Dong's raiding the Yardies' flat in Kittybrewster.'

'Aye, I gathered that. What I want to know is why you're down here keeping tabs on it, and no' upstairs in your beddie-byes.'

Logan placed Steel's tea on the breakfast bar, the smell of mint curling through the air, the little paper tag dangling over the side of the mug like the tail on a herbal tampon. 'Told you: couldn't sleep.'

She hauled a stool out and settled down opposite. 'Do I look like a sodding idiot?'

'Here we go: five, four, three, two, one. Do it.'

The bang and crack of a Big Red Door Key smashing into wood crackled out of the handset.

Steel's eyes narrowed to wrinkly slits. 'You think they're the ones who torched your house, don't you?'

'I didn't—'

'Oh, for fuck's sake, Laz – do you *never* bloody listen? Finnie'll do his nut when he finds out!' She buried her head in her hands. 'Why did I let that wee jobbie Rennie talk me into helping you come back to work today?'

Logan stared out of the window. There was a hollow-eyed face staring back at him. 'I couldn't get them on my own. Not both of them. . .'

'So what, you thought Finnie would let you grab an MP5 and go *shoot* the wee buggers?' She looked up. 'What about Shuggie Webster?'

The ghost in the glass shrugged. 'I don't think I want to be a police officer any more.'

'Fuck's sake, Laz. Are you the one beat the poor sod up?'

'I. . .' He rubbed a hand over his eyes. 'It's. . .'

'You bloody idiot! Soon as they question him, he'll land you in it. Do you no' remember what happened to Insch? They'll lock you up, you daft bastard.'

'Probably. Maybe. I don't know.' There was nothing funny about it, but Logan couldn't help laughing, just a little bit, the sound bitter and cold. 'Might not be a bad idea.'

Steel hunched over her mug. 'I can't get you out of this one. I mean . . . fucking hell, Laz.'

'I know.'

'ON THE FLOOR! ON THE FLOOR NOW!'

They both turned and looked at the handset.

'You sure they're the ones who torched your flat?'

'Find out soon enough.'

She sighed. 'Then what? You go for them in the cells? Get yourself up on a couple of murders as well as the assault? You really think that's what Samantha wants?'

'What would you do if someone tried to kill Susan, or Jasmine? Bake them a cake?'

'GOOD. NOW MOVE AND I'LL BLOW YOUR ARSE OFF!'

'I'd. . .' She fiddled with her mug, making it click against the working surface. 'Doesn't make you any less of a daft bastard.'

'Team One: clear.'

'Team Four: clear.'

He stared down at his hands. 'Don't think I can do this any more.'

'Team Three: we have the suspects.'

'Team Two: Guv, we've got enough smack, coke, speed, and weed up here to keep Keith Richards stoned off his tits till he's ninety! Holy crap, Cath, you ever see so much weed in your life?'

Steel dumped her teabag on the draining board. 'Don't be an arse: you can't quit. What the hell would you do? Go be a rentacop down the Trinity Centre? Shoplifting and old ladies who've peed themselves?'

'Believe it or not, I got a job offer this morning.'

If you ever decide police work is no longer the career for you. . . Well, as I said, it would be nice to know that my legacy was in good hands.

Go from a police officer to heading up Aberdeen's biggest criminal empire. . . Let's face it, he was already halfway there.

Strange how much could change in just twenty-four hours.

42

Logan straightened his tie. 'OK.'

Steel looked him up and down. 'I still think you're a bloody idiot. Get a Federation rep in there with you!'

The summons to DCI Finnie's lair had been sitting on his desk when he got in, gritty-eyed and yawning, feeling as if someone had replaced his insides with burning snakes. 'MCRAE ~ MY OFFICE ~ ASAP!'

'What good's a rep going to do? If Shuggie's made a complaint I'm screwed anyway.'

Of course he'd complained – Urquhart was right, Shuggie Webster was a junkie. . . And he had every right to complain.

Logan closed his eyes. They were going to suspend him, arrest him, and lock him away for four-to-six years. Maybe by the time he was up for parole, Samantha would have woken up.

Deep breath.

He knocked on the head of CID's door.

Finnie's voice came from inside: 'Enter.'

Logan marched into the office, DI Steel slouching along behind him. 'You wanted to see me, sir?'

Finnie glanced at the clock, mounted on the wall, then sat back in his seat and steepled his fingers.

'Sir, I—'

'DI Bell picked up your Marley brothers last night. They came gift-wrapped with half a million pounds' worth of drugs. It's a significant result.'

'With all due respect, sir—'

'I know, I know.' Finnie held up a hand. 'You wanted to be there when the firearms team went in, running the operation. But I couldn't allow it, not after everything you'd been through yesterday. You needed to go home and get some rest.'

'But, sir—'

'Don't worry. Even though DI Bell made the arrests, we're all aware that it's only because *you* supplied the information. Nightshift ran their prints and DNA through the system: Robert and Jacob are wanted in connection with one death in Lothian and Borders, and two in Greater Manchester. Their capture represents a considerable feather in Grampian's police cap, at a time when we're not *exactly* covering ourselves in glory with the McGregor case.'

The bastard was drawing it out, making him suffer.

Logan shifted his feet. 'I'd like to—'

'Then there's *this*.' He held up that morning's *Press and Journal*.

And here it was: 'POLICE DISGRACE AS FORMER HERO HOSPITALIZES ADDICT IN REVENGE ATTACK. . .' only that wasn't the headline. The front page read, 'MOTHER ABDUCTED FROM KINCORTH STREET'. There was a photo of a smiling teenager, one eye squinted shut, a bottle of beer in her hand. It almost looked like— Finnie ruffled the paper. 'Trisha Brown's mother is telling everyone we're not taking her daughter's disappearance seriously. That while *Alison McGregor* gets TV tributes and the Chief Constable making statements, all her daughter gets is one *lowly* sergeant.'

Logan frowned at the photo again. It was her: Trisha Brown, taken before the heroin sank its manky-brown claws into her. She couldn't have been much older than thirteen.

Finnie's face curled down at the edges. 'Not exactly a step in the right direction, is it?'

'Sir, I want to explain—'

'And *then* there's Shuggie Webster. DI Bell went up to the hospital and took his statement last night.'

Too slow. No point jumping when you've already been pushed.

Logan raised his chin and straightened his shoulders, staring out through the window behind Finnie's head. 'Yes, sir.'

Goodbye career: hello suspension, arrest, prosecution, and jail time.

'Mr Webster has been kind enough to give us the names and addresses of three of his other suppliers and half a dozen dealers, as well as coughing to nearly twenty unlawful removals.' Finnie smiled. 'Isn't that *nice* of him?'

Logan closed his eyes, waiting for the punchline.

'I understand Mr Webster told DI Bell that you'd convinced him to turn his life around and come clean.'

Logan risked one eye. 'He did?'

'Yes. Said you were very persuasive when you rescued him from the three hoodies who attacked him yesterday morning.'

Hoodies. . .?

'. . . so remember: tempers are going to be running high today. All it'll take is one idiot and we could have a riot on our hands.' Acting DI Mark McDonald shuffled the papers in his hands, and shifted from foot to foot at the front of the crowded briefing room – every single member of day-shift CID, and more than two-dozen uniformed constables

360

staring at him. 'The media are out in force, waiting for something to kick off, so *please* make sure you keep your eyes and ears open.' He cleared his throat. 'Thank you.' Then sat down.

Someone had updated the countdown on the whiteboard behind him. Now it read, 'DEADLINE: TOMORROW!!!'

Finnie got to his feet. 'As *Acting* Detective Inspector MacDonald says, the media are wetting themselves with anticipation. But that does *not* excuse this.' He clicked the remote and the front page of today's *Aberdeen Examiner* filled the projection screen. 'DID MISSING PAEDOPHILE KIDNAP ALISON AND JENNY?' above a photo of Frank Baker.

Finnie glowered around the room. 'When I find out which unprofessional, unscrupulous *bastard* talked to the press I will make Hannibal Lecter look like Tinky-Bloody-Winky. Do I make myself clear?'

Uncomfortable silence.

He curled his top lip. 'Need I remind you *boys* and *girls* that we have less than twenty-four hours to find Alison and Jenny McGregor? Let's try to concentrate on doing our *jobs*.'

Rennie stuck his hand up. 'What if the kidnappers decide we haven't raised enough cash?'

'Mr Maguire from Blue-Fish-Two-Fish informs me that the official freedom fund now stands at just over six million pounds.'

Someone whistled.

'If we fail to find these people it's going to be open season on every D-list celebrity in the country. *After all*, if the guys who snatched *Alison and Jenny* can get away with six point three million pounds, maybe *I* can too?'

Finnie glowered at them all again. 'Now tell me, ladies and gentlemen, do we really want to be responsible for that, because I don't think we do. Do you?'

No one answered that.

He nodded at Superintendent Green and the man from SOCA stood. 'As soon as Jenny and Alison McGregor are released, a report will be submitted to the Independent Police Complaints Commission asking them to review Grampian Police's handling of the investigation, which is *standard policy* for high-profile cases like this.' Green held up his hands, as if he was about to bless them all, instead of crap on them from a great height. 'The Serious Organized Crime Agency will, at that point, move from an advisory capacity to an executive role.'

'Let me guess,' DI Steel hauled up her trousers, 'that means you're going to take over.'

Angry noises filled the briefing room.

Finnie banged his coffee mug on the nearest desk. 'All right, that's enough. Let's try to behave like grown-ups and *professionals*.'

Superintendent Green sat back down again.

'We have one last item of business.' A smile spread across Finnie's face. 'You'll have heard we made a significant seizure of drugs last night – thanks to DS McRae – and expect to make further inroads into the supply chain over the next few days. You'll *also* have heard that DI McPherson met with an unfortunate accident yesterday. As he's going to be out of commission for at least three weeks, I'm promoting DS McRae to the rank of Detective Inspector effective immediately. I'm sure you'll *all*. . .' he turned his smile on Green for a moment, then back to the rest of the room, 'join me in wishing him every success in this challenging role.'

Logan stared. 'What. . .?'

'Woohoo!' Rennie started a round of applause that rippled around the room, then grew.

Logan stared at his hands. The knuckles were still slightly swollen, the skin around them mottled with faint bruises. That was what they were clapping for – because he beat the crap out Shuggie Webster, a crippled junkie with his hands cable-tied behind his back.

Go Team Logan.

He should have resigned when he'd had the chance.

'I know, OK?' Logan covered his head with his hands, then slumped back in his seat in the make-shift office. 'It's not like I planned it, is it?'

He could hear Steel sighing. 'You're a sodding lucky bugger, Laz. But if Shuggie changes his mind. . .'

'He won't.' Not unless he wanted to feel the wrath of Wee Hamish Mowat. And Jonny Urquhart had made it quite clear what that would involve.

There was a pause. Then her voice went cold. 'That what you were doing up the hospital yesterday afternoon? Threatening him to keep his gob shut?'

'No. . .' Logan crumpled forward until his elbows touched the desk. 'I spoke to Trisha's mum, I sat with Samantha. That's *all*.'

'You used to be. . .' Steel grunted. He could picture her, standing behind him, shaking her head, eyes closed, chewing on her top lip. 'Fuck's sake, Laz.'

The door banged open. 'Celebrations!' Rennie danced into the room – a one man conga line. 'Da-da-dada-da, *da*! Da-da-dada-da, *da*!'

He grabbed Steel's hips and kept on dancing. 'Da-da-dada-da, *da*! Da-da-dada-da, *da*!'

'Get off me you daft wee sod!' She smacked his hands away.

'Oh, come on, Guv, not every day one of our own gets bumped up the ranks.' He performed a little curtsey. 'Detective *Inspector* McRae, may I be the first to tell you how gargantuanly sexy you look as a DI, and if you ever need a sidekick—'

'Thanks, but—'

'I think Detective Sergeant Simon Rennie has a certain ring to it, don't you? I mean, if you're being promoted, they'll need someone to fill in for you at the Wee Hoose, yeah?' He grinned, his teeth sparkling white against the unnaturally orange tan. 'Then *I* can get some poor sod to make the tea for a change.'

'Good idea.' Steel clicked her e-cigarette into life and sooked on it. 'Latte: three sugars, extra chocolate, and some of that hazelnut syrup if they've got it. DI McRae'll have decaf: two and a coo.'

Rennie's grin slipped. 'Can't I get someone else to—'

'If you're no' back in two minutes with those coffees, you're going to spend the rest of the day as Biohazard's bitch, understand?'

Rennie pretty much sprinted from the room.

Steel waited until the door was closed and they were alone once more. 'I'm no' going to say this twice, so pin back your lugs: you ever, *ever* do anything like this again, I'll hang your arse out like a pair of scabby knickers, understand?'

'Then let me *quit*.'

She thumped him on the shoulder. 'You're no' getting off that lightly.'

Of course he wasn't.

'Now what?'

Steel sent a perfect smoke ring crashing against his computer monitor. 'I mean it, Laz. I'll no' have wee Jasmine growing up with a bent copper for a dad.'

Logan logged into his email, scrolling through the backlog of messages. 'Anything else?' Not looking at her.

'Yes.'

'What?' He clicked on an email from DI Bell – an update on the interviews conducted overnight with the 'Marley brothers'.

'I'm sorry about Samantha. If you need to talk to anyone. . .'

'I don't need to—'

''Cause if you do, you can call your pet psychologist. All that touchy-feely bollocks gives me the dry boak.' She sniffed. 'Now, maybe we should—'

Logan's mobile burst into song.

'Laz?' Colin Miller. *'We got another message from the wankers in the white sperm-suits. You near your computer?'*

The email package chimed at him, a little window popping up in the bottom left corner of the screen: 'COLIN MILLER. FWD: ONE DAY TO GO.'

The door banged open and Rennie lurched over the threshold, breathing like a pervert, clutching his side. 'They've. . . They've got a . . . got a . . . a new video!'

Logan opened the message: a link to YouTube. He clicked on it.

'No' more toes, is it?' Steel pulled the fake cigarette from her mouth.

The video finally downloaded enough to start playing. Logan hauled the headphones out of the socket and the speakers crackled with static, then that cold computer voice boomed into the room.

43

Steel tapped the screen. 'Play it again.'

'You have twenty-four hours left to save Jenny's life.'

On the screen a fuzzy image snapped into focus – Jenny McGregor lying curled up on a bare mattress. A chain was wrapped around her neck, the other end padlocked to the metal bed frame. Her Winnie the Pooh pyjamas were grubby, but the bandages on her feet looked fresh – a faint stain marking where her little toes had been hacked off.

Steel bared her teeth. 'Bastards.'

'Some newspapers insist on telling you that this is all a hoax: it is not. I promise you Jenny will die if you fail to raise enough money.'

A figure stepped into shot, dressed in the familiar white SOC outfit with gloves and a plastic mask that distorted their features. They held up an eight-inch carving knife.

'She will die, and the police will receive a different part of her dismembered body every day for fourteen days: one piece for every day you failed to raise enough money.'

The speakers crackled. A woman screamed, *'Don't hurt my baby!'* and the camera swung around to show Alison McGregor, scrabbling at the bare floorboards with her fingernails, trying to drag herself away from the radiator they'd chained her to. Her hair was a mess, face bright pink, tears streaming down her cheeks. Then the sound cut off, leaving Alison screaming and shouting in silence.

Jenny filled the screen again.

`'If you fail her, she will die. Then we will start the process all over again with her mother.'`

The white-suited figure took a handful of hair and hauled the little girl's head up, then held the knife against her throat.

The picture zoomed in. Jenny's nose bright pink and shiny, her bottom lip trembling. Her eyes darted up to the right, probably looking at the bastard with the knife, then she nodded. It wasn't a big nod, but it was still enough for the blade to make a little crease in her skin. She looked straight into the lens, and fat tears sparked in the corners of her eyes.

Her voice came from the laptop's speakers, small and trembling. *'I don't... I don't want... to die...'*

`'You have until midnight.'`

The screen went dark, then YouTube's little line of 'if you liked that, you'll love these' videos appeared, along with an option to play the thing again.

'Lights.' DCI Finnie pointed the remote at the projector mounted on the roof of the briefing room, freezing the picture as the man in the SOC suit pressed the knife against Jenny's throat.

Someone flipped the switch and a cold fluorescent glow filled the room. The audience shifted in their seats. It was a much more select group than earlier, just the top brass and senior CID officers.

Finnie placed the remote down on the lectern next to him. 'At least we now have a timeframe: midnight.'

Chief Constable Anderson swore, light glinting off the polished silver buttons on his dress uniform and the top of his shiny head. 'What's the pot standing at?'

'Er. . .' Acting DI Mark McDonald fidgeted his way through a small stack of paper. 'It's about—'

'Six point three million.' Superintendent Green lounged in his chair, staring up at the screen. 'Conservative estimates put the total at about seven million by midnight.'

'Dear lord.' The Chief Constable shook his head. 'Any idea how they're planning on getting their hands on the money?'

'It has to be electronic transfer.' Green tapped his pen against the palm of his hand. 'They can't ask for it in cash – we can't get that much together by midnight; then they'd have to launder it. Not to mention the risk involved with picking it up.'

'I see. And what about this Frank Baker?'

DI Steel narrowed her eyes at Green for a moment. 'We've got sightings from Nairn to Portsmouth and back again. His face is in every regional newspaper in the UK, and most of the nationals as well; posters up at every ferry terminal, bus station, and airport.'

Green nodded. 'I knew he was involved from the moment I spoke to him.'

'Oh aye? And did you no' think it'd be a good idea to let *us* know so we could keep an eye on him *before* you scared him off?'

'I can't be expected to do your job for you, Inspector.'

Then followed five minutes of arguing, moaning, and trying to pass the buck.

Logan stared at the screen. The Knife Man had a stick-on

conference-style name badge just like the two in the abduction video. It was difficult to make out, but it sort of looked like 'Sylv—' something. Sylvia? Sylvester?

Logan tried them both out on his notepad. Sylvia, David, and Tom. Sylvester, Tom, and David.

Didn't really make any difference – they were fake names. No one went to all the trouble of producing forensically-neutral crime scenes and notes, then stuck a big sticky label on their chest with their real name scrawled across it.

No, this was *Reservoir Dogs* territory.

The badges were so they could tell who they were talking to, when they were all done up in their SOC suits and masks. All humanity obscured.

Sylvia, Tom, and David.

Sylvester, Tom, and David—

Someone elbowed him in the ribs.

Logan looked up from his notepad. The whole room was staring at him.

Finnie pinched the bridge of his nose, and sighed. 'I *know* you're new to this, Detective *Inspector* McRae, but *generally* we like to pay attention in case strategy meetings.'

Logan could feel the heat prickling at the back of his neck. 'Yes, sir.' He glanced down at the notepad in front of him. He'd been doodling – a Dalek, complete with sink-plunger arm, and beady eye.

Not Sylvester, Tom, and David. Put them in the right order—

'For goodness' sake, DI McRae, are you *listening* to a word I'm—'

'*Doctor Who*.' Logan stood. 'Tom Baker, Sylvester McCoy, David Tennant all actors who've played the Doctor. It's their naming system.'

That got him a sea of blank looks.

Superintendent Green raised an eyebrow. 'Yes well, that's *fascinating*. But it still doesn't help us determine—'

'Hold on a second. . .' Logan flipped back through his notebook.

Green snorted. 'Sergeant, I mean *Inspector* McRae, a little career advice: if you can't focus for two minutes, how—'

'Here.' Logan poked the page with a finger. 'Stephen Clayton, he's on the same psychology course as Alison McGregor. He tried to chat her up, but she knocked him back pretty hard. He called her – and I quote – "a stuck up, holier than thou, lying, two-faced bitch." Said, "getting kidnapped was the best thing that ever happened to that manipulative cow". And he's a Doctor Who fan: signed posters, remote-controlled Dalek, the works.'

The Chief Constable sat forward, silver buttons sparkling on uniform black. 'Is he a viable suspect?'

'Who else have we got?'

No one leapt in with any helpful suggestions.

Steel had a scratch under the table. 'How's a wee psychology student tosser pull all this off?'

'Well. . .' Logan looked up at the screen. 'What if Clayton gets other students to help him? We know one of them has medical training: he could be studying to be a doctor.'

Acting DI Mark McDonald shook his head. 'Couldn't be. I've been over McPherson's case notes half a dozen times – the hospital say access to the pharmacy's restricted to doctors and authorized nurses. No exceptions.'

I've got a mate who's a medical student, fixes me up now and then.

Steel leant over and rapped her knuckles on the top of Mark's head. 'Hello? This thing on? Testing, testing.'

'Get off!'

'McPherson couldn't investigate shite for sweetcorn. Sticky-fingered medical student helps himself to a bunch of surgical drugs, does a wee bit of amputation, and Bob's your builder. No' like it's open heart surgery, is it?'

370

'Right, Andy,' the Chief Constable pointed at DCI Finnie, 'I want this Clayton brought in for questioning. I'll sort out the warrant with Sheriff McNab personally, you just make sure Clayton's in custody within the hour.'

'Yes, sir. I'll get a firearms—'

'Actually,' Green folded his arms across his chest, puffing himself up, 'that might not be the *best* course of action.' He narrowed his eyes and stared off into the middle distance. 'If we snatch him, he'll just clam up. The deadline will come and go, and he doesn't have to tell us anything. Why would he cooperate?'

The Chief Constable shook his head. 'Grampian Police will *not* stand idly by and do nothing while a little girl and her mother are killed!'

'I'm not suggesting you do nothing, sir.' A flash of perfect white teeth. 'I'm suggesting we establish surveillance on DI McRae's student: like DI Steel should have done with Frank Baker. If he really *is* one of the kidnappers, he'll lead us right to them. After all, they'll want to regroup before the midnight deadline, won't they?' Green nodded, agreeing with himself. 'Then we swoop.'

Logan stared at him.

Swoop? The silly bastard really did think he was in a TV cop show. 'With all due respect—'

'Tell me,' Steel fiddled with her fake cigarette, 'this "watch and wait" approach's no' got anything to do with stringing things out, would it? SOCA hang on till the deadline's past, take over the investigation; Alison and Jenny get released; then you "swoop", pick up the only suspect we've had in a fortnight, and take all the sodding credit while we get our arses kicked in every newspaper in the country?' She smiled at him. 'How am I doing?'

Green scowled back. 'You have a very strange idea of collaborative policing, Inspector.'

'Coming from you?' She turned to the Chief Constable. 'We *could* sit about on our thumbs, waiting for Clayton to lead us to his nasty wee Doctor Who appreciation society, or we can go kick in his door and actually do something about it.'

'And what happens when the rest of the gang find out we've snatched him?' Green leaned on the desk. 'They abandon the whole enterprise, kill Alison and Jenny, then disappear. At least my way we have some chance of getting the McGregors out alive.'

The Chief Constable sat back in his seat. 'I think we need to take a break and consider our options. In the meantime, DCI Finnie, get surveillance organized on Mr Clayton ASAP. If we *do* decide to take him, I want to know where he is. We reconvene back here in twenty minutes.'

Robert 'Marley' was lying on the cell's blue plastic mattress. The nightshift had obviously confiscated his clothes for forensic analysis, because he was partially dressed in a white paper SOC suit. He'd stripped off the top half, tying the arms around his waist, exposing a broad brown chest and the kind of washboard abs that didn't belong on real people. One hand behind his head, the other tucked into the make-shift waistband.

He didn't look in the least bit worried about being banged up in a holding cell, facing three counts of murder, one of animal cruelty, and skinning Shuggie Webster's fingers. . .

And somehow Logan couldn't work up the enthusiasm to congratulate him on that last one.

Robert Marley looked up from his bed. He'd dyed his hair red and fluorescent orange, as if his head was on fire. 'The fuck you lookin' at, mon. I an' I ain't some fuckin' peepshow for whitey.'

Logan slammed the hatch shut.

The Police Custody and Security officer standing next to him in the corridor puffed out her cheeks. 'Pfff. . . Don't let the fake Jamaican accent fool you; heard the pair of them talking last night in broad Mancunian – had to split them up in the end. Probably never been south of London in their lives.'

Logan's phone rang. He ignored it.

'They're up before the Sheriff at half-two. You want me to stick Bobby the Pseudo-Yardie in an interview room?'

He flexed his right hand, feeling the skin pull tight over his swollen knuckles. 'Not yet.'

'Want to see the other one? Got him downstairs?'

His phone was ringing again. 'Hold on.' He pulled it out. 'McRae.'

'LoganDaveGoulding.' The psychologist pronounced it as if it was all one big Liverpudlian word. *'I've been trying to get in touch with—'*

'You heard about the fire.' Of course he had, it'd been in all the evening papers.

'Well, yeah, but I wanted to know how you're doing. I'm sorry about Samantha.'

Everyone was sorry about Samantha. Every bastard he passed in the corridor was *sorry* about her, as if that helped.

Logan held the phone against his chest, and turned to the PCSO. 'Thanks, I'll get back to you.'

She wandered off, twirling her big bunch of keys like Charlie Chaplin's cane.

He put the phone back to his ear.

'. . . be mad as hell at the bastards.' A small pause. *'Look, I've got to give a lecture at ten on "pluralism in regard to the self", but I'm free from eleven if that's any good?'*

Logan stared at the closed cell door. 'I'm kinda busy right now.'

'*Of course you are: sorting out home insurance, visiting the hospital...?*'

He scrubbed a hand across his face. 'You know, don't you?'

'*That you're at work? Well, let's call it an educated guess. You need time to grieve, Logan.*'

'She's – not – dead!'

'*It's not about death, Logan: most times grief's about change. And I know it's a cliché, but sometimes it really* does *help to talk about it. Rant. Shout. Throw things.*' Goulding sighed. '*You know you're not alone, so why shut yourself off?*'

'Excuse me, sir...' The PCSO was back, pulling a gaunt-faced teenager by the arm. 'Emily here needs a word.'

Emily looked like she needed a meal, and a bath, and to stop shooting heroin into every vein she had. She licked her lips and stared at him. 'You the copper looking for that Trisha Brown, yeah?'

Logan stuck the phone against his chest. 'You a friend?'

'There a reward for, you know, information and that?'

'Depends on the information.'

She rubbed a hand up and down her needle-tracked arm. 'You got them Marley fucks in, right?'

'Why?'

'They're going down, right? You're not gonna let the fuckers out?'

Logan stared at her. 'What've you got?'

Her left leg trembled, as if it wasn't really connected to the rest of her. 'You ask them about Trisha?'

'Why would—'

'Bob, right? Big ginger-haired darkie bastard. He did this...' She pulled up her 'BRITAIN'S NEXT BIG PORN STAR' T-shirt, showing off a set of xylophone ribs covered in green-and-blue bruising. 'Fucker said I should be grateful. If I wasn't careful I'd end up like Trisha Brown.'

374

Logan stared at the cell door again. Then went back to his phone call. Goulding was still talking. '. . . *point being the strong silent type, it's not*—'

'Speak to you later.' He hung up.

'So, you know, do I get a reward or something?'

'We'll see. . .'

'Whatever you want, it'll have to wait. We're swamped.' The IB tech took off his dusty plastic goggles and wiped them on the tails of his lab coat. He nodded over his shoulder at a stack of blue plastic crates loaded with evidence bags. 'You got any idea how much drugs Ding-Dong brought in last night? Like Pete Docherty's bathroom cabinet in here today.'

'Where's Elaine?'

'Ah.' The tech nodded. 'Give us a sec. . .' He was back two minutes later with a manila folder. He placed it carefully on the light table. 'I'm off for a cup of tea, or a pee, or something.' Then backed up, turned around, and walked out of the room. The lab door closed, leaving Logan alone with half a million pounds' worth of drugs.

He opened the folder. Inside were the preliminary forensic results from the flat fire. Traces of accelerant in the hall, no fingerprints on the door or letterbox. The DNA result was hidden away at the back: Elaine Drever had been right, they'd swabbed the door and managed to find viable samples.

Logan read the conclusion twice. It didn't make any sense – they'd run the profile through the database and not made a single match. Not one.

That wasn't possible. Bob and Jacob Marley were in the cells, they were in the system, their DNA was on file from two murder scenes.

How could there not be a match?

He rammed the results back into the folder and stormed

out into the corridor. Elaine Drever's office was two doors down – he barged in without knocking.

Logan waved the folder at her. 'Who fucked up?'

The head of the Identification Bureau pursed her lips. 'Sorry, sir, something's come up. I'll have to call you back.' She hung up. 'Sergeant McRae, I—'

'Who was it? Who screwed with the DNA sample?'

A long pause. 'No one screwed with anything.'

'Run the match again.'

'It's not going to—'

He slammed the folder down on her desk. 'Run – it – again!'

Elaine Drever stared at him. 'We did. Six times. Then we went back and redid the samples. *Twice*. There wasn't—'

'Then why didn't you find a bloody match!'

Her eyes narrowed. 'Samantha's one of ours; you really think we're not doing everything we can to catch the bastards? There wasn't a match. No match. Zero. Whoever did it, they're not in the database.'

'They have to be! They—'

'We've been over the scene with a nit comb; we can't find what isn't there.' She picked up the folder. 'You catch the bastard and this'll convict him. One hundred percent. Not even Hissing Sid could get him off. But whoever did it, they're *not* in the system.'

44

It had to be them. Had to be. If it wasn't. . . Logan ran a hand across his face. If it wasn't them, then everything he'd done to Shuggie Webster was. . .

His pulse thumped in his ears, heart beating hard enough to make his whole body rock. Thump. Thump. Thump. Oh Jesus.

'You OK, Sarge?' Someone sat down on the other side of the canteen table. 'I mean, you know, Inspector?' A cough. 'Sorry, Guv.'

Logan looked up from his coffee and the canteen snapped back into focus. The sound of officers and support staff gossiping and laughing. He blinked.

PC Guthrie shrugged, his shoulders coming up to touch his red-tipped ears. 'Force of habit.'

'Yes.' Logan took a sip of coffee. Cold. God knew how long he'd been sitting here.

The constable unwrapped a Tunnock's Teacake, carefully smoothing out the paper until it was mirror-smooth. 'Going for a record attempt later, thought I'd get some practice in.' He put his hands behind his back and loomed over the teacake. It looked like a little brown breast – a circle of biscuit topped with a dome of marshmallow and dipped in chocolate. 'Sergeant Downie's on four point five seconds.'

Logan pushed his mug away. 'Have you done the door-to-doors?'

Guthrie licked his lips, not taking his eyes off the teacake. 'Trisha Brown? Yup – no one recognized the e-fit. Did a search for other properties Edward Buchan had access to, like you asked: allotments, lock-ups, garages, caravans, friends on holiday, that kind of thing. Doesn't look like he's got anywhere to keep her.'

'No one recognized the e-fit at all?'

'Sorry, Guv. Did two streets either side and put up a couple of "have you seen this man?" posters as well. Nothing.' He lined the teacake up with the edge of the canteen table. 'OK, we ready?'

Maybe no one recognized the e-fit because Edward Buchan had made the whole abduction story up to hide the fact he'd killed Trisha and dumped her body somewhere. Unless. . . Logan frowned. According to 'Britain's Next Big Porn Star', Robert Marley told her if she wasn't careful she'd end up like Trisha Brown.

'OK: three, two, one— Hey!'

He grabbed the teacake and took a big bite. 'We've got two Yardies in the cells downstairs: I want the one calling himself "Robert" in an interview room in ten minutes.'

'I ain't sayin' nothin' without me lawyah.' Robert Marley lounged back in his plastic chair, bare arms and chest shining with a faint sheen of sweat, flame-coloured hair glowing in the light from the interview room's narrow window. 'I knows me rights.'

'Do you now?' Logan tilted his head on one side and stared, letting the silence stretch.

Standing with his back to the wall, Guthrie unwrapped

the replacement teacake Logan had bought to stop him moaning.

Outside, the wail of a patrol car's siren rose, then faded.

Logan tapped the scarred Formica tabletop. 'What about Trisha Brown's rights?'

'Eh, mon, I told you: I an' I ain't sayin'—'

'Oh grow up, Charles, you're not kidding anyone with the mock-Jamaican patois. You sound like a stereotype from a seventies sitcom.'

The Yardie bared his teeth, showing off a line of gold crowns. 'You got no bizzzzness disrespectin' me cultural heritage, *white* boy.'

'Cultural heritage?' Logan checked his notes. 'You were born in Manchester, you did two years at Leeds University studying political science, your mum's Welsh, and your dad's in the Rotary Club. Have you even *been* to Jamaica?'

'I an' I is honourin' me roots.'

'Then why didn't you become a quantity surveyor like your dear old dad?'

Charles Robert Collins, AKA Robert Marley, narrowed his eyes. 'I don't have to answer any of your questions without a legal representative.' He raised his chin, all trace of Jamaican accent gone. He didn't even sound Mancunian, so he'd probably been putting that on too. 'This is an infringement of my civil liberties.'

'Scottish legal system, Charlie. You should have done your research before you decided to sell drugs here.' Logan dug a photo out of a blue folder and slapped it down on the table between them. A bruised face glowered out from an ID shot – Trisha Brown, holding up a board with her name spelled out in magnetic letters. 'What did you do to her?'

Charles looked away, a crease between his eyebrows. 'I've never seen this woman before.'

'Really? Because we've got a witness who saw you snatch her off the street.'

'No you don't.' But he wouldn't look Logan in the eye.

'Oh, but we *do*.' Logan went back into the folder. No sign of the e-fit. He waved PC Guthrie over. 'Go get the e-fit.'

The constable shifted. 'Guv?'

God help us. Logan stood and whispered in Guthrie's ear. 'The e-fit. The one you did with Edward Buchan. Go get it.'

'Oh. . . But I left a copy on your desk.'

Logan frowned at him. 'That was you? The e-fits with no bloody case numbers? You have to fill in all the details – how's anyone supposed to know what they're looking at?'

Pink rushed up the constable's cheeks. 'Thought they were meant to be anonymous so the witnesses don't—'

'Not the internal copies, you idiot.'

'Oh.' Guthrie's shoulders slumped.

'Now go get me a copy of the bloody e-fit!'

'But. . .' The constable leaned in close, his voice carried on a warm chocolaty whisper, 'It doesn't look anything like him. The guy Edward Buchan saw was white.'

'You made me look a complete prick!' Logan slammed his hand against the cell door, and the boom reverberated around the small room, echoing back from the bare concrete walls.

Sitting on the blue plastic mattress with her knees drawn up against her chest, Emily – Britain's Next Big Porn Star – flinched. She was backed up into the corner, keeping her head down, like a dog waiting to be beaten. Another victory for Team Logan.

He sighed and tried to soften his voice. 'You told me they'd used Trisha Brown as a threat.'

Emily nodded, still keeping her eyes on her chewed fingers.

'What happened?'

She glanced at him, then away again. 'There was some

380

drugs went missing, Shuggie got them on credit, like. Some cop raided them and he couldn't pay them back. . .'

Logan leant back against the cell door. 'And?'

'Bob and Jacob thought Shuggie needed a lesson.'

She went back to chewing at her nails.

Silence.

'Emily, I'm going to need more than that.'

'Way I heard it, they invite Shuggie and Trisha over to discuss spreading the repayments, only when they get there, Bob takes this knife and he. . .' She shuddered. 'He, you know.' Emily stuck out the little finger on her left hand, then pretended to skin it with an invisible knife. 'Then the bastards make Shuggie watch them taking turns. You know: raping her.'

Emily wrapped her arms around her knees, fingertips stroking the bruises beneath her T-shirt. 'Wrote the cop's name on her chest and told her to fuck off and get the drugs back if she didn't want to swap places with Shuggie.'

'Fuck me.' Acting DI Mark MacDonald closed the door to Logan's makeshift office and slumped against it. 'Like a bloody bear pit down there.' He peered at the packet of shortbread sitting next to Logan's in-tray. 'Any chance. . .?'

'Not mine, Rennie left them.'

'Good enough for me.' He tore open the wrapper and helped himself to a couple. 'I hate media briefings.' He perched himself on the edge of Logan's desk. 'How come you're not off with the cavalry?'

Logan brushed the bits of shortbread from his mouse and scrolled onto the next page of the interview report form – typing up his meeting with Robert Marley. 'You're getting crumbs everywhere.'

'Anyway, if you're not off arresting this Clayton tosser, do you want to give me a hand with a risk assessment for the hostage handover?'

Logan sat back. 'They're arresting Stephen Clayton? Who's arresting Stephen Clayton? *When*?'

'Thought you knew. Finnie and the tosser Green set off with a firearms team fifteen minutes ago.'

Bastards!

Logan opened his desk drawer. His Airwave handset was nesting in a collection of witness statements and check-lists. He punched in Finnie's number.

The head of CID's voice crackled out of the speaker, nearly drowned out by the roar of an engine. *'Ah, Inspector McRae, how nice of you to report for duty. What, were you busy getting your hair done?'*

'You've gone after Clayton! Why the—'

'Where were you? We've been calling you for the last forty minutes.'

Logan closed his eyes and swore. He pulled out his mobile phone and swore again: he'd switched it off for the interview with the flame-haired 'Marley' brother. He turned the thing back on and it bleeped at him, the screen flickering with little alerts. 'You Have 12 New Messages'. Perfect.

'I've been interviewing suspects in the Trisha Brown abduction.'

'I want your pet psychologist at the station in half an hour, ready to downstream on the Clayton interview.'

'I can be out at Hillhead in fifteen minutes, if. . .' A solid tone came from the speaker, then silence. Finnie had hung up on him. 'Great.' He dumped the handset back in the drawer and slammed it shut. 'I do all the work and they waltz in and make the arrest.' He scowled at Mark. 'What's *that* look for?'

'How come, you're "Detective Inspector McRae", but I'm always, "*Acting* Detective Inspector MacDonald"?'

'Because Finnie's a dick, that's why.' He turned back to his screen. 'Can't believe they went after Clayton without me.'

'You're only DI till bloody McPherson gets back, I'm—'

'Did anyone else find a suspect for Alison and Jenny's abduction? Did they buggery.' Logan hauled everything out of his in-tray and dumped it on the desk, rifling through the pile of letters and forms. 'But do I get to be part of the pick-up team? *No*. That'd be too much to ask for.'

Burglary, burglary, unlawful removal, complaint about someone's dog barking, memo from Baldy Bain about not parking personal vehicles on the Rear Podium. . . Where the hell was Guthrie's e-fit?

The door thumped shut. Logan looked up – Mark was gone. Flounced off in a huff.

How could Finnie go after Stephen Clayton without him?

The anonymous trio of e-fits were wedged between reports of a flasher and complaints about a gang of kids dressed in Cub Scout uniforms running riot in Bridge of Don. Logan laid the three computer-generated identikits side by side on his desk. Two looked as if a drunken monkey had been operating the software, but the third actually bore a passing resemblance to a human being.

A man, mid-fifties to early sixties, long hair, goatee beard, glasses, a Brothers Grimm fairytale nose, lopsided ears of different sizes. Vaguely familiar. Logan held the e-fit out at arm's length and squinted at it, blurring his vision. . .

Nope.

He trundled his chair back from the desk and headed downstairs.

A middle-aged man was standing on the grey terrazzo floor in front of the reception desk, waving his arms about like an angry windmill, his brown suit stained and splattered with scarlet. As if he'd stood too close to someone who'd exploded. '. . . little bastards! What sort of people *raise* children like that?'

Big Gary was standing on the other side of the desk, behind the glass partition, nodding – every gesture setting his collection of chins wobbling. 'I know, sir. Dreadful. If you'd like to take a seat, I'll get someone down to take your statement. . .' His eyes locked on Logan, then a grin pulled at his chubby cheeks. 'Ah, DS McRae: there's a gentleman here who's—'

'They need a damn good slap. If I did that when I was a kid, my mum would've battered the shite out of me!'

Logan slipped the e-fit through the gap between the glass partition and the desk. 'He look familiar to you?'

'This is what you get for being a concerned bloody citizen. Who wants to use a bus shelter covered in graffiti?'

Big Gary scratched at his big pink head. 'Kind of. . .' He squinted one eye shut. 'Who did it?'

'Guthrie.'

'When I was in the Cubs we *respected* our elders, now it's *Lord of the Bloody Flies*!'

'That explains it.' Big Gary stuck his tongue out and frowned. 'Might be Darren McInnes? If it is, he's not been well. . .' He handed the e-fit back to Logan. 'You could try the Horny Grolloch Squad; but I'm pretty sure it's him.'

'It's a bloody disgrace. Who's going to pay for my suit, that's what I want to know!'

'Aye, weil, I suppose it does kinda look a bittie like him.' DC Paul Leggett held the e-fit up next to his computer screen. A familiar wrinkled face stared out of the monitor: Darren McInnes (52) – Exposing Children to Harm/Danger or Neglect, Possessing Indecent Images of Children, Theft by Housebreaking, Serious Assault.

No wonder he'd looked familiar: he was one of the first registered sex offenders they'd interviewed in the Munro House Hotel.

Leggett ran a hand through his collar-length hair. 'Aye, maybe. . .'

The stocky wee man wouldn't have got away with the bohemian look in uniform or CID, but in the Mong Squad it helped not to look like a police officer.

The Offender Management Unit office was cramped, every available surface covered in box files and bits of paper. The bitter-burnt smell of cheap coffee filled the air; an oscillating fan whirred and clicked its way left to right, ruffling the stack of forms nearest to it.

Leggett made humming noises. 'The ears is all tae buggery, and the nose is three times too big, but other than that, it's him.'

Logan took the e-fit back, folded it in thirds, and slipped it back into his pocket. 'Thanks.'

'Fit's he done?'

'McInnes? We think he might've snatched Trisha Brown off the street in Kincorth.'

'Trisha Brown?' Leggett curled his top lip. 'And Dodgy Darren? Nah, he's strictly into the younger woman. Did eight years for molesting a three-year-old girl doon the beach. He wouldnae know whit tae do wi' a fully grown one.'

'You don't think he's—'

'Oh, dinna get me wrong, he's a cantankerous dirty auld bugger and I wouldn't put anything past him, but. . .' Leggett shrugged. 'Never can tell, I suppose. You want to go gie him a wee knock?'

Tempting. But then, what if Finnie came back with Stephen Clayton. . .? Not that Logan would get a look in at the interrogation – not if Superintendent 'I'm A Prick' Green had anything to do with it.

'Give me a minute.' Logan wandered over to the corner of the cramped office, looking out of the window while he dialled. Three storeys down, on the opposite side of the road, someone was peeing into the open top of an illegally parked Porsche in full view of Grampian Police Force Headquarters. You had to admire that level of stupidity.

The psychologist picked up on the third ring. *'Dr Dave Goulding?'*

'Can you get down to FHQ in about. . .' Logan checked his watch. 'Fifteen, twenty minutes? We're picking up a suspect in the McGregor case.'

'Ah. . .' There was a pause. *'And how do you feel about that?'*

'I feel you should get your arse over—'

'Logan, the thing about being a professional psychologist is that you learn to pick up on the tone of someone's voice.'

'Can you make it or not? Finnie needs you to do downstream monitoring and advice.'

'Are you're feeling excluded?'

'Yes or no?'

Silence.

'I've got a client at half ten. I'll be—'

'Cancel it.'

'That's not exactly—'

'We're talking about saving a little girl and her mum here, Dave.'

This time the silence stretched on and on and. . . *'On one condition: you and I sit down for half an hour to talk. We do that, or you wait till I'm finished with Mrs Reid.'*

Down on the street below, a man in a dark-blue suit stopped in the middle of the road to stare at the Porsche piddler. He dropped the collection of green Marks & Spencer bags he'd been carrying and ran at the guy who was using his pride-and-joy as a urinal.

'That's blackmail.'

'Sauce for the goose. Take it or leave it.'

The piddler lurched back and sideways, his legs looking as if they weren't really under control. And then the Porsche's owner cracked a fist into his face. The pair of them tumbled to the pavement, arms and rebellious legs flailing.

'Just make sure you tell the front desk you're here to interview Stephen Clayton. If I'm not about you can start working up some questions.'

'Half an hour, Logan. That's the deal.'

A pair of uniform charged across the road, peaked caps held down with one hand. Logan watched them haul the piddler and the piddlee apart.

Logan glanced over at DC Leggett. He was holding up a set of car keys.

'I'll be back soon as I can. Just got to take care of something first.'

45

'. . . want to thank all your listeners for their generous donations. Really, on behalf of Alison and Jenny: you guys are terrific. With your help, we're going to get them back.'

The beige council van grumbled to a halt outside a shabby bungalow in Blackburn.

'I'm here with Gordon Maguire of Blue-Fish-Two-Fish. You're listening to Original FM, and here's Alison and Jenny McGregor with Wind Beneath My Wings. . .'

The van's engine gave one last diesel rattle, and there was silence.

DC Leggett pulled the keys out of the ignition. 'Sure your witness wasn't taking the piss?'

'Nope.' Logan climbed out into the warm morning.

The bungalow's grey-harled walls were streaked with green and brown; the front garden a jungle of knee-high grass and bright-yellow dandelions, bordered by mis-shapen bushes. A red helicopter droned by overhead, taking a detour around Kirkhill Forest on the way out to the rigs.

Logan marched up the path, raised his finger to the door-bell, then stopped. There was an old blue Citroën parked on the driveway beside the house, in front of a single garage with a heavy wooden door.

Leggett sniffed. 'Fits up?'

'Edward Buchan – the guy who sat on his arse and watched Trisha Brown getting beaten up and abducted – said they were driving a blue saloon.'

The doorbell made a dull buzzing noise deep inside the house.

'I'm still no' seeing Dodgy Darren grabbing a fully grown woman.' The constable scuffed his shoe through a tuft of green, whipping the head off a daisy, then sighed. 'His poor auld dad would have a fit if he knew what a state the place wis in noo.'

Logan tried the doorbell again.

'Nice couple, his mum and dad – could nivver figure out fit they did to end up wi' a child molester fir a son.'

This time he kept his finger on the button, letting the buzz drone on and on.

'Wis his mum who dobbed him in the first time. Found a bunch of filthy photos under his mattress when he was sixteen. Wee girls. No' pretty.'

The door yanked open and there he was: Darren McInnes, fists and jaw clenched, lips flecked with spittle, lank yellow-grey hair flying about his head. 'Bugger off out of it!' His breath stank like an ashtray.

He must have had the television and radio turned up full volume, because the noise was almost deafening, a TV advert for toothpaste fighting against Jenny and Alison's version of *Wind Beneath My Wings*.

Strange – they hadn't heard it through the closed door. . .

Logan held up his warrant card. 'Remember me, Mr McInnes?'

McInnes took a step back, eyes narrowed, goatee beard jutting out. 'I told you: I've never even *met* Alison and Jenny McGregor.'

389

'That's not why we're here.'

DC Leggett waved. 'Fit like the day, Darren: keepin' well?'

'What do *you* want?'

The constable stepped over the threshold into the hallway, forcing McInnes to back up again. 'You'll no' mind if we come in for a fly cup, eh? Thirsty work keeping tabs on registered sex offenders.'

'On the scrounge, are you? Well you can bugger off. I'm not running a soup kitchen.'

Leggett backed him up another couple of paces, making enough room for Logan to step inside and close the front door. The hallway was crowded with stacks of dusty cardboard boxes, piled up between the doors – high enough to brush the ceiling.

'Now, now, Darren, you're no' refusing to cooperate with a supervising authority, are you?'

'You've got no business barging in here. This is my home. I've got rights.'

'Aye.' Another couple of steps and they were in the kitchen. A portable radio sat on top of a stained fridge, blaring out the instrumental bit of the song. Leggett flipped the switch, killing the racket. Now it was just the television, shouting to itself in the lounge. 'And right now you have the right to stick the kettle on and produce a packet of chocolate biscuits.' He leant back against the working surface as McInnes stuck a dirty kettle under the cold tap, then slammed the thing down on the worktop and plugged it in. 'Not supposed to be having a visit till next week. . .'

Logan stared at him, keeping his face neutral. 'We know.'

McInnes froze for a moment, then opened a cupboard and pulled out three chipped mugs. 'Don't play clever buggers with me, Sergeant. I'm not some moron you can intimidate and manipulate. I haven't done anything wrong, and you know it.' He dropped a teabag in each mug. 'You're fishing.'

'Trisha Brown.'

There wasn't even a pause. 'Never heard of her.'

'Really? Because we've got a witness who saw you assault and abduct her.'

'They're lying.' The kettle gave a low growl.

'When we take your car down to the station, how much do you want to bet it's full of her DNA, hair, fibres, blood?'

The theme tune to *Friends* blared out of the lounge.

McInnes cleared his throat. 'So what if there is? She's a prostitute, isn't she? Maybe I picked her up?'

'Thought you said you'd never heard of her?'

'I don't have any milk.'

Leggett shook his head. 'Darren, you silly sod. She's no' even your type.'

'Maybe I like to pick up prostitutes now and then. I thought you'd be pleased.'

'Where is she?'

'Would you rather I was hanging around the school gates like some dirty-mac-wearing pervert?'

'Darren. . .'

Logan turned and headed back out into the hall. The TV and radio couldn't have been on earlier – the only noise coming from inside the house had been the doorbell. That meant McInnes had switched them on and turned the volume up full before he answered the door.

He was trying to hide something. . .

In the lounge, on the telly, a collection of tossers were dancing about in a fountain. Logan picked up the remote and thumbed the standby button.

Silence.

The room was littered with newspapers and magazines, a handful of tatty dog-eared paperbacks, the wallpaper and roof stained a mottled orangey-brown. There was a tin of tobacco balanced on the arm of the sagging sofa, empty pouches of Golden Virginia lying on the carpet like fallen leaves.

Logan closed his eyes, listening.

He could hear them in the kitchen: 'If I want to use prostitutes it's my business, nobody else's.'

'You swore blind last week you'd no' had a shag for three years!'

'Why should I indulge your prurient interest?'

A click and the radio burst into deafening life again. *'. . . to say that everyone at Scotia Lift are rooting for Alison and Jenny. We've raised two thousand pounds for the fund!'*

Logan stuck his head back into the kitchen. 'Turn that bloody radio off.'

'This is my home, you can't come in here and—'

'Where is she? She's here, isn't she?'

'And it's the weather and traffic coming up, right after Bohemian Rhapsody. . .'

'I want you both to leave. You've no right—'

Logan tried the first door off the hallway: a bathroom, the pale-blue suite streaked with muddy green beneath the taps. The next door opened on a bedroom that had the earthy, choking smell of mildew. Then a single bedroom, the duvet a rumpled heap on top of the sagging mattress.

McInnes marched out into the hall. 'What are you doing? You've got no right to search my home! I demand you leave—'

'Why's this one locked?' Logan gave the door handle a rattle.

'It's the garage. I don't want anyone breaking in.'

'Open it.'

'I. . . I don't have the key. I lost it.'

Leggett nodded. 'That's nae a problem: I can kick it in for you in a jiffy.'

'No, no, it's. . . Hold on.' He walked over to a little wooden

392

box mounted on the wall, opened it, pulled out a Yale key on a yellow plastic tag and handed it to the constable. 'This is harassment.'

'Ta.' A rattle, a clunk, and the door swung open.

It was a garage. Bare breezeblock walls, concrete floor, a fluorescent striplight dangling from the roof beams. Empty. No Trisha Brown.

McInnes folded his arms. 'See?' His voice echoed back from the featureless space. 'I told you she wasn't here. Now I want you to leave my home so I can make a formal complaint to your bosses.'

Brilliant – another disaster.

Logan turned on the spot, looking around the box-crowded hallway. 'Have you got an allotment? Shed? Anything like that?'

'No.' McInnes pulled his shoulders back, one arm flung towards the front door. 'Now get out.'

The sound of Frank Sinatra crackled through a tinny little speaker somewhere in Leggett's jacket. He dug out a scuffed mobile phone and flipped it open. 'Guv? . . . Aye. . . No, we're paying Darren McInnes a visit, says he's sworn off wee girls for prostitutes. . . Aye, that's fit I said. . . Aye. . .'

Logan ran a hand through his hair. 'We're still going to take your car in for testing.'

'I told you – I picked her up and paid for sex.'

A frown. 'Fit? Henry MacDonald?' Leggett stepped back into the kitchen, his voice barely audible over the radio. 'Did he? Whit, frank and beans? . . . Just the beans. Ah weil, least he's left himself something tae pee through.'

Logan took another look into the garage. How could she not be here? 'Does this place have an attic?'

'No. And before you ask, there's no basement either. Now are you going to leave or not?'

'Aye, I think so. . . Did you?' Leggett stuck his head out

of the kitchen and stared at McInnes. 'Oh aye. . .? Hud oan.'
He held the phone against his chest. 'DI Ingram says he
knows you fine, Darren. Says he supervised you when you
got oot of Peterheed the first time and they gave you that
cooncil hoose in Kincorth.'

Logan stared at the kitchen doorway, then the next one
along. Then at the huge stack of cardboard boxes in between.

'Says you've never had a hoor in your life.'

'What would he know about it? The man's an idiot. I
used to go with them all the time. Now are you going to
leave, or do I have to call my lawyer?'

There was something wrong. . . Logan peered past Leggett
into the kitchen, then in through the next door to the
manky bathroom. The space *between* the two doors – the
space full of floor-to-ceiling boxes – was too wide. Both
rooms should have shared a dividing wall, but they had to
be at least eight foot apart. He reached up and took a box
from the top of the pile, exposing a section of white-painted
architrave. There was another door, hidden away behind
the boxes. And these ones didn't look anywhere near as
dusty as the others stacked up in the hallway. As if they'd
been recently moved.

Logan dumped the box on the musty carpet and grabbed
another one.

'Aye. . . I'll tell him it's—'

A dull clunk.

He stuck the box on top of the first, then hauled the next
off the pile. 'Leggett: give me a hand.' One more box.
'Leggett?'

Another box on the pile. He could just see the door handle.
'Constable, any time you want to lend a hand, you can. . .'
Logan turned.

Constable Paul Leggett was sprawled out on the kitchen
floor, one arm reaching through into the hallway, a patch

of dark sticky red oozing down his forehead, his mobile phone lying against the skirting board opposite.

Shite. . .

Where the hell was—

A shadow, moving fast. He ducked and a whatever it was crumped into a cardboard box, tearing straight through to the insides, sending the whole pile tumbling down on top of him. Its weight battered into him, sending him crashing to the carpet, the bulky shapes thumping into his legs, arms and chest. A clang of hidden metal as a box bounced off his shoulder.

One of them burst open spilling books across the mildewed carpet, the corner of a hardback cracked into the bridge of Logan's nose. Sharp flaring pain, a bright yellow glow, and the smell of burning pepper.

He scrambled backwards, trying to get out from under the pile.

McInnes grabbed the end of his makeshift club and pulled it free. It was some sort of trophy: a white marble plinth, with a golden pillar, and a little man mounted on the very top. The dusty figurine looked as if he was playing bowls.

'I told you to leave my house.' McInnes hefted the trophy like a hammer. 'Told you, but you wouldn't listen. Nobody ever listens.'

Logan's nose was full of burning pepper, his eyes watering. 'Darren McInnes, I'm arresting you for obstructing, assaulting, molesting or hindering an officer in the course of their duty. You do not have to say anything—'

The heavy stone plinth took a gouge out of the plasterboard.

McInnes lunged, swinging the trophy, following Logan down the hall, backing him towards the door, not giving him time to do anything but dodge the next blow.

'Cut it out! Don't make me—' The edge caught him just

above the right elbow. Burning needles exploded up and down his arm. *'Agh, fuck!'*

'I TOLD YOU TO GET OUT!'

Logan whipped back his foot, then pistoned it forward, slamming his heel into McInnes's knee.

McInnes squealed and collapsed into a stack of cardboard boxes, clutching his knee with one hand, the bowling trophy hanging limp in the other, face creased up, teeth bared.

Logan struggled upright, grabbed the first thing he saw – the collected works of William Shakespeare – and smashed it into McInnes's face. The bowling trophy clattered to the floor; blood spurted from the old man's mouth. He raised a hand, but Logan rammed the book, spine-first, into his nose.

McInnes went down, covering his face and head, bleating as Logan smashed the book into his ribs. He curled one leg up against his chest, the other sticking out at an awkward angle.

Logan dropped the book, breathing hard. He spat; a glob of red-flecked foam trickled down the wall. He wiped a hand across his mouth and chin: it came away dripping with blood.

DC Leggett groaned.

Logan lurched over. 'Paul?' He slid down the wall until he was sitting on the dusty carpet next to him. 'You OK?'

'No. . .' Leggett reached up and touched the gash in his forehead. Flinched. 'Ayabastard. . .'

'You'll live.' The avalanche of boxes had almost cleared the space in front of the hidden door. Logan crawled over and hauled the last box out of the way, leaving a bloody hand print on the cardboard. He glanced back at McInnes – curled up on the floor, crying, clutching his knee – then turned the door handle.

Locked.

It flew open on the second kick, the boom reverberating around the house.

Logan stepped into an L-shaped room with bare breeze-block walls, loops of grey electrical cable protruding from metal ducting, one corner done up with plasterboard nailed to raw wooden struts. Modular metal shelves lined several of the walls, a washing machine and tumble dryer sitting beside a big chest freezer, sheets of water-bloated chipboard nailed up where windows should have been.

He picked his way across the bare concrete floor to the corner, glanced back at McInnes again – still crying, still trying to hold his ruptured knee together – then stepped into the long leg of the L-shaped room.

Trisha Brown was crumpled against a storage radiator, naked, one arm handcuffed to the supports. Her wrist was a solid ring of raw flesh, blood smeared from her fingertips halfway to her elbow. Her other arm. . . Logan looked away. Human limbs weren't meant to bend like that. Her legs were worse: twisted and broken and covered in scabs and weals, pale thighs dotted with little red burns and bite marks.

The sharp smell of urine and pine disinfectant, overlaid with BO and shit.

'Trisha?' He swallowed. 'Trisha, can you hear me?' He knelt beside her, felt for a pulse. Strong, pounding. 'Trisha, it's going to be OK.' He put a hand under her chin and raised her head. 'Fuck. . .' Her nose was buckled to the left, both eyes swollen shut, her chin lopsided, her lips cracked and bleeding, her cheek misshapen – probably broken – every inch of skin covered in a violent rainbow of bruises. 'Are you—'

Her head snapped forward, mouth wide, jagged stumps of teeth flashing in bloody gums.

Logan flinched back, snatching his hand out of the way. She wobbled, shoulders twitching, then slumped back against the battered radiator. A cross between a growl and a hiss escaped her battered lips.

Jesus.

Logan turned away, marched around the corner and back into the hall. 'YOU!' He took a handful of McInnes's long greasy grey hair. 'Where's the key?'

'I don't—'

Logan hauled. 'Where's the *fucking* key?'

The old man screamed, let go of his knee and grabbed at Logan's hand, trying to keep it from hauling the scalp off his head. 'In the box! In the box!'

Logan dragged him across the hall to the little wooden box mounted on the wall – the one the garage door key had come from – McInnes screaming and crying, his good leg scrabbling at the carpet, the other one dragging through the debris.

It wasn't difficult to spot the handcuff key – Logan snatched it from its hook and hauled McInnes through the door with him, into the unfinished room.

46

'What was I supposed to do?' Darren McInnes sat in the back of the patrol car, hands cuffed behind his back, a medical cool-pack strapped to his swollen knee.

The front door opened and someone in a green jumpsuit backed out onto the garden path, holding up one end of a metal-framed stretcher.

McInnes gave a little laugh, then winced, watching as Trisha was carried over to the waiting ambulance. 'She was my first, did you know that? My first real life little girl.'

Logan looked at him. 'Shut up.'

'Before her it was just pictures, but then I got out of prison and they gave me a council flat just round the corner from her house. . . She was so small and so pretty and I remember she fell off her bike and broke her arm, and I just wanted to make her feel loved, so I—'

'If you don't start exercising your right to remain silent, I swear to God. . .'

A sigh. 'Her mother was out of her face most of the time, or desperate for a fix, or down the docks renting her arse out so she could pay for the next high. Busy single mother like that needs a babysitter.'

'McInnes—'

'I'm dying.' He turned and smiled at Logan. The skin around his right eye was already an angry dark blue and purple, the lid swollen and puffy, the white stained with red. 'Cancer – all through my liver and kidneys. Doctor gave me three months, that was four weeks ago. Funny, isn't it? Smoked like a chimney all my life; everyone always said it'd be lung cancer that did it.'

'That supposed to make me feel sorry for you?'

'I don't care what you think.' McInnes's smile turned into a grin. 'Oh, I knew you'd find me eventually – but I'll be dead long before it gets anywhere near court. Can't blame me for going out in style.'

'You think this is *funny*?'

'Took me two weeks to track Trisha down, and in the end there she was: not two hundred yards from her mum's house. Staggering along, begging for money.' He sighed as they shut the ambulance doors. 'Thought it would be rather fitting – to end my life the way it started, with *her*. But. . .' McInnes shook his head. 'She was a lot more fun when she was five.'

Logan climbed out into the warm morning sun and slammed the door shut before McInnes had another accident.

One of the paramedics walked around the side of the ambulance, spotted Logan, and headed over. He nodded towards the patrol car, with its greasy-haired black-eyed occupant. 'You the one buggered his knee?'

Logan could feel the heat rushing up his cheeks. 'It was self defence. He—'

'Bastard should be taken out and shot.' The paramedic scowled through the windscreen. 'She'll be lucky if they can save her legs, forget walking again. Had to give her three times as much morphine to get her settled.'

Logan didn't tell him that probably had as much to do

with Trisha's tolerance for opiates as the amount of pain she was in.

The *Danse macabre* sounded in Logan's pocket as the ambulance pulled away, lights flashing.

'McRae?'

DI Steel's gravelly voice hissed in his ear: *'Where the sodding hell are you?'*

'We found Trisha Brown.'

A pause. *'Alive?'*

'Only just.'

'Hold on. . .' There was an echoey hiss – probably Steel holding a hand over the mouthpiece of her phone – then the muffled sound of people talking.

Logan watched a uniformed PC help DC Leggett limp out of McInnes's house. There was a patch of gauze on Leggett's forehead, held in place with bright-white sticking tape. For some *unfathomable* reason, his symptoms seemed to get a lot worse as soon as the pretty constable turned up.

'You still there?'

'The suspect's coughed for abduction, rape, and breaking pretty much every bone in her arm and legs. Thinks the cancer's going to get him before the courts do.'

Logan could hear someone talking to her in the background.

'Couldn't agree more, Guv.' Then she was back. *'Get yourself over here, we've got the president of the Doctor Who Appreciation Society in an interview room, and your mate the Liverpudlian nutwrangler's being a dick. Says he's no' doing bugger all till he's talked to you.'*

Logan stared up at the crystal blue sky and swore.

'Tell Goulding I'll be right there.'

Logan shifted in his creaking plastic chair. The Observation Suite was gloomy, the only light coming from the TV screen:

401

interview room number two; Superintendent Green and DI Steel sitting across the table from Stephen Clayton.

The student flicked his head to the side, getting the long dark hair out of his eyes. *'One more time, for the hard of thinking: I didn't do anything to Alison and Jenny McGregor. I asked Alison out, she said no. End of story.'*

Goulding rested the fingertips of his left hand against the screen, pinning Clayton to the cathode ray tube. 'Look at the body language – arms open, legs spread, leaning back in his seat, keeping eye contact. "I'm confident and comfortable. You do not threaten me."'

'Yes, well. . .' Logan shifted again, trying to stop his leg from going to sleep. 'He's a psychology student, isn't he? Don't they teach you lot how to do this kind of thing?'

'What,' Goulding threw a glance in Logan's direction, 'you mean: how to lie?'

Logan crossed his arms, then unfolded them again. If Clayton could do it, so could he. 'Aren't you supposed to be prompting them with questions?'

'How long have we known each other, Logan?'

'I mean, that was the whole point of getting you in here, wasn't it?'

'Don't you think you can trust me?'

'She rejected you, didn't she?' On the little screen, Superintendent Green tapped his knuckles against the tabletop. *'You loved her, and she shot you down in flames.'*

'I didn't love her. I thought she'd be a decent shag. You know what these single mothers are like: gagging for it.'

Steel nodded. *'He's got a point.'*

'Do you think I'll judge you, or think less of you if you admit you're having problems?'

'I'm *not* having problems!'

'She shot you down and it hurt, didn't it? You wanted revenge.'

402

Clayton leant forward. *'You don't do a lot of interviewing, do you?'*

'Logan, if you don't talk about it, how's it ever going to get better?'

'I mean, you haven't even tried to establish a rapport with me, just straight in with the cod psychology. Now your colleague here,' he pointed at Steel, *'she's doing much better.'*

'We talked about it – we spent *half an hour* talking about it. Now will you just do your bloody job!'

Goulding smiled. 'That's what I'm trying to do.' He picked up the little microphone and pressed the red 'TALK' button. 'Ask him about his parents – how does he think they'll react when they find out he's been arrested?'

Steel had a wee scratch below the table. *'What's your mum and dad going to think about you being dragged in here? Steve?'*

Green scowled at her. Probably thought *he* should be the one asking the questions.

Clayton shrugged. *'You see, Superintendent, you're either an alpha male, or you're not. The inspector here: she is, but you. . .'* He made a side-to-side see-saw motion with one hand.

'If it was me: if someone had set fire to my flat while I was sleeping, if my girlfriend had ended up in a coma, I'd want to kill someone.'

Logan stared at Goulding. 'Leave it.'

'My mother and father were loving and supportive. They're proud of everything I've achieved.'

'If I'd stood there and watched her fall—'

'Fine, you *really* want to know? I thought Shuggie Webster did it, OK? So I tracked him down and I beat the crap out of him.' Logan turned away. 'Could've killed him. . .'

'That's a perfectly natural feeling. We all—'

'I don't mean figuratively: I had the option. I could have killed him, got rid of the body, no one would have known.'

'Ah. . . Now *that's* more like it.' Goulding picked up the microphone. 'If his parents are so wonderful, why has he been rebelling against them all his life?'

On the little screen, Superintendent Green blurted out the question, desperate to get there before Steel.

'So, for a brief moment you held the power of life and death.' The psychologist scribbled something in his notepad. 'And you chose to be merciful.' He tilted his head to the side. 'How did that make you feel?'

Logan looked away. 'Sick.'

'Really? Interesting. . . Interesting. . .'

On the little screen, Clayton ran a hand through his long brown hair. *'Tell me, Inspector, when did you discover you were a lesbian? Was it sudden, a gradual process, or have you always known?'*

Goulding smiled. 'You know, I'm beginning to think your friend Mr Clayton might be a bit too much of a challenge for the inspector and DSI Green. He's playing with them, like he's got all the time in the world. He's in no rush to give us the McGregors.'

Steel shook her head. *'Nice try, sunshine, but you're no' even in the same league as Hannibal Lecter. Now unless you're looking for a size-nine hand-stitched leather enema, tell us what you did with Alison and Jenny?'*

'How you doing, kiddo?' SYLVESTER lifts Jenny's chin till her eyes are level with the narrow slits where *his* eyes should be.

She looks away. 'Want my mummy.'

'Yeah, well. . .' He pats her on the head, like she's a doggie. 'Soon be over; then you can go home. That'll be nice, won't it?'

The room's hot. Sunlight makes streaks across the bare floorboards, stopping at the foot of the bed. Stopping short of her sore feet. Jenny bites her lip as he strokes her hair with his rubbery fingers.

'Will you leave that bloody kid alone?' TOM's sitting on the windowsill, reading a newspaper with a photo of Mummy on the front. 'Look like a paedophile: pawing at her the whole time.'

'Screw you.' SYLVESTER's robot voice turns into a metal whisper. 'I'm really sorry about . . . well,' his eyes drift down, towards her bandaged feet, 'everything. You know?' He shrugs and his white paper suit rustles.

She doesn't say anything, just sits quietly as the door opens and the monster with the 'PATRICK' sticker comes in, the big camera slung over her shoulder. Jenny can hear Mummy crying in the other room, and then PATRICK closes the door, shutting it out. 'He's not answering his phone.'

SYLVESTER's still stroking Jenny's hair. 'You try email?'

'Of course I tried bloody email.' PATRICK stops and stares. 'What are you doing?'

TOM looks over the top of his newspaper. 'Kiddie-fiddling.'

'I'm not a bloody paedo!' SYLVESTER stands. 'You try to be nice, show a wee kid some compassion, and—'

'I know what *you* want to show her. You want to show her your—'

'Enough!' PATRICK stomps her foot. 'Shut up, the pair of you!'

TOM shrugs. 'What if the cops picked him up? I mean, they were all over the place today—'

'They speak to you too?'

'Was out. Did my flatmates though; asking all kinds of stuff about Alison and Jenny.'

PATRICK waves a hand. 'Doesn't matter.'

'But what if—'

'As long as you keep your mouths *shut*, they can't prove anything. They've got nothing: no witnesses, no motive, no DNA, no fingerprints, nothing. If we torch this place before we go Sherlock Holmes couldn't catch us.'

'Yeah, but suppose—'

'Are you retarded?' She walks over to the bed, picks up Teddy Gordon and turns him upside down so his horrible fuzzy bottom is sticking in the air, the white washing tag poking out like a worm. 'We're talking about over eight *million* pounds, Sylvester.'

'Yeah, no: it'll be fine, I'm working on it. No one'll see a thing.'

'Make sure they don't.' PATRICK shoves the teddy bear at Jenny, those dead black eyes glittering at her. 'After all, you don't want to end up like Colin, do you?'

SYLVESTER doesn't say anything, he just stands there staring at PATRICK. Even TOM is silent.

47

'He's in there laughing at us!' Superintendent Green thumped his fist against the boardroom table's polished mahogany surface. 'I told you we should have followed him – he would've led us straight to Alison and Jenny McGregor. Bringing him in like this was *wilfully* reckless.'

Logan checked his watch. Two minutes into the catch-up session and Green was already throwing blame around.

Steel narrowed her eyes. 'At least we're *doing* something. You'd still be sitting in here with your thumb up your—'

'Inspector!' Finnie slumped back in his seat. 'We appreciate your passion, but now's not the time. Perhaps we could focus on finding solutions *instead* of pointing fingers?'

'Well,' Acting DI Mark MacDonald fidgeted with his pen, 'what if we let Clayton go? Pretend it was just a mistake, and we're dropping all the charges? Then we could keep him under surveillance and he would think he was in the clear? You know, best of both worlds?'

Finnie stared at him until Mark's ears went bright pink. 'Don't be stupid. What do the IB say?'

Logan checked the file he'd grabbed on the way to the boardroom. 'They're still going through his laptop – Clayton's

407

got about two gig of encrypted files that could be anything. Unless he gives us the key, it's going to take months, maybe years.'

'That's *not* an option. Door-to-doors?'

Steel had a dig at her bra. 'Ongoing. Halls of residence are huge; has to be hundreds of students living at Hillhead.'

'I see. . .' Finnie buried his face in his hands for a moment. Then surfaced again. 'Options?'

'We're no' letting Clayton go – the media would skin us alive.'

'Superintendent Green?'

The man from SOCA crossed his arms. 'I think I've said my piece.'

Finnie turned back to Logan. 'What about the psychologist, Goulding?'

'He wants some off-the-record time with Clayton. Thinks it might help to build a rapport and—'

Green's chin came up. 'It's out of the question. You can't leave a civilian alone with the only suspect you've managed to produce: nothing Clayton says will be admissible. I won't allow you to compromise the whole investigation. The Independent Police Complaints Commission—'

'Blah, blah, blah.' Steel gave her left boob an extra hard jiggle. 'You know what, Superintendent? You're about as welcome round here as a blowjob off your own granddad.'

His eyes went wide. 'How *dare*—'

'All right, all right.' Finnie rubbed at his face. 'Just for a moment, could we all *pretend* that we're on the same side?'

Green made a big show of taking a deep breath, then aligning the cuffs of his shirt sleeves. 'You need to find Frank Baker. You need to come up with a strategy for recovering Alison and Jenny. You need to come up with a strategy for following the money when it's handed over. You need to sort this out now. Not tomorrow, not next week: *now*.'

Steel let go of her bra. 'I say we give Goulding fifteen minutes with Clayton. Not like we've got anything to lose, is it?'

Finnie nodded. 'Agreed. Do it in an interview room, with the cameras running. And make sure Clayton knows he's being filmed so his defence can't moan about it afterwards. Any objections, Superintendent?'

'I suppose.'

'Good. McRae, set it up. Acting DI MacDonald: I want that risk assessment on my desk by three. Steel: find out where we are with Frank Baker. I'll see what we can do about tracking the ransom payment.'

Dr Dave Goulding sat in Finnie's office, a mug of tea in one hand, a Jaffa Cake in the other. 'I'd say it's . . . possibly not as clean-cut as that.'

The head of CID closed his eyes and massaged the bridge of his nose. 'This *might* come as a bit of a shock, but I just want to know "yes" or "no".'

Logan rested his back against the bank of filing cabinets, the metal cool through the white cotton of his shirt. Steel stifled a yawn.

'It's not as simple as that.' Goulding turned his Jaffa Cake into a crescent moon. 'Stephen Clayton feels comfortable playing with us because he's not worried about slipping up. That means he's either incredibly arrogant, or he had nothing to do with Alison and Jenny's abduction.' The rest of the Jaffa Cake disappeared. 'I just don't think he's the right personality type. Oh, he's bright enough, but he couldn't keep it secret. He'd want to shout it from the top of Marischal College: "Look at me! Look how clever I am!"'

Finnie pursed his rubbery lips. 'He's *definitely* not involved?'

'It's not impossible, but it's unlikely.'

'Then we're back to square one. And we've wasted a

whole morning, and *hundreds* of man-hours on a bloody *student.*' Finnie massaged his nose again. 'Inspector McRae, can you tell that I'm *slightly* disappointed?'

'He was a Doctor Who fan, he had history with Alison McGregor—'

'That doesn't matter if he didn't have *anything* to do with their abduction!'

No, it didn't.

Steel puffed out her cheeks. 'Well, look on the bright side, at least Green's got something new to whinge about.'

'*. . . join us next week for more* Britain's Next Big Star*!*' Canned applause filtered through the house, echoing up the stairwell from the television in the lounge.

Logan sat on Alison McGregor's bed and stared at the photos he'd found in a shoebox at the back of the cupboard: Alison in a bikini, Alison in T-shirt and jeans, Alison at the beach . . . He held up one of her in a school uniform. She was sitting on a low brick wall, a tin of extra-strong cider in one hand, a cigarette in the other, her school blouse unbuttoned so far her bra was on display, school tie disappearing into cleavage.

Everything was completely fucked up. Stephen Clayton *had* to be involved. If he wasn't . . . what else did they have?

Logan turned the photo over, 'My Birthday ~ 14 Today!!!' was picked out in blue biro on the back. She didn't look fourteen.

'*Welcome to* Britain's Next Big Star*!*' Cheering. '*We've got a terrific show for you this week, but remember: only four of tonight's contestants can go through to the next round, so make sure you vote for your favourites!*'

Alison's DVD recorder was full of the stuff – *Britain's Next Big Star*, the *X-Factor*, *Britain's Got Talent*, *Strictly Come Dancing*, three different things with 'Andrew Lloyd Webber' in the title. . .

Logan laid the photograph on the bed, next to the others, and pulled another one from the box: Alison in the pub with another girl and a pair of gormless-looking blokes. The other girl . . . looked a bit like Vicious Vikki, only a lot thinner. One of the blokes was definitely Doddy McGregor.

Logan placed it next to the schoolgirl shot. Then frowned.

Alison McGregor looked identical in every single picture.

Her clothes changed, her hair changed, her make-up changed, but her face didn't. It was exactly the same smile in every picture – mouth, teeth, eyes, eyebrows all *exactly* the same.

It wasn't a bad smile: it was open, warm, wholesome, and a little bit sexy all at the same time. . . It suited her. But seen like this, all these photos spread out on the duvet cover, it just looked as if she was wearing a mask. As if whenever a camera came out, the real Alison McGregor disappeared.

Sitting on his own, in an empty house, Logan knew how she felt.

'Where the hell have you been?' TOM stands in the middle of the room, with his hands on his hips.

Jenny looks up from the bed as DAVID walks in, swinging his legs like he's a cowboy in a movie.

'Don't be so fucking gay.' DAVID dumps a plastic bag from the supermarket on the floor. 'Got stuck with our friendly neighbourhood plod this afternoon. Took forever to get rid of the bastards.' He pulls a newspaper from the bag and throws it to TOM. 'Front page.'

TOM fumbles, then unfolds the paper and stares at it. 'Holy *shit*.'

'I know. Where's Sylvester?'

'Lecture.'

'Cool. Cool.' DAVID nods at the bed. 'End game, Alison. You ready?'

He pulls a bottle out of the bag – a big bottle with a big cork. 'I think celebrations are in order. Tom?'

'Spectacular!' TOM turns the newspaper around until they can all see it. There's a picture of Jenny and Mummy on the cover. 'Nine point four million. Ca-fucking-ching!'

Mummy sits up and the chain around her ankle rattles. 'We just want to go home.'

'Well, here's the problem,' DAVID holds the bottle in his hand like it's a doll, 'we've had a change of plan. Tom?'

'What?'

'You got the duct tape?'

'Bingo.' TOM holds up a thick grey hoop.

'Cool.' DAVID snaps his fingers. 'Let's see it.'

'Nine point four *million*.' TOM skips across the room. 'Shit that is a load of—'

THUNK. DAVID swings the bottle like a hammer, right into the back of TOM's head.

Don't bottles break when you hit them on things? Like when the Queen launches a ship and she has to thump the bottle on the ship and it breaks and there's all this foam everywhere and the ship slides away into the sea.

'Nnnnng. . .' TOM wobbles. The silvery tape falls from his hand, hits the floorboards and rolls away.

DAVID hits him with the bottle again. *Thunk*.

TOM's legs stop working and he falls to the floor. His left foot twitches, the fingers of one purple-gloved hand shaking. Something dark seeps down inside his mask, making the clear plastic go red.

Jenny scrambles backwards until she bashes into the bedpost, not caring about the burny pain in her feet.

DAVID puts the bottle on the floor. He goes back to his shopping and pulls out a big black bin-bag. Shakes it so it's all puffy. Then puts it over TOM's head. 'Don't want to get blood on our nice clean floor, do we?'

He holds it tight around TOM's neck for ages and ages, till TOM stops moving. Then he stands and turns to them. 'And then . . . there were four.'

Mummy shakes her head. 'I just want this to be over with.'

'About that. . .' DAVID grabs her hair and drags her off the bed. Mummy screams, hands clawing at him.

'NO!' Jenny can't back away any further, the metal bedpost digs into her back. Teddy Gordon smiles up at her with his dead crow eyes. Laughing. She grabs him by the throat and throws him with all her might. 'DON'T HURT MY MUMMY!'

Teddy Gordon bounces off DAVID's chest.

He looks down at the bear lying on the floor beside TOM. 'Yeah, cute.'

DAVID hauls Mummy over onto her stomach, and kneels on her back. Then catches her hands, holding them in one big purple-gloved fist as he wraps her wrists in shiny silver tape.

'GET OFF ME! GET THE FUCK OFF ME!'

He tears off another bit of tape, and now Mummy only mumbles and hisses.

Jenny jumps onto the floor and runs at him, her feet stabby and aching and sore. Brave Little Girl. . . She snatches the bottle off the floor. I name this ship DAVID. She swings it with all her might.

It bounces off his shoulder.

He turns to look at her, his head on one side, like next door's cat watching a bird with a broken wing. 'Mistake.' His hand snaps out, thumping down on Jenny's left foot.

Something sharp bursts inside her, tearing up her leg, she opens her mouth to scream, but there's no breath left. She falls, clutching her ankle in both hands, staring as a poppy blooms on the white bandage. The broken thing catches fire.

And now she *can* scream, over and over again. So loud it makes her throat rattle.

'Fuck's sake. Shut up.' He grabs her face – stinky rubber fingers clamping her jaw shut – then forces the sticky tape over her mouth. 'There we go, *much* better.'

Mummy wriggles on the floor, eyes small and sparkly, making noises that don't count as words.

Tears make everything blurry. Jenny's bandage drips red. She doesn't even move when DAVID tapes her wrists together, then does the same with her ankles.

He stands, towering over them. 'Like I said: change of plan. Sylvester's figured out a way to get away with it all. Nine point four million. Completely untraceable. So you're surplus to fucking requirements, *Alison*. A liability. Yeah, we *could* let you go, trust you to keep your trap shut. . .' He laughs. 'A publicity whore like you? Soon as people start forgetting about you, soon as you're not on the cover of *Hello!* any more, it'll be all,' DAVID throws his arms out wide, '"My secret kidnap hell!" Plucky Alison McGregor reveals all!'

He drops his arms. 'Not going to happen. Jenny does one last video, and then. . . Well, I'll make it quick, OK? I'm not a *complete* fucking monster after all.'

48

'*And what are you going to sing for us?*' The ex-Blue-Peter presenter hunkered down so he was on the same level as the little girl with the curly blonde hair.

Jenny McGregor looked at him with those big blue eyes of hers. '*We're going to sing a song about my Daddy.*'

Logan sat back on the couch, the remote control for the TV balanced on his knee. He'd found a can of Diet Irn-Bru lurking at the back of the fridge. That's what happened when you got kidnapped – Grampian Police came round and helped themselves to the contents of your kitchen.

They sure as hell didn't rescue you.

Alison McGregor put a hand on her daughter's shoulder. '*It's called* Wind Beneath My Wings.' They were wearing matching costumes, covered in sequins.

'*OK, well, good luck.*' Mr Blue Peter turned his smile on the camera. '*And remember, if you want to vote for Alison and Jenny, we'll be putting up the number to call at the end of the show.*'

The music swelled and the McGregors walked hand in hand to the front of the stage. A big projection screen sat on one side – the words 'In Loving Memory Of John "Doddy" McGregor' faded up for a couple of bars, then was replaced by the photo they'd used in the papers when his body was transported back from Iraq.

As they sang, the image changed: Doddy at the beach with Jenny; Doddy sitting on an armoured vehicle, somewhere hot and dusty; Doddy holding a small pink baby. . . And then the first instrumental break came and Doddy was replaced by a video clip of a pair of injured squaddies, talking about how he'd saved their lives. Then back to the montage for the next verse.

No wonder Alison and Jenny got the most votes of the entire series. Everyone loved them.

Logan's phone went off, the *Danse macabre* clashing with the saccharine song. He thumbed the power button on the remote, shutting the TV off. 'McRae.'

'Where are you?' DI Steel.

He picked himself off the couch and wandered out into the hall. 'Alison McGregor's house.'

'Find anything?'

'No.' He headed up the stairs, back through into Alison's bedroom. 'We're screwed, aren't we?'

'Just got off the phone to Tayside.' A pause. *'Frank Baker's turned up. Ninewells Hospital. Made it as far as Dundee before a bunch of neds recognized him.'*

Logan made a little gap in the lace curtains and peered out. The same two old ladies were camped out on the pavement, with their folding chairs and their thermos of tea. Soon it'd be a sea of faces and television cameras, all gathered together to be part of the moment as the deadline expired.

'He OK?'

'What do you think? Be lucky if he lives to see tomorrow.'

Logan let the curtain fall back into place. 'As if thing's weren't. . .'

There was a clunk from somewhere downstairs.

'And is Stupidintendent Green taking responsibility for his cock-up? Is he buggery – apparently it's all my fault for no' having Baker under surveillance in the first place.'

Another clunk.

'Hold on a minute.' Logan pressed the mute button. . .

Nothing. Maybe it was the house settling, or something outside, or—

Clunk.

There was someone in the house.

He crept down the stairs and froze at the bottom.

This time the clunk was a clink, then a scraping sound coming from the kitchen.

He reached for the handle and turned it slowly, one hand pressed against the door as he eased it open.

A shadow moved across the floor, then paused. Another clunk.

He stepped inside.

A woman was kneeling beside the cooker, a holdall open on the floor beside her. Bleached blonde hair; pink T-shirt; hipster jeans riding about mid-buttock. She was picking her way through one of the kitchen cupboards. 'Baked beans, baked beans, baked beans. . . Where's the caviar and fancy shit?'

Logan slammed his hand on the working surface. 'Can I help you?'

She screamed, jumped, banged her head off the inside of the cupboard, then fell on her backside, clutching her centre parting. The pink T-shirt had 'LITTLE MISS NAUGHTY' printed across the front. 'Ow. . . *Fuck*. What did you do that for?'

Logan frowned at her. 'Do I know you?'

She looked up at him, her eyes going wide, mouth hanging open, chin disappearing into the skin of her neck. 'No.'

'You're her, aren't you? Thingy Wallace, Shona – I

417

interviewed you – you're not allowed to work with children any more.'

She blushed. Looked at the floor. 'Don't know what you're talking about.'

'On your feet.'

'I'm supposed to be here. I'm, like, Alison's best friend and she . . . asked me to make sure she had, you know, enough food and that for when they let her go.'

'So you're saying she's spoken to you since she's been abducted.'

'Well. . . erm. . . It's. . .'

Idiot.

'I was only trying to help!'

The Police Custody and Security Officer slammed the cell door in Shona Wallace's face, then held his clipboard out for Logan to sign. 'They get worse, don't they?'

Logan scrawled his name across the custody form, then headed upstairs to the third floor. Elaine Drever wasn't in her office, so he tried the lab.

She was standing by the light table in the middle of the room, frowning at a stack of print-outs. 'What about fingerprints?'

A lumpy young man with a squinty face cricked his jaw from side to side. 'Doing them next.'

'Thanks, Tim.' Elaine Drever tucked the report under her arm, then turned and flinched. 'Sergeant. . . Sorry I mean, DI McRae. . .' She reached out and touched his arm. 'Logan. How you holding up?'

'Did you find a match yet?'

The lab phone rang, and Tim shuffled over to answer it.

'Hold on.' She crossed to the in-tray perched on top of the fridge-freezer and rifled through some forms. 'Tim? What happened to that blood sample we got last night? From the hospital? The one for DI McRae?'

Tim looked up from the phone. 'The ASAP one? Ben's running it now.'

'What?' Logan held up a hand. 'No – the DNA from the flat door. Did you find a match yet?'

'Oh.' Elaine checked her watch. 'We've done it a dozen times and it's still not coming up with anything. And we're not getting any fibres off the door either. Well, besides ones from the hall carpet, and given how hard the door must've hit him. . . It's odd: I would have expected to find *something*.'

Another glance at her wrist. 'Sorry, I've got to attend a bloody prize-giving at Robert Gordon University. I swear to God, these forensic students get younger every year. It's like visiting a playschool.'

'Boss?' Tim clamped his hand over the mouthpiece. 'We got a hit.'

Elaine shook her head. 'Well, it's just going to have to wait till I get back. Late already.' She patted Logan on the arm again. 'Really, we're doing everything we can.' And then she was gone.

'Yeah, thanks, Ben.' Tim hung up. 'DI McRae?'

Logan stopped, halfway out the door.

'That blood sample: it's a DNA match for the big toe you brought in.'

He frowned, drumming his fingers on the door frame. The DNA matched. . . 'Tim – did you get anything from the tip-off note? The one that said Alison and Jenny were snatched by paedophiles?'

'Don't think so.' He hauled a drawer out of a battleship-grey filing cabinet. 'Here we go. . .' A hanging file with an evidence bag and a single sheet of paper. 'Nope.'

'Nothing at all?'

'No prints, no fibres, no DNA. Sorry, Inspector.'

'. . .and another four letters of complaint.' Big Gary placed a stack of paper in the middle of Finnie's desk. 'Bloody law students are the worst – getting their eye in for a lifetime selling other buggers' houses.'

Finnie picked up the paperwork and dumped it in his pending-tray. Then looked up and scowled at Logan. 'Two weeks. Two weeks and all we've managed to do is piss off a bunch of students and get a paedophile hospitalized. *Remind* me again, Inspector, why do I pay you lot?'

Logan stepped into the office. 'Did anyone get anywhere with the ex-police-officer angle?'

There was a moment's silence. 'Tell me, DI McRae, do you really think I've got *nothing* better to do than sit here answering asinine questions? Or might I *just* have something slightly more *important* to do today?'

'Sorry, sir.'

'Should think so too.' He turned in his seat. 'Anything else, Sergeant McCormack?'

Big Gary produced a clipboard and held it out. 'Need you to approve the overtime plan. Acting DI MacDonald's got half the station down for a green shift: riot patrol.'

'God help us. . .' He signed the form.

'Thank you, sir.' Big Gary squeezed his way out of the room.

Logan shut the door. 'I think we're being screwed with.'

Finnie didn't even look up. 'Inspector, this *might* surprise you, but I don't have time to listen to you moaning about Superintendent Green today.'

'The tip-off – the one that had us interviewing every sex offender in Grampian – I think it's a fake.'

The head of CID picked the next report from his in-tray.

'Some people think it's fun to waste police time, Inspector. Like you're doing right now.'

'No, I mean it was the kidnappers trying to distract us. The tip-off note's forensically neutral, just like everything they've ever sent us.' Logan sank into the visitor's chair. 'And we found out who the big toe belongs to: five-year-old girl, car accident, they amputated her leg at ARI. It was supposed to be cremated. She's not dead.'

A frown. 'Are you sure it's not—'

'Just got a DNA match. Whoever they are, they've got access to Aberdeen Royal Infirmary.'

Finnie punched a button on his office phone. 'Acting DI MacDonald – my office, *now*. And bring everything you have from the hospital investigation.'

'*But I'm*—'

'*Now*, Mr MacDonald.'

'*Yes, sir.*'

Finnie pressed the button again and the phone went silent. *I swear to God, these forensic students get younger every year.*

Logan scooted forward until he was leaning over the desk. 'It's a teaching hospital, right? What if they're all students?'

Finnie shook his head. 'MacDonald and McPherson both ruled out—'

'Think about it: the medical student gets them the drugs and amputates Jenny's toes. The IT student makes the videos and emails untraceable. And the forensic student keeps them all from getting caught.' Logan pulled out his phone and dialled. 'Bob?'

'*If you're calling to complain, it wasn't me, OK?*'

'I need to. . .' Frown. '*What* wasn't you?'

'*. . . Nothing.*' A cough. '*What can I do you for?*'

'Did you find the dealer who sold your suicide that morphine?'

'"*Stumpy the Dwarven Queen*"? *No one in Tayside's ever heard of her. Why the sudden interest in Bruce Sangster?*'

Of course no one had heard of her – she didn't exist. Craig 'Arrogant-Patronizing-Prick' Peterson made her up. That's why none of Bruce's friends knew anything about his alleged drug problem. Sangster didn't buy the morphine, he stole it from the hospital, along with some thiopental sodium and a little girl's severed leg.

'You still got that list of his friends?'

'*. . . Why?*'

'Did you take a note of what courses they were doing?'

'*Course I did. Now why do you—*'

'I'm looking for someone doing computer science and someone doing forensics.'

'*Hold on. . .*' Some rustling.

The door to Finnie's office creaked open and Acting DI Mark MacDonald lurched in, arms loaded down with box files. He took one look at Logan and sniffed.

'*Yeah, here we go: three computer scientists; and one Davina Pearce, BSc Hons, Forensic Science with Law. She's doing Media Studies too.*'

Mark dumped the files on the corner of the desk. 'That's everything. But I've been through it all dozens of times. There's nothing there.'

Logan stuck his phone back in his pocket and grinned at Finnie. 'Bingo.'

49

Logan climbed out into the warm evening, mobile phone clamped to his ear. 'Any luck?'

The Woolmanhill halls of residence was a lopsided grey canyon of three five-storey buildings set at angles to each other around a lopsided car park, just off the Denburn roundabout.

Bob gave a big wet sigh. *'Peterson's not in.'*

'Anyone know where he's gone?'

Rennie scanned the intercom entry system next to a freshly-painted stairwell door, then pressed the button for flat six. The intercom buzzed.

'Flatmates say he's out with his mates: cinema, pizza, pints.'

'Mobile?'

'Went straight to voicemail.'

A high, singsongy voice crackled out of the speaker. *'Hello?'* Very girly.

Rennie pressed the talk button. 'Yeah, is Davina in? It's Simon.'

'What would you have us do now, your temporarily-promoted-to-inspectorship?'

'See if he's got a car, then get onto CCTV: I want every

Automatic Number Plate Recognition camera in the north-east looking for him. And find out what he's been doing for the last two weeks: where he's been going, who he's been talking to, that kind of thing.'

'Hi, Simon. Yeah, Davina's in her room, but she's sulking.'

'God, you're not asking for much, are you? See when it's my go at being DI—'

'Yeah, "the wrath of Bob". I know.' Logan killed the connection.

'Oh. . . Well, can I come up?' The intercom buzzed again, and when Rennie leant against the door it swung open. 'Ta.' He winked at Logan. 'We have lift-off.'

A plump young woman opened the door to flat six. She was growing her very own curly brown halo, held in place with a golden scrunchie. She smiled, showing off a mouthful of metalwork. 'You're Simon, right? So nice to *meet* you. I'm Robin, bet Davina's told you *all* about me!'

'Yeah, hi. She about?'

Robin rolled her eyes. 'God, you *know* what she's like; went storming off to her room yesterday, slammed the door, and hasn't been out since; honestly, it's like a soap opera in here some weeks; you want a cup of coffee? I'm making anyway, think we've got some biscuits too.' All done in two breaths.

'Cool. Can my mate have one too?'

The smile slipped a little as she caught sight of Logan, then she rallied with a cheery, 'More the merrier.' She turned and bustled down the hallway, pausing to knock on one of the internal doors. 'Davina, your friends are here. Davina? I'm making them coffee, you want some?' Pause. Another knock. 'Davina?'

No response.

She did the eye-rolling thing again. 'Some people, eh?

Didn't even go to lectures today, and we were doing blood spatter analysis; I love blood spatters, does that make me weird? Suppose it does, but then I am a bit *loopy*. . .' She stuck her tongue out and circled a finger beside her head. 'Now, coffee!'

Logan stopped outside Davina Pearce's door. She'd decorated it with photos of a young Asian woman: big smile, serious glasses, long black hair. Some were taken in pubs, others at parties, a few in snow-smothered woods. He knocked as the human whirlwind dragged Rennie off to the kitchen.

'Davina? Davina, we need to talk.'

Still nothing, but he could hear music coming from the other side of the door, something upbeat and rocky. 'Davina? Can you hear me?' He rested his ear against the cool wood. Not so much as a rustle, just that cheery music, then the sound of raucous laughter cackled out of the kitchen. Either Rennie had said something very, *very* funny or Little Miss Motor Mouth was desperate.

He tried the kitchen. 'Are you *sure* she's in?'

'Oh yes, I've got the room at the end, by the front door, and I always hear everyone coming and going and coming and going, and I swear she's not been out of that room since yesterday lunchtime. It has to be a man, right? Only men can make you *that* miserable.' She offered Rennie a tin of biscuits. 'No offence, I'm sure you're really nice to your girlfriend; do you have a girlfriend? Listen to me prattling on; I'll get some mugs washed.'

Logan pointed down the corridor. 'Do you have a spare key for Davina's room?'

'Well. . . Yes, *but* I couldn't just go barging into someone's room; I mean keys are for emergencies only and what would Davina think if I let two men into her room; I wouldn't like it if I was her and I'm not sure it's fair of you to ask, because I've never. . .' She stared at Logan's warrant card. 'Oh.'

'Are you *sure* she hasn't left the building? She could have sneaked out when you were asleep, or when you were off doing your blood spatters?'

'Wow, you're *police* officers? That's so exciting, I've always wanted to work with the police; that's why I'm doing forensic science; I think it's really fascinating what you can—'

'Where would she have gone to?'

'Nowhere. Davina's the world's biggest environmentalist; I mean she switches *all* the lights off and if you've got the fridge door open for more than three seconds you get a lecture about polar bears and she never ever leaves her music playing if she's going out, she just wouldn't do it; she's like this total eco-ninja.'

Rennie put a hand on Robin's round shoulder. 'What if something's happened to her?'

'Something. . .'

'What if she's fallen and hurt herself? What if Davina needs our help?'

'Oh God, that would be *terrible*; I'll get the key.'

Rennie waited until Robin disappeared into the room at the end of the corridor then grinning at Logan. 'Said I'd make a great sidekick.'

She was back a minute later, clutching a key with a yellow-haired gonk dangling off the end of it. 'Here.' She passed it to Rennie, blushing slightly as her hand touched his.

Rennie slipped the key into the lock, turned it, then tried the door handle. 'Open sesame!'

Logan knocked and stepped inside, then froze. The room was slightly bigger than the ones at Hillhead, with space for an Ikea-style single bed, cabinet, desk, wardrobe, and a little sink in the corner. The wall above the bed was covered with photographs: a mix of landscapes, portraits, and industrial wastelands. . . Most done in arty black-and-white.

He cleared his throat. 'Robin, I think you should go back through to the kitchen.'

'Is she OK? Davina? Are you OK? I didn't want to unlock the door, but we thought you might be hurt and I thought—'

'Rennie, take her back to the kitchen. *Now*.'

'Why, what's. . .' Rennie peered over Logan's shoulder, then backed up quickly. 'OK: come on, Robin, why don't we finish making that coffee?'

'But I don't—'

'I know, but I'm really thirsty, aren't you? I love your hair by the way. . .'

Logan listened to their voices fading down the corridor, then the clunk of the kitchen door shutting. He took another step, keeping his feet as close to the skirting board as possible.

Davina Pearce: BSc (Hons) Forensic Science with Law and Media Studies was sitting on the beige carpet with one leg tucked under her, the other sticking out into the middle of the room, her back against the wall. She was naked, except for the leather belt around her neck – one end fastened to the window catch. An orange in her mouth, juice sticky and drying on her chin. A black, rubbery vibrator lying on the floor by her knee.

Her skin was pale as butter, but the underside of her thighs and legs were stained dark pink where the blood had pooled after death. Eyes open, glassy, and bloodshot.

'Fuck. . .'

Logan pulled out his phone and called it in.

She wriggles closer, tears hot on her damp cheeks. Her left foot is on fire, burning and stabbing like a million bee stings all in the one spot. She's getting blood all over the mattress, but she doesn't care.

Golden sunlight makes wiggly shapes across the floor, sneaking in through the cracks in the boarded-up windows.

Ice cream and lemonade in the garden, listening to the bees bumble and Mummy singing a song while Daddy makes a wooden thing for the kitchen. A sandpit full of castles, and princesses, and the little black poops left by next-door's cat that Mummy can't know about or she'll get angry. Jenny likes next-door's cat. She doesn't want anything bad to happen to it.

The silvery tape is thick and sticky, but she manages to tease a corner free around Mummy's mouth with her fingernails.

Jenny picks and pulls and tugs until Mummy takes in a huge breath and coughs. There's a pink rectangle around her lips, tiny hairs sticking to the underside of the duct tape.

'Oh God, oh my baby, I'm so sorry. . .' Mummy's crying. 'We have to get out of here, we have to get out of here *right now*, before they come back! They're not going to let us go. . .'

Jenny rests her head against Mummy's chest, just for a moment, feeling the warm softness, the thumpita-thumpita of her heart.

'You have to untie Mummy's hands.'

It takes forever. Every time she finds an end it tears and rips and Mummy's crying and Jenny's crying and it's hard and her foot hurts so much. . . And then the tape's gone and Mummy's sitting up.

Jenny is a Good Little Girl. She just needs to rest for a minute. Close her eyes and let the burny pain go away. Good Little Girl. . .

'Sweetie?'

Someone shakes her shoulder.

'Come on we need to go. Quickly.' Mummy unwraps Jenny's wrists. 'Can you walk?' She looks down. 'Oh Christ, all that blood. . .'

Mummy rips the tape off Jenny's face, it hurts for a bit, but not as much as her burning foot. 'I want Daddy. . .'

'We have to get out of here.'

'I'm *tired*.'

Mummy presses the palm of her hand against Jenny's head. 'You're cold. . .'

She hauls her arms up and Mummy hugs her. Holds her so close she can't breathe. But that's OK. Just want to rest a while. Be warm. Be loved.

There's a rattle, then the chain around her neck slithers away like a cold metal snake.

Another rattle. Jenny forces her eyes open and sees Mummy holding up a little shiny key. Top lip curled, showing off her teeth, like an angry dog.

'They're not so bloody clever after all. Are they?' She stands and holds out her hand. 'Let's go.'

'What a waste.' Rennie's shoulders slumped as the IB carried Davina Pearce out of the room in a white body-bag. He plucked a photo from the wall above the bed – Davina in arty black-and-white, posing in front of a big chunk of machinery. 'She was pretty. I mean, it wouldn't be OK if she was a munter, but . . . you know.' He held the photo out to Logan. 'Do we have to tell her parents?'

'Depends where she's from.' Logan turned the photo over. Four little blobs of Blu-Tack lurked in each corner, around a laser-printed sticker: 'Self-Portrait, B&W, 18-55mm 1/80sec at f/4 ~ Equipment Yard Wellheads Industrial Estate' along with a date/time stamp. 'It's a bit convenient, isn't it?'

'Autoerotic asphyxiation? Don't fancy it myself.'

'No, you idiot, I mean, that's two of Craig Peterson's friends dead in less than a week. Bruce Sangster takes an overdose with a bag over his head, Davina Pearce has a "sexual accident".'

'I heard about sixty people snuff it during a strangle-wank

every year. Silly sods. Only takes seven pounds of pressure to collapse your carotid artery and that's you. True story.'

Logan stuck the photo back on the wall. Davina Pearce had a good eye for light and shadow, specializing in moody black-and-whites. Urban decay was a recurring theme – boarded-up tenements, rusting cars, skips full of random shapes, sagging chain-link fencing, a broken bottle, the sun setting over a burnt-out Volkswagen.

The portraits were good too, but they didn't have the same intensity as the landscapes and still lifes. Davina *did* like to pose for her own photographs though. There was one of her in jeans and a bra, looking back over her shoulder at the camera in some derelict house: walls covered with graffiti, the floorboards stippled with bars of light. Artistic and a bit sinister at the same time. A tattoo sprawled across her shoulder, a Chinese dragon, breathing fire. . . Samantha would've loved it.

Logan pulled the photo off the wall.

Still not been up to see her today. Still not worked up the courage to sit in that little room and listen to the machines breathing for her. Hold her cold hand and pretend everything was going to be OK.

That was what happened when you were completely useless. When you couldn't protect the people you loved. When you couldn't even find the bastards responsible. . .

He stared at the photograph in his hands, felt his eyes widen.

Maybe not quite so fucking useless after all.

Logan flipped it over, and there, between the blobs of Blu-Tack was another sticker: 'SELF-PORTRAIT, B&W, 18-55MM 1/2SEC AT F/16 ~ DERELICT INDUSTRIAL UNIT, FARBURN INDUSTRIAL PARK'.

He grabbed all the exterior shots, checking the stickers for one that matched the time stamp on the other image.

There was only one that came anywhere near: a high, padlocked gate outside a blocky grey building with boarded-up windows and one of those big up-and-over doors you could get a forklift through. The company name was partially obscured by a birch tree growing through the fence. But that didn't matter – all they had to do was drive through the industrial estate until they found the building in the picture.

He shoved the picture of Davina posing in the graffiti-covered room into Rennie's hands. 'Recognize the backdrop?'

The constable leaned forward, squinting. 'Yeah. . . Erm, no. Kinda. . .?'

'Here's a clue for you: it was in the video where they cut off Jenny McGregor's toes.'

50

Every step's like someone's jamming burning ice into her feet, but she grits her teeth and swallows the screams down, keeping them deep inside where they can boil and shake.

Mummy holds a finger up to her lips and makes a ssssssssshing noise. Then opens the door slow and quiet. It's another room, all covered in scribbles and paint like the one they had to stay in, but there's no bed, just a bunch more doors. She marches over to one on the far side.

Jenny wipes her damp eyes with her grubby sleeve, takes a deep wobbly breath and shuffles after her. The bandage on her left foot's soggy, like she's stepped in a puddle of tomato sauce, every step leaving a smeared footprint on the dirty carpet.

And it *hurts*.

'Come on, baby; nearly there; who's Mummy's good little girl?'

Good Little Girl. She's a Good Little Girl.

Jenny stops for a moment, breath hissing in and out between her teeth, tears rolling down her cheeks.

Mummy tries the door, then says a bad word. She grabs the handle and twists it left and right, pulls, snarls, shakes it back and forward. Then steps back and gives the door a kick with her bare foot.

She tries another door. Locked. And another. It's locked too. 'You BASTARD!' Mummy slams her hand into the wood and it BOOMs around the dark, smelly room.

Then a cold metal voice rattles in the shadows. 'Come on, I mean: you've got to be fucking kidding, right?' A monster steps out of the gloom, his white suit glowing as he moves into a beam of sunlight. His name badge says ROGER. 'Like I'm going to leave the place unlocked so you can just walk out? How thick do you think I am, Alison?'

Mummy turns and flattens herself against the door. 'You have to let us go.'

'I have to do fuck all.' He holds up a shiny thing. It takes Jenny a moment to realize it's a big knife. 'Now, are you going to get back in your room like a good little girl, or do I have to drag you back there in bits?'

Logan grabbed the handle above the passenger door as Rennie threw the car into a hard left, the Vauxhall's back end drifting out as they jumped the lights onto George Street. A white van blared its horn, an old lady in a Mini made wanking gestures.

'Repeat, we need a firearms team out at Farburn Industrial Estate, Stoneywood ASAP.'

'Hud oan. . .'

There was a click, a pause, and then Finnie's voice boomed out of the Airwave handset. *'What's going on?'*

Logan told him about the photograph from Davina Pearce's wall.

'And you think that's enough to get a firearms team scurrying—'

'I'm telling you, it's the *exact* same room from the video—Watch out for the bus!'

'You sure I can't use the siren?' The car jerked out into the middle of the road and back again. Shops and taxis and lorries and people blurred past the passenger window.

'Look, it's half-seven: we've got less than five hours till the deadline. If they're—'

'Hold on.' The line went quiet. And then Finnie was back: *'This better not be another wild goose chase like Stephen Clayton.'*

'Tell you what: if it is you've got my resignation on your desk first thing tomorrow.' Not as if he was throwing much away with that one.

Another pause. *'Deal. A firearms team is on its way.'*

'How about that one?' Rennie pointed through the windscreen at a disused mini-warehouse.

Logan compared it to the photograph. 'Keep going.'

The pool car kerb-crawled its way through the industrial estate. That was the trouble with somewhere like this at quarter to eight on a Wednesday evening – almost every single building looked deserted: everything closed up and dark, chain-link fences and padlocked gates.

The purple-black clouds had spread across the sky, a faint drizzle specked the car windows, a rainbow arcing over the massive, ugly, abandoned 1970s-style complex of concrete and glass that used to house BP.

'Charlie Delta Twelve, this is Foxtrot Tango Two ... where the hell are you?'

Logan thumbed the button. 'Wellheads Road. Still looking for the target unit.'

'Turning onto Riverview Drive now.' The voice on the other end dropped to a whisper. *'Word to the wise: we've got that SOCA tosser following in a car with DS Taylor, Steel, and Finnie. Just so you know.'*

Steel and Green in a car together – poor bloody Doreen, there was no way that would end well.

Rennie took a left, down a little road between two hulking warehouses. 'You know, Guv, we could always engineer a wee *incident* where someone accidentally shoots Green in the bollocks. In all the confusion.'

'Don't tempt me. . . There!' Logan smacked his hand on the dashboard. 'There: the one with the green roof!'

It even had the tree growing through the fence.

A big faded sign was bolted to the front of the building, 'CAMBERTOOLS ~ THE DOWNHOLE E.O.R. SOLUTION SPECIALISTS'. The bottom floor was harled in dirty grey; a couple of boarded-up windows stared blindly out into the rubbish-strewn car park. The upper floor was clad in the same green corrugated iron as the roof, the paint chipped and peeling in places, stained with seagull droppings. The big warehouse door wore a dirt-streaked sign, 'CONDEMNED BUILDING. NO ENTRY'. The one on the fence read, 'WARNING: THIS SITE PATROLLED BY GUARD DOGS'.

'Foxtrot Tango Two, we have a winner.' Logan gave the firearms team directions then told Rennie to park fifty yards down the street, behind a locked-up burger van.

'What now?' Rennie massaged the steering wheel.

'We go charging in like the A-team, beat up all the bad guys, rescue Alison and Jenny.'

He sat up straight, eyes shining. 'Cool! We can—'

Logan hit him. 'Don't be a prick. We wait for the firearms team, we set up a perimeter, and we figure out how to get the hostages out without killing anyone. What's wrong with you?'

'Well, it. . . Ahem. . .' He turned off the engine. 'Yes, Guv.'

Three minutes later a filthy, unmarked Transit van growled into sight. It drifted to a halt in front of the pool car and a plainclothes officer grinned and waved through the wind-shield at Logan. *'Aye, aye. Nice day for a shoot-out?'*

'You know what's going to happen if Finnie hears you, don't you, Brian?'

An unmarked Vauxhall pulled up on the other side of the road. The grin disappeared from Brian's face. *'Speak of the Devil.'*

Logan climbed out of the pool car and hurried over to the back of the Transit van, keeping the burger van between himself and the Cambertools industrial unit. Finnie, Green, and Steel got out of the other car. Doreen stayed behind, waiting until her passengers weren't looking before bouncing her head off the steering wheel.

The man from SOCA stuck his chest out, then snapped his fingers. 'Situation Report?'

You're a wanker. Logan pointed at the industrial unit. 'We think that's where they shot the video after amputating Jenny McGregor's toes.'

'I see. And you haven't ascertained if the suspects are in the building yet?'

Steel twisted her e-cigarette on and set it dangling from the corner of her mouth. 'When *exactly* were they meant to do that? They only got here a minute before us. Want to whinge about how we're no' psychic enough now?'

'I'm getting pretty bloody tired of your attitude, Inspector.'

'You've moaned about everything else.' She sent a plume of fake cigarette smoke his way.

'Was *five minutes* too much to ask for?' Finnie looked at the sky for a moment, then back to earth. 'DI McRae, I want a risk analysis: what's the layout of the building, where are the points of entry and exit, where are our victims likely to be held, how many targets are we looking at, what kind of weapons are they likely to—'

'We don't have time for this.' Green unbuttoned his jacket, slipped it off, and thrust it at Logan. He was wearing a bulletproof vest underneath, and a shoulder holster.

'Shouldn't we—'

'Cover me!' The superintendent pulled a snub-nosed

436

semi-automatic from his holster and ran in a crouch towards the padlocked gates.

'Come back here!' Finnie's eyes bugged, his mouth crimped into an angry cat's bum as Green kept on going. 'Who gave him a bloody gun?'

A clink and Green was through the gates, heading for the main doors.

'Oh you silly bastard. . .' Logan dumped the tailored jacket on the damp road and banged on the side of the Transit van. 'OPEN UP!' He stuck his head around the side. 'RENNIE!'

'On it, Guv.'

The van's back doors popped open and a sweaty firearms-trained officer wheezed out into the light drizzle. He was dressed from head to toe in black, from his heavy-duty steel-toecapped boots to his thick bulletproof vest and crash helmet, a submachine gun dangling on a strap around his neck. 'Bloody roasting in there.'

'Give me your sidearm.' Logan stuck his hand out.

The man in black backed off a step. 'What?'

'Give me your gun!'

He unholstered his Glock, a chunky rectangular thing that smelled of warm oil and plastic, holding it close to his chest. 'Erm. . . Actually, I had to sign for this, so—'

Logan grabbed it. Ejected the clip. It was full, so he slid it back into the handgrip and hauled the slide back, racking the first round into the breach.

Finnie tapped him on the shoulder. 'DI McRae, what *exactly* do you think you're doing? We need a plan, a strategy!'

Rennie puffed his way around the side of Foxtrot Tango Two, holding a pair of heavy black vests covered in pockets. 'Only got stab-proof, that OK?'

'It'll have to be. . .'

'DI McRae!'

Logan pulled one of the vests on over his suit jacket. 'If

he goes in on his own he'll get killed. If we're *lucky*. If we're not, he'll take Alison and Jenny with him.'

'We're not in the business of throwing good idiots after bad! You can't—'

'You! Give Rennie your MP5.'

The firearms officer pouted. 'But then I won't have any—'

'*Now*!'

He held out his submachine gun and Rennie snatched it from his hands. 'You've cleaned this, right? Better not jam.'

'Inspector McRae, do you *actually* think this—'

'What choice have we got? We go in, we grab him, and we drag him back out here before he sods everything up. We don't engage the targets, we don't pull any heroics – we stop Green.' Logan looked around the side of the Transit. Green was flattening himself against the wall beside the industrial unit's front door. 'Oh, Christ: the moron really does think he's on telly. . .'

Rennie hauled back the slide on his Heckler & Koch MP5. 'Ready when you are, Guv.'

The head of CID shook his head, then turned and marched back towards his car. 'Sergeant McIver: I want a tactical briefing, and I want it *now*!'

Logan ran for the abandoned industrial unit, Rennie clattering along behind him.

51

Rennie stopped beside the open front door to the abandoned Cambertools industrial unit. 'I still say we should shoot him in the balls, you know, by *accident*?'

Logan glanced back towards Foxtrot Tango Two, where the firearms team were all thumping out into the drizzle. 'We go in on three.'

'How did someone like Green get promoted to superintendent?'

'Maybe they had a raffle. Two, one. . .' Logan gave the nod and Rennie ducked through the open door, MP5 held at half-mast.

'Clear.'

Logan followed him into a boxy corridor covered with graffiti. Four doors off it, all closed.

'What do you think?'

Logan nodded towards the nearest door, raised his borrowed gun, and took up a firing stance.

Rennie tried the handle. 'Locked.' So was the next one, and the one after that.

Last door.

Rennie hauled open the door and charged in, bent double,

Logan behind him, swinging his Glock above the constable's back. It was the room from the video; the room in Davina Pearce's self portrait – a graffiti-scrawled office with a single, wrought-iron bed against one wall, a low table in the middle of the room. One door on the opposite wall.

Blood made a scuffed track across the wooden floorboards.

Superintendent Green was slumped against the bed, both hands clutching his right thigh – a dark red stain spread out across his trouser leg. His Glock lay on the floor by his knee. The silly sod hadn't even got off a single shot. 'Oh God, oh Christ, oh fuck. . .'

Alison McGregor was standing, very still and silent, in front of the boarded-up window, arms by her sides. Trembling. There was someone behind her, dressed in full SOC gear and a plastic mask. He had a six-inch knife pressed to Alison's throat, the shiny blade speckled with crimson. The other hand was wrapped in Jenny McGregor's blonde curly hair, holding her close.

Logan inched to the side. 'Armed police officers: drop the knife.'

The man in the SOC suit shrugged, his speech distorted by some sort of filter in the mask into an electronic pseudo-robot: 'Now *why* would I do something like that?'

'Oh God,' Green's voice had jumped an octave, 'he *cut* me!'

Logan kept his eyes on the knife. 'Well what the hell did you expect, charging in here like an idiot?'

'You have to get me to a hospital!'

'Drop – the – knife.'

'No.' The man in the SOC suit tilted his head to one side. 'Here's how it's going to work: you're going to take your moron and fuck off. You're going to clear the road north. You're going to get me a car and you're not going to follow it.

If you do that Alison and Jenny will live. If you don't they will die.'

'I'm bleeding. . .'

'It's over.' Logan shifted his grip on the gun. 'The building's surrounded by armed police. You're not going anywhere.'

'Then they're both going to die.'

'No they're not.'

'Oh God, I need an ambulance. . .'

'WILL YOU SHUT UP?' Logan nodded and Rennie shuffled the other way, MP5 up to his shoulder like a sniper. 'Now put the knife down and no one else needs to get hurt.'

'You're familiar with the concept of IEDs, aren't you, Sergeant? Well, I'm wearing an improvised explosive device right now, and all it takes is one little twitch and we all end up spread across the fucking walls, ceiling, floor. . . You get the picture. Now be good little officers and do what you're told.'

Sergeant: the man in the SOC suit recognized him. He'd been right, it *was* Peterson.

'Can't do that, Craig. Put the knife down.'

'Ah. . .' He stared at the floor for a moment. 'I'm not "Craig", my name's Roger. And if you don't do what I tell you, everyone's going to die.' He rocked the bloody knife back and forth, leaving a red line across Alison's throat. 'Starting with Goldilocks here.'

She bared her teeth. 'He's lying.'

'Shut up.'

'He doesn't have a bomb.'

Craig/ROGER laughed. 'Believe me, you can't trust a single word she says.'

'Shoot him. He wasn't going to let us go, he was always going to kill us both!'

'I really, really need an ambulance. . .'

'Guv?' Rennie shifted right another pace. 'Got a firing solution.'

'Come on, Craig, give it up. No one has to die.'

The white SOC suit rustled. 'You spoke to Vicious Vikki, right? She tell you the squirrel story? When she was ten, Alison here made some squirrel traps, caught about six of them in the woods behind her house. Know what she did with them?'

'Just put the knife down and we can all walk out of here.'

'She drowned them in a bucket. One by one. Lined the traps up so they could watch their mates dying. That's the kind of person she is – a complete fucking psycho.'

'He's lying.'

'Think that's bad? Ask her what happened to Doddy's parents. They hated her: who wants a gold-digging sociopath marrying their son?'

'It was an accident!'

'*Sure* it was. Come on, Sergeant, who do you think told David to torch your flat.'

Logan stared at him. '*What*?'

'You heard.' ROGER tilted his head to one side. 'Now back – the fuck – up, both of you, and get me that car, or I slit her throat and we go through the whole thing again with the brat.'

He jiggled the knife again and blood seeped down Alison's neck.

'Aaagh. . .'

'DON'T HURT MY MUMMY!' Jenny grabbed the hand wrapped in her hair and yanked. Then sank her teeth into ROGER's leg.

'Fucking bitch!'

He must have loosened his grip, because Alison twisted to the side, driving her elbow into his stomach. A grunt.

ROGER slashed the knife at her, but she was out of reach.

Rennie lunged forward, going for Jenny, but ROGER hauled her back – off her feet, the two of them thumping back into the boarded-up window. Now the SOC suited figure was cornered, the knife glinting in a slice of golden sunlight.

Logan pushed Alison behind him, keeping the gun pointing straight at ROGER's face. 'On your knees, *now*.'

ROGER cleared his throat, then lowered the blade. 'It was *her* idea. All of it. She—'

A loud boom reverberated around the room. Logan flinched. Jenny screamed. Rennie swore.

Red blossomed in the middle of ROGER's chest.

52

Logan eased the gun out of Alison's hands.

'He was going to hurt my little girl. . .'

Jenny was sitting on the floor by the window, knees drawn up to her chest, bandaged feet scrabbling on the blood-slicked floorboards. *Screaming*.

Rennie scooped her up, backing off into the middle of the room. ROGER lay crumpled on the floor. The semi-transparent plastic of his mask darkened, speckles of red spraying out around the voice modifier with every breath. His purple-gloved fingers twitched above the hole in his chest. Blood seeped through his SOC suit. 'Gachhhh. . .'

'Rennie, get her out of here.' Logan glanced down at Green. 'And *take* that with you.' He pulled out his phone as the constable hauled Green to his feet.

'MUMMY!' Jenny reached out, but Rennie held on tight and carried her out through the door, Green limping and snivelling and moaning along behind him.

'I need an ambulance here ASAP – kidnapper has gunshot wound to the chest.'

Alison McGregor raised her chin. 'I did what any mother would've done to protect her baby.'

'*Fit aboot Alison and Jenny, they OK?*'

'Just get the bloody ambulance sorted!' Logan gave him the address then hung up.

ROGER twitched and spasmed. 'Oh fuck. . .' The words came out in a gurgle of red. 'We were . . . going to stick the money in . . . in a charity fund . . . siphon . . . siphon it off. . .'

Logan stared at Alison. 'You *told* someone to set fire to my flat?'

'He's lying.' She wrapped her arms around her chest. 'He'd say anything to save himself.'

ROGER's left foot banged against the wooden floor, beating out a tattoo. 'Gaaaach. . .'

Logan knelt beside the trembling man and eased off the plastic mask.

It wasn't Craig Peterson.

'Any news?' Dr Goulding closed the door.

Logan looked over his shoulder, then back out of the window of his makeshift incident room. 'Still in surgery.'

'Well, look on the bright side – if he *does* survive, how long do you think he'll last in prison?'

Logan just shrugged, watching the crowds outside the front of FHQ. There had to be at least five hundred people out there, all clutching their 'WE LOVE YOU JENNY!' 'WE NEVER GAVE UP!' banners, or just waving their mobile phones about, as if it was some kind of rock concert. The TV people must be loving this.

'So,' Goulding patted him on the shoulder, 'why aren't you down there, enjoying all the glory and adulation? This is your moment in the sun.'

'They found Craig Peterson.'

'Did they now?'

'Sitting in his Renault; hose from the exhaust in through

445

the driver's window. Bob said the whole car reeked of whisky. There was a text message in his phone for his mum, telling her he was sorry for letting her down. Never sent it.'

'Hmm. . . Did you notice how the deaths are all about being unable to breathe? Bruce Sangster with a plastic bag over his head, Davina Pearce with a belt around her neck, Craig Peterson with the exhaust fumes? I really hope Gordon Maguire survives, it's going to be fascinating finding out what it means to him.' A frown. 'I wonder if it's a common fantasy for television producers. . .'

'He was losing his business, investors waiting for him to go bankrupt so they could buy up the assets.' Logan rested his head against the window. 'Maguire said it was all Alison's idea. That she came up with the whole thing.'

How could *anyone* be that manipulative? So completely callous and amoral that they'd mutilate their own daughter just to become a little bit more famous?

The psychologist ran the tips of his fingers across the glass. 'I always thought there was something funny about the toes. Why amputate two little toes, when one *big* toe would've been much easier?' He smiled. 'Did you know some women in the US have their pinkie toes removed so they can wear expensive high heels? Looked at a certain way, what happened to Jenny isn't so much a disfigurement as a cosmetic enhancement.'

'How am I supposed to prove it? It's his word against hers, *if* he lives. Everyone else in the gang's dead: no witnesses, no forensics. There's sod all to tie her to. . .' He picked up the dusty blue folder he'd got Guthrie to dig out of the archives. A house fire in Kincorth six and a half years ago. Two fatalities – Doddy McGregor's parents. 'Maybe that's why her house was so tidy – she knew she was going to be abducted. Didn't want us to take crime scene photos of the place looking like a pigsty.'

The crowd on the Front Podium roared and cheered. Must be Alison McGregor making her triumphant exit from the station. Logan scowled. 'And nine point four million's peanuts compared to what she's going to rake in from sponsorship, movie, and publishing deals.'

From his commandeered office, Logan watched her wave and glad-hand her way into the throng. She could've sneaked out the back in an unmarked car if she'd wanted to, but no: she wanted to bask in the love of her fans.

Oh – my – God! She's here, she's finally here. God she looks great, she's so *brave*.

Beatrice Eastbrook gives herself a quick once-over. Hair: going a little frizzy with all the FUCKING drizzle, but other than that, OK. Make-up: good. Outfit: perfect. It's the one Alison helped her pick out on what was, swear to God, the greatest day of her whole life.

Alison stands in the middle of the crowd, surrounded by microphones and cameras. 'I just want to thank you all for never stopping believing!'

A cheer.

'And, if it's OK with you guys, we're going to put the Freedom Fund to good use – setting up a charity to support the families of our brave troops. To show them that *we'll* never stop believing either!'

Another cheer.

Alison's got a couple of minders with her, big ugly blokes in black suits. They clear a path in front of her, moving really slowly so she can talk to all her fans. All the people who love her.

But not the way Beatrice loves her. No one loves Alison McGregor like she does.

She's getting closer. It's just like in her dreams. Beatrice has prayed every night for two whole weeks that the bastards who took Alison away from her would die horrible deaths. That's the kind of friend she is. The kind that doesn't give up on someone.

Here she is – so close, so close. . .

Beatrice elbows her way to the front. Don't these bastards know who she is? She's Alison's best friend!

Alison looks right at her and smiles.

Beatrice's heart almost stops. Right then and there. Bang. Dead. Killed with a smile.

She steps forward and wraps her arms around Alison. 'God, I'm so glad you're safe!'

Beatrice holds her tight. Never let go. Best friends forever.

And then Alison leans forward and whispers something in her ear.

Beatrice blinks. 'I've got a present for you. . .'

Thump, thump, thump, THUMP, THUMP – the blade's a living thing, flashing and biting and there's blood everywhere and people are screaming and the two big thugs in their black suits just stand there with their mouths hanging open and Beatrice keeps on going, stabbing and stabbing.

Then someone grabs her by the throat, someone else by the arm, hauling the blade from her hand. They drag her to the ground, kicking and punching as she laughs and laughs and laughs.

53

Eleven o'clock and the hospital sounds were muted. Just that constant humming throb, as if the place was one huge machine designed to chew people up and leave nothing but pale shells behind.

Logan stood beside Helen Brown's bed, hands behind his back, watching a woman barely older than he was crying quietly because her grandson was going into care and her daughter was going to lose both legs.

'The doctors say she's comfortable, and—'

'Get out. Just. . .' Helen Brown ground her fists into her eye sockets. 'Just leave me alone. . .'

'Darren McInnes will die in prison, I promise he'll—'

'YOU SHOULD'VE FOUND HER SOONER! YOU SHOULD'VE FUCKING CARED!' Her voice echoed around the small ward.

'All right, Helen, calm down. He's leaving.' The big nurse squeaked to a halt on the terrazzo floor, face large and pink. She scowled at Logan. 'Aren't you?'

The uniformed constable shook Logan's hand. With the pointy nose and go-faster cheekbones, he looked like a

449

shaved whippet. 'I know it's all fucked up and that, sir, but I wanted to tell you: you did a great job.'

Then why did he feel like shit? 'Mr Webster in?'

'Shuggie? Aye, he's not going nowhere till they sort out his hand. Hate to think how much these skin grafts are costing, like he ever paid taxes in his life.' Constable Whippet shifted his feet. 'Here, sir, if you're stopping for a bit, any chance I can nip off for a piss?'

'Sure.' Logan stepped into the room and closed the door.

Shuggie was sitting in the chair beside his bed. The bruising hadn't gone down much, if anything it looked worse – the blues and purples evolving into sickening greens and yellows. His right hand was encased in some sort of cage, probably keeping pressure off the raw meat and bare bones inside.

Logan cleared his throat. 'How are you feeling?'

Shuggie looked up, then squealed, shrinking back into his chair. 'I didn't say anything! I didn't, I swear to God. . .' He held the cage against his chest.

So *that* was the kind of person Logan was now: the kind people were terrified of.

'I just wanted to tell you that I'm sorry. For everything.'

Shuggie kept his eyes on the cage around his hand. 'I promise I won't say anything. . .'

'Yes, well. . .' The nurse curled her top lip, exposing off-white teeth. 'Don't worry – she'll pull through. Bastards like her always do. It's the good ones who die young.'

On the other side of the glass, Beatrice Eastbrook lay in a private room, hooked up to a bank of monitors. Her head was wrapped in bandages, the few patches of visible skin bruised and scabbed.

The nurse cleared her throat. 'We've. . . Well, someone

450

has to tell Jenny that her mummy's gone.' Silence. A cough. 'You know.'

Logan nodded.

'Hi.' He stood at the foot of the hospital bed.

She was tiny, dwarfed by the scratchy sheets and the big metal frame, lying on top of the covers. They'd changed the dressings on her feet – swapping filthy, blood-soaked bandages for fresh white.

Jenny stared at him, her mouth a hard little line.

'Yes. . . Anyway. . .' Logan reached into the plastic bag the IB had given him, and pulled out a blue teddy bear. 'We found this in. . . well, I thought you'd like him back. For company.' He held the bear out, but she didn't move. 'Right. I'll just put him here.'

He sat it at the bottom of the bed, where she could see it. Something familiar from home. She'd like that. 'Are you OK?'

She stopped staring at him and stared at the bear instead.

'There's a little girl who got knocked down by a car; the doctors had to cut off her leg, and the people who kidnapped you stole it. They sent her big toe to the police, pretending it was yours.'

Logan scratched the fur between the bear's ears. 'There's going to be a ceremony later and the Lord Provost's going to give it back to her. I think her mum and dad want to bury it. . . Anyway, the little girl would like to meet you, if you're free later? Would you like that?'

Silence.

He swallowed. Let out a long breath. Then pulled up a plastic chair. 'Jenny, the doctors want me to tell you about your mummy. . .'

'So, the Chief Constable made an official complaint, and now Green's buried under a mountain of paperwork, trying to explain why he charged into a hostage situation and let someone shoot someone else with the gun he wasn't supposed to have.'

No reply.

Logan stared at the ceiling. 'The caravan still smells like a mouldy tramp, by the way. You should see the size of the spiders – bastards are demanding squatters' rights. . .'

He squeezed Samantha's hand. The skin was cold.

The machine hissed and pinged, breathing for her. Another bleeped, displaying her heartbeat. Everything stank of disinfectant, boiled cauliflower, and despair. Even Wee Hamish Mowat's huge bunch of flowers couldn't cover that up.

'They found out who torched the flat.' He cleared his throat. 'When they ran Craig Peterson's DNA through the system, it matched the stuff on the outside of the flat door. It. . . That's why there was no fibres or fingerprints. I picked on him because I thought he needed taking down a notch, and he. . .' A deep breath. 'He must've thought I was on to them. So he tried to get us out of the way. It was my fault: all of it. All of this. . .'

Logan bent forward until his forehead rested on the scratchy blanket.

'I don't want to be a police officer any more. I don't fucking *deserve* to be one any more.'

The machines bleeped and hissed. The building throbbed.

'I'm sorry.'

'It's OK. Shhhh. . .' A hand stroked the back of his neck. 'It's OK.'

He looked up and Samantha smiled down at him from her nest of pillows.

'God, Logan, you make such a *fuss* about stuff.'

'I thought you were—'

'I'm fine. Didn't think you were going to get rid of me that easily, did you?' She pulled the wires from her wrist and chest. 'Come on, let's blow this corrugated craphole before they decide to stick me in another sodding coma.' Samantha swung her legs out of bed and hopped down onto the linoleum. . .

Logan blinked, jerked upright in his seat. Wiped a hand across his mouth, clearing away the drool.

Samantha just lay there, hooked to the machines with tubes and wires, not moving, not saying anything.

Because in real life there were no happy endings – in real life there was just pain and shattered bones.

Read the
series from

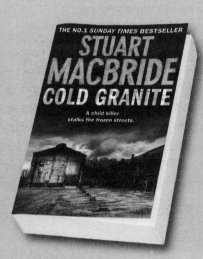

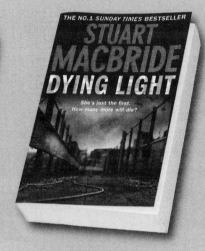

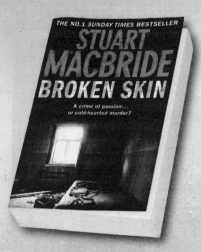

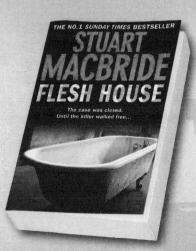

Logan McRae
the beginning

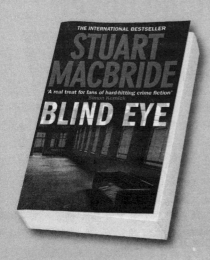

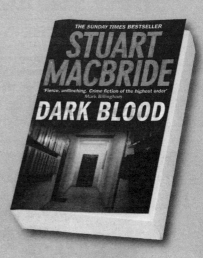

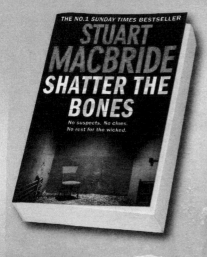

BLOODY.
BRILLIANT.
MACBRIDE.

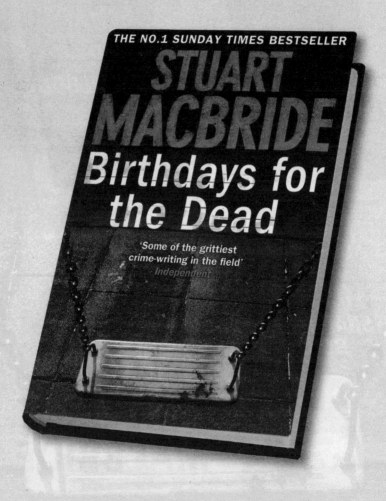